Pr

THE IN
TRILOGY:

"Many books are good, some are great, but few are truly important. Add to this last category *The Hundred Thousand Kingdoms*, N. K. Jemisin's debut novel... In this reviewer's opinion, this is the must-read fantasy of the year."

—Bookpage

"A complex, edge-of-your-seat story with plenty of funny, scary, and bittersweet twists."

—Publishers Weekly (Starred Review)

"An offbeat, engaging tale by a talented and original newcomer."

—Kirkus

"The very best kind of sequel: as lush and evocative and true as the first, with all the same sense of mystery, giving us the world and characters we already love, and yet with a new story and a wonderfully new perspective on the whole dazzling world and pantheon the author has built."

—Naomi Novik

"An astounding debut novel...the worldbuilding is solid, the characterization superb, the plot complicated but clear."

—RT Book Reviews (Top Pick!)

"The key is just to tell a great, exciting, engaging story that keeps you turning pages long past your bedtime. And Jemisin has definitely done that here."
—io9.com

"N. K. Jemisin has written a fascinating epic fantasy where the stakes are not just the fate of kingdoms but of the world and the universe."
—sfrevu.com

"A similar blend of inventiveness, irreverence, and sophistication—along with sensuality—brings vivid life to the setting and other characters: human and otherwise....*The Hundred Thousand Kingdoms* definitely leaves me wanting more of this delightful new writer."
—*Locus*

"A compelling page-turner."
—The Onion A.V. Club

"Jemisin's talent as a storyteller should make her one of the fantasy authors to watch in the coming years."
—*Library Journal*

"*The Broken Kingdoms* had everything I loved about the first book in this trilogy—an absorbing story, an intriguing setting and world mythology, and a likable narrator with a compelling voice. The next book cannot come out soon enough."
—fantasybookcafe.com

"*The Broken Kingdoms* is an excellent sequel to *The Hundred Thousand Kingdoms* because it expands the universe of the series geographically, historically, magically and in the range of characters, while keeping the same superb prose and gripping narrative that made the first one such a memorable debut."

THE
KINGDOM
OF GODS

By N. K. Jemisin

The Inheritance Trilogy

The Hundred Thousand Kingdoms
The Broken Kingdoms
The Kingdom of Gods

Dreamblood

The Killing Moon
The Shadowed Sun

THE
KINGDOM
OF GODS

BOOK THREE OF THE INHERITANCE TRILOGY

N. K. JEMISIN

www.orbitbooks.net

Copyright © 2011 by N.K. Jemisin
"Not the End" copyright © 2011 by N.K. Jemisin
Excerpt from *The Killing Moon* copyright © 2012 by N.K. Jemisin
All rights reserved. In accordance with the U.S. Copyright Act of 1976, the scanning, uploading and electronic sharing of this book without the permission of the publisher is unlawful piracy and theft of the author's intellectual property. If you would like to use material from the book (other than for review purposes), permission must be obtained by contacting the publisher. We appreciate your support of the author's rights.

Orbit
Hachette Book Group
237 Park Avenue
New York, NY 10017
www.orbitbooks.net

Orbit is an imprint of Hachette Book Group. The Orbit name and logo are trademarks of Little, Brown Book Group Limited.

The publisher is not responsible for websites (or their content) that are not owned by the publisher.

Printed in the United States of America

Originally published in trade paperback by Hachette Book Group
First mass market edition: April 2012

10 9 8 7 6 5 4 3 2 1
OPM

BOOK ONE

Four Legs in the Morning

SHE LOOKS SO MUCH LIKE ENEFA, *I think, the first time I see her.*

Not this moment, as she stands trembling in the lift alcove, her heartbeat so loud that it drums against my ears. This is not really the first time I've seen her. I have checked in on our investment now and again over the years, sneaking out of the palace on moonless nights. (Nahadoth is the one our masters fear most during those hours, not me.) I first met her when she was an infant. I crept in through the nursery window and perched on the railing of her crib to watch her. She watched me back, unusually quiet and solemn even then. Where other infants were fascinated by the world around them, she was constantly preoccupied by the second soul nestled against her own. I waited for her to go mad, and felt pity, but nothing more.

I next visited when she was two, toddling after her mother with great determination. Not mad yet. Again when she was five; I watched her sit at her father's knee, listening raptly to his tales of the gods. Still not mad. When she was nine, I watched her mourn her father. By that point, it had become clear that she was not, and would never go, insane.

Yet there was no doubt that Enefa's soul affected her. Aside from her looks, there was the way she killed. I watched her climb out from beneath the corpse of her first man, panting and covered in filth, with a bloody stone knife in her hand. Though she was only thirteen years old, I felt no horror from her—which I should have, her heart's fluctuations amplified by her double souls. There was only satisfaction in her face, and a very familiar coldness at her core. The warriors' council women, who had expected to see her suffer, looked at each other in unease. Beyond the circle of older women, in the shadows, her watching mother smiled.

I fell in love with her then, just a little.

So now I drag her through my dead spaces, which I have never shown to another mortal, and it is to the corporeal core of my soul that I take her. (I would take her to my realm, show her my true soul, if I could.) I love her wonder as she walks among my little toy worlds. She tells me they are beautiful. I will cry when she dies for us.

Then Naha finds her. Pathetic, isn't it? We two gods, the oldest and most powerful beings in the mortal realm, both besotted by a sweaty, angry little mortal girl. It is more than her looks. More than her ferocity, her instant maternal devotion, the speed with which she lunges to strike. She is more than Enefa, for Enefa never loved me so much, nor was Enefa so passionate in life and death. The old soul has been improved, somehow, by the new.

She chooses Nahadoth. I do not mind so much. She loves me, too, in her way. I am grateful.

And when it all ends and the miracle has occurred and she is a goddess (again), I weep. I am happy. But still so very alone.

1

Trickster, trickster
Stole the sun for a prank
Will you really ride it?
Where will you hide it?
Down by the riverbank!

THERE WILL BE NO TRICKS in this tale. I tell you this so that you can relax. You'll listen more closely if you aren't flinching every other instant, waiting for the pratfall. You will not reach the end and suddenly learn I have been talking to my other soul or making a lullaby of my life for someone's unborn brat. I find such things disingenuous, so I will simply tell the tale as I lived it.

But wait, that's not a real beginning. Time is an irritation, but it provides structure. Should I tell this in the mortal fashion? All right, then, linear. Slooooow. You require context.

Beginnings. They are not always what they seem. Nature is cycles, patterns, repetition—but of what we believe, of the beginning I understand, there was once only Maelstrom, the unknowable. Over a span of uncountable aeons, as none of us were here yet to count, It churned forth endless substances and concepts and creatures. Some of those must have been glorious, because even today the Maelstrom spins forth new life with regular randomness, and many of those creations are indeed beautiful and wondrous. But most of them last only an eyeblink or two before the Maelstrom rips them apart again, or they die of instant old age, or they collapse in on themselves and become tiny Maelstroms in turn. These are absorbed back into the greater cacophony.

But one day the Maelstrom made something that did not die. Indeed, this thing was remarkably like Itself—wild, churning, eternal, ever changing. Yet this new thing was ordered enough to think, and feel, and dedicate itself to its own survival. In token of which, the first thing it did was get the hells away from the Maelstrom.

But this new creature faced a terrible dilemma, because away from the Maelstrom there was nothing. No people, no places, no spaces, no darkness, no dimension, no EXISTENCE.

A bit much for even a god to endure. So this being—whom we shall call *Nahadoth* because that is a pretty name, and whom we shall label male for the sake of convenience if not completeness—promptly set out to create an existence, which he did by going mad and tearing himself apart.

This was remarkably effective. And thus Nahadoth found himself accompanied by a formless immensity of separate substance. Purpose and structure began to cohere around it simply as a side effect of the mass's presence, but only so much of that could occur spontaneously. Much like the Maelstrom, it churned and howled and thundered; unlike the Maelstrom, it was not in any way *alive*.

It was, however, the earliest form of the universe and

the gods' realm that envelops it. This was a wonder—but Nahadoth likely did not notice, because he was a gibbering lunatic. So let us return to the Maelstrom.

I like to believe that It is aware. Eventually It must have noticed Its child's loneliness and distress. So presently, It spat out another entity that was aware and that also managed to escape the havoc of its birth. This new one—who has always and only been male—named himself Bright Itempas, because he was an arrogant, self-absorbed son of a demon even then. And because Itempas is also a gigantic screaming twit, he attacked Nahadoth, who... well. Naha very likely did not make a good conversation partner at the time. Not that they talked at all, in those days before speech.

So they fought, and fought, and fought times a few million jillion nillion, until suddenly one or the other of them got tired of the whole thing and proposed a truce. Both of them claim to have done this, so I cannot tell which one is joking. And then, because they had to do *something* if they weren't fighting and because they were the only living beings in the universe after all, they became lovers. Somewhere between all this—the fighting or the lovemaking, not so very different for those two—they had a powerful effect on the shapeless mass of substance that Nahadoth had given birth to. It gained more function, more structure. And all was well for another Really Long Time.

Then along came the Third, a she-creature named Enefa, who should have settled things because usually three of anything is better, more stable, than two. For a while this was the case. In fact, EXISTENCE became the universe, and the beings soon became a family, because it was Enefa's nature to give meaning to anything she touched. I was the first of their many, many children.

So there we were: a universe, a father and a mother and

a Naha, and a few hundred children. And our grandparent, I suppose—the Maelstrom, if one can count It as such given that It would destroy us all if we did not take care. And the mortals, when Enefa finally created them. I suppose those were like pets—part of the family and yet not really—to be indulged and disciplined and loved and kept safe in the finest of cages, on the gentlest of leashes. We only killed them when we had to.

Things went wrong for a while, but at the time that this all began, there had been some improvement. My mother was dead, but she got better. My father and I had been imprisoned, but we'd won our way free. My other father was still a murdering, betraying bastard, though, and nothing would ever change that, no matter how much penance he served—which meant that the Three could never be whole again, no matter that all three of them lived and were for the most part sane. This left a grating, aching void in our family, which was only tolerable because we had already endured far worse.

That is when my mother decided to take things into her own hands.

I followed Yeine one day, when she went to the mortal realm and shaped herself into flesh and appeared in the musty inn room that Itempas had rented. They spoke there, exchanging inanities and warnings while I lurked incorporeal in a pocket of silence, spying. Yeine might have noticed me; my tricks rarely worked on her. If so, she did not care that I watched. I wish I knew what that meant.

Because there came the dreaded moment in which she looked at him, really *looked* at him, and said, "You've changed."

And he said, "Not enough."

And she said, "What do you fear?" To which he said nothing, of course, because it is not his nature to admit such things.

So she said, "You're stronger now. She must have been good for you."

The room filled with his anger, though his expression did not change. "Yes. She was."

There was a moment of tension between them, in which I hoped. Yeine is the best of us, full of good, solid mortal common sense and her own generous measure of pride. Surely she would not succumb! But then the moment passed and she sighed and looked ashamed and said, "It was...wrong of us. To take her from you."

That was all it took, that acknowledgment. In the eternity of silence that followed, he forgave her. I knew it as a mortal creature knows the sun has risen. And then he forgave himself—for what, I cannot be sure and dare not guess. Yet that, too, was a palpable change. He suddenly stood a little taller, grew calmer, let down the guard of arrogance he'd kept up since she arrived. She saw the walls fall—and behind them, the him that used to be. The Itempas who'd once won over her resentful predecessor, tamed wild Nahadoth, disciplined a fractious litter of child-gods, and crafted from whole cloth time and gravity and all the other amazing things that made life possible and so interesting. It isn't hard to love that version of him. I know.

So I do not blame her, not really. For betraying me.

But it hurt so much to watch as she went to him and touched his lips with her fingers. There was a look of dazzlement on her face as she beheld the brilliance of his true self. (She yielded so easily. When had she become so weak? Damn her. Damn her to her own misty hells.)

She frowned a little and said, "I don't know why I came here."

"One lover has never been enough for any of us," said
Itempas, smiling a sad little smile, as if he knew how
unworthy he was of her desire. Despite this, he took her
shoulders and pulled her close and their lips touched and
their essences blended and I hated them, I hated them, I
despised them both, how dare he take her from me, how
dare she love him when I had not forgiven him, how dare
they both leave Naha alone when he'd suffered so much,
how could they? I hated them and I loved them and gods
how I wanted to be with them, why couldn't I just be one
of them, it wasn't fair—

—no. No. Whining was pointless. It didn't even make
me feel better. Because the Three could never be Four,
and even when the Three were reduced to two, a godling
could never replace a god, and any heartbreak that I felt in
that moment was purely my own damned fault for wanting what I could not have.

When I could bear their happiness no more, I fled. To a
place that matched the Maelstrom in my heart. To the
only place within the mortal realm I have ever called
home. To my own personal hell...called Sky.

I was sitting corporeal at the top of the Nowhere Stair,
sulking, when the children found me. Total chance, that.
Mortals think we plan everything.

They were a matched set. Six years old—I am good at
gauging ages in mortals—bright-eyed, quick-minded,
like children who have had good food and space to
run and pleasures to stimulate the soul. The boy was
dark-haired and -eyed and -skinned, tall for his age, solemn. The girl was blonde and green-eyed and pale, intent.
Pretty, both of them. Richly dressed. And little tyrants, as
Arameri tended to be at that age.

"You will assist us," said the girl in a haughty tone.

Inadvertently I glanced at their foreheads, my belly clenched for the jerk of the chains, the painful slap of the magic they'd once used to control us. Then I remembered the chains were gone, though the habit of straining against them apparently remained. Galling. The marks on their heads were circular, denoting fullbloods, but the circles themselves were mere outlines, not filled in. Just a few looping, overlapping rings of command, aimed not at us but at reality in general. Protection, tracking, all the usual spells of safety. Nothing to force obedience, theirs or anyone else's.

I stared at the girl, torn between amazement and amusement. She had no idea who—or what—I was, that much was clear. The boy, who looked less certain, looked from her to me and said nothing.

"Arameri brats on the loose," I drawled. My smile seemed to reassure the boy, infuriate the girl. "Someone's going to get in trouble for letting you two run into me down here."

At this they both looked apprehensive, and I realized the problem: they were lost. We were in the underpalace, those levels beneath Sky's bulk that sat in perpetual shadow and had once been the demesne of the palace's lowblood servants—though clearly that was no longer the case. A thick layer of dust coated the floors and decorative moldings all around us, and aside from the two in front of me, there was no scent of mortals anywhere nearby. How long had they been wandering down here alone? They looked tired and frazzled and depleted by despair.

Which they covered with belligerence. "You will instruct us in how we might reach the overpalace," said the girl, "or guide us there." She thought a moment, then lifted her chin and added, "Do this now, or it will not go well with you!"

I couldn't help it: I laughed. It was just too perfect, her

fumbling attempt at hauteur, their extremely poor luck in meeting me, all of it. Once upon a time, little girls like her had made my life a hell, ordering me about and giggling when I contorted myself to obey. I had lived in terror of Arameri tantrums. Now I was free to see this one as she truly was: just a frightened creature parroting the mannerisms of her parents, with no more notion of how to *ask* for what she wanted than how to fly.

And sure enough, when I laughed, she scowled and put her hands on her hips and poked out her bottom lip in a way that I have always adored—in children. (In adults it is infuriating, and I kill them for it.) Her brother, who had seemed sweeter-natured, was beginning to glower, too. Delightful. I have always been partial to brats.

"You have to do what we say!" said the girl, stamping her foot. "You will help us!"

I wiped away a tear and sat back against the stair wall, exhaling as the laughter finally passed. "You will find your own damn way home," I said, still grinning, "and count yourselves lucky that you're too cute to kill."

That shut them up, and they stared at me with more curiosity than fear. Then the boy, who I had already begun to suspect was the smarter if not the stronger of the two, narrowed his eyes at me.

"You don't have a mark," he said, pointing at my forehead. The girl started in surprise.

"Why, no, I don't," I said. "Imagine that."

"You aren't...Arameri, then?" His face screwed up, as if he had found himself speaking gibberish. *You curtain apple jump, then?*

"No, I'm not."

"Are you a new servant?" asked the girl, seduced out of anger by her own curiosity. "Just come to Sky from outside?"

I put my arms behind my head, stretching my feet out in front of me. "I'm not a servant at all, actually."

"You're dressed like one," said the boy, pointing.

I looked at myself in surprise and realized I had manifested the same clothing I'd usually worn during my imprisonment: loose pants (good for running), shoes with a hole in one toe, and a plain loose shirt, all white. Ah, yes—in Sky, servants wore white every day. Highbloods wore it only for special occasions, preferring brighter colors otherwise. The two in front of me had both been dressed in deep emerald green, which matched the girl's eyes and complemented the boy's nicely.

"Oh," I said, annoyed that I'd inadvertently fallen prey to old habit. "Well, I'm not a servant. Take my word for it."

"You aren't with the Teman delegation," said the boy, speaking slowly while his eyes belied his racing thoughts. "Datennay was the only child with them, and they left three days ago, anyway. And they dressed like Temans. Metal bits and twisty hair."

"I'm not Teman, either." I grinned again, waiting to see how they handled that one.

"You *look* Teman," said the girl, clearly not believing me. She pointed at my head. "Your hair barely has any curl, and your eyes are sharp and flat at the corners, and your skin is browner than Deka's."

I glanced at the boy, who looked uncomfortable at this comparison. I could see why. Though he bore a fullblood's circle on his brow, it was painfully obvious that someone had brought non-Amn delicacies to the banquet of his recent heritage. If I hadn't known it was impossible, I would have guessed he was some variety of High Norther. He had Amn features, with their long-stretched facial lines, but his hair was blacker than Nahadoth's void and as straight as windblown grass, and he was indeed a rich all-over brown that had nothing to do with a suntan. I had seen infants like him drowned or head-staved or tossed off the Pier, or marked as lowbloods and given over to servants to raise. Never had one been given a fullblood mark.

The girl had no hint of the foreign about her—no, wait. It was there, just subtle. A fullness to her lips, the angle of her cheekbones, and her hair was a more brassy than sunlit gold. To Amn eyes, these would just be interesting idiosyncracies, a touch of the exotic without all the unpleasant political baggage. If not for her brother's existence, no one would have ever guessed that she was not pure-blooded, either.

I glanced at the boy again and saw the warning-sign wariness in his eyes. Yes, of course. They would have already begun to make his life hell.

While I pondered this, the children fell to whispering, debating whether I looked more of this or that or some other mortal race. I could hear every word of it, but out of politeness I pretended not to. Finally the boy stage-whispered, "I don't think he's Teman at *all*," in a tone that let me know he suspected what I really was.

With eerie unity they faced me again.

"It doesn't matter if you're a servant or not, or Teman or not," said the girl. "*We're* fullbloods, and that means you have to do what we say."

"No, it doesn't," I said.

"Yes, it does!"

I yawned and closed my eyes. "Make me."

They fell silent again, and I felt their consternation. I could have pitied them, but I was having too much fun. Finally, I felt a stir of air and warmth nearby, and I opened my eyes to find that the boy had sat down beside me.

"Why won't you help us?" he asked, his voice soft with

honest concern, and I nearly flinched beneath the onslaught of his big dark eyes. "We've been down here all day, and we ate our sandwiches already, and we don't know the way back."

Damnation. I'm partial to cuteness, too. "All right," I said, relenting. "Where are you trying to go?"

The boy brightened. "To the World Tree's heart!" Then his excitement flagged. "Or at least, that was where we *were* trying to go. Now we just want to go back to our rooms."

"A sad end to a grand adventure," I said, "but you wouldn't have found what you were looking for anyhow. The World Tree was created by Yeine, the Mother of Life; its heart is her heart. Even if you found the chunk of wood that exists at the Tree's core, it would mean nothing."

"Oh," said the boy, slumping more. "We don't know how to find her."

"I do," I said, and then it was my turn to sag, as I remembered what had driven me to Sky. Were they still together, she and Itempas? He was mortal, with merely mortal endurance, but she could renew his strength again and again for as long as she liked. How I hated her. (Not really. Yes, really. Not really.)

"I do," I said again, "but that wouldn't help you. She's busy with other matters these days. Not much time for me or any of her children."

"Oh, is she your mother?" The boy looked surprised. "That sounds like our mother. She never has time for us. Is your mother the family head, too?"

"Yes, in a way. Though she's also new to the family, which makes for a certain awkwardness." I sighed again, and the sound echoed within the Nowhere Stair, which descended into shadows at our feet. Back when I and the other Enefadeh had built this version of Sky, we had created this spiral staircase that led to nothing, twenty feet down to dead-end against a wall. It had been a long day spent listening to bickering architects. We'd gotten bored.

"It's a bit like having a stepmother," I said. "Do you know what that is?"

The boy looked thoughtful. The girl sat down beside him. "Like Lady Meull, of Agru," she said to the boy. "Remember our genealogy lessons? She's married to the duke now, but the duke's children came from his first wife. His first wife is the mother. Lady Meull is the stepmother." She looked at me for confirmation. "Like that, right?"

"Yes, yes, like that," I said, though I neither knew nor cared who Lady Meull was. "Yeine is our queen, sort of, as well as our mother."

"And you don't like her?" Too much knowing in both the children's eyes as they asked that question. The usual Arameri pattern, then, parents raising children who would grow up to plot their painful deaths. The signs were all there.

"No," I said softly. "I love her." Because I did, even when I hated her. "More than light and darkness and life. She is the mother of my soul."

"So, then..." The girl was frowning. "Why are you sad?"

"Because love is not enough." I fell silent for an instant, stunned as realization moved through me. Yes, here was truth, which they had helped me find. Mortal children are very wise, though it takes a careful listener or a god to understand this. "My mother loves me, and at least one of my fathers loves me, and I love them, but that just isn't *enough*, not anymore. I need something more." I groaned and drew up my knees, pressing my forehead against them. Comforting flesh and bone, as familiar as a security blanket. "But what? What? I don't understand why everything feels so wrong. Something is changing in me."

I must have seemed mad to them, and perhaps I was.

All children are a little mad. I felt them look at each other. "Um," said the girl. "You said *one* of your fathers?"

I sighed. "Yes. I have two. One of them has always been there when I needed him. I have cried for him and killed for him." Where was he now, while his siblings turned to each other? He was not like Itempas—he accepted change—but that did not make him immune to pain. Was he unhappy? If I went to him, would he confide in me? Need me?

It troubled me that I wondered this.

"The other father…" I drew a deep breath and raised my head, propping my folded arms on my knees instead. "Well, he and I never had the best relationship. Too different, you see. He's the firm disciplinarian type, and I am a brat." I glanced at them and smiled. "Rather like you two, actually."

They grinned back, accepting the title with honor. "We don't have any fathers," said the girl.

I raised my eyebrows in surprise. "*Someone* had to make you." Mortals had not yet mastered the art of making little mortals by themselves.

"Nobody important," said the boy, waving a hand dismissively. I guessed he had seen a similar gesture from his mother. "Mother needed heirs and didn't want to marry, so she chose someone she deemed suitable and had us."

"Huh." Not entirely surprising; the Arameri had never lacked for pragmatism. "Well, you can have mine, the second one. I don't want him."

The girl giggled. "He's your father! He can't be ours."

She probably prayed to the Father of All every night. "Of course he can be. Though I don't know if you'd like him any more than I do. He's a bit of a bastard. We had a falling-out some time ago, and he disowned me, even though he was in the wrong. Good riddance."

The girl frowned. "But don't you miss him?"

I opened my mouth to say *of course I don't* and then realized that I did. "Demonshit," I muttered.

They gasped and giggled appropriately at this gutter talk. "Maybe you should go see him," said the boy.

"I don't think so."

His small face screwed up into an affronted frown. "That's silly. Of course you should. He probably misses you."

I frowned, too taken aback by this idea to reject it out of hand. "What?"

"Well, isn't that what fathers do?" He had no idea what fathers did. "Love you, even if you don't love them? Miss you when you go away?"

I sat there silent, more troubled than I should have been. Seeing this, the boy reached out, hesitating, and touched my hand. I looked down at him in surprise.

"Maybe you should be happy," he said. "When things are bad, change is good, right? Change means things will get better."

I stared at him, this Arameri child who did not at all look Arameri and would probably die before his majority because of it, and I felt the knot of frustration within me ease.

"An Arameri optimist," I said. "Where did you come from?"

To my surprise, both of them bristled. I realized at once that I had struck a nerve, and then realized which nerve when the girl lifted her chin. "He comes from right here in Sky, just like me."

The boy lowered his eyes, and I heard the whisper of taunts around him, some in childish lilt and some deepened by adult malice: *where did you come from did a barbarian leave you here by mistake maybe a demon dropped you off on its way to the hells because gods know you don't belong here.*

I saw how the words had scored his soul. He had made me feel better; he deserved something in recompense for that. I touched his shoulder and sent my blessing into him, making the words just words and making him stronger against them and putting a few choice retorts at the tip of his tongue for the next time. He blinked in surprise and smiled shyly. I smiled back.

The girl relaxed once it became clear that I meant her brother no harm. I willed a blessing to her, too, though she hardly needed it.

"I'm Shahar," she said, and then she sighed and unleashed her last and greatest weapon: politeness. "Will you *please* tell us how to get home?"

Ugh, what a name! The poor girl. But I had to admit, it suited her. "Fine, fine. Here." I looked into her eyes and made her know the palace's layout as well as I had learned it over the generations that I had lived within its walls. (Not the dead spaces, though. Those were mine.)

The girl flinched, her eyes narrowing suddenly at mine. I had probably slipped into my cat shape a little. Mortals tended to notice the eyes, though that was never the only thing that changed about me. I put them back to nice round mortal pupils, and she relaxed. Then gasped as she realized she knew the way home.

"That's a nice trick," she said. "But what the scriveners do is prettier."

A scrivener would have broken your head open if they'd tried what I just did, I almost retorted, but didn't because she was mortal and mortals have always liked flash over substance and because it didn't matter, anyway. Then the girl surprised me further, drawing herself up and bowing from the waist. "I thank you, sir," she said. And while I stared at her, marveling at the novelty of Arameri thanks, she adopted that haughty tone she'd tried to use before. It really didn't suit her; hopefully she would figure that out soon. "May I have the pleasure of knowing your name?"

"I am Sieh." No hint of recognition in either of them. I stifled a sigh.

She nodded and gestured to her brother. "This is Dekarta."

Just as bad. I shook my head and got to my feet. "Well, I've wasted enough time," I said, "and you two should be getting back." Outside the palace, I could feel the sun setting. For a moment I closed my eyes, waiting for the familiar, delicious vibration of my father's return to the world, but of course there was nothing. I felt fleeting disappointment.

The children jumped up in unison. "Do you come here to play often?" asked the boy, just a shade too eagerly.

"Such lonely little cubs," I said, and laughed. "Has no one taught you not to talk to strangers?"

Of course no one had. They looked at each other in that freakish speaking-without-words-or-magic thing that twins do, and the boy swallowed and said to me, "You should come back. If you do, we'll play with you."

"Will you, now?" It *had* been a long time since I'd played. Too long. I was forgetting who I was amid all this worrying. Better to leave the worry behind, stop caring about what mattered, and do what felt good. Like all children, I was easy to seduce.

"All right, then," I said. "Assuming, of course, that your mother doesn't forbid it"—which guaranteed that they would never tell her—"I'll come back to this place on the same day, at the same time, next year."

They looked horrified and exclaimed in unison, "Next *year*?"

"The time will pass before you know it," I said, stretching to my toes. "Like a breeze through a meadow on a light spring day."

It would be interesting to see them again, I told myself, because they were still young and would not become as foul as the rest of the Arameri for some while. And, because I had already grown to love them a little, I mourned, for the day they became true Arameri would most likely be the day I killed them. But until then, I would enjoy their innocence while it lasted.

I stepped between worlds and away.

The next year I stretched and climbed out of my nest and stepped across space again, and appeared at the top of the Nowhere Stair. It was early yet, so I amused myself conjuring little moons and chasing them up and down the steps. I was winded and sweaty when the children arrived and spied me.

"We know what you are," blurted Deka, who had grown an inch.

"Do you, now? Whoops—" The moon I'd been playing with made a bid to escape, shooting toward the children because they stood between it and the corridor. I sent it home before it could put a hole in either of them. Then I grinned and flopped onto the floor, my legs splayed so as to take up as much space as possible, and caught my breath.

Deka crouched beside me. "Why are you out of breath?"

"Mortal realm, mortal rules," I said, waving a hand in a vague circle. "I have lungs, I breathe, the universe is satisfied, hee-ho."

"But you don't sleep, do you? I read that godlings don't sleep. Or eat."

"I can if I want to. Sleeping and eating aren't that interesting, so I generally don't. But it looks a bit odd to forgo breathing—makes mortals very anxious. So I do that much."

He poked me in the shoulder. I stared at him.

"I was seeing if you were real," he said. "The book said you could look like anything."

"Well, yes, but all of those things are *real*," I replied.

"The book said you could be fire."

I laughed. "Which would also be real."

He poked me again, a shy grin spreading across his face. I liked his smile. "But I couldn't do *this* to fire." He poked me a third time.

"Watch it," I said, giving him A Look. But it wasn't serious, and he could tell, so he poked me again. With that I leapt on him, tickling, because I cannot resist an invitation to play. So we wrestled and he squealed and struggled to get free and complained that he would pee if I kept it up, and then he got a hand free and started tickling me back, and it actually did tickle awfully, so I curled up to escape him. It was like being drunk, like being in one of Yeine's newborn heavens, so sweet and so perfect and so much delicious fun. I *love* being a god!

But a hint of sour washed across my tongue. When I lifted my head, I saw that Deka's sister stood where he had left her, shifting from foot to foot and trying not to look like she yearned to join us. Ah, yes—someone had already told her that girls had to be dignified while boys could be rowdy, and she had foolishly listened to that advice. (One of many reasons I'd settled on a male form myself. Mortals said fewer stupid things to boys.)

"I think your sister's feeling left out, Dekarta," I said, and she blushed and fidgeted more. "What shall we do about it?"

"Tickle her, too!" Dekarta cried. Shahar threw him a

glare, but he only giggled, too giddy with play-pleasure to be repressed so easily. I had a fleeting urge to lick his hair, but it passed.

"I'm not feeling left out," she said.

I petted Dekarta to settle him and to satisfy my grooming urge, and considered what to do about Shahar. "I don't think tickling would suit her," I said at last. "Let's find a game we can all play. What about, hmm…jumping on clouds?"

Shahar's eyes widened. "What?"

"Jumping on clouds. Like jumping on a bed but better. I can show you. It's fun, as long as you don't fall through a hole. I'll catch you if you do—don't worry."

Deka sat up. "You can't do that. I've been reading books about magic and gods. You're the god of childhood. You can only do things children do."

I laughed, pulling him into a headlock, which he squealed and struggled to get free of, though he didn't struggle all that hard. "Almost anything can be done for play," I said. "If it's play, I have power over it."

He looked surprised, going still in my arms. I knew then that he had read the family records, because during my captivity, I had never once explained to the Arameri the full implications of my nature. They had thought I was the weakest of the Enefadeh. In truth, with Naha swallowed into mortal flesh every morning, I had been the strongest. Keeping the Arameri from realizing this had been one of my best tricks ever.

"Then let's go cloud jumping!" Deka said.

Shahar looked eager, too, as I offered her my hand. But just as she reached for my hand, she hesitated. A familiar wariness came into her eyes.

"L-Lord Sieh," she said, and grimaced. I did, too. I hated titles, so pretentious. "The book about you—"

"They wrote a book about me?" I was delighted.

"Yes. It said..." She lowered her eyes, then remembered that she was Arameri and looked up, visibly steeling herself. "It said you liked to kill people, back when you lived here. You would do tricks on them, sometimes funny tricks... but sometimes people would die."

Still funny, I thought, but perhaps this was not the time to say such things aloud. "It's true," I said, guessing her question. "I must've killed, oh, a few dozen Arameri over the years." Oh, but there had been that incident with the puppies. A few hundred, then.

She stiffened, and Deka did, too, so much that I let him go. Headlocks are no fun when they're real. "Why?" asked Shahar.

I shrugged. "Sometimes they were in the way. Sometimes to prove a point. Sometimes just because I felt like it."

Shahar scowled. I had seen that look on a thousand of her ancestors' faces, and it always annoyed me. "Those are bad reasons to kill people."

I laughed—but I had to force it. "Of course they're bad reasons," I said. "But how better to remind mortals that keeping a god as a slave is a bad idea?"

Her frown faltered a little, then returned in force. "The book said you killed *babies*. Babies didn't do anything bad to you!"

I had forgotten the babies. And now my good mood was broken, so I sat up and glared at her. Deka drew back, looking from one to the other of us anxiously. "No," I snapped at Shahar, "but I am the god of *all* children, little girl, and if I deem it fitting to take the lives of some of my chosen, then who the hells are you to question that?"

"I'm a child, too," she said, jutting her chin forward. "But *you're* not my god—Bright Itempas is."

I rolled my eyes. "Bright Itempas is a coward."

She inhaled, her face turning red. "He is not! That's—"

"He is! He murdered my mother and abused my father—and killed more than a few of his own children, I'll thank you to know! Do you think the blood is any thicker on my hands than on his? Or for that matter, on your own?"

She flinched, darting a look at her brother for support. "I've never killed anyone."

"*Yet.* But it doesn't matter, because everything you do is stained with blood." I rose to a crouch, leaning forward until my face was inches from hers. To her credit, she did not shrink away, glaring back at me—but frowning. Listening. So I told her. "All your family's power, all your riches, do you think they come from nowhere? Do you think you *deserve* them, because you're smarter or holier or whatever they teach this family's spawn these days? Yes, I killed babies. Because their mothers and fathers had no problem killing the babies of other mortals, who were heretics or who dared to protest stupid laws or who just didn't breathe the way you Arameri liked!"

Appropriately, I ran out of breath at that point and had to stop, panting for air. Lungs were useful for putting mortals at ease but still inconvenient. Just as well, though. Both children had fallen silent, staring at me in a kind of horrified awe, and belatedly I realized I had been ranting. Sulking, I sat down on a step and turned my back on them, hoping that my anger would pass soon. I liked them—even Shahar, irritating as she was. I didn't want to kill them yet.

"You...you think we're bad," she said after a long moment. There were tears in her voice. "You think *I'm* bad."

I sighed. "I think your family's bad, and I think they're going to raise you to be just like them." Or else they would kill her or drive her out of the family. I'd seen it happen too many times before.

"I'm not going to be bad." She sniffed behind me. Deka, who was still within the range of my eyesight, looked up and inhaled, so I guessed that she was full-out crying now.

"You won't be able to help it," I said, resting my chin on my drawn-up knees. "It's your nature."

"It isn't!" She stamped a foot on the floor. "My tutors say mortals aren't like gods! We don't have *natures*. We can all be what we *want* to be."

"Right, right." And I could be one of the Three.

Sudden agony shot through me, firing upward from the small of my back, and I yelped and jumped and rolled halfway down the steps before I regained control of myself. Sitting up, I clutched my back, willing the pain to stop and marveling that it did so only reluctantly.

"You kicked me," I said in wonder, looking up the steps at her.

Deka had covered his mouth with both hands, his eyes wide; of the two of them, only he seemed to have realized that they were about to die. Shahar, fists clenched and legs braced and hair wild and eyes blazing, did not care. She looked ready to march down the steps and kick me again.

"I *will* be what I want to be," she declared. "I'm going to be head of the family one day! What I say I'll do, I'll do. I *am* going to be good!"

I got to my feet. I wasn't angry, in truth. It is the nature of children to squabble. Indeed, I was glad to see that Shahar was still herself under all the airs and silks; she was beautiful that way, furious and half mad, and for a fleeting instant I understood what Itempas had seen in her foremother.

But I did not believe her words. And that put me in an altogether darker mood as I went back up the steps, my jaw set and tight.

"Let's play a game, then," I said, and smiled.

Deka got to his feet, looking torn between fear and a desire to defend his sister; he hovered where he was, uncertain. There was no fear in Shahar's eyes, though some of her anger faded into wariness. She wasn't stupid. Mortals always knew to be careful when I smiled a certain way.

I stopped in front of her and held out a hand. In it, a knife appeared. Because I was Yeine's son, I made it a Darre knife, the kind they gave to their daughters when they first learned to take lives in the hunt. Six inches straight and silvery, with a handle of filigreed bone.

"What is this?" she asked, frowning at it.

"What's it look like? Take it."

After a moment she did, holding it awkwardly and with visible distaste. Too barbaric for her Amn sensibilities. I nodded my approval, then beckoned to Dekarta, who was studying me with those lovely dark eyes of his. Remembering one of my other names, no doubt: *Trickster*. He did not come at my gesture.

"Don't be afraid," I said to him, making my smile more innocent, less frightening. "It's your sister who kicked me, not you, right?"

Reason worked where charm had not. He came to me, and I took him by the shoulders. He was not as tall as I, so I hunkered down to peer into his face. "You're really very pretty," I said, and he blinked in surprise, the tension going out of him. Utterly disarmed by a compliment. He probably didn't get them often, poor thing. "In the north, you know, you'd be ideal. Darre mothers would already be haggling for the chance to marry you to their daughters.

It's only here among the Amn that your looks are something to be ashamed of. I wish they could see you grown up; you would have broken hearts."

"What do you mean, 'would have'?" asked Shahar, but I ignored her.

Deka was staring at me, entranced in the way of any hunter's prey. I could have eaten him up.

I cupped his face in my hands and kissed him. He shivered, though it had been only a fleeting press of lips. I'd held back the force of myself because he was only a child, after all. Still, when I pulled back, I saw his eyes had glazed over; blotches of color warmed his cheeks. He didn't move even when I slid my hands down and wrapped them around his throat.

Shahar went very still, her eyes wide and, finally, frightened. I glanced over at her and smiled again.

"I think you're just like any other Arameri," I said softly. "I think you'll want to kill me rather than let me murder your brother, because that's the good and decent thing to do. But I'm a god, and you know a knife can't stop me. It'll just piss me off. Then I'll kill him *and* you." She twitched, her eyes darting from mine to Deka's throat and back. I smiled and found my teeth had grown sharp. I never did this deliberately. "So I think you'll let him die rather than risk yourself. What do you think?"

I almost pitied her as she stood there breathing hard, her face still damp from her earlier tears. Deka's throat worked beneath my fingers; he had finally realized the danger. Wisely, though, he held still. Some predators are excited by movement.

"Don't hurt him," she blurted. "Please. Please, I don't—"

I hissed at her, and she shut up, going pale. "Don't beg," I snapped. "It's beneath you. Are you Arameri or not?"

She fell silent, hitching once, and then—slowly—I saw the change come over her. The hardening of her eyes and will. She lowered the knife to her side, but I saw her hand tighten on its hilt.

"What will you give me?" she asked. "If I choose?"

I stared at her, incredulous. Then I burst out laughing. "That's my girl! Bargaining for your brother's life! Perfect. But you seem to have forgotten, Shahar, that that's not one of your options. The choice is very simple: your life or his—"

"No," she said. "That's not what you're making me choose. You're making me choose between being bad and, and being myself. You're trying to *make* me bad. That's not fair!"

I froze, my fingers loosening on Dekarta's throat. In the Maelstrom's unknowable name. I could feel it now, the subtle lessening of my power, the greasy nausea at the pit of my belly. Across all the facets of existence that I spanned, I diminished. It was worse now that she had pointed it out, because the very fact that she understood what I had done made the harm greater. Knowledge was power.

"Demonshit," I muttered, and grimaced ruefully. "You're right. Forcing a child to choose between death and murder—there's no way innocence can survive something like that intact." I thought a moment, then scowled and shook my head. "But innocence never lasts long, especially for Arameri children. Perhaps I'm doing you a favor by making you face the choice early."

She shook her head, resolute. "You're not doing me a favor; you're cheating. Either I let Deka die, or I try to save him and die, too? It's not fair. I can't win this game, no matter what I do. You better do something to make up for it." She did not look at her brother. He was the prize in this game, and she knew it. I would have to revise my opinion of her intelligence. "So...I want you to give me something."

Deka blurted, "Just let him kill me, Shar; then at least you'll live—"

"Shut up!" She snapped it before I would have. But she closed her eyes in the process. Couldn't look at him and keep herself cold. When she looked back at me, her face was hard again. "And you don't have to kill Deka, if I...if I take that knife and use it on you. Just kill me. That'll make it fair, too. Him or me, like you said. Either he lives or I do."

I considered this, wondering if there was some trick in it. I could see nothing untoward, so finally I nodded. "Very well. But you *must choose*, Shahar. Stand by while I kill him, or attack me, save him, and die yourself. And what would you have of me, as compensation for your innocence?"

At this she faltered, uncertain.

"A wish," said Dekarta.

I blinked at him, too surprised to chastise him for talking. "What?"

He swallowed, his throat flexing in my hands. "You grant one wish, anything in your power, for...for whichever one of us survives." He took a shaky breath. "In compensation for taking *our* innocence."

I leaned close to glare into his eyes, and he swallowed again. "If you dare wish that I become your family's slave again—"

"No, we wouldn't," blurted Shahar. "You can still kill me—or...or Deka—if you don't like the wish. Okay?"

It made sense. "Very well," I said. "The bargain is made. Now *choose*, damn you. I don't feel like being—"

She lunged forward and shoved the knife into my back so fast that she almost blurred. It hurt, as all damage to the body does, for Enefa in her wisdom had long ago established that flesh and pain went hand in hand. While I froze, gasping, Shahar let go of the knife and grabbed Dekarta instead, yanking him out of my grasp. "Run!" she cried, pushing him away from the Nowhere Stair toward the corridors.

He stumbled a step away and then, stupidly, turned back to her, his face slack with shock. "I thought you would pick...you should have..."

She made a sound of utter frustration while I sagged to my knees and struggled to breathe around the hole in my lung. "I *said* I would be good," she said fiercely, and I would have laughed in pure admiration if I'd been able. "You're my brother! Now go! Hurry, before he—"

"Wait," I croaked. There was blood in my mouth and throat. I coughed and fumbled behind me with one hand, trying to reach the knife. She'd put it high in my back, partially through my heart. Amazing girl.

"Shahar, come with me!" Deka grabbed her hands. "We'll go to the scriveners—"

"Don't be stupid. They can't fight a god! You have to—"

"*Wait*," I said again, having finally coughed out enough blood to clear my throat. I spat more into the puddle between my hands and still couldn't reach the knife. But I could talk, softly and with effort. "I won't hurt either of you."

"You're lying," said Shahar. "You're a trickster."

"No trick." Very carefully I took a breath. Needed it to talk. "Changed my mind. Not going to kill...either of you."

Silence. My lung was trying to heal, but the knife was

in the way. It would work its way free in a few minutes if I couldn't reach it, but those minutes would be messy and uncomfortable.

"Why?" asked Dekarta finally. "Why did you change your mind?"

"Pull this . . . mortalfucking knife, and I'll tell you."

"It's a trick—" Shahar began, but Dekarta stepped forward. Bracing a hand on my shoulder, he took hold of the knife hilt and yanked it free. I exhaled in relief, though that almost started me coughing again.

"Thank you," I said pointedly to Dekarta. When I glared at Shahar, she tensed and took a step back, then stopped and inhaled, her lips pressed tightly together. Ready for me to kill her.

"Oh, enough with the martyrdom," I said wearily. "It's lovely, just lovely, that you two are all ready to die for each other, but it's also pretty sickening, and I'd rather not throw up more than blood right now."

Dekarta had not taken his hand from my shoulder, and I realized why when he leaned to the side to peer at my face. His eyes widened. "You weakened yourself," he said. "Making Shahar choose . . . It hurt you, too."

Far more than the knife had done, though I had no intention of telling them that. I could have willed the knife out of my flesh or transported myself away from it, if I had been at my best. Shaking off his hand, I got to my feet, but I had to cough one or two times more before I felt back to normal. As an afterthought, I sent away the blood from my clothing and the floor.

"I destroyed some of her childhood," I said, sighing as I turned to her. "Stupid of me, really. Never wise to play adult games with children. But, well, you pissed me off."

Shahar said nothing, her face hollow with relief, and

my stomach did an extra turn at this proof of the harm
I'd done her. But I felt better when Dekarta moved to her
side, and his hand snaked out to take hers. She looked at
him, and he gazed back. Unconditional love: childhood's
greatest magic.

With this to strengthen her, Shahar faced me again.
"Why did you change your mind?"

There had been no reason. I was a creature of impulse.
"I think because you were willing to die for him," I
said. "I've seen Arameri sacrifice themselves many
times—but rarely by choice. It intrigued me."

They frowned, not really understanding, and I
shrugged. I didn't understand it, either.

"So, then, I owe you a wish," I said.

They looked at each other again, their expressions mirrors of consternation, and I groaned. "You have no idea
what you want to wish for, do you?"

"No," said Shahar, ducking her eyes.

"Come back in another year," said Dekarta, quickly.
"That's more than enough time for us to decide. You can
do that, can't you? We'll…" He hesitated. "We'll even
play with you again. But no more games like this one."

I laughed, shaking my head. "No, they're not much
fun, are they? Fine, then. I'll be back in a year. You'd better be ready."

As they nodded, I took myself away to lick my wounds
and recover my strength. And to wonder, with dawning
surprise, what I'd gotten myself into.

2

Run away, run away
Or I'll catch you in a day
I can make you scream and play
'Til my father goes away
(Which one? Which one?
That one! That one!)
Just run, just run, just run.

As always when I was troubled, I sought out my father, Nahadoth.

He was not difficult to find. Amid the vastness of the gods' realm, he was like a massive, drifting storm, terrifying for those in his path and cathartic in his wake. From any direction, one could look into the distance and there he was, defying logic as a matter of course. Almost as noticeable were the lesser presences that drifted nearby, drawn toward all that heavy, dark glory even though it might destroy them. I beheld my siblings in all their variety and sparkling beauty, elontid and mnasat and even a few of my fellow niwwah. Many lay prostrate before our dark father or strained toward the black unlight that was his core, their souls open for the most fleeting droplets of his approval. He played favorites, though, and many of them had served Itempas. They would be waiting a long time.

For me, however, there was welcome on the wind as I traveled through the storm's outermost currents. The layered walls of his presence shifted aside, each in a different direction, to admit me. I caught the looks of envy from my less-favored siblings and gave them glares of contempt in return, staring down the stronger ones until they turned away. Craven, useless creatures. Where had they been when Naha needed them? Let them beg his forgiveness for another two thousand years.

As I passed through the last shiver, I found myself taking corporeal form. A good sign, that; when he was in a foul mood, he abandoned form altogether and forced any visitors to do the same. Better still, there was light: a night sky overhead, dominated by a dozen pale moons all drifting in different orbits and waxing and waning and shifting from red through gold through blue. Beneath it, a stark landscape, deceptively flat and still, broken here and there by line-sketched trees and curving shapes too attenuated to qualify as hills. My feet touched ground made of tiny mirrored pebbles that jumped and rattled and vibrated like frenzied living things. They sent a delicious buzz through my soles. The trees and hills were made of the glittering pebbles, too—and the sky and moons, for all I knew. Nahadoth was fond of playing with expectations.

And beneath the sky's cool kaleidoscope, shaping himself in an aimless sort of way, my father. I went to him and knelt, watching and worshipping, as his shape blurred through several forms and his limbs twisted in ways that had nothing to do with grace, though occasionally he grew graceful by accident. He did not acknowledge my presence, though of course he knew I was there. Finally he finished, and fell, purposefully, onto a couchlike throne that formed itself as I watched. At this, I rose and went to stand beside him. He did not look at me, his face turned toward the moons and shifting only slightly now, mostly just reacting to the colors of the sky. His eyes were shut, only the long dark lashes remaining the same as the flesh around them changed.

"My loyal one," he said. The pebbles hummed with the low reverberations of his voice. "Have you come to comfort me?"

I opened my mouth to say yes—and then paused, startled, as I realized this was not true. Nahadoth glanced at me, laughed softly and not without cruelty, and widened his couch. He knew me too well. Shamed, I climbed up beside him, nestling into the drifting curve of his body. He petted my hair and back, though I was not in the cat's shape. I enjoyed the caresses anyhow.

"I hate them," I said. "And I don't."

"Because you know, as I do, that some things are inevitable."

I groaned and flung an arm over my eyes dramatically, though this only served to press the image into my thoughts: Yeine and Itempas straining together, gazing at each other in mutual surprise and delight. What would be next? Naha and Itempas? All three of them together, which existence had not seen since the demons' time? I lowered my arm and looked at Nahadoth and saw the same sober contemplation on his face. Inevitable. I bared my teeth and let them grow cat-sharp and sat up to glare at him.

"You *want* that selfish, thickheaded bastard! Don't you?"

"I have always wanted him, Sieh. Hatred does not exclude desire."

He meant the time before Enefa's birth, when he and Itempas had gone from enemies to lovers. But I chose to interpret his words more immediately, manifesting claws and digging them into the drifting expanse of him.

"Think of what he did to you," I said, flexing and sheathing. I could not hurt him—would not even if I could—but there were many ways to communicate frustration. "To us! Naha, I know you will change, must change, but you need not change *this* way! Why go back to what was before?"

"Which before?" That made me pause in confusion, and he sighed and rolled onto his back, adopting a face that sent its own wordless message: white-skinned and black-eyed and emotionless, like a mask. The mask he had worn for the Arameri during our incarceration.

"The past is gone," he said. "Mortality made me cling to it, though that is not my nature, and it damaged me. To return to myself, I must reject it. I have had Itempas as an enemy; that holds no more appeal for me. And there is an undeniable truth here, Sieh: we have no one but each other, he and I and Yeine."

At this I slumped on him in misery. He was right, of course; I had no right to ask him to endure again the hells of loneliness he had suffered in the time before Itempas. And he would not, because he had Yeine and their love was a powerful, special thing—but so had been his love with Itempas, once. And when all Three had been together...How could I, who had never known such fulfillment, begrudge him?

He would not be alone, whispered a small, furious voice in my most secret heart. *He would have me!*

But I knew all too well how little a godling had to offer a god.

Cold white fingers touched my cheek, my chin, my chest. "You are more troubled by this than you should be," said Nahadoth. "What is wrong?"

I burst into frustrated tears. "I don't know."

"Shhhh. Shhhh." She—Nahadoth had changed already, adapting to me because she knew I preferred women for some things—sat up, pulling me into her lap, and held me against her shoulder while I wept and hitched fitfully. This made me stronger, as she had known it would, and when the squall passed and nature had been served, I drew a deep breath.

"I don't know," I said again, calm now. "Nothing is right anymore. I don't understand the feeling, but it's troubled me for some while now. It makes no sense."

She frowned. "This is not about Itempas."

"No." Reluctantly I lifted my head from her soft breast and reached up to touch her more rounded face. "Something is changing in me, Naha. I feel it like a vise gripping my soul, tightening slowly, but I don't know who holds it or turns it, nor how to wriggle free. Soon I might break."

Naha frowned and began to shift back toward male. It was a warning; *she* was not as quick to anger as *he* was. He was male most of the time these days. "Something has caused this." His eyes glinted with sudden suspicion. "You went back to the mortal realm. To Sky."

Damnation. We were all, we Enefadeh, still sensitive to the stench of that place. No doubt I would have Zhakkarn on my doorstep soon, demanding to know what madness had afflicted me.

"*That* had nothing to do with it, either," I said, scowling at his overprotectiveness. "I just played with some mortal children."

"Arameri children." Oh, gods, the moons were going dark, one by one, and the mirror-pebbles had begun to rattle ominously. The air smelled of ice and the acrid sting of dark matter. Where was Yeine when I needed her? She could always calm his temper.

"Yes, Naha, and they had no power to harm me or even to command me as they once did. And I felt the wrongness *before* I went there." It had been why I'd followed Yeine, feeling restless and angry and in search of excuses for both. "They were just children!"

His eyes turned to black pits, and suddenly I was truly afraid. "You love them."

I went very still, wondering which was the greater blasphemy: Yeine loving Itempas, or me loving our slavemasters?

He had never hurt me in all the aeons of my life, I reminded myself. Not intentionally.

"Just children, Naha," I said again, speaking softly. But I couldn't deny his words. *I loved them.* Was that why I had decided not to kill Shahar, breaking the rules of my own game? I hung my head in shame. "I'm sorry."

After a long, frightening moment, he sighed. "Some things are inevitable."

He sounded so disappointed that my heart broke. "I—" I hitched again, and for a moment hated myself for being the child I was.

"Hush now. No more crying." With a soft sigh, he rose, holding me against his shoulder effortlessly. "I want to know something."

The couch dissolved back into the shivering bits of mirror, and the landscape vanished with it. Darkness enclosed us, cold and moving, and when it resolved, I gasped and clutched at him, for we had traveled via his will into the blistering chasm at the edge of the gods' realm, which contained—insofar as the unknowable could be contained—the Maelstrom. The monster Itself lay below, far below, a swirling miasma of light and sound and matter and concept and emotion and moment. I could hear Its thought-numbing roar echoing off the wall of torn stars that kept the rest of reality relatively safe from Its ravenings. I felt my form tear as well, unable to maintain coherence under the onslaught of image-thought-music. I abandoned it quickly. Flesh was a liability in this place.

"Naha..." He still held me against him, yet I had to shout to be heard. "What are we doing here?"

Nahadoth had become something like the Maelstrom, churning and raw and formless, singing a simpler echo of Its toneless songs. He did not answer at first, but he had no sense of time in this state. I schooled myself to patience; he would remember me eventually.

After a time he said, "I have felt something different here, too."

I frowned in confusion. "What, in the Maelstrom?" How he could comprehend anything of this morass was beyond me—quite literally. In my younger, stupider days, I had dared to play in this chasm, risking everything to see how deeply I could dive, how close I could get to the source of all things. I could go deeper than all my siblings, but the Three could go deeper still.

"Yes," Nahadoth said at length. "I wonder..."

He began to move downward, toward the chasm. Too stunned to protest at first, I finally realized he was actually taking me in. "Naha!" I struggled, but his grip was steel and gravity. "Naha, damn you, do you want me dead? Just kill me yourself, if so!"

He stopped, and I kept shouting at him, hoping reason would somehow penetrate his strange thoughts. Eventually it did, and to my immense relief, he began to ascend.

"I could have kept you safe," he said with a hint of reproof.

Yes, until you lost yourself in the madness and forgot I was there. But I was not a complete fool. I said instead, "Why were you taking me there anyhow?"

"There is a resonance."

"What?"

The chasm and the roar vanished. I blinked. We stood in the mortal realm, on a branch of the World Tree, facing the unearthly white glow of Sky. It was nighttime, of course, with a full moon, and the stars had shifted fractionally. A year had passed. It was the night before I was to meet the twins a third time.

"There is a resonance," Nahadoth said again. He was a darker blotch against the Tree's bark. "You, and the Maelstrom. The future or the past, I cannot tell which."

I frowned. "What does that mean?"

"I don't know."

"Has it ever happened before?"

"No."

"Naha..." I swallowed my frustration. He did not think as lesser beings did. It was necessary to move in spirals and leaps to follow him. "Will it hurt me? I suppose that's all that matters."

He shrugged as if he did not care, though his brows had furrowed. He wore his Sky face again. This close to the palace where we had both endured so many hells, I did not like it as much.

"I will speak to Yeine," he said.

I shoved my hands into my pockets and hunched my shoulders, kicking at a spot of moss on the bark beneath my feet. "And Itempas?"

To my relief, Nahadoth uttered a dry, malicious laugh. "*Inevitable* is not the same as *immediate*, Sieh—and love does not mandate forgiveness." With that he turned away, his shadows already blending with those of the Tree and the night horizon. "Remember that, with your Arameri pets."

Then he was gone. The clouds above the world wavered for an instant with his passing, and then reality became still.

Troubled beyond words, I became a cat and climbed the branch to a knot the size of a building, around which clustered several smaller branches that were dotted with the Tree's triangle-shaped leaves and silvery flowers. There I curled up, surrounded by Yeine's comforting scent, to await the next day. And I wondered—with no surcease since I no longer had to sleep—why my insides felt hollow and shaky with dread.

With time to kill before the meeting, I amused myself—if one can call it amusing—by wandering the palace in the hours before dawn. I started in the underpalace, which had so often been a haven for me in the old days, and discovered that it had indeed been entirely abandoned. Not just the lowest levels, which had always been empty (save the apartments I and the other Enefadeh had inhabited), but all of it: the servants' kitchens and dining halls, the nurseries and schoolrooms, the sewing salons and haircutters'. All the parts of Sky dedicated to the lowbloods who made up the bulk of its population. By the look of things, no one had been in the underpalace to do more than sweep in years. No wonder Shahar and Dekarta had been so frightened that first day.

On the overpalace levels, at least, there were servants about. None of them saw me as they went about their duties, and I didn't even bother to shape myself an Amn form or hide in a pocket of silence. This was because even though there were servants, there weren't *many* of them—not nearly as many as there had been in my slave days. It was a simple matter to step around a curve of corridor when I heard one walking toward me, or spring up to cling to the ceiling if I was caught between two. (Useful fact: mortals rarely look up.) Only once was I forced to use magic, and that not even my own; faced with an inescapable convergence of servants who would surely spot me otherwise, I stepped into one of the lift alcoves, where some long-dead scrivener's activation bounced me up to another level. Criminally easy.

It should not have been so easy for me to stroll about, I mused as I continued to do so. I had reached the high-blood levels by this point, where I did have to be a bit more careful. There were fewer servants here, but more guards, wearing the ugliest white livery I'd ever seen—and swords, and crossbows, and hidden daggers, if my fleshly eyes did not deceive me. There had always been guards in Sky, a small army of them, but they had taken pains to remain unobtrusive in the days when I'd lived here. They had dressed the same as the servants and had never worn weapons that could be seen. The Arameri preferred to believe that guards were unnecessary, and they hadn't been, in truth, back then. Any significant threat to the palace's highbloods would have forced us Enefadeh to transport ourselves to the site of danger, and that would've been the end of it.

So, I considered as I stepped through a wall to avoid an unusually attentive guard, it seemed the Arameri had been forced to protect themselves more conventionally. Understandable—but how did that account for the diminished number of servants?

A mystery. I resolved to find out, if I could.

Stepping through another wall, I found myself in a room that held a familiar scent. Following it—and tiptoeing past the nurse dozing on the sitting room couch—I found Shahar, asleep in a good-sized four-poster bed. Her perfect blonde curls spread prettily over half a dozen pillows, though I stifled a laugh at her face: mouth open, cheek mashed on one folded arm, and a line of drool down that arm forming a puddle on the pillow. She was snoring quite loudly and did not stir when I went over to examine her toy shelf.

One could learn a great deal about a child from her play. Naturally I ignored the toys on the highest shelves; she would want her favorites within easy reach. On the lower shelves, someone had been cleaning the things and keeping them in good order, so it was hard to spot the most worn of the items. Scents revealed much, however, and three things in particular drew me closer. The first was a large stuffed bird of some sort. I touched my tongue to it and tasted a toddler's love, fading now. The second was a spyglass, light but solidly made so as to withstand being dropped by clumsy hands. Perhaps she used it to look down at the city or up at the stars. It had an air of wonder that made me smile.

The third item, which made me stop short, was a scepter.

It was beautiful, intricate, a graceful, twisting rod marbled with bright jewel tones down its length. A work of art. Not made of glass, though it appeared to be; glass would have been too fragile to give to a child. No, this was tinted daystone, the same substance as the palace's walls—very difficult to shatter, among its other unique properties. (I knew that very well, since I and my siblings had created it.) Which was why, centuries ago, a family head had commissioned this and other such scepters from his First Scrivener, and had given it to the Arameri heir as a toy. *To learn the feel of power,* he had said. And since then, many little Arameri boys and girls had been given a scepter on their third birthday, which most of them promptly used to whack pets, other children, and servants into painful obedience.

The last time I had seen one of these scepters, it had been a modified, adult version of the thing on Shahar's shelf. Fitted with a knife blade, the better to cut my skin to ribbons. The perversion of a child's toy had made each slice burn like acid.

I glanced back at Shahar—fair Shahar, *heir* Shahar, someday Lady Shahar Arameri. A very few Arameri children would not have used the scepter, but Shahar, I felt certain, was not so gentle. She would have wielded it with glee at least once. Deka had probably been her first victim. Had her brother's cry of pain cured her of the taste for sadism? So many Arameri learned to treasure the suffering of their loved ones.

I contemplated killing her.

I thought about it for a long time.

Then I turned and stepped through the wall into the adjoining room.

A suite, yes; that, too, was traditional for Arameri twins. Side-by-side apartments, connected by a door in the bedroom, ostensibly so that the children could sleep together or apart as they desired. More than one set of Arameri twins had been reduced to a singlet thanks to such doors. So easy for the stronger twin to creep into the weaker one's room unnoticed, in the dark of the night while the nurses slept.

Deka's room was darker than Shahar's, as it was positioned on the side of the palace that did not get moonlight. It would get less sunlight, too, I realized, for through the window-wall I could see one of the massive, curling limbs of the World Tree stretching into the distance against the night horizon. Its spars and branches and million, million leaves did not completely obscure the view, but any sunlight that came in would be dappled, unsteady. Tainted, by Itempan standards.

There were other indicators of Deka's less-favored status: fewer toys on the shelves, not as many pillows on the bed. I went to the bed and gazed down at him, thoughtful. He was curled on his side, neat and quiet even in rest. His nurse had done his long black hair in several plaits, perhaps in an awkward bid to give it some curl. I bent and ran my finger along one plait's smooth, rippling length.

"Shall I make you heir?" I whispered. He did not wake, and I got no answer.

Moving away, I was surprised to realize none of the toys on his shelves tasted of love. Then I understood when I came to the small bookcase, which practically reeked of it. Over a dozen books and scrolls bore the stamp of childish delight. I ran my fingers along their spines, absorbing their mortal magic. Maps of faraway lands, tales of adventure and discovery. Mysteries of the natural world—of which Deka probably experienced little, stuck here in Sky. Myths and fancies.

I closed my eyes and lifted my fingers to my lips, breathing the scent and sighing. I could not make a child with such a soul heir. It would be the same as destroying him myself.

I moved on.

Through the walls, underneath a closet, over a jutting spar of the World Tree that had nearly filled one of the dead spaces, and I found myself in the chambers of the Arameri head.

· The bedroom alone was as big as both the children's apartments combined. Large, square bed at the center, positioned atop a wide circular rug made from the skin of some white-furred animal I could not recall ever having hunted. Austere, by the standards of the heads I had known: no pearls sewn into the coverlet, no Darren black-wood or Kenti hand carving or Shuti-Narekh cloudcloth. What little other furniture there was had been positioned about the edges of the vast room, out of the way. A woman who did not like impediments in any part of her life.

The Lady Arameri herself was austere. She lay curled on her side, much like her son, though that was as far as the similarity went. Blonde hair, surprisingly cut short. The style framed her angular face well, I decided, but it was not at all the usual Amn thing. Beautiful, icy-pale face, though severe even in sleep. Younger than I'd expected: late thirties at a guess. Young enough that Shahar would come of age long before she was elderly. Did she intend for Shahar's children to be the true heirs, then? Perhaps this contest was not as foregone as it seemed.

I looked around, thoughtful. No father, the children had said, which meant the lady had no husband in the formal sense. Did she deny herself lovers, too, then? I bent to inhale her scent, opening my mouth slightly for a better taste, and there it was, oh, yes. The scent of another was embedded deep in her hair and skin, and even into the mattress. A single lover of some duration—months, perhaps years. Love, then? It was not unheard of. I would hunt amid the palace denizens to see if I could find the match to that lilting scent.

The lady's apartment told me nothing about her as I visited its other chambers: a substantial library (containing nothing interesting), a private chapel complete with Itempan altar, a personal garden (too manicured to have been cared for by anything but a professional gardener), a public parlor and a private one. The bath alone showed signs of extravagance: no mere tub here but a pool wide and deep enough to swim, with separate adjoining chambers for washing and dressing. I found her toilet in another chamber, behind a crystal panel, and laughed. The seat had been inscribed with sigils for warmth and softness. I could not resist; I changed them to ice-cold hardness. Hopefully I could arrange to be around to hear her shout when she discovered them.

By the time I finished exploring, the eastern sky was growing light with the coming dawn. So with a sigh I left Lady Arameri's chambers, returned to the Nowhere Stair, and lay down at the bottom to wait.

It seemed an age before the children arrived, their small feet striking a determined cadence as they came through the silent corridors. They did not see me at first, and exclaimed in dismay—then, of course, they came down the steps and found me. "You were hiding!" Shahar accused.

I had arranged myself on the floor, with my legs propped up against the wall. Smiling at her upside down, I said, "Talking to strangers again. Will you two never learn?"

Dekarta came over to crouch beside me. "Are you a stranger to us, Sieh? Even still?" He reached out and poked my shoulder again, as he had done before he learned I was dangerous. He smiled shyly and blushed as he did it. Had he forgiven me, then? Mortals were so fickle. I poked him back and he giggled.

"*I* don't think so," I said, "but you lot are the ones who worship propriety. The way I see it, a stranger feels like a stranger; a friend feels like a friend. Simple."

To my surprise, Shahar crouched as well, her small face solemn. "Would you mind, then?" she asked with a peculiar sort of intent that made me frown at her. "Being our friend?"

I understood all at once. The wish they'd earned from me. I'd expected them to choose something simple, like toys that never broke or baubles from another realm or wings to fly. But they were clever, my little Arameri pets. They would not be bribed by paltry material treasures or fleeting frivolities. They wanted something of real worth.

Greedy, presumptuous, insolent, *arrogant* brats.

I flipped myself off the wall with an awkward, ugly movement that no mortal could have easily replicated. It startled the children and they fell back with wide eyes, sensing my anger. On my hands and toes, I glared at them. "You want *what*?"

"Your friendship," said Deka. His voice was firm, but his eyes looked uncertain; he kept glancing at his sister. "We want you to be our friend. And we'll be yours."

"For how long?"

They looked surprised. "For as long as friendship lasts," said Shahar. "Life, I guess, or until one of us does something to break it. We can swear a blood oath to make it official."

"Swear a—" The words came out as a bestial growl. I could feel my hair turning black, my toes curling under. "How dare you?"

Shahar, damn her and all her forbears, looked innocently confused. I wanted to tear her throat out for not understanding. "What? It's just friendship."

"The friendship of a god." If I'd had a tail, it would have lashed. "If I did this, I would be obligated to play with you and enjoy your company. After you grow up, I'd have to look you up every once in a while to see how you're doing. I'd have to *care* about the inanities of your life. At least *try* to help you when you're in trouble. My gods, do you realize I don't even offer my worshippers that much? I should kill you both for this!"

But to my surprise, before I could, Deka sat forward and put his hand on mine. He flinched as he did it, because my hand was no longer fully human; the fingers had shortened, and the nails were in the process of becoming retractable. I kept the fur off by an effort of will. But Deka kept his hand there and looked at me with more compassion than I'd ever dreamt of seeing on an Arameri's face. All the swirling magic inside me went still.

"I'm sorry," he said. "We're sorry."

Now two Arameri had apologized to me. Had that ever happened when I'd been a slave? Not even Yeine had said those words, and she had hurt me terribly once during her mortal years. But Deka continued, compounding the miracle. "I didn't think. You were a prisoner here once—we read about it. They made you act like a friend then, didn't they?" He looked over at Shahar, whose expression showed the same dawning understanding. "Some of the old Arameri would punish him if he wasn't nice enough. We can't be like them."

My desire to kill them flicked away, like a snuffed candle.

"You...didn't know," I said. I spoke slowly, reluctantly,

forcing my voice back into the boyish higher registers where it belonged. "It's obvious you don't mean...what I think you meant by it." A backhanded route to servitude. Unearned blessings. I moved my nails back into place and sat up, smoothing my hair.

"We thought you would like it," Deka said, looking so crestfallen that I abruptly felt guilty for my anger. "I thought...we thought..."

Yes, of course, it would have been his idea; he was the dreamer of the two.

"We thought we were almost friends anyway, right? And you didn't seem to mind coming to see us. So we thought, if we asked to be friends, you would see we weren't the bad Arameri you think we are. You would see we weren't selfish or mean, and maybe"—he faltered, lowering his eyes—"maybe then you would keep coming back."

Children could not lie to me. It was an aspect of my nature; they could lie, but I would know. Neither Deka nor his sister were lying. I didn't believe them anyway—didn't want to believe them, didn't trust the part of my own soul that tried to believe them. It was never safe to trust Arameri, even small ones.

Yet they meant it. They wanted my friendship, not out of greed but out of loneliness. They truly wanted me for myself. How long had it been since anyone had wanted me? Even my own parents?

In the end, I am as easy to seduce as any child.

I lowered my head, trembling a little, folding my arms across my chest so they would not notice. "Um. Well. If you really want to...to be friends, then...I guess I could do that."

They brightened at once, scooching closer on their knees. "You mean it?" asked Deka.

I shrugged, pretending nonchalance, and flashed my famous grin. "Can't hurt, can it? You're just mortals." Blood-brother to mortals. I shook my head and laughed, wondering why I'd been so frightened by something so trivial. "Did you bring a knife?"

Shahar rolled her eyes with queenly exasperation. "You can make one, can't you?"

"I was just asking, gods." I raised a hand and made a knife, just like the one she'd used to stab me the previous year. Her smile faded and she drew back a little at the sight of it, and I realized that was not the best choice. Closing my hand about the knife, I changed it. When I opened my hand again, the knife was curved and graceful, with a handle of lacquered steel. Shahar would not know, but it was a replica of the knife Zhakkarn had made for Yeine during her time in Sky.

She relaxed when she saw the change, and I felt better at the grateful look on her face. I had not been fair to her; I would try harder to be so in the future.

"Friendships can transcend childhood," I said softly when Shahar took the knife. She paused, looking at me in surprise. "They can. If the friends continue to trust each other as they grow older and change."

"That's easy," said Deka, giggling.

"No," I said. "It isn't."

His grin faded. Shahar, though—yes, here was something she understood innately. She had already begun to realize what it meant to be Arameri. I would not have her for much longer.

I reached up to touch her cheek for a moment, and she blinked. But then I smiled, and she smiled back, as shy as Deka for an instant.

Sighing, I held out my hands, palms up. "Do it, then."

Shahar took my nearer hand, raising the knife, and then frowned. "Do I cut the finger? Or across the palm?"

"The finger," said Deka. "That was how Datennay said you do blood oaths."

"Datennay is an idiot," Shahar said with the reflexiveness of an old argument.

"The palm," I said, more to shut them up than to take any real stance.

"Won't that bleed a lot? And hurt?"

"That's the idea. What good is an oath if it doesn't cost you something to make?"

She grimaced, but then nodded and set the blade against my skin. The cut she made was so shallow that it tickled and did not make me bleed at all. I laughed. "Harder. I'm not a mortal, you know."

She threw me an annoyed look, then sliced once across the palm, swift and hard. I ignored the flash of pain. Refreshing. The wound tried to close immediately, but a little concentration kept the blood welling.

"You do me, I do you," Shahar said, giving the knife to Dekarta.

He took the knife and her hands and was not at all hesitant or shy about cutting his sister. Her jaw flexed, but she did not cry out. Nor did he when she made the cuts for him.

I inhaled the scent of their blood, familiar despite three generations removed from the last Arameri I had known. "Friends," I said.

Shahar looked at her brother, and he gazed back at her, and then they both looked at me. "Friends," they said together. They took each other's hands first, then mine.

Then—

* * *

Wait. What?

They held my hands, tight. It hurt. And why were both children crying out, their hair whipping in the wind? Where had the wind—

I didn't hear you. Speak louder.

This made no sense, our hands were *sealed*, *sealed together*, I could not let them go—

Yes, I am the Trickster. Who calls...?

They were screaming, the children were screaming, both of them had risen off the floor, only I held them down and why was there a grin on my face? Why—

Silence.

3

I SLEPT, and while I did, I dreamt. I did not remember some of these dreams for a long time. I was aware of very little, in fact, aside from

something

being

wrong

and perhaps a little bit of

wait

I

thought

what.

Vague awareness, in other words. A most unpleasant state for any god. None of us is all knowing, all seeing—that is mortal nonsense—but we know *a lot* and see *quite a bit*. We are used to a near-constant infusion of information by means of senses no mortal possesses, but for a time there was nothing. Instead, I slept.

Suddenly, though, in the depths of the silence and vagueness, I heard a voice. It called my name, my *soul*, with a fullness and strength that I had not heard in several mortal lifetimes. Familiar pulling sensation. Unpleasant.

I was comfortable, so I rolled over and tried to ignore it at first, but it pricked me awake, slapped me in the back to prod me forward, then shoved. I slid through an aperture in a wall of matter, like being born—or like entering the mortal realm, which was pretty much the same thing. I emerged naked and slippery with magic, my form reflexively solidifying itself for protection against the soul-devouring ethers that had once been Nahadoth's digestive fluids, in the time before time. My mind dragged itself out of stupor at last.

Someone had called my name.

"What do you want?" I said—or tried to say, though the words emerged from my lips as an unintelligible growl. Long before mortals had achieved a form worthy of imitation, I had taken the likeness of a creature that loved mischief and cruelty in equal measure, as quintessential an encapsulation of my nature as my child shape. I still tended to default to it, though I preferred the child shape these days. More fine control and nuance. But I had not been fully conscious when I took form in the mortal realm, and so I had become the cat.

Yet that shape was clumsy when I tried to rise, and something about it... felt wrong. I wasted no time trying to understand it, simply became the boy instead—or tried to. The change did not go as it should have. It took real effort, and my flesh remolded itself with molasses-slow reluctance. By the time I had clothed myself in human skin, I was exhausted. I flopped where I had materialized, panting and shaking and wondering what in the infinite hells was wrong with me.

"Sieh?"

The voice that had summoned me from the vague place. Female. Familiar and yet not. Puzzled, I tried to lift my head and turn to face the voice's owner, and found to my amazement that I could not. I had no strength.

"It *is* you. My gods, I never imagined..." Soft hands touched my shoulders, pulled at me. I groaned softly as she rolled me onto my side. Something pulled at my head, painful. Why the hells was I cold? I was never cold.

"By the endless Bright! This is..."

She touched my face. I turned toward her hand instinctively, nuzzling, and she gasped, jerking away. Then she stroked me again and did not pull away when I pressed against her this time.

"Sh-Shahar," I said. My voice was too loud and sounded wrong. I opened my eyes as wide as I could and stared at her, buglike. "Shahar?"

She was Shahar. I was certain of it. But something had happened to her. Her face was longer, the bones finer, the nose bridge higher. Her hair, which had been shoulder length when I'd last seen her—a moment ago? The day before?— now tumbled around her body, disheveled as if she'd just woken from sleep. Waist length at least, maybe longer.

Mortal hair did not grow so quickly, and not even Arameri would waste magic on something so trivial. Not these days, anyhow. Yet when I tried to find the nearby stars to know how much time had passed, what came back to me was only a blank, unintelligible rumble, like the jabbering of memory-worms.

"Cold," I murmured. Shahar got up and went away. An instant later, something covered me, warm and thick with the scents of her body and bird feathers. It should not have warmed me, any more than my body should have been cold to begin with, but I felt better. By this point I could move a little, so I curled up under it gratefully.

"Sieh..." She sounded like she was regaining her

composure after a deep shock. Her hand fell on my shoulder again, comforting. "Not that I'm not glad to see you"—she did not sound glad, not at all—"but if you were ever going to come back, why now? Why here, like this? This...gods. Unbelievable."

Why now? I had no idea, since I had no idea what *now* meant. Of *then*, I remembered less thoughts than impressions: holding her hand, holding Deka's hand. Light, wind, something out of control. Shahar's face, wide-eyed with panic, mouth open and—

Screaming. She had been screaming.

Some of my strength had returned. I used it to reach for her knee, which was a few inches from my face. My fingers slid over smooth, hot skin to reach thin, fine cloth—a sleep shift. She gasped and jerked away. "You're freezing!"

"I'm *cold*." So cold that I could feel the room's moisture beginning to cling to my skin, wherever the blanket didn't cover it. I pulled my head under the blanket, or tried to. That pulling sensation again. It held my head in place, though I could move somewhat against its tension. "Demonshit! What is that?"

"Your hair," said Shahar.

I froze, staring up at her.

She pushed at my arm, then pulled up a lock of hair for me to see. Loose-waved, dark brown, thick, and longer than her arm. *Feet* long. I couldn't move because I was half tangled in it.

"I didn't tell my hair to get that long," I said. It was a whisper.

"Well, tell it to get short again. Or quit flopping about so I can get you loose." She flipped up the blanket and started gathering my hair, tugging and finger combing.

When she turned me onto my side, my head was freed. I'd been lying on the bulk of it.

My hair should not have grown. *Her* hair should not have grown. "Tell me what's happened," I said as she shifted me about like an oversized doll. "How much time has passed since we took the oath?"

"Took the oath?" She stared down at me, an incredulous look on her face. "Is that all you remember? My gods, Sieh, you broke the oath almost the instant you made it—"

I cursed in three mortal languages, loudly, to cut her off. "Just tell me how much time has passed!"

Fury reddened her cheeks, though the pale light around us—Sky's glowing walls—made this difficult to see. "Eight years."

Impossible. "I would have remembered eight years."

I should have understood the anger in her voice as she snapped, "Well, that's how long it's been. Not my fault if you don't remember it. I suppose you must have so many important things to do, you gods, that mortal years pass like breaths for you."

They did, but we were *aware* of the breaths. I wanted to know more, like why she sounded so angry and hurt. Those things called to me like the sting of broken innocence, and they felt important. But they also felt like the sorts of things that needed to be softened with silence before they were brought forth sharp, so I pushed them aside and asked, "Why am I so weak?"

"How should I know?"

"Where was I? While I was gone?"

"Sieh"—she let out a hard exhalation—"I don't know. I haven't seen you once since the day eight years ago when you and I and Deka agreed to become friends. You tried to kill us and disappeared."

"Tried— I didn't try to kill you." Her face hardened further, full of hate. That meant I *had* tried to kill her, or at least she believed I had. "I didn't *intend* to. Shahar—" I reached for her again, instinctive this time. I could pull strength from mortal children if I had to, but when I touched her knee again, there was only a trickle of what I needed. Of course; eight years. She would be sixteen now—not yet a woman, but close. I whimpered in frustration and pulled away.

"I remember nothing from that moment until now," I said, to take my mind off fear. "I took your hands and then I was here. Something is wrong."

"Obviously." She pinched the bridge of her nose between her fingers and let out a heavy sigh. "Hopefully your arrival didn't trip the boundary scripts in the walls, or there will be a dozen guards breaking down the door in a minute. I'm going to have to think of some way to explain your presence." She paused, frowning at me hopefully. "Or can you leave? That would really be the easiest solution."

Yes, good for me and for her. It was obvious she didn't want me here. I didn't want to be here, either, weak and heavy and wrong-feeling like this. I wanted to be with, with, wait, was that— Oh, no.

"No," I whispered, and when she sighed in exasperation, I realized she thought I'd been responding to her question. I made a heroic effort and grabbed her hand as tight as I could, startling her. "*No.* Shahar, how did you bring me here? Did you use scrivening, or—or did you command it somehow?"

"I didn't bring you here. You just showed up."

"No, you made me come, I felt it, you pulled me out of him—" And oh demons, oh hells, I could feel him coming. His fury made the whole mortal realm throb like an open wound. How could she not feel it? I shook her hand in lieu of shouting at her. "You pulled me out of him and *he's going to kill you if you don't tell me right now what you did*!"

"Who—" she began. And then she froze, her eyes going wide, because even she could feel it now. Of course she could, because he was in the room with us, taking shape as the glowing walls went suddenly dark and the air trembled and hushed in reverence.

"Sieh," said the Lord of Night.

I closed my eyes and prayed Shahar would stay silent.

"Here," I said. An instant later he was beside me, the drifting dark of his cloak settling around him as he knelt. Chilly fingers touched my face, and I fought the urge to laugh at my own obtuseness. I should have realized at once why I was so cold.

He turned my face from side to side, examining me with more than eyes. I permitted this, because he was my father and it was his right to be concerned, but then I caught his hand. It solidified beneath my touch, and strength flowed into me from the limitless furnace of his soul. I exhaled in relief. "Naha. Tell me."

"We found you adrift, like a soul with no home. Damaged. Yeine attempted to heal you and could not. I took you into myself to do the same."

And Nahadoth's womb was a cold, dark place. "I don't feel healed."

"You aren't. I could not find a cure for your condition, nor could I preserve you." His voice, usually inflectionless, turned bitter. It was Itempas's gift to halt the progression of processes that depended on time; Nahadoth lacked this power entirely. "The best I could do was keep you safe while Yeine sought a cure. But you were taken from me. I had no idea where you had gone... at first."

And then his dark, dark eyes lifted to settle on Shahar. She flinched, quite reasonably.

I had no reason to want to save her, other than my own childish sense of honor. I had taken her innocence; I owed her. And however wrong it seemed to have gone, I had taken an oath to be her friend. So I sat up carefully—not into his line of sight, because that was never safe, but enough to get his attention. "Naha, whatever she did, she didn't do it intentionally."

"Her intentions do not matter," he said very softly. He did not look away from her. "When you were pulled from me, it felt much like the days of our incarceration. A summons that could be neither ignored nor denied."

Shahar made a soft sound, not quite a whimper, and Nahadoth's expression turned sharp and hungry. I did not blame him for his anger, but Shahar was not like the Arameri of old; she had not been raised to know the ways of gods. She did not realize that her fear could spur him to attack, because night was the time of predators and she was acting too much like prey.

Before I could think of some way to distract him, the worst occurred: she spoke.

"L-Lord Nahadoth," she said. Her voice shook, and he leaned closer to her, his breath quickening and the room growing darker. Demonshit. But then, to my surprise, she drew a deep breath and her fear receded. "Lord Nahadoth," she said again. "I assure you, I did nothing to... to *summon* Lord Sieh here. I was thinking of him, yes...." She glanced at me, her expression suddenly bleak, which confused me. "I spoke his name. But not because I wanted him here—quite the opposite. I was angry. It was a curse."

I stared at her. *A curse?* But her shift of mood had done what I could not; Naha exhaled and sat back.

"A curse is much like a prayer," he said, thoughtful. "If you knew his nature well enough…"

"A prayer wouldn't have snatched me from your void," I said, looking down at myself. The length of my limbs was obscene. My palms were half again as large as they had been! I was meant to have small, clever child fingers, not these monstrous paws. "And it couldn't have done *this* to me. Nothing should have done this." Now that Naha had renewed my strength, I could correct the error. I willed myself back to normal.

"Stop." Nahadoth's will clamped down on mine like a vise before I could begin the shaping. I froze, startled. "It is no longer safe for you to alter your form."

"No longer *safe*?"

He sighed. "You do not understand." So he looked into my eyes and made me know what he and Yeine had come to realize in the eight years since everything had gone wrong.

There is a line between god and mortal that has nothing to do with immortality. It is *material*: a matter of substance, composition, flexibility. This was what ultimately made the demons weaker than us, though some of them had all our power: they could cross this line, become god-stuff, but it took great effort, and they could not do it for long. It was not their natural state. Other mortals could not cross the line at all. They were locked to their flesh, aging as it aged, drawing strength from its strength and growing weak with its failure. They could not shape it or the world around them, save with the crude power of their hands and wits.

The problem, Nahadoth willed me to know, was that I

was no longer quite like a god. The substance of me was somewhere between godstuff and mortality—but I was becoming more mortal as time passed. I could still shape myself if I wished, as I had done when I arrived as the cat. But it would not go easily. There might be pain, damage to my flesh, permanent distortion. And there would come a day, perhaps today, perhaps another, when I would no longer be able to shape myself at all. If I tried then, I would die.

I stared at him and felt truly afraid.

"What are you saying?" I whispered, though he had said nothing. Mortal figure of speech. "Naha, what are you saying?"

"You are becoming mortal."

I was breathing harder. I had not willed myself to breathe harder. Or tremble, or sweat, or grow larger, or mature into manhood. My body was doing all that on its own. My body: alien, tainted, out of control.

"I'm going to die," I said. My mouth was dry. "Naha, growing older defies my nature. If I stay like this, if I keep aging, if I *trip and fall* hard enough, I'll die the way mortals do."

"We will find a way to heal you—"

My fists clenched. *"Don't lie to me!"*

Naha's mask cracked, replaced by sorrow. I remembered ten million nights in his lap, begging him for stories. His beautiful lies, I had called them. He had held me and told me of wonders real and imagined, and I had been so happy to never grow up. So that he could keep lying to me forever.

"You will grow older," he said. "As you leave childhood behind, you will grow weaker. You will begin to require sustenance and rest as mortals do, and your awareness of

things beyond mortal senses will fade. You will become…
fragile. And, yes, if nothing is done, you will die."

I could not bear the softness of his voice, no matter
how hard the words. He was always so soft, always yield-
ing, always tolerant of change. I did not want him to tolerate this.

I threw off the blanket and got to my feet—awkwardly,
as my limbs were longer than I was used to and I had too
much hair—and stumbled over to Shahar's windows. I put
my hands on the glass and leaned on it with all my weight.
Mortals rarely did this, I had observed during my centuries in Sky. Even though they knew that Sky's glass was
reinforced by magic and inhumanly precise engineering,
they could not rid themselves of the fear that just once, the
glass might break or the pane come loose. I braced my
feet and shoved. I needed *something* in my presence to be
unmoving and strong.

Something touched my shoulder and I turned fast, irra-
tionally aching for hard sunset eyes and harder brown
arms and brick-wall flexibility. But it was only the mortal,
Shahar. I glared at her, furious that she wasn't who I
wanted, and thought of batting her aside. It was somehow
her fault this had happened to me. Maybe killing her
would free me.

If she had looked at me with compassion or pity, I
would have done it. There was none of that in her face,
though—just resentment and reluctance, nothing at all
comforting. She was Arameri. That wasn't something
they did.

Itempas had failed me, but Itempas's chosen had been
magnificently predictable for two thousand years. I
yanked her closer and locked my arms around her, so
tight that it couldn't have been comfortable for her. She

turned her face away and her cheek pressed against my shoulder. She did not bend, though—didn't speak, didn't return my embrace. So I held her and trembled and ground my teeth together so that I would not simply start screaming. I glared at Nahadoth through the screen of her curls.

He gazed back at me, still and rueful. He knew full well why I had turned away from him, and he forgave me for it. I hated him for that, just as I'd hated Yeine for loving Itempas and just as I hated Itempas for going mad and not being here when I needed him. And I hated all three of them for squandering each other's love when I would give anything, *anything*, to have that for myself.

"Go away," I whispered through Shahar's hair. "Please."

"It isn't safe for you here."

I laughed bitterly, guessing his intent. "If I'm to have only a few more decades of life, Naha, I won't spend them asleep inside you. Thanks."

His expression tightened. He was not immune to pain, and I supposed I was driving the knives in deeper than usual. "You have enemies."

I sighed. "I can take care of myself."

"I will not lose you, Sieh. Not to death, and not to despair."

"Get out!" I clutched Shahar like a teddy bear and shut my eyes, shouting, "Get out, demons take you, go away and leave me the hells alone!"

There was an instant of silence. Then I felt him go. The walls resumed their glow; the room felt suddenly looser, airy. Shahar relaxed, minutely, against me. But not all the way.

I kept her against me anyway because I was feeling selfish and I did not want to care what she wanted. But I was older now, more mature whether I wanted to be or not, so after a moment I stopped thinking solely about myself. She stepped back when I let her go, and there was a distinctly wary look in her eyes.

"What are you going to do?" she asked.

I laughed, leaning back against the glass. "I don't know."

"Do you want to stay here?"

I groaned and put my hands on my head, tangling my fingers in all my unwanted hair. "I don't know, Shahar. I can't think right now. This is a bit much, all right?"

She sighed. I felt her come to stand beside me at the window, radiating thought. "You can sleep in Deka's room for tonight. In the morning I'll speak with Mother."

I was so soul-numb that this did not bother me nearly as much as it should have. "Fine," I said. "Whatever. I'll try not to wake him as I pace the floors and cry."

There was a moment's silence. That did not catch my attention so much as the ripple of hurt that rode in the silence's wake. "Deka isn't here. You'll have the room to yourself."

I looked at her, frowning. "Where is he?" Then it occurred to me: Arameri. "Dead?"

"No." She didn't look at me and her expression didn't change, but her voice went sharp and contemptuous of my assumption. "He's at the Litaria. The scriveners' college? In training."

I raised both eyebrows. "I didn't know he wanted to become a scrivener."

"He didn't."

Then I understood. Arameri, yes. When there was more than one potential heir, the family head did not *have* to pit them against one another in a battle to the death. She could keep both alive if she put one in a clearly subordinate position. "He's meant to be your First Scrivener, then."

She shrugged. "If he's good enough. There's no guarantee. He'll prove himself if he can, when he comes back. *If* he comes back."

There was something more here, I realized. It intrigued me enough to forget my own troubles for a moment, so I turned to her, frowning. "Scrivener training lasts years," I said. "Ten or fifteen, usually."

She turned to face me, and I flinched at the look in her eyes. "Yes. Deka has been in training for the past eight years."

Oh, no. "Eight years ago..."

"Eight years ago," she said in that same clipped, edged tone, "you and I and Deka took an oath of friendship. Immediately upon which you unleashed a flare of magic so powerful that it destroyed the Nowhere Stair and much of the underpalace—and then you vanished, leaving Deka and me buried in the rubble with more bones broken than whole."

I stared at her, horrified. She narrowed her eyes, searching my face, and a flicker of consternation diluted her anger. "You didn't know."

"No."

"How could you not know?"

I shook my head. "I don't remember anything after we joined hands, Shahar. But...you and Deka were wise to ask for my friendship; it should have made you safe from me for all time. I don't understand what happened."

She nodded slowly. "They pulled us out of the debris and patched us up, good as new. But I had to tell Mother about you. She was furious that we'd concealed something so important. And the heir's life had been threatened, which meant someone had to be held accountable." She folded her arms, holding her shoulders ever-so-slightly stiff. "Deka had fewer injuries than I. Our fullblood relatives started to hint that Deka—only Deka, never me—might have done something to antagonize you. They didn't come right out and accuse him of plotting to use a godling as a murder weapon, but..."

I closed my eyes, understanding at last why she had cursed my name. I had stolen her innocence first and then her brother. She would never trust me again.

"I'm sorry," I said, knowing it was wholly inadequate.

She shrugged again. "Not your fault. I see now that what happened was an accident."

She turned away then, pacing across her room to the door that adjoined her suite to the one that had been Dekarta's. Opening it, she turned back to look at me, expectant.

I stayed by the window, seeing the signs clearly now. Her face was impassive, cool, but she had not completely mastered herself yet. Fury smoldered in her, banked for now, but slow burning. She was patient. Focused. I would think this a good thing, if I hadn't seen it before.

"You don't blame me," I said, "though I'll wager you did, until tonight. But you still blame *someone*. Who?"

I expected her to dissemble. "My mother," she said.

"You said she was pressured into sending Deka away."

Shahar shook her head. "It doesn't matter." She said nothing for a moment more, then lowered her eyes. "Deka...I haven't heard from him since he left. He returns my letters unopened."

Even with my senses as muddled as they were, I could feel the raw wound in her soul where a twin brother had been. A wound like that demanded redress.

She sighed. "Come on."

I took a step toward her and stopped, startled as I

realized something. Arameri heads and heirs had loathed one another since the Bright's dawning. Unavoidable, given circumstances: two souls with the strength to rule the world were rarely good at sharing or even cohabitating, for that matter. That was why the family's heads had been as ruthless about controlling their heirs as they were about controlling the world.

My eyes flicked to Shahar's odd, incomplete blood sigil. None of the controlling words were there. She was free to act against her mother, even plot to kill her, if she wanted.

She saw my look and smiled. "My old friend," she said. "You were right about me, you know, all those years ago. Some things are my nature. Inescapable."

I crossed the room to stand beside her on the threshold. I was surprised to find myself uncertain as I considered her. I should have felt vindicated to hear her plans of vengeance. I should have said, and meant it, *You'll do worse before you're done.*

But I had tasted her childish soul, and there had been something in it that did not fit the cold avenger she seemed to have become. She had loved her brother, enough to sacrifice herself for him. She had sincerely yearned to be a good person.

"No," I said. She blinked. "You're different from the rest of them. I don't know why. You shouldn't be. But you are."

Her jaw flexed. "Your influence, maybe. As gods go, you've had a greater impact on my life than Bright Itempas ever could."

"That should've made you worse, actually." I smiled a little, though I did not feel like it. "I'm selfish and cruel and capricious, Shahar. I've never been a good boy."

She lifted an eyebrow, and her eyes flicked down. I wore nothing but my ridiculously long hair, which fell to my ankles now that I was standing. (My nails, however, had kept to my preferred length. Partial mortality, partial growth? I would live in dread of my first manicure.) I thought Shahar was looking at my chest, but my body was longer now, taller. Belatedly I realized her gaze had settled lower.

"You're not a *boy* at all anymore," she said.

My face went hot, though I did not know why. Bodies were just bodies, penises were just penises, yet she had somehow made me feel keenly uncomfortable with mine. I could think of nothing to say in reply.

After a moment, she sighed. "Do you want food?"

"No…" I began, but then my belly churned in that odd, clenching way that I had not felt in several mortal generations. I had not forgotten what it meant. I sighed. "But I will by morning."

"I'll have a double tray brought up. Will you sleep?"

I shook my head. "Too much on my mind, even if I was exhausted. Which I'm not." Yet.

She sighed. "I see."

Suddenly I realized *she* was exhausted, her face lined and paler than usual. My time sense was returning—murky, sluggish, but functional—so I understood it had been well past midnight when she'd summoned me. Cursed me. Had she been pacing the floor herself, her mind cluttered with troubles? What had caused her to remember me, however hatefully, after all this time? Did I want to know?

"Does our oath stand, Shahar?" I asked softly. "I didn't mean to harm you."

She frowned. "Do you want it to stand? I seem to recall

you were less than thrilled by the idea of two mortal friends."

I licked my lips, wondering why I was so uneasy. *Nervous.* She made me nervous. "I think perhaps...I could use friends, under the circumstances."

She blinked, then smiled with one side of her mouth. Unlike her earlier smiles, this one was genuine and free of bitterness. It made me see how lonely she was without her brother—and how young. Not so far removed, after all, from the child she had been.

Then she stepped forward, putting her hands on my chest, and kissed me. It was light, friendly, just a warm press of her lips for an instant, but it rang through me like a crystal bell. She stepped back and I stared at her. I couldn't help it.

"Friends, then," she said. "Good night."

I nodded mutely, then went into Deka's room. She shut the door behind me, and I slumped back against it, feeling alone and very strange.

4

Sleep, little little one
Here is a world
With hate on every continent
And sorrow in the fold.
Wish for a better life
Far, far from here
Don't listen while I talk of it
Just go there.

I DIDN'T SLEEP THAT NIGHT, though I could have. The urge was there, itchy. I imagined the craving for sleep as a parasite feeding on my strength, just waiting for me to grow weak so that it could take over my body. I had liked sleep, once, before it became a threat.

But I did not like boredom, either, and there was a great deal of that in the hours after I left Shahar. I could only ponder my troubling condition for so long. The only way to vent my frustration was to do something, anything, so I got up from the chair and wandered about Deka's room, peering into the drawers and under the bed. His books were too simple to interest me, except one of riddles that actually contained a few I hadn't heard before. But I read it in half an hour and then was bored again.

There is nothing more dangerous than a bored child— and though I had become a bored adolescent, that old mortal adage still rang true. So as the small hours stretched into slightly longer hours, I finally got up and opened a wall. That much, at least, I could do without expending any of my remaining strength; all it took was a word. When the daystone had finished rolling aside to make room for me, I went through the resulting opening into the dead spaces beyond.

Roaming my old territory put me in a better mood. Not everything was the same as it had been, of course. The World Tree had grown both around and through Sky, filling some of its old corridors and dead spaces with branchwood and forcing me to make frequent detours. This, I knew, had been Yeine's intent, for without the Enefadeh, and more importantly without the constant empowering presence of the Stone of Earth, Sky needed the Tree's support. Its architecture broke too many of Itempas's laws for the mortal realm; only magic kept it in the sky and not smashed on the ground.

So down seventeen levels, around a swirling rise of linked globules that only resembled a tunnel in dreams, and underneath an arched branch spur, I found what I'd sought: my orrery. I moved carefully between the protective traps I'd set, out of habit stepping around the patches of moonstone that lined the floor. It looked like daystone—mortals had never been able to tell the difference—but on cloudy, new-moon nights, the pieces of moonstone transformed, opening into one of Nahadoth's favorite hells. I had made it as a little treat for our masters, to remind them of the price to be paid for enslaving their gods, and we had all seeded it through the palace. They had blamed—and punished—Nahadoth for it, but he'd thanked me afterward, assuring me the pain was worth it.

But when I spoke *atadie* and the orrery opened, I stopped on its threshold, my mouth falling open.

Where there should have been more than forty globes floating through the air, all turning around the bright yellow sphere at the orrery's center, there were only four still floating. *Four*, counting the sun sphere. The rest lay scattered about the floor and against the walls, corpses in the aftermath of a systemic carnage. The Seven Sisters, identical small goldenworlds I had collected after searching billions of stars, lay strewn about the edges of the room. And the rest—Zispe, Lakruam, Amanaiasenre, the Scales, Motherspinner with its six child moons linked by a web of rings, and oh, Vaz, my handsome giant. That one, once a massive stark-white sphere I had barely been able to get my arms around, had hit the floor hard, splitting down the middle. I went to the nearer of the shattered halves and picked it up, moaning as I knelt. Its core was exposed, cold, still. Planets were resilient things, far more than most mortal creatures, but there was no way I could repair this. Even if I'd had the magic left to spare.

"No," I whispered, clutching the hemisphere to myself and rocking over it. I couldn't even weep. I felt as dead as Vaz inside. Nahadoth's words had not driven home the horror of my condition, but this? This I could not deny.

A hand touched my shoulder, and so great was my misery that I did not care who it was.

"I'm sorry, Sieh." Yeine. Her voice, a soft contralto, had deepened further with grief. I felt her kneel beside me, her warmth radiant against my skin. For once, I took no comfort in her presence.

"My fault," I whispered. I had always meant to disperse the orrery, returning its worlds to their homes when I'd tired of them. Only I never had, because I was a selfish brat. And when I'd been incarcerated in mortal form, desperate to feel like a god because my Arameri masters treated me like a thing, I had brought the orrery here despite the danger that they might be discovered. I had spent strength I didn't have, killing my mortal body more than once, to keep the orrery alive. And now, after all that, I hadn't even noticed that I'd failed them.

Yeine sighed and looped her arms around my shoulders, pressing her face to my hair for a moment. "Death comes to all, in time."

But this had been too soon. My orrery should have lasted a sun's lifetime. I drew a deep breath and set the hemisphere down, turning to look up at her. Her face did not show the shock that I knew she felt at the sight of my older shape. I was grateful for that, because she could have flinched at my withered beauty, but of course that was not her way. She still loved me, would always love me, even if I could no longer be her little boy. I lowered my eyes, ashamed that I had ever begrudged Itempas her affection.

"There are some survivors," I said softly. "They..." I drew a deep breath. What would I do without them? I would truly be alone then...but I would do what was right. They deserved that, these truest friends of mine. "Will you help them, Yeine? Please?"

"Of course." She closed her eyes. One by one, the planets that still floated about the sun sphere, and a couple of the ones on the floor, vanished. I followed with her as best I could, watching her carefully deposit each where I had found it: this one spinning around a bright golden sun, which was delighted to have it back; that one near twin suns that sang in harmony; that one in the heart of a stellar nursery, surrounded by howling infant planets and hissing, cranky magnetars, where it sighed and resigned itself to the noise.

But when Yeine reached for the sun sphere, En, it fought her. Surprised, we both opened our eyes back in the orrery to find that En had shed its ordinary yellow kickball disguise. It had begun to spin and burn, expending itself in a dangerous way given that I could not replenish it. At this rate, it would fail and die like the rest in minutes.

"What the hells are you doing?" I demanded of it. "Quit that; you're being rude."

It responded by darting out of its place and whisking over to boot me in the stomach. I *oof*ed in surprise, wrapping my arms around it inadvertently, and felt its outrage. How dare I try to send it away? It was older than many of my siblings. Had it not always been there when I needed it? It would not be sent away like some disgraced servant.

I touched its hot, pale-yellow surface, trying not to cry. "I can't take care of you anymore," I said. "Don't you understand? If you stay with me, you'll die."

It would die, then. Did not care it would die did not care.

"Stubborn ball of hot air!" I shouted, but then Yeine touched my hand where it rested on En's curve. When she did, En glowed brighter; she was feeding it as I could not.

"A true friend," she said gently, with only a hint of censure, "is something to be treasured."

"Not to death," I said, looking up at her for support. "Yeine, please; it's crazy. Send it away."

"Shall I deny its wishes, Sieh? Force it to do what you want? Am I Itempas now?"

And at that I faltered, silent, because of course she knew of my earlier anger. Perhaps she had even known I was there, spying on her with Itempas until I'd flounced off. I hunched, ashamed of myself and then ashamed that I felt ashamed.

"You use force when it suits you," I muttered, trying to cover the shame with sullenness.

"And when I must, yes. But it doesn't suit me now."

"I don't want more death on my conscience," I said, both to her and to En. "Please, En. I couldn't bear to lose you. Please!"

En—the demonshitting, lightfarting gasbag—responded by turning red and bloating with each passing second. Gathering itself to explode, as if that was somehow better than starving to death! I groaned.

Yeine rolled her eyes. "A tantrum. I suppose that's to be expected, given your influence, but really…" She shook her head and sat back on her knees, looking around thoughtfully. For an instant her eyes darkened, from their usual faded green to something deep and shadowed, like a thick, wet forest, and then suddenly the orrery chamber was empty. All my dead toys vanished. En, too, for which I felt sudden regret.

"I'll keep the rest safe for you," she said, reaching up to smooth a hand over my hair as she had always done. I closed my eyes and relaxed into the comfort of familiarity, pretending for a moment that I was still small and all was well. "Until the day you can reclaim them and send them home yourself."

I exhaled, grateful despite the bitterness her words triggered in me. It hurt her to make dead things live again; it went against her nature, a perversion of the cycle Enefa had designed at the beginning of life. She did not do it often, and we never asked it of her. But... I licked my lips. "Yeine... this thing that's happening to me..."

She sighed, looking troubled, and belatedly I realized there was no need to ask. If she'd had the power to reverse my transformation into a mortal, she would have used it, no matter what harm it did her. But what did it mean, then, that the goddess who had supreme power over mortality could not erase mine?

"If I were older," she said, and I felt guilty for making her doubt herself. She lowered her eyes, looking small and vulnerable, like the mortal girl she resembled. "If I knew myself better, perhaps I would be able to find some solution."

I sighed and shifted to lie on my side, putting my head in her lap after awkwardly pushing my hair out of the way. "This may be beyond all of us. Nothing like it has ever happened before. It's pointless to rail against what you can't stop." I scowled. "*That* would make you Itempas."

"Nahadoth is unhappy," she said.

I suspected she wanted to change the subject. I sighed. "Nahadoth is overprotective."

She stroked my hair again, then lifted the tangled mass and began to finger comb it. I closed my eyes, soothed by the rhythmic movements.

"Nahadoth loves you," she said. "When we first found you in this... condition... he tried so hard to restore you that it damaged him. And yet..." She paused, her tension suddenly prickling the air between us.

I frowned, both at her description of Nahadoth's behavior and at her hesitation. "What?"

She sighed. "I'm not certain you can be any more reasonable about this than Naha."

"*What*, Yeine?" But then I understood, and as she had

predicted, I grew unreasonably angry. "Oh gods and demons, no, no you don't. You want to talk to Itempas."

"Resisting change is his nature, Sieh. He may be able to do what Nahadoth could not: stabilize you until I find a cure. Or if we joined again, as Three—"

"No! You'd have to set him free for that!"

"Yes. For your sake."

I sat up, scowling. "I. Don't. Care."

"I know. Neither does Nahadoth, to my surprise."

"Naha—" I blinked. "What?"

"He is willing to do anything to save you. Anything, that is, except the one thing that might actually work." Abruptly she was angry, too. "When I asked, he said he would rather let you die."

"Good! He knows *I* would rather die than ask for that bastard's help! Yeine"—I shook my head but forced the words out—"I understand why you're drawn to him, even though I hate it. Love him if you must, but don't ask the same of me!"

She glared back, but I did not back down, and after a moment, she sighed and looked away. Because I was right, and she knew it. She was still so young, so mortal. She knew the story, but she had not *been there* to see what Itempas had done to Nahadoth, or to the rest of us Ene-fadeh. She lived with the aftermath—as did we all, as would every living thing in the universe, forever and ever—but that was entirely different from knowing firsthand.

"You're as bad as Nahadoth," she said at last, more troubled than angry. "I'm not asking you to forgive. We all know there's no forgiving what he did, the past can't be rewritten, but someday you're going to have to *move on*. Do what's necessary for the world, and for yourselves."

"Staying angry is necessary for me," I said petulantly, though I forced myself to take a deep breath. I did not want to be angry with her. "One day, maybe, I'll move on. Not now."

She shook her head, but then took me by the shoulders and guided me down so that my head lay in her lap again. I had no choice but to relax, which I wanted to do, anyway, so I sighed and closed my eyes.

"It's irrelevant in any case," she said, still sounding a bit testy. "We can't find him."

I did not want to talk about him, either, but I dredged up interest. "Why not?"

"I don't know. But he's been missing for several years now. When we seek his presence in the mortal realm, we feel nothing, find nothing. We aren't worried ... yet."

I considered this but could offer no answer. Even together, the Three were not omniscient, and Yeine and Nahadoth alone were not the Three. If Itempas had found some scrivener to craft an obscuration for him ... But why would he do that?

For the same reason he does anything else, I decided. *Because he's an ass.*

"I don't," Yeine said softly after a while. I frowned in confusion. She sighed and stroked my hair again. "Love him, I mean."

So many unspokens in her words. *Not yet* the most obvious among them, and perhaps a bit of *not ever, because I am not Enefa*, though I did not believe that. She was too drawn to him already. Most relevant was *not until you love him, too*, which I could live with.

"Right." I sighed, weary again. "Right. I don't love him, either."

We both fell silent at that, for a long while. Eventually

she began to touch my hair here and there, causing the excess length to fall away. I closed my eyes, grateful for her attention, and wondered how many more times I would be privileged to experience it before I died.

"Do you remember?" I asked. "The last day of your mortal life. You asked me what would happen when you died."

Her hands went still for a moment. "You said you didn't know. Death wasn't something you'd thought much about."

I closed my eyes, my throat tightening for no reason I could fathom. "I lied."

Her voice was too gentle. "I know."

She finished my hair and gathered the shed length of it in one hand. I felt the flick of her will, and then she put her hand in front of my face to show me what she'd done. My hair had become a thin woven cord short enough to loop about my neck, and threaded onto this cord was a small, yellow-white marble. A different size and substance, but I would recognize its soul anywhere: En.

I sat up, surprised and pleased, lifting the necklace to grin at my old friend. (It did not like being smaller. It missed being a kickball, bouncy and fat. Did it have to be this puny, rigid shape just because I wasn't a child anymore? Surely adult mortals liked to kick balls sometimes. I stroked it to still its whining.) Then I touched my shorter hair and found that she'd reshaped that, too, giving me a style that suited the older lines of my face.

I looked up at her. "You've made me very pretty— thank you. Did you play with dolls as a mortal girl?"

"I was Darre. Dolls were for boys." She got to her feet, unnecessarily dusting off her clothes, and looked around the now-empty chamber. "I don't like you being here, Sieh. In Sky."

I shrugged. "This place is as good as any other."
Nahadoth had been right about that. I couldn't leave the
mortal realm in my condition; too much of the gods' realm
was inimical to flesh. Naha could have kept me safe by
taking me into himself, but I would not tolerate that again.

"This place has Arameri."

Resisting the urge to bat at the marble on its cord, I
slipped it over my head and let it settle under my shirt
instead. (En liked that, being near my heart.) "I'm not a
slave anymore, Yeine. They're no threat to me now." She
shot me a look of such disgust that I recoiled. "What?"

"Arameri are *always* a threat."

I raised my eyebrows. "Really, daughter of Kinneth?"

At this she looked truly annoyed, her eyes turning a
yellowy, acid peridot. "They cling to power by a thread,
Sieh. Only their scriveners and armies allow them to keep
control—mortal magic, mortal strength, both of which
can be subverted. What do you think they'll do, now that
they have a god in their power again?"

"I can't see how a weak, dying god will do them much
good. I can't even take another form safely. I'm pathetic."
She opened her mouth to protest again, and I sighed to
interrupt her. "I will be careful. I promise. But truly,
Yeine, I have more important concerns right now."

She sobered. "Yes." After another moment's silence,
she uttered a heavy sigh and turned away. "See that you
are careful, Sieh. A mortal lifetime may seem like nothing to you...." She paused, blinked, and smiled to herself.
"To me, too, I suppose. But don't squander it. I mean to
use every moment of yours to try and find a cure."

I nodded. So lucky I was to have such devoted, determined parents. Two out of three of them, anyhow.

"I will see you again when I know more," she said. She

leaned forward to pull me into an embrace. I was still sitting on my knees; I did not rise as she did this. If I had, I would have been taller than her, and that did not feel at all right.

Then she vanished, and I sat alone in the empty orrery for a long time.

Judging by the angle of the sun, it was well into the afternoon when I returned to Dekarta's room. I didn't care about that for long, however, because as I stepped through the hole in the wall, I found that I had visitors. They rose to greet me as I stopped in surprise.

Shahar, more demure than I had ever seen her, stood near the door to her own room. She was dressed in what passed for daily wear among fullbloods: a long gown of honey-lattice, bright blue satin slippers, and a cloak, with her hair tucked and looped into an elaborate chignon. Beside Shahar stood a woman whose demeanor immediately cried *steward* to me. She stood the tallest of the three women in the room, broad-shouldered and handsome and marvelously direct in her gaze, with a churning avalanche of thick, coily black hair falling about her shoulders and back. Yet despite her commanding presence, she was not as well dressed as the other two, and her mark was only that of a quarterblood. She kept silent and looked through me with her hands behind her back, in the posture of detached attention that all her successful predecessors had mastered.

Between these two stood a third woman: the most high Lady Arameri herself, head of the family and ruler of the Hundred Thousand Kingdoms, resplendent in a deep red shawl-collared gown. Then to my further shock, all three women dropped to one knee—the steward smoothly, the lady and her heir somewhat less so. At the sight of their bowed heads, I couldn't help laughing.

"Well!" I said, putting my hands on my hips. "Now *this* is a welcome. I had no idea I was so important. Have you actually been waiting here all day for me to come back?"

"It's no less a welcome than we would offer to any god," said the lady. Her voice was low, surprisingly like Yeine's. She looked older awake, with a ruler's troubles and her own personality influencing the lines of her face, but she was still beautiful in a chilly, powerful way. And she was not afraid of me at all.

"Yes, yes, I know," I said, going to stand before her. I had not bothered to conjure or steal clothing for myself, which put certain parts of me right at the lady's eye level, should she choose to look up. Could I needle her into doing so? "Very diplomatic, Lady Arameri, given that half my family wants to kill you and the other half couldn't care less if the first half did. I assume Shahar told you everything?"

She didn't take the bait, damn her, keeping her gaze downcast. "Yes. My condolences on your loss of immortality, Lord Sieh."

Bitch. I scowled and folded my arms. "It's not *lost*; it's just mislaid for a while, and I am still a god whether I live forever or die tomorrow." But now I sounded petulant. She was manipulating me, and I was a fool for letting her do it. I went to the windows, turning my back on them to hide my annoyance. "Oh, get up. I hate pointless formality, or false humility, whichever this is. What's your name, and what do you want?"

There was a whisper of cloth as they rose. "I am Remath Arameri," the lady said, "and I want only to welcome you back to Sky—as an honored guest, of course.

We will extend you every courtesy, and I have already set the scrivener corps to the task of researching your...condition. There may be little we mortals can do that the gods haven't already attempted, but if we learn anything, we will share it with you, naturally."

"Naturally," I said, "since if you can figure out how it happened to me, you might be able to do it to any god who threatens you."

I was pleased that she did not attempt to deny it. "I would be remiss in my duties if I didn't try, Lord Sieh."

"Yes, yes." I frowned as something she'd mentioned caught my attention. "Scrivener *corps*? You mean the First Scrivener and his assistants?"

"The mortal world has changed since you last spent time among us, Lord Sieh," she said. A nice touch, that, making my centuries of slavery sound like a vacation. "As you might imagine, the loss of the Enefadeh—of your magic—was a great blow to our efforts to maintain order and prosperity in the world. It became necessary that we assume greater control over all the scriveners that the Litaria produces."

"So you have an army of scriveners, in other words. To go with your more conventional army?" I hadn't paid attention to the mortal realm since T'vril's death, but I knew he'd been working on that.

"The Hundred Thousand Legions." She did not smile—I got the impression she didn't do that often—but there was a hint of wry irony in her voice. "There aren't really a hundred thousand, of course. It just sounds impressive that way."

"Of course." I had forgotten what a pain it was, dealing with Arameri family heads. "So what do you *really* want? Because I highly doubt you're actually glad to have me here."

She did not dissemble, either, which I liked. "I'm neither glad nor displeased, Lord Sieh—though, yes, your presence does serve several useful purposes to the family." There was a pause, perhaps while she waited to see my reaction. I did wonder why the Arameri could possibly want me around, but I imagined that would become clear soon enough. "To that end, I have informed Morad, our palace steward, to ensure that all your material needs are met while you're here."

"It would be my honor and pleasure, Lord Sieh." This from the black-haired woman. "We could begin with a wardrobe."

I snorted in amusement, liking her already. "Of course."

Remath continued. "I have also informed my daughter Shahar that you are now her primary responsibility. For the duration of your time here in Sky, she is to obey you as she would me and see to your comfort at any cost."

Wait. I frowned, turning back to Remath at last. The expression on Remath's face—or rather, the intent lack of expression—made it clear that she knew full well what she had just done. The shocked look that Shahar threw at her back confirmed it.

"Let me be sure I understand you," I said slowly. "You're offering me *your daughter* to do with as I please." I glanced at Shahar again, who was beginning to look murderous. "What if it pleases me to kill her?"

"I would prefer that you not do so, naturally." Remath delivered this with sculptured calm. "A good heir represents a substantial investment of time and energy. But she is Arameri, Lord Sieh, and our fundamental mission has not changed since the days of our founding Matriarch. We rule by the grace of the gods; therefore, we serve the gods in all things."

Shahar threw me a look more raw than anything I'd seen since her childhood, full of betrayal and bitterness and helpless fury. Ah—now that was the Shahar I remembered. Not that this was as terrible as she seemed to think; our oath meant she had nothing to fear from me. Had she told Remath about that? Was Remath counting on a childhood promise to keep her heir safe?

No. I had lived among the Arameri for a hundred generations. I had seen how they raised their children with careful, calculated neglect; that was why Shahar and Dekarta had been left to wander the palace as children. They believed any Arameri stupid enough to die in a childhood accident was too stupid to rule. And I had also seen, again and again, how Arameri heads found ways to test their heirs' strength, even at the cost of their heirs' souls.

This, however... I felt my fists clench and had to work hard not to become the cat. Too dangerous, and a waste of magic.

"How dare you." It came out a snarl, anyway. "You think I'm some petty, simpleminded mortal, delighting in the chance to turn the tables? You think I need someone else's humiliation to know my own worth? *You think I'm like you?*"

Remath lifted an eyebrow. "Given that mortals are made in the gods' image, no, I think *we* are like *you*." That infuriated me into silence. "But very well; if it doesn't please you to use Shahar, then don't. Tell her what *will* please you. She'll see it done."

"And is this to take precedence over my other duties, Mother?" Shahar's voice was as cool as Remath's, though higher pitched; they sounded much alike. But the fury in her eyes could have melted glass.

Remath glanced over her shoulder and seemed pleased by her daughter's anger. She nodded once, as if to herself. "Yes, until I inform you otherwise. Morad, please make certain Shahar's secretary is informed." Morad murmured a polite affirmative, while Remath kept watching Shahar. "Have you any questions, Daughter?"

"No, Mother," Shahar replied quietly. "You've made your wishes quite clear."

"Excellent." In what I considered a brave gesture, Remath turned her back on her daughter and faced me again. "One more thing, Lord Sieh. Rumors are inevitable, but I would advise that you not make your presence—or rather, your nature—known during your time here. I'm sure you can imagine what sort of attention that would draw."

Yes, every scrivener and godphile in the palace would drive me to distraction with questions and worship and requests for blessings. And since this was Sky, there would also be the inevitable highbloods who wanted a little godly assistance with whatever schemes they had going, and a few who might try to harm or exploit me to gain prestige for themselves, and...I ground my teeth. "Obviously it would make sense for me to keep a low profile."

"It would, yes." She inclined her head—not the bow of a mortal to a god, but a respectful gesture between equals. I wasn't sure what she meant by that. Was she insulting me by not bothering to show reverence, or was she paying me the compliment of honesty? Damn, I couldn't figure this woman out at all. "I'll take my leave of you now, Lord Sieh."

"Wait," I said, stepping closer so that I could look her in the eye. She was taller than me, which I liked; it made me feel more my old self. And she was at least wary of me, I saw when I stood closer. I liked that, too.

"Do you mean me harm, Remath? Say you don't. *Promise* it."

She looked surprised. "Of course I don't. I'll swear any oath you like on that."

I smiled, showing all my teeth, and for the barest instant I did smell fear in her. Not much, but even an Arameri is still human, and humans are still animals, and animals know a predator when one draws near.

"Cross your heart, Remath," I said. "Hope to die. Stick a needle in your eye."

She lifted an eyebrow at my nonsense. But the words of a god have power, regardless of what language we speak, and I was not quite mortal yet. She felt my intent, despite the silly words.

"Cross my heart," she replied gravely, and inclined her head. Then she turned and swept out, perhaps before she could reveal more fear, and certainly before I could say anything else. I stuck my tongue out at her back as she left.

"Well." Morad drew a deep breath, turning to regard me. "I believe I can find suitable garments for your size, though a proper fitting with the tailor would make things easier. Would you be willing to stand for that, Lord Sieh?"

I folded my arms and conjured clothing for myself. A small and petty gesture, and a waste of magic. The slight widening of her eyes was gratifying, though I pretended nonchalance as I said, "I suppose it wouldn't hurt to work with a tailor, too. Never been much for keeping up with fashion." Then I wouldn't need to expend more magic.

She bowed—deeply and respectfully, I was pleased to see. "As for your quarters, my lord, I—"

"Leave us," snapped Shahar, to my surprise.

After the slightest of startled pauses, Morad closed her mouth. "Yes, lady." With a measured but brisk stride, she,

too, left. Shahar and I gazed at each other in silence until
we heard the door of Dekarta's apartment shut. Shahar
closed her eyes, drawing a deep breath as if for strength.

"I'm sorry," I said.

I expected her to be sad. When she opened her eyes,
however, the fury was still burning. Coldly. "Will you
help me kill her?"

I rocked back on my heels in surprise and slid hands
into my pockets. (I always made clothes with pockets.)
Considering for a moment, I said, "I could kill her for you
right now, if you want. Better to do it while I still have
magic to spare." I paused, reading the telltale signs in her
posture. "But are you sure?"

She almost said yes. I could see that, too. And I was
willing to do it, if she asked. It had never been my way to
kill mortals before the Gods' War, but my enslavement
had changed everything. Arameri weren't ordinary mortals, anyway. Killing them was a treat.

"No," she said at last. Not reluctantly. There was no
hint of squeamishness in her—but then, I had been the
one to teach her to kill, long ago. She sighed in frustration. "I'm not strong enough to take her place, not yet. I
have only a few allies among the nobles, and some of my
fullblood relatives...." She grimaced. "No. I'm not ready."

I nodded slowly. "You think she knows that?"

"Better than I do." Shahar sighed and slumped into a
nearby chair, putting her head in her hands. "It's always
like this with her, no matter what I do. No matter how
well I prove myself. She thinks I'm not strong enough to
be her heir."

I sat down on the edge of a beautifully worked wooden
desk. My butt settled more heavily than I intended, partly
because my butt was bigger now and partly because I was

feeling a little winded. Why? Then I remembered: the clothing I'd conjured.

"That's standard for Arameri," I said to distract myself. "I can't remember how many times I saw family heads put their children through all manner of hells to make sure they were worthy." Fleetingly I wondered what the Arameri did for a succession ceremony now, since the Stone of Earth no longer existed and there was no need for a life to be spent in its inheritance. Remath's master sigil, I'd noticed, had been the standard kind, complete with the old commanding language even though it was now useless. Clearly they maintained at least a few of the old traditions, however unnecessarily. "Well, it should be easy enough to prove you're not weak. Just order the annihilation of a country or something."

Shahar threw me a scathing look. "You think the slaughter of innocent mortals is funny?"

"No, it's horrific, and I will hear their screams in my soul for the rest of existence," I said in my coldest tone. She flinched. "But if you're afraid of being seen as weak, then you have limited options. Either do something to prove your strength—and in Arameri terms, *strength* means *ruthlessness*—or quit now and tell your mother to make someone else heir. Which she should do, in my opinion, if she's right and you aren't strong enough. The whole world will be better off if you never inherit."

Shahar stared at me for a moment. Hurt, I realized, because I'd been deliberately cruel. But I'd also told the truth, however unpleasant she might find it. I'd seen the carnage that resulted when a weak or foolish Arameri took over the family. Better for the world and for Shahar, because otherwise her relatives would eat her alive.

She rose from the chair and began to pace, folding her

arms and nibbling her bottom lip in a way that I might have found endearing on another day and under better circumstances.

"What I don't understand is why your mother wants me here," I said. I stretched out my offensively long legs and glared down at them. "I'm not even a good figurehead, if that's what she's thinking. My magic is dying; anyone who looks at me can see that something's wrong. And she wants me to keep my godhood secret anyhow. This makes no sense."

Shahar sighed, stopping her pacing and rubbing her eyes. "She wants to improve relations between the Arameri and the gods. It's a project her father began—mostly because *you* stopped visiting Sky when her grandfather, T'vril Arameri, died. She's been sending gifts to the city's godlings, inviting them to events and so on. Sometimes they actually show up." She shrugged. "I'm told she even courted one as a potential husband. He didn't accept, though. They say that's why she never married; after being turned down by a god, she couldn't settle for anything less without being seen as weak."

"Really?" I grinned at the idea of cold Remath trying to win one of my siblings' love. Some of them might have been amused enough to allow a seduction. Which one had she propositioned? Dima, maybe; he would mount anything that held still long enough. Or Ellere, who could match any Arameri for hauteur and preferred stiff types like Remath—

"Yes. And I suspect that's why she tried to give me to you." I blinked in surprise, and Shahar smiled thinly. "Well, you're too young for her tastes. But not mine."

I leapt to my feet, taking several quick steps back from her. "That's insane!"

She stared at me, surprised by my vehemence. "Insane?" Her jaw tightened. "I see. I had no idea you found me so repellent."

I groaned. "Shahar, I'm the god of *childhood*. Would you please think about that for a moment?"

She frowned. "Children are perfectly capable of marriage."

"Yes. And some of them even have children themselves. But childhood doesn't last long under those conditions." I shuddered before I could stop myself, folding my arms over my chest to match her posture. Paltry, inadequate protection. Impossible not to think of groping hands, grunting breaths. So many of Shahar's forbears had loved having a pretty, indestructible, never-aging boy around—

Gods, I was going to be sick. I leaned against the desk, trembling and panting.

"Sieh?" Shahar had drawn near, and now she touched me, her hand warm against my back. "Sieh, what's wrong?"

"What do you do for fun?" I took deep breaths.

"What?"

"Fun, damn you! Do you do anything but scheme in your spare time, or do you actually have a life?"

She glowered at me, and her petulance made me feel just a little better. I turned and grabbed her hand and dragged her across the room, onto Deka's modestly sized bed. She gasped and tried to pull free of me. "What the hells are you doing?"

"Jumping on the bed." I didn't take my shoes off. Worked better with them on. I stood awkwardly in the soft middle of the mattress and hauled her up with me.

"*What?*"

"You're supposed to try and keep me happy, right?" I took her by the shoulders. "Come on, Shahar. It's only been eight years. You used to love trying new things, remember? I offered to take you cloud jumping once and you leapt at the chance, until you remembered that I was a baby-killing monster." I grinned, and she blinked, outrage fading as she remembered that day. "You kicked me down the stairs so hard I actually got bruises!"

She uttered a weak, uncertain laugh. "I'd forgotten about that. Kicking you."

I nodded. "It felt good, didn't it? You didn't care that I was a god, that I might get angry and hurt you. You did what you wanted, damn the consequences."

Yes, at last, the old light was in her eyes. She was older, wiser, she would never do something so foolish today— but that didn't mean she didn't *want* to. The impulse was there, buried but not dead. That was enough.

"Now try it again," I said. "Do something fun." I bounced a little on the bed's soft, springy surface. She yelped and stumbled, trying to get her footing—but she laughed. I grinned, the nausea gone already. "Don't think! Just do what feels good!"

I jumped, really jumped this time, and the force of my landing nearly threw her off the bed. She shrieked in terror and excitement and sheer giddy release, and finally jumped in self-defense, wobbling badly because my jumping had thrown her off. I laughed and grabbed her and made her jump with me, as high as I could go without using magic. She cried out again when we actually got within arm's reach of the room's arched ceiling. Then we came down fast and hard, and something in Deka's bed groaned in protest and I took us up again and she was laughing, laughing, her face alight, and on impulse I pulled her close and we overbalanced and went sideways and I had to use magic to make sure we landed safely on our backs, but that was fine because suddenly magic was easy again and I felt so good that I laughed and kissed her.

I truly hadn't meant anything by it. Jumping felt good and laughing felt good and she felt good and kissing her felt good. Her mouth was soft and warm, her breath a tickle against my upper lip. I smiled as I let it end and sat up.

But before I could, her hands gripped the cloth at the back of my shirt, pulling me down again. I started as her mouth found mine again, more delicious sweetness like flower nectar; then her tongue slipped between my lips. Now the sweetness turned to honey, thick and golden, sliding down my throat in a slow caress, spreading molten through my body. She shifted a little to press her small breasts against my chest. (Wait, little girls didn't have breasts, did they?) Oh, gods, her hands on my back felt so good, I hadn't liked a mortal this much in ages, could it be the love that Remath schemed for? No, I loved Shahar already, had loved her since childhood, oh yes oh yes oh yes. *Exquisite mortal, here is my soul; I want you to know it.*

We parted then, her gasping and jerking away, me letting out a slow, trembling sigh.

"Wh-what…" She put a hand to her mouth, her green eyes wide and so clear in the afternoon sunlight that I could count every spoke of her irises. "Sieh, what—"

I cupped her cheek, sighing languidly. "That was me." I closed my eyes, relaxing into the moment. "Thank you."

"For what?"

I didn't feel like explaining, so I didn't. I just rolled onto my back and let myself drift. Thankfully, she said nothing for a long while, lying still beside me.

Such moments of peace never last, so I didn't mind when she finally spoke. "It's your antithesis, isn't it? Marriage, things like that. Anything to do with adulthood."

I yawned. "Duh."

"Just talking about it made you sick."

"No. Finding out that I'm dying *and* worrying about my orrery *and* talking about marriage made me sick. If I'm already strong, a little thing like that can't hurt me."

"Your orrery?" I felt the bed shift as she sat up on her elbows, her breath tickling my face.

"Nothing important. It's gone now."

"Oh." She was silent a moment longer. "But how do you keep yourself from thinking about things like dying?"

I opened my eyes. She was on her side now, head propped on her fist. Her hair had come partially loose from its swept-up chignon, and her eyes were softer than I'd ever seen them. She looked thoroughly rumpled and a bit naughty, not at all the poised and controlled family heir.

"How do *you* keep yourself from thinking about death?" I touched her nose with a fingertip. "You mortals have to live with that fear all the time, don't you? If you can do it, I can, too." I would have to, or I would die even sooner. But I did not say this aloud; it would have spoiled the mood.

"I see." She lifted a hand, hesitated, and then yielded to impulse, resting it on my chest. I couldn't purr in this form, but I could sigh in pleasure and arch a little beneath her hand, which I did. "So... what was that, just now?"

"Why, Lady Shahar, I believe it's called a *kiss* in Senmite. In Teman it's *umishday*, and in Oubi it's—"

She swatted my chest hard enough to sting, then blanched as she realized what she'd done, then got over it. Her cheeks had gone that blotchy pink that either meant sickness or strong emotion in Amn; I guessed she was feeling shy. "What I mean is, *why* did you do it?"

"Why did you kiss me last night?"

She frowned. "I don't know. It felt right."

"Same for me." I yawned again. "Damn. I think I need to sleep."

She sat up, though she did not immediately leave the bed. Her back was to me, so I could see the tension in her shoulders. I thought she was going to ask another question, and perhaps she meant to. But what she said instead was, "I'm glad you came back, Sieh. Really. And I'm glad...what happened that day wasn't..." She drew a deep breath. "I hated you for a long time."

I folded my hands under my head, sighing. "You probably still hate me a little, Shahar. I took your brother from you."

"No. Mother did that." But she did not sound wholly certain, and I knew the mortal heart was not always logical.

"Wounds need time to heal," I said, thinking of my own.

"Maybe so." After another moment, she stood with a sigh. "I'll be in my room."

She left. I was tempted to lie there awhile longer and fight the urge to sleep, but there are times to be childish and times when wisdom takes precedence. Sighing, I rolled over and curled up, giving in.

5

Above mortals are the gods, and above us is the unknowable, which we call Maelstrom. For some reason It likes the number three. Three are Its children, the great gods who made the rest of us, who named themselves and encompass existence. Three also are the rankings of us lesser gods—though that is only because we killed the fourth.

First came the niwwah, the Balancers, among whose ranks I am honored to be counted. We were born of the Three's earliest efforts at intercourse, for they had other ways of lovemaking long before reproduction had anything to do with it. They did not know how to be parents then, so they did many things wrong, but it was long ago and most of us have forgiven them for it.

We are called Balancers not because we balance anything, mind, but because each of us has two of the Three as parents in what we have come to realize is a balanced combination: Nahadoth and Enefa in my case, Itempas and Enefa in others. We do not like each other much, Nahadoth's children and our half siblings who belong to Itempas, but we do love each other. So it goes with family.

Next are the elontid, the Imbalancers. Again, this name

is not because they take any active role in the maintenance or destruction of existence, but because they were born of *imbalance*. We did not know at first that certain mixes among us are dangerous. Nahadoth and Itempas, first and foremost—Enefa made them able to breed together, but they are both too similar and too different to do so easily. (Gender has nothing to do with this difficulty, mind you; that is only a game for us, an affectation, like names and flesh. We employ such things because you need them, not because we do.) On the rare occasions that Naha and Tempa bear children together, the results are always powerful, and always frightening. Only a few have lived to adulthood: Ral the Dragon, Ia the Negation, and Lil the Hunger. Also counted among the elontid are those born of unions between gods and godlings, reflecting the inequity of the merging that created them. They are gods of things that ebb and wane, like the tides, fashion, lust and liking.

Nothing is wrong with them, I must emphasize, though some among my fellow niwwah treat them as pitiable creatures. This is a mistake; they are merely different.

Third we count the mnasat: those children we godlings have produced among ourselves. Here there is weakness, in the relative sense of things, for even the mnasat can destroy a world if pressed. Countless numbers have been born over the aeons, but most are culled in their first few centuries—caught in the cross fire of the Three's endless battling and copulating, or dragged into the Maelstrom by accident, or lost through any of the other legion hazards that might befall a young god. The War in particular decimated their ranks—and I will admit that I took my share of their lives. Why shouldn't I have, if they were so foolish as to interfere in the concerns of their betters? Yet there were a few whom I could not kill, and who proved themselves worthy through that trial-by-apocalypse. The mnasat have shown us by the harsh example of their deaths that it is *living true*, not mere strength, which dictates matters among us. Those who submitted to their natures gained power to match even the strongest of us niwwah—and those who forgot themselves, no matter how much innate power they possessed, fell.

There is another lesson in this: life cannot exist without death. Even among gods there are winners and losers, eaters and eaten. I have never hesitated to kill my fellow immortals, but I sometimes mourn the necessity.

The demons were the fourth ranking of us, if you're wondering. But there is no point in speaking of them.

I awakened with a rude snarfle and a groan. Dreams. I had forgotten those, a plague of mortal flesh. Bad enough mortals wasted so much of their lives insensible, but Enefa had also given them dreams to teach them about themselves and their universe. Few of them ever listened to the lessons—a total waste of creation in my eyes—but thanks to that, I would have to endure these mind-farts every time I slept. Lovely.

It was late in the night, nowhere near morning. Though I had been asleep for only three or four hours, I felt no further urge to rest, perhaps because I wasn't yet fully mortal. So what to do with the hours until Shahar was awake to entertain me?

I got up and went roaming again in the palace, this time not bothering to conceal myself. The servants and guards said nothing when I passed them, despite my nondescript clothing and unmarked forehead, but I felt their eyes on my back. What had Morad, or whoever served as the captain of the guard now, told them about me? There was no flavor of adoration or revulsion to their stares. Just curiosity—and wariness.

I went into the underpalace first, to the Nowhere Stair. Which no longer existed, to my shock.

In its place was an open atrium. Three levels of wide circular balconies ringed a space that had been reworked with sculptures and potted plants of the sort that needed little care. (At least it wasn't dusty anymore. The Arameri no longer neglected the underpalace, having realized it could hide secrets.) The atrium lacked the intentionally carefree feel of most Sky architecture, and I could see where the edges of each balcony had been too-hastily molded by the scriveners, leaving them uneven and not as smooth as they should have been. Servants had cleaned up the rubble, but signs of the disaster were still there, for one who knew how to see.

I crouched at the edge of one of the balconies, bracing one hand on the thin railing, and touched the rough day-stone of the floor. Echoes still reverberated in the stone— not echoes of sound, since those had long since moved on, but echoes of *event*. I closed my eyes and saw again what the stone had witnessed.

The Nowhere Stair. At the bottom of it, three children holding hands. (I marveled at how small Shahar had been then; already I had grown used to her older shape.) I watched the mortals' faces change from smiles to alarm, felt the rising rush of wind, saw their hair and clothing begin to whip about as if they'd been caught in a tornado. They screamed as their feet rose from the floor; then they flipped entirely, twisting upside down. Only I did not budge, my feet seemingly rooted to the ground. Only their grip on each other and me held them down.

And the look on my face! In the memory, I stood with mouth slack, eyes distant and confused, brow ever-so-slightly furrowed and head cocked, as if I heard something no one else could, and whatever I heard had obliterated my wits.

Then my body blurred, flesh interspersing with white lines. My mouth opened and the stone beneath my fingertips gave one last microscopic shiver as a concussion of force tore loose from my throat. The Nowhere Stair shattered like glass, as did all the daystone around it and beneath it and above it. What saved the children was that the energy blasted outward in a spherical wave; they fell amid the rubble, bleeding and still, but not much of the rubble landed on them.

And when the dust cleared, I had vanished.

Taking my fingers off the stone, I frowned to myself. Then I said to the mortal who had hovered somewhere behind me, watching for the past ten minutes, "What do you want?"

He came forward, preceded by the familiar mingled scent of books and chemical phials and incense; by that I knew what he was before he ever spoke. "My apologies, Lord Sieh. I did not mean to disturb you."

I rose, dusting off my hands, and turned to take his measure. An island man of late middle years, with salt-sprinkled red hair and a lined saturnine face that showed a hint of beard stubble. There was a fullblood mark on his brow, but he didn't look Arameri or even Amn. And full-bloods rarely smelled of hard work. An adoptee, then.

"You the First Scrivener?" I asked.

He nodded, obviously torn between fascination and unease. Finally he offered me an awkward bow—not deep enough to be properly respectful but too deep for the kind of disdain a devout Itempan should have shown. I laughed, remembering Viraine's cool, nuanced poise, and then sobered as I remembered why Viraine had been so good at things like that.

"Forgive me," the man said again. "But the servants passed word that you were abroad in the palace, and...I thought...well, it seems natural that you would come to the scene of the crime, so to speak."

"Mmm." I slipped my hands into my pockets, trying very hard not to feel uneasy in his presence. These were not the old days. He had no power over me. "It's late, First Scrivener, or early. Don't you Itempans believe in a full night's rest before your dawn prayers?"

He blinked; then his surprise faded into amusement. "They do, but I'm not Itempan, Lord Sieh. And I wanted to meet you, which necessitated staying up late, or so my research suggested. You were known to be decidedly nocturnal during your"—his confidence faltered again—"time here."

I stared at him. "How can you not be Itempan?" All scriveners were Itempan priests. The Order gave anyone with a knack for magic a single choice: join or die.

"About—hmm—fifty years ago? The Litaria petitioned the Nobles' Consortium for independence from the Order of Itempas. The Litaria is a secular body now. Scriveners may devote themselves to whichever god, or gods, they wish." He paused, then smiled again. "As long as we serve the Arameri, regardless."

I looked him up and down, opened my mouth a little to get a better taste of his scent, and was stymied. "So which god do you honor?" He certainly wasn't one of mine.

"I *honor* all the gods. But in terms of spirituality, I prefer to worship at the altars of knowledge and artistry." He made an apologetic little gesture with his hand, as if he worried about hurting my feelings, but I had begun to grin.

"An atheist!" I put my hands on my hips, delighted. "I haven't seen one of you since before the War. I thought the Arameri wiped all of you out."

"As well as they did all the other gods' worshippers, Lord Sieh, yes." I laughed at this, which seemed to hearten him. "Heresy is actually rather fashionable among the commonfolk, though here in Sky I am more circumspect about it, of course. And the, ah, *polite* term for people like me is *primortalist*."

"Ugh, what a mouthful."

"Unfortunately, yes. It means 'mortals first'—neither an accurate nor complete representation of our philosophy, but as I said, there are worse terms. We believe in the gods, naturally." He nodded to me. "But as the Interdiction has shown us, the gods function perfectly well whether we believe in them or not, so why devote all that energy to a pointless purpose? Why not believe most fervently in mortalkind and its potential? We, certainly, could benefit from a little dedication and discipline."

"I agree wholeheartedly!" And if I didn't miss my guess, there were probably a few of my siblings involved in his mortal-worshipping movement. But I refrained from pointing this out, lest it disturb him. "What's your name?"

He bowed again, more easily this time. "Shevir, Lord Sieh."

I waved a hand. "I make the Arameri call me 'lord.' It's just Sieh."

He looked uneasy. "Er, well—"

"Arameri is a state of mind. I've known some adoptees who fit right into this family. You, sir, are a die among the jacks." I smiled to let him know that had been meant as a compliment, and he relaxed. "Remath told you all about me, then?"

"The Lady Arameri informed me of your . . . condition, yes. I and my staff, including those in the city below, are already hard at work trying to determine what might have caused the change. We'll inform Lady Remath at once if we find anything."

"Thank you." I refrained from pointing out that telling Remath wouldn't do me any good unless Remath chose to pass the information along. He probably knew that and was just letting me know where his loyalties lay. Mortals first. "Were you here in Sky, eight years ago?"

"Yes." He came to stand beside me, staring avidly at my profile, my posture, everything. Studying me. Knowing his beliefs, I did not mind for once. "I was head of the healing squadron then; it was I and my colleagues who treated Lord Dekarta and Lady Shahar after their injury. I was promoted to First Scrivener for saving their lives." He hesitated. "The previous First Scrivener was removed from office for failing to realize that a god had visited Sky."

I rolled my eyes. "There is no scrivening magic that can detect a god's presence if we don't want to be detected." I had never wanted to be detected.

"The lady was informed of this." He was smiling thinly, not bitter at least. I supposed there was no point in laying blame.

"If you were here back then, you—or your predecessor— would have conducted an investigation."

"Yes." He straightened as if giving a report. "The incident occurred in early afternoon. There was a tremor throughout the palace, and all of the boundary scripts sounded an alarm, indicating unauthorized active magic within the palace's walls. Guards and service staff arrived to find this." He gestured at the atrium. The debris had been removed, but that changed nothing; it was painfully clear to anyone who had seen it before that the atrium was really just an enormous sunken pit. "No one knew what had happened until three days later, when first Dekarta, then Shahar awakened."

More than enough time for rumors to gain traction and ruin Deka's life. Poor boy, and his sister, too.

"What sort of magic was it?" I asked. Scriveners loved to classify and categorize magic, which somehow helped them grasp it with their unmagical mortal minds. There might be something in their convoluted logic that would help me understand.

"Unknown, Lord—" He caught himself. "Unknown."

"Unknown?"

"Nothing like it has been observed in the mortal realm, at least not within recorded history. The Litaria's best scholars have confirmed this. We even consulted several of the friendlier godlings of the city; they weren't able to explain it, either. If *you* don't know—" He shut his mouth with an audible snap, in palpable frustration. He had plainly hoped I would have more answers.

I understood entirely. Sighing, I straightened. "I didn't intend to hurt them. Nothing that happened makes any sense."

"The children's hands were bloody," Shevir said, his tone neutral. "Both hands, cut in the same way, inflicted on each other to judge by the angles and depth. Some of my colleagues believed they may have attempted some sort of ritual...."

I scowled. "The only ritual involved was one that children the world over have enacted to seal promises." I lifted my hand, gazing at my own smooth, unscarred palms. "If *that* could cause what happened, there would be a great many dead children lying about."

He spread his hands in that apologetic gesture again. "You must understand, we were desperate to come up with some explanation."

I considered this and hoisted myself up onto the railing, reveling in the ability to kick my feet at last. This seemed to make Shevir very uncomfortable, probably because the drop into the atrium was far enough to kill a mortal. Then I remembered that I was becoming mortal, and with a heavy sigh, I dropped back to the floor.

"So you decided one of the children—Deka—had summoned me, annoyed me, and I blew them to the hells in retaliation."

"*I* didn't believe that." Shevir grew sober. "But certain parties would not be put off, and ultimately Dekarta was sent to the Litaria. To learn better control of his innate talents, his mother announced."

"Exile," I said softly. "A punishment for getting Shahar hurt."

"Yes."

"What's he like now? Deka."

Shevir shook his head. "No one here has seen him since he left, Lord Sieh. He doesn't come home at holidays or vacation breaks. I'm told he's doing well at the Litaria; ironically, he turned out to have a genuine talent for the art. But...well...rumor has it that he and Lady Shahar hate each other now." I frowned, and Shevir shrugged. "I can't say I blame him, really. Children don't see things the way we do."

I glanced at Shevir; he was lost in thought and hadn't noticed the irony of talking about childhood to me. He was right, though. The gentle Deka I'd known would not have understood that he was being sent away for reasons that had very little to do with Shahar being injured. He would have drawn his own conclusions about why the friendship oath had gone wrong and why he'd been separated from his beloved sister. Self-blame would have been only the beginning.

But why had Remath even bothered exiling him? In the old days, the family had been quick to kill any member who'd transgressed in some way or another. They should have been even quicker with Deka, who broke the Arameri mold in so many ways.

Sighing heavily, I straightened and turned away from the atrium railing. "Nothing in Sky has ever made sense. I don't know why I keep coming here, really. You'd think being trapped in this hell for centuries would've been enough for me."

Shevir shrugged. "I can't speak for gods, but any mortal who spends enough time in a place grows... acclimated. One's sense of what is normal shifts, even if that place is filled with unpleasantness, until separation feels wrong."

I frowned at this. Shevir caught my look and smiled. "Married seventeen years. Happily, I might add."

"Oh." This reminded me, perversely, of the previous night's conversation with Shahar. "Tell me more about her," I said.

I hadn't specified the "her," but of course Shevir was as good at parsing language as any scrivener. "Lady Shahar is very bright, very mature for her age, and very dedicated to her duties. I've heard most of the other fullbloods express confidence in her ability to rule after her mother—"

"No, no," I said, scowling. "None of that. I want to know..." Suddenly I was uncertain. Why was I asking him about this? But I had to know. "About *her*. Who are her friends? How did she handle Deka's exile? What do you think of her?"

At this flood of questions, Shevir raised his eyebrows. Suddenly I realized two horrifying things: first, that I was developing a dangerous attraction to Shahar, and second, that I had just revealed it.

"Ah... well... she's very private," Shevir began awkwardly.

It was too late, but I waved a hand and tried to repair the damage I'd done. "Never mind," I said, grimacing. "These are mortal affairs, irrelevant. All I should concentrate on now is finding the cure for whatever's happened to me."

"Yes." Shevir seemed relieved to change the subject. "Er, to that end... the reason I sought you out was to ask if you might be willing to provide some samples for us. My fellow scriveners—that is, of the palace contingent— thought we might share this information with the previts in Shadow and the Litaria."

I frowned at this, unpleasantly recalling other First Scriveners and other examinations and other samples over the centuries. "To try and figure out what's changed in me?"

"Yes. We have information on your, ah, prior tenure...." He shook his head and finally stopped trying to be tactful. "When you were a slave here, immortal but trapped in mortal flesh. Your present state appears to be very different. I'd like to compare the two."

I scowled. "Why? To tell me that I'm going to die? I know that already."

"Determining *how* you're turning mortal may give us some insight into what caused it," he said, speaking briskly now that he was in his element. "And perhaps how to reverse it. I would never presume that mortal arts can surpass godly power, but every bit of knowledge we can gather might be useful."

I sighed. "Very well. You'll want my blood, I presume?" Mortals were forever after our blood.

"And anything else you would be willing to give. Hair, nail parings, a bit of flesh, saliva. I'll want to record your current measurements, too—height and weight and so forth."

I could not help growing curious at this. "How could that possibly matter?"

"Well, for one thing, you appear to be no more than sixteen years old to my eye. The same age as Lady Shahar and Lord Dekarta, now—but initially, I understand, you looked significantly older than both of them. Approximately ten years to their eight. If you had merely aged eight years in the intervening time—"

I caught my breath, understanding at last. I had grown up before, hundreds of times; I knew the pattern that my body normally followed. I should have been heavier, taller, more finished, with a deeper voice. Eighteen years old, not sixteen. "Shahar and Dekarta," I breathed. "My aging has slowed to match theirs."

Shevir nodded, looking pleased at my reaction. "You do seem rather thin, so perhaps you lacked nourishment while you were...away...and this stunted your growth. More likely, however—"

I nodded absently, quickly, because he was right. How had such a crucial detail escaped me?

Because it is the sort of thing only a mortal would notice.

I had suspected that my condition was somehow linked to the friendship oath I'd taken with Shahar and Dekarta. Now I knew: their mortality had infected me, like a disease. But what kind of disease slowed its progress to match that of other victims? There was something *purposeful* about that sort of change. Something intentional.

But whose intent, and for what purpose?

"Let's go to your laboratory, Scrivener Shevir," I said, speaking softly as my mind raced with inferences and implications. "I believe I can give you those samples right now."

I was getting hungry by the time I left Shevir's laboratory, just after dawn. It wasn't bad yet—not the sort of raw, precarious ache I'd known a few times during my slave years, whenever my masters had starved me—but it made me irritable, because it was more proof of my oncoming mortality. Would I starve to death if I ignored it now? Could I still sustain myself with games and disobedience, as I normally did? I was tempted to find out. Then again, I considered as I rubbed my upper arm, where a bandage and healing script concealed the divot of flesh Shevir had taken from me, there was no point in making myself suffer unnecessarily. As a mortal, there would be pain enough in my life, whether I sought it out or not.

Noise and commotion distracted me from grimness. I stepped quickly to the side of a corridor as six guardsmen ran by, hands on their weapons. One of them carried a messaging sphere, and through this I heard the speaker—their captain, I assumed—issuing rapid commands in a low tone. Something about "clear the north-seven corridors" and "forecourt," and most clearly, "Tell Morad's people to bring something for the smell."

I could no more resist such temptation than I could Shahar's summons—maybe less so. So I hummed a little ditty and slid my hands into my pockets and skipped as I headed down a different corridor. When the guards were out of sight, I opened a wall and tore off running.

I was almost thwarted by the Tree, which had grown through one of the most useful junctures in the dead spaces, and by my stupid, infuriatingly lanky body, which could no longer squeeze through the tighter passages. I knew plenty of alternate routes but still arrived at the courtyard late and out of breath. (That annoyed me, too. I was going to have to make my mortal body stronger, or it would be completely useless at this rate.)

It was worth it, however, for what I saw.

Sky's forecourt had been designed by my late sister, Kurue, who had understood two key elements of the mortal psyche: they hate being reminded of their own insignificance, yet they simultaneously and instinctively expect their leaders to be overwhelmingly dominant. This was why visitors were confronted with magnificence at four cardinal points as they arrived on the Vertical Gate. To the north was Sky's vaulted, cavernous entryway, taller than many buildings in the city below. To the east and west lay the twin lobes of the Garden of the Hundred Thousand, a mosaic of ordered flower beds each crowned by an exotic tree. Beyond these one could see a branch of the World Tree, wild and miles vast, spreading a million leaves against the blue sky. Kurue had never planned for the Tree, but it was a testament to her skill that it looked like she had. For those who dared to look south, there was nothing. Only the lonely Pier and an otherwise unimpeded view of the landscape and very, very distant horizon.

Now the forecourt had been defiled by something hideous. As I emerged from the garden via the servants' ground entrance, no one noticed me. Soldiers were all over the place, disorganized, in a panic. I saw the captain of the guard on one side of the gate mosaic, shouting at the coach driver to take the coach away, away, away for the Father's sake, take it to the ground station at the cargo gate and let no one touch it.

I ignored all this as I walked forward through the

hubbub, my eyes on twin lumps on the ground. Someone had had the sense to lay them on a square of cloth, but that barely contained the mess. Pieces of the lumps spilled and scattered every which way, not helped at all by soldiers who stumbled around retching even as they tried to scrape everything back onto the cloth. As I got close enough to get a good look at the mess—flesh gone gelatinous, so rotten the only thing solid in it was spongy bone—the captain turned and spotted me. He was warrior enough to drop his hand to the sword at his side, but sensible enough to avoid drawing it as he realized who I must be. He cursed swiftly, then caught himself and threw a quick glance to be sure his men weren't looking before he bowed quickly. Not a subtle man.

"Sir," he said carefully, though I could see he would rather have used *my lord*. He was no Itempan, either, though his forehead bore an Arameri mark. He held up a hand, and I stopped a few feet from the outermost edges of the foulness. "Please, it's dangerous."

"I don't think the maggots are likely to attack, do you?" My joke fell flat because there were no maggots. It was easy to see that what lay on the blanket were the remains of two very, very dead mortals, but that peculiarity did puzzle me. And the smell was wrong. I stepped closer, opening my mouth a little, though the last thing I wanted was a better taste of it. I had never liked carrion. But that taste gave me nothing but ammonia and sulfur and all the usual flavors of death.

"Arameri, I take it?" I crouched for a better look. I could not make out marks on their foreheads, or their faces at all for that matter, which were oddly blackened and featureless. Almost flat. "Who were they? These look long-enough dead that I might've known them."

Stiffly, the captain said, "They are—we believe—Lord Nevra and Lady Criscina, second cousins of Lady Remath. Fullbloods. And they died—we believe—last night."

"What?"

He didn't repeat himself, though he did stir from his pose in order to kick over a globule of Nevra. Or Criscina. The soldiers had by now managed to get all the scattered bits onto the cloth and were wrapping it carefully for transport. I could see smears along the ground between the Vertical Gate and the cloth. They had brought the bodies up to Sky in the coach, but they hadn't bothered to wrap them first? That made no sense...unless they hadn't realized the couple inside were dead before they'd opened the door.

I went over to the captain, who stiffened again at my approach, but held firm. I was surprised to see a low-bloods' simple bar symbol on his forehead, though it was also hollowed out at the center in the manner of all the blood sigils I'd seen, except Remath's. It was rare for low-bloods to achieve high rank within Sky. That meant this man either had a powerful patron—not a parent, or he wouldn't be a lowblood—or he was very competent. I hoped the latter.

"I must admit I pay little attention to mortals once they're dead," I said, keeping my voice low. "No fun, corpses. But I was under the impression it normally took them a few months, if not years, to reach this state."

"Normally, yes," he said tersely.

"Then what caused this?"

His jaw flexed. "Please forgive me, sir, but I am under orders to keep this matter private. This *family* matter." Which meant that Remath had ordered his silence, and nothing short of my dangling him off the Pier would make him talk. Perhaps not even that; he seemed the stubborn type.

I rolled my eyes. "You know as well as I do that only magic could cause such a horror. A scrivener's activation gone wrong, or perhaps they aggravated one of my siblings." Though I doubted that. Any godling was capable of such a thing, even the ones with gentler natures, but I could think of no godling who *would*. We killed; we did not desecrate. We respected death. To do otherwise was an offense to Enefa, and probably Yeine, too.

"I cannot say, sir."

Stubborn, indeed. "Why did you say it was dangerous?"

He looked hard at me then, to my surprise. Not angrily, though I was pestering him and I knew it. He had the most remarkable gray eyes. Rare in Sky, and almost unheard of among Maroneh, though he looked brown enough to be fully of that race. Probably part Amn, if he was Arameri.

"As you said, my lord." He spoke softly but emphatically. "Only magic could have done such a thing. This magic works on contact."

He lifted his chin in the direction of the bodies' faces, which were still visible as the soldiers worked to wrap the loose limbs. I peered closer and realized that what I had taken for just more decay was something different. The blackness of their faces was not rot, but char. Not faces at all, in fact: each of the dead mortals wore some sort of mask over their features. The masks had burned so badly as to fuse with the flesh, leaving only eyes and a line of jaw of the original faces.

Then the soldiers were done bundling. Six of them set off, carrying the bodies slowly between them. As they reached the palace entrance, a phalanx of servants emerged, carrying cleaning implements and censers. They would cleanse the forecourt of its taint quickly so that no highblood would know such horror had ever lain here.

"I must make my report to the Lady Arameri," said the captain, turning.

"What's your name?" I asked.

The captain paused, looking wary, and by that I guessed he'd heard something of my reputation. I grinned.

"No singsongs, I promise," I said. "No games or tricks. You've done nothing to offend me, so you have nothing to fear."

He relaxed minutely. "Wrath Arameri."

Definitely Maroneh, with a name like that. "Well, Captain Wrath, since you're going to tell the lady I turned up here, anyway, you might also tell her that I'd be happy to assist in determining the cause of...this." I gestured vaguely at the place where the corpses had lain.

He frowned again. "Why?"

"Boredom." I shrugged. "Curiosity killed the cat. I'm too old to play with toys now."

A flicker of confusion crossed his face, but he nodded. "I will convey your message, sir." He turned on his heel and left, heading into the palace, but he paused on the steps and bowed as a slim, white-clad figure appeared in the entryway. Shahar.

I followed him more slowly, nodding to the servants out of habit (which seemed to startle them) and stopping at the foot of the wide steps. Shahar wore a simple morning robe of plush white fur, and a forbidding expression that made me hunch sheepishly, out of long habit.

"I awoke to find you missing," she said, "and since I'm now judged on how well I serve your needs"—oh, marvelous, just the lightest glaze of venom on those words; she was very good—"it became imperative that I find you before completing any of my other, many, duties. I was at a loss, however, until I was informed of this incident. I knew you would be wherever there was trouble."

I flashed her my most winning smile, which made her eyes even colder. Perhaps I was too old for that to work anymore. "You could simply have called me," I said. "Like you did two nights ago."

She blinked, distracted from her own anger so easily that I knew she wasn't that upset. "Do you think that would work?"

I shrugged, though I was less nonchalant about it than I let her see. "We're going to have to try it sometime, I suppose."

"Yes." She let out a deep sigh, but then her eyes drifted to the servants now assiduously attacking the soiled area around the Vertical Gate. One of them was even cleaning the gate itself, though carefully, using a clear solution and taking great pains not to step on any of the black tiles.

"You knew them?" I asked. Softly, in case she'd cared for them.

"Of course," she said. "Neither was any threat to me." As near a declaration of friendship as it got with this family. "They managed our shipping concerns in High North and on the islands. They were competent. Sensible. Brother and sister, like—" *Deka and me*, I suspected she would have said. "A great loss to the family. Again."

By the bleakness of her expression, I realized suddenly that she was not surprised by the manner of their deaths. And her wording had been another clue, as had Wrath's warning.

"I'm hungry," I said. "Take me somewhere with food and eat with me."

She glared. "Is that a command?"

I rolled my eyes. "I'm not forcing you to obey it, so no."

"There are many kinds of force," she said, her gaze as hard as stone. "If you tell my mother—"

I groaned in exasperation. "I'm not a tattletale! I'm just hungry!" I stepped closer. "And I want to talk about this somewhere private."

She blinked, then flushed—as well she should have, because she should've caught my hints. Would have, if her pride hadn't interfered. "Ah." She hesitated, then looked around the forecourt as if it were full of eyes. It usually was, one way or another. "Meet me at the cupola of the library in half an hour. I'll have food brought." With that she turned away in a swirl of fur and whiteness, her shoes clicking briskly on the daystone as she walked.

I watched her walk away, amused until I realized my eyes were lingering on the slight curves of her hips and their even slighter sway, thanks to her stiff, haughty walk. That unnerved me so badly that I stumbled as I backed down the steps. Though there were only servants to see me—and they were carefully not looking, probably on Morad's orders—I still quickly righted myself and slipped into the garden as a cover, pretending to look at the boring trees and flowers with great fascination. In truth, however, I was shaking.

Nothing to be done for it. Shevir had gauged my age at sixteen, and I knew full well what that age meant for mortal boys. How long before I found myself curled in a sweating knot, furiously caressing myself? And now I knew whose name I would groan when the moment struck.

Gods. How I *hated* adolescence.

Nothing to be done for it, I told myself again, and opened a hole in the ground.

It did not take long to reach the library. I emerged between two of the massive old bookshelves in a disused corner, then made my way along the stacks until I reached the half-hidden spiral staircase. Kurue had built the library's cupola as a reward for those palace denizens who loved the written word. They usually found it only by browsing the stacks and sitting quietly for a while, losing themselves in some book or scroll or tablet. It made me obscurely proud that Shahar had found it—and then I grew annoyed at that pride and more annoyed at my annoyance.

But as I reached the top of the staircase, I stopped in surprise. The cupola was already occupied, and not by Shahar.

A man sat on one of its long cushioned benches. Big, blond, dressed in a suggestively martial jacket that would have looked more so if it hadn't been made out of pearlescent silk. The cupola's roof was glass, its walls open to the air (though as magically protected from the winds and thinner air as the rest of the palace). A shaft of sunlight made a churning river of the man's curly hair, and jewels of his jacket buttons, and a sculpture of his face. I knew him at once for Arameri Central Family even without looking at the mark on his brow, because he was too beautiful and too comfortable.

But when he turned to me, I saw the mark and stared, because it was *complete*. All the scripts I remembered: the contract binding the Enefadeh to the protection and service of Shahar's direct descendants, the compulsion that forced Arameri to remain loyal to their family head…all of it. But why did only this man, out of all the Central Family, wear the mark in its original form?

"Well, well," he said, his eyes raking me with the same quick analysis.

"Sorry," I said uneasily. "Didn't know anyone was up here. I'll try someplace else."

"You're the godling," he said, and I stopped in surprise. He smiled thinly. "I think you must remember how difficult it is to keep a secret in this place."

"I managed, in my day."

"Indeed you did. And a good thing that was, or you would never have gotten free of us."

I lifted my chin, feeling annoyed and belligerent. "Is that really a good thing in the eyes of a fullblood?"

"Yes." He shifted then, setting aside the large, handsomely bound book that had been in his lap. "I've just been reading about you and your fellow Enefadeh, actually, in honor of your arrival. My ancestors really had a monster by the tail, didn't they? I feel exceedingly fortunate that you were released before I had to deal with you."

I narrowed my eyes at him, trying to understand my own wariness. "Why don't I like you?"

The man blinked in surprise, then smiled again with a hint of irony. "Maybe because, if you were still a slave and I your master, *you're* the one I would put the shortest leash on."

I wasn't sure if that was it, but it didn't help. I had never trusted mortals who guessed at how dangerous I was. That usually meant they were just as dangerous. "Who are you?"

"My name is Ramina Arameri."

I nodded, reading the lines of his face and the frame of his bones. "Remath's brother?" No, that wasn't quite right.

"Half brother. Her father was the last family head. Mine wasn't." He shrugged dismissively. "How could you tell?"

"You look Central Family. You smell like her. And you feel"—I glanced at his forehead—"like power that has been leashed."

"Ah." He touched his forehead with a self-deprecating little smile. "This does make it obvious, doesn't it? True sigils were the norm in your day, I understand."

"*True* sigils?" I frowned. "What do they call those trimmed-down ones, then?"

"Theirs are called semisigils. Aside from Remath, I am the only member of the family who currently wears a true sigil." Ramina looked away, his gaze falling on a flock of birds swirling around a Tree branch in the distance. They took off, gliding away, and he followed their slow, steady flight. "It was given to me when my sister took her place as head of the family."

I understood then. The true sigil enforced loyalty to the family head at the cost of the wearer's will. Ramina could no more act against his sister's interests than he could command the sun to set.

"Demons," I said, feeling an unexpected pity for him. "Why didn't she just kill you?"

"Because she hates me, I suppose." Ramina was still watching the birds; I couldn't read his expression. "Or loves me. Same effect either way."

Before I could reply, I heard footsteps on the spiral staircase. We both fell silent as two servants came up, bowing quickly toward Ramina and throwing me uncomfortable looks as they set up a wooden tray and put a large platter of finger foods on it. They left quickly, whereupon I went over to the tray and crammed several items into my mouth. Ramina lifted an eyebrow; I bared my teeth at him. He sniffed a bit and looked away. Good. Bastard.

I was full after only that mouthful, which made me happy because it proved I wasn't fully mortal yet. So I belched and began licking my fingers, which I hoped would disgust Ramina. Alas, he did not look at me. But a moment later, he glanced toward the steps again as Shahar emerged from the floor entrance. She nodded to me, then spotted Ramina and brightened. "Uncle! What are you doing up here?"

"Plotting to take over the world, obviously," he said, smiling broadly at her. She went over and hugged him with real affection, which he returned with equal sincerity. "And having a lovely conversation with my new young friend here. Did you come to meet him?"

Shahar sat down beside him, glancing from him to me and back. "Yes, though it's just as well you're here. Do you know what's happened?"

"Happened?"

She sobered. "Nevra and Criscina. They—Soldiers brought the bodies this morning."

Ramina grimaced, closing his eyes. "How?"

She shook her head. "The masks, again. This time it…" She made a face. "I didn't see the result, but I smelled it."

I sat down on a bench opposite them, in the cupola's shadows, and watched them. The light making an aura of their curls. Their identical looks of sorrow. Yes, it was so obvious I wondered why Remath bothered to try and keep it secret.

Ramina got to his feet and began pacing, his expression ferocious. "Demons and darkness! All the highbloods will be livid, and rightly so. They'll blame Remath for not finding these bastards." He stopped abruptly and turned to Shahar, his eyes narrowing. "And you will be in greater danger than ever, Niece, if these attackers have grown that bold. I wouldn't advise travel for some time."

She frowned a little at this, but not in a surprised way. No doubt she had been thinking the same thing since the forecourt. "I'm scheduled to go to the Gray this evening, to meet with Lady Hynno."

The Gray? I wondered.

"Reschedule it."

"I can't! I asked for the meeting. If I reschedule, she'll know something's wrong, and Mother has decreed that any news of these murders is to remain secret."

Ramina stopped and looked pointedly at me. I flashed him a winning smile.

Shahar made a sound of exasperation. "She also decreed that I'm to give him whatever he wants." She glowered at me. "He saw the bodies, anyway."

"Yes," I said, "but I would appreciate an explanation to go with those bodies. I take it this sort of thing has happened before?"

Ramina frowned at my forwardness, but Shahar only slumped, not bothering to hide her despair. "Never a full-blood before. But others, yes."

"Other *Arameri*?"

"And those who support our interests, sometimes, yes. Always with the masks and always deadly. We're not even sure how the culprit gets the victims to put the mask on. The effects are different every time, and the masks burn up afterward, as you saw."

Amazing. In the old days, no one would have dared to kill an Arameri, for fear of the Enefadeh being sent to find and punish the killers. Had the world overcome its fear of the Arameri to that degree in just a few generations? The resilience—and vindictiveness—of mortals would never cease to astound me.

"Who do you think is doing it, then?" I asked. They both threw me irritated looks, and I raised my eyebrows. "Obviously you don't *know*, or you would have killed them. But you must *suspect* someone."

"No," said Ramina. He sat down, crossing his legs and

tossing his long mane of hair over the back of the seat. He regarded me with active contempt. "If we suspected someone, we would kill them, too."

I grew annoyed. "You have the masks, however damaged. Have the scriveners forgotten how to craft tracking scripts?"

"This is not the same," said Shahar. She sat forward, her eyes intent. "This isn't scrivening. The scriveners have no idea how this, this...false magic works, and..." She hesitated, glancing at Ramina, and sighed. "They can't stop it. We are helpless against these attacks."

I yawned. I didn't time it that way, didn't do it deliberately to suggest that I didn't care about their plight, but I saw them both scowl at me, anyway. When I closed my mouth, I glowered back. "What do you want me to say? 'I'm sorry'? I'm not, and you know it. The rest of the world has had to live with this kind of terror—murders without rhyme or reason, magic that strikes without warning—for centuries. Thanks to you Arameri." I shrugged. "If some mortal has figured out a way to make you know the same fear, I'm not going to condemn them for it. Hells, you should be glad I'm not cheering them on."

Ramina's expression went blank, in that way Arameri think is so inscrutable when it really just means they're pissed and trying not to show it. Shahar, at least, was honest enough to give me the full force of her anger. "If you hate us so much, you know what to do," she snapped. "It should be simple enough for you to kill us all. Or"—her lip curled, her tone turning nasty—"ask Nahadoth or Yeine to do it, if you don't have the strength."

"Say that again!" I shot to my feet, feeling quite strong enough to slaughter the whole Arameri family because she was being a brat. If she'd been a boy, I would have slugged her one. Boys could beat each other and remain friends, however; between boys and girls the matter was murkier.

"Children," said Ramina. He spoke in a mild tone, but he was looking at me, palpably tense despite that oh-so-calm face. I appreciated his acknowledgment of my nature. It did help to calm me, which was probably what he'd hoped for.

Shahar looked sulky, but she subsided, and after a moment I, too, sat down, though I was still furious.

"For your information," I spat, crossing my legs and *not* sulking, thank you, "what you're describing isn't false magic. It's just *better* magic."

"Only the gods' magic is better than scrivener magic," Shahar said. I could hear her trying for calm dignity, which immediately made me want to torment her in some way.

"No," I said. To alleviate the urge to annoy her, I shifted to lie down on the bench, putting my feet up on one of the delicate-looking columns that supported the roof. I wished my feet had been dirty, though I supposed that would only have inconvenienced the servants. "Scrivening is only the best thing you mortals—pardon me, you *Amn*—have come up with thus far. But just because *you* haven't thought of anything better doesn't mean there can't *be* anything better."

"Yes," said Ramina with a heavy sigh, "Shevir has already explained this. Scrivening merely approximates the gods' power, and poorly. It can only capture concepts that are communicated via simple written words. Spoken magic works better, when it works."

"The only reason it doesn't work is because mortals don't say it right." The bench was surprisingly comfortable. I would try sleeping up here some night, in the open air, beneath the waning moon. It would feel like resting in

Nahadoth's arms. "You get the pronunciation right, and the syntax, but you never master the *context*. You say the words at night when you should only say them by day. You speak them when we're on this side of the sun, not that side—all you have to do is consider the seasons, for gods' sake! But you don't. You say *gevvirh* when you really mean *das-ankalae*, and you take the *breviranaeno-ket* out of the..." I glanced at them and realized they weren't following me at all. "...You say it wrong."

"There's no way to say it better," said Shahar. "There's no way for a mortal to understand all that... context. You know there isn't."

"There's no way for you to speak as we do, no. But there are other ways to convey information besides speech and writing. Hand signs, body language"—they glanced at each other and I pointed at them—"meaningful looks! What do you think magic is? *Communication*. We gods call to reality, and reality responds. Some of that is because we made it and it is like limbs, the outflow of our souls, we and existence are one and the same, but the rest..."

I was losing them again. Stupid, padlock-brained creatures. They were smart enough to understand; Enefa had made certain of that. They were just being stubborn. I gave up and sighed, tired of trying to talk to them. If only some of my siblings would come to visit me... but I dared not risk word getting out about my condition. As Nahadoth had said, I had enemies.

"Would you consent to work with Shevir, Lord Sieh?" asked Ramina. "To help him figure out this new magic?"

"No."

Shahar made a harsh, irritated sound. "Oh, of course not. We're only giving you a roof over your head and food and—"

"You have *given* me nothing," I snapped, turning my head to glare at her. "In case you've forgotten, *I built the roof.* If we're going to get particular about obligations, Lady Shahar, how about you tell your mother I want two thousand years of back wages? Or offerings, if she prefers; either will keep me in food for the rest of my mortal life." Her mouth fell open in pure affront. "No? Then shut the hells up!"

Shahar stood so fast that on another world she would have shot into the sky. "I don't have to take this." In a flurry of fur and smolder, she went down the steps. I heard the click of her shoes along the library's floors, and then she was gone.

Feeling rather pleased with myself, I folded my arms beneath my head.

"You enjoyed that," said Ramina.

"Whatever gave you that impression?" I laughed.

He sighed, sounding bored rather than frustrated. "It might amuse you to bicker with her—in fact, I'm sure it does amuse you—but you have no idea of the pressure she's under, Lord Sieh. My sister has not been kind to her in the years since you almost killed her and caused her brother to be sent away."

I flinched, reminded of the debt I owed to Shahar— a reminder that Ramina had no doubt meant to deliver. Uncomfortable now, I took my feet off the column and turned onto my belly, propping myself up on my elbows to face him.

"I understand why Remath sent the boy away," I said, "though I'm still surprised that she did it. Usually, when there's more than one prospective heir, the family head pits them against each other."

"That wasn't possible in this case," Ramina said. He had turned his gaze away again, this time toward the vast open landscape on the palace's other side. I followed his eyes, though I had seen the view a million times myself: patchwork farmland and the sparkling blot of the Eyeglass, a local lake. "Dekarta has no chance of inheriting. He's safer away from Sky, quite frankly."

"Because he's not fully Amn?" I gave him a hard look. "And how, exactly, did that happen, *Uncle* Ramina?"

He turned back to me, his eyes narrowing, and then he sighed. "Demonshit."

I grinned. "Did you really lie with your own sister, or did a scrivener handle the fine details with vials and squeeze bulbs?"

Ramina glared at me. "Is tact simply not in your nature, or are you this offensive on purpose?"

"On purpose. But remember that incest isn't exactly unknown to gods."

He crossed his legs, which might have been defensiveness or nonchalance. "It was the politic solution. She needed someone she could trust. And we are only half siblings, after all." He shrugged, then eyed me. "Shahar and Dekarta don't know."

"Shahar, you mean. Who's Deka's father?"

"I am." When I laughed, his jaw tightened. "The scriveners were most careful in their tests, Lord Sieh. Believe me. He and Shahar are full siblings, as Amn as I am."

"Impossible. Or you aren't as Amn as you think."

He bristled, elegantly. "I can trace my lineage unbroken back to the first Shahar, Lord Sieh, with no taint of lesser races at any point. The problem, however, is Remath. Her half-Ken grandfather, for one..." He shuddered dramatically. "I suppose we're lucky the children didn't turn up redheads on top of everything else. But that wasn't the only problem."

"His soul," I said softly, thinking of Deka's smile, still shy even after I'd threatened to kill him. "He is a child of earth and dappled shadows, not the bright harsh light of day."

Ramina looked at me oddly, but I was tired of adapting myself to mortals' comfort. "If by that you mean he's too gentle... well, so is Shahar, really. But she at least looks the part."

"When will he be allowed to return?"

"In theory? When his training is complete, two years from now. In actuality?" Ramina shrugged. "Perhaps never."

I frowned at this, folding my arms and resting my chin on them. With a heavy sigh, Ramina got to his feet as well. I thought he would leave and was glad for it; I was tired of plodding mortal minds and convoluted mortal relationships. But he stopped at the top of the stairwell, gazing at me for a long moment.

"If you won't help the scriveners find the source of these attacks," he said, "will you at least agree to protect Shahar? I feel certain she will be a target for our enemies—or those among our relatives who may use the attacks as a cover for their own plots."

I sighed and closed my eyes. "She's my friend, you fool."

He seemed annoyed, probably because of the "you fool." "What does that—" He paused, then sighed. "No, I should be grateful. The one thing we Arameri have always lacked is the gods' friendship. If Shahar has managed to win yours... well, perhaps she has a better chance of surviving to inherit than I'd first thought."

With that, Ramina left. I still didn't like him.

6

I sent a letter to my love
And on the way I dropped it,
A little puppy picked it up
And put it in his pocket.
It isn't you,
It isn't you,
But it is you.

Sᴋʏ ɪs ʙᴏʀᴇᴅᴏᴍ. That was the thing I had hated the most about it, back when I'd been a slave. It is a massive palace, each spire of which could house a village; its chambers contain dozens of entertainments. All of these become tedious to the point of torment after two thousand years. Hells, after twenty.

It was quickly becoming obvious that I would not be able to endure Sky for much longer. Which was fine; I needed to be out in the world anyhow, searching for the means to cure myself, if such a thing existed in the mortal realm. But Sky was a necessary staging ground for my efforts at life, allowing me relative safety and comfort in which to consider important logistical questions. Where

would I live when I left? *How* would I live, if my magic
would soon desert me? I had no resources, no particular
skills, no connections in mortal society. The mortal realm
could be dangerous, especially given my new vulnerability. I needed a plan, to face it.

(The irony of my situation did not escape me; it was
the nature of all mortal adolescents to experience such
anxiety at the prospect of leaving their childhood home
for the harsh adult world. Knowing this did not make me
feel better.)

I had come to no conclusion by the afternoon, but since
I guessed that Shahar might have gotten over her fury
with me by this point, I went in search of her.

When I walked into Shahar's quarters, I found her surrounded by three servants who seemed to be in the middle
of dressing her. As I appeared in the parlor doorway, she
turned around so fast that her half-done hair whipped
loose; I saw a flash of dismay cross one servant's face
before the woman masked it.

"Where in the infinite hells have you been?" Shahar
demanded as I leaned against the doorjamb. "The servants said you left the cupola hours ago."

"Good to see you, too," I drawled. "What are you getting all polished up for?"

She sighed, submitting once again to the servants'
attentions. "Dinner. I'm meeting with Lady Hynno of the
Teman Protectorate's ruling Triadice, and her *pymexe*."

She pronounced the word perfectly, which was fitting,
as she'd probably been taught to speak Teman since childhood. The word meant something like "heir," though with
a masculine suffix. "Prince," then, in Amn parlance,
though unless the Temans had rewritten their charter
again in the centuries since I'd last paid attention to them,

it was not a hereditary role. They chose their leaders from among their brighter young folk, then trained them for a decade or so before actually letting them be in charge of anything. That sort of sensible thinking was why I'd chosen the Temans as my model, back when I'd first crafted a mortal appearance for myself.

Then I noticed the gown they were wrapping around Shahar. Quite literally: the gown seemed to consist of bands of subdued gold cloth, palm wide, being woven over and under other bands until a herringbone pattern had been achieved. The overall effect was very elegant and cleverly emphasized Shahar's still-developing curves. I whistled, and she threw a wary look at me. "If I didn't know any better," I said, "I would think you were courting this prince. But you're too young, and since when have Arameri *married* foreigners? So this must be something else."

She shrugged, turning to gaze at herself in the bedroom mirror; the dress was almost done. They needed to wrap only the bottom few layers around her legs. But how was she going to get out of the thing? Perhaps they would cut it off her.

"The Triadic likes beauty," she said, "and she controls the tariffs on shipping from High North, so it's worthwhile to impress her. She's one of the few nobles who can actually make things difficult for us." She turned to the side, inspecting her profile; now that the servant had repaired her hair, she looked perfect and knew it. "And Prince Canru is an old childhood friend, so I don't mind looking nice for him."

I raised my eyebrows in surprise. Arameri usually didn't let their children have friends. Though I supposed friends were necessary, now that they had no gods. I went over to the parlor's couch and flopped onto it, not caring about the servants' glances. "So your dinner will be business and pleasure, then."

"Mostly business." The servants murmured something, and there was a pause as Shahar examined herself. Satisfied, she nodded, and the servants filed out. Once they were gone, Shahar slid on a pair of long, pale yellow gloves. "I mean to ask her about what happened to my cousins, in fact."

I rolled onto my side to watch her. "Why would she know?"

"Because the Temans are part of a neutral group in the Nobles' Consortium. They support us, but they also support progressive efforts like a revised tithe system and secular schools. The Order of Itempas can no longer afford to educate children beyond the age of nine, you see—"

"Yes, yes," I said, rubbing my eyes. "I don't care about the details, Shahar. Just tell me the important part."

She sighed in exasperation, coming over to the couch to gaze haughtily at me. "I believe Hynno has alliances with those High Norther nobles who consistently vote against the interests of the Arameri in the Consortium," she said. "And *they*, I believe, are the source of the attacks on my family."

"If you think that, then why haven't you killed them?" Not even a handful of generations ago, her forbears would have done it already.

"Because we don't know which nations are involved. The core of it is in High North, that much we're certain of, but that still encompasses two dozen nations. And I suspect some involvement by Senmite nations as well, and even some of the islands." She sighed, putting her hands on her hips and frowning in consternation. "I want the head of this snake, Sieh, not just its fangs or scales. So I'm taking your advice and issuing a challenge. I'm going to tell them to kill me before I assume leadership of the family, or I will destroy the whole of High North to deal with the threat."

I rocked back, duly impressed, though a knot of cold anger tightened in my stomach as well. "I see. I assume you're bluffing in order to lure them out into the open."

"Of course I am. I'm not even certain we *can* destroy a continent anymore, and the attempt would certainly exhaust the scrivener corps. Weakening ourselves at a time like this would be foolish." Looking pleased with herself, Shahar sat down beside me. Her dress made a pleasant harmony of sounds as it flexed with her body, a carefully designed effect of its peculiar construction. It probably cost the treasury of a small nation. "Still, I've already spoken with Captain Wrath, and we will coordinate an operation that can put on a suitably threatening display—"

"So you won't use your ancestors' methods," I snapped, "because you still want to be a good Arameri. But you're not above using their *reputation* to advance your goals. Do I have that right?"

She stared at me, startled into momentary silence. "What?"

I sat up. "You threaten people with genocide, and then you wonder why they scheme against you. Really, Shahar; I thought you wanted to change things."

Her face darkened at once. "I would never actually do it, Sieh. Gods, that would make me a monster!"

"And what does it make you to threaten all that they know and love?" She fell silent in confusion and growing anger, and I leaned close so that my breath would caress her cheek. "A monster too cowardly to accept her own hideousness."

Shahar went pale, though two flaring spots of color rose

on her cheeks as fury warred with shock in her eyes. To her credit, however, she did not launch an immediate attack, and she did not move away from me. Her nostrils twitched. One of her hands tightened, then relaxed. She lifted her chin.

"Clearly you aren't suggesting that I actually inflict some calamity on them," she said. Her voice was soft. "What, then, do you suggest, Trickster? Let them continue with these assassination attempts until every full-blood is dead?" Her expression tightened further. "Never mind. I don't know why I'm even asking. You don't care whether any of us live or die."

"Why should I?" I gestured around us, at Sky. "It's not as though there aren't plenty of Arameri—"

"No, there aren't!" Her temper broke with an almost palpable force. She shifted to her hands and knees, glowering. "You've looked around this place, Sieh. They tell me the underpalace was full, back in your day. They tell me there were once as many Arameri living abroad as there were here in Sky, and we could take our pick from among the best of the family to serve us. These days we've actually been adopting people into the family who aren't related at all! Tell me what that means to you, O eldest of godlings!"

I frowned. What she was saying made no sense. Humans bred like rabbits. There had been thousands of Arameri in the days when I'd been a slave... but she was right. The underpalace should never have been empty. No mostly-Maroneh lowblood should have been able to rise to captain of the guard. And Remath had mated with her own brother—that had never happened in the old days. Incest, certainly, constantly, but never *for children*. Yet if Remath, herself diluted in some hidden way, sought to concentrate the Central Family's strengths...

The signs had been there since I'd first returned to Sky,

but I hadn't seen them. I was so used to thinking of the Arameri as powerful and numerous, but in fact they were dwindling. Dying.

"Explain," I said, inexplicably troubled.

Shahar's anger faded; she sat down again, her shoulders slumping. "The targeting of highbloods is a recent thing," she said, "but the attacks were happening for a long time before that. We just didn't notice until the problem became acute." Her expression grew sour.

"Lowbloods," I guessed. Those Arameri least-closely related to the Central Family, lacking in resources or social status to give them greater value to the family head. The servants, the guards. The expendable ones.

"Yes." She sighed. "It started long ago. Probably a few decades after you and the other Enefadeh broke free. All the collateral lines of the family, the ones we left free to manage businesses or simply bring in new blood— It was subtle at first. Children dying of odd diseases, young wives and husbands turning up infertile, accidents, natural disasters. The lines died out. We apportioned their estates to allies or resumed control of them ourselves."

I was already shaking my head. "No. Accidents can be arranged, gods know children are easy to kill, but *natural disasters*, Shahar? That would mean..." Could a scrivener do it? They knew the scripts for wind and rain and sunlight, but storms were demonishly hard to control. Too easy to trigger a tsunami when trying for a flash flood. But the alternative—no. No.

She smiled, following my worst thoughts. "Yes. It *could* mean that a god has been working to kill us for the past fifty years or more."

I leapt to my feet, beginning to pace. My mortal skin suddenly felt constricting, choking; I wanted to shed it.

"If I wanted to kill the Arameri, I would *do* it," I snapped. "I would fill this place with soap bubbles and bury you in bath toys. I would put spiked holes in all the floors and cover them with rugs. I would will every Arameri under twelve to just fall down and die—I can do it, too!" I rounded on her, daring her to challenge me.

But Shahar was still nodding, wearily, her smile gone. "I know, Sieh."

Her capitulation bothered me. I was not used to seeing her despair. I was not used to regarding any Arameri as helpless or vulnerable, let alone all of them.

"Yeine forbade any of us to retaliate against the Arameri," I said softly. "She didn't care about you—she hates you as much as the rest of us do—but she didn't want war everywhere, and..." The Arameri, foul as they were, had been the best hope for keeping the world from collapsing into chaos. Even Nahadoth had gone along with Yeine, and none of my siblings would defy her.

Would they?

I turned away, going to the window so that Shahar would not see my fear.

She sighed and got to her feet. "I've got to go. We're leaving early so as to fool any potential assassins...." She paused, noticing my stillness at last. "Sieh?"

"Go on," I said softly. Beyond the window, the sun had begun to set, scattering a crimson spectrum across the sky. Did Itempas feel the end of day, wherever he was, the way Nahadoth had once died with every dawn? Did some part of him quail and gibber into silence, or did he fade slowly, like the bands of color in the sky, until his soul went dark?

At my silence, Shahar headed for the door, and I roused myself enough to think. "Shahar." I heard her stop. "If something happens, if you're in danger, call me."

"We never tested that."

"It will work." I felt that instinctively. I didn't know how I knew, but I did. "I don't care if most of the Arameri die, it's true. But you are my friend."

She went still behind me. Surprised? Touched? Once upon a time, I would have been able to taste her emotions on the air. Now I could only guess.

"Get some rest," she said at last. "I'll have food sent up. We'll speak again when I return." Then she left.

And I leaned back against the window, trembling now that she was gone, left alone to ponder the most terrible of possibilities.

A godling defying a god. It seemed impossible. We were such low things compared to them; they could kill us so easily. Yet we were not powerless. Some among us—myself, once upon a time—were strong enough to challenge them directly, at least for a few moments. And even the least of us could keep secrets and stir up trouble.

One godling's mischief did not trouble me. But if *many* of us were involved, conspiring across mortal generations, implementing some complex plan, it was no longer mischief. It was a revolt. One far more dangerous than whatever the northerners planned for the Arameri.

Because if the godlings revolted against the gods, the gods would fight back, as they had done when threatened by the demons long ago. But godlings were not as fragile as demons, and many of us had no vested interest in keeping the mortal realm safe. That would mean a second Gods' War, worse than the first one.

This had been brewing right under my nose for fifty years, and I hadn't had a clue.

Beyond me, in silent rebuke, the bloody sky went gradually black.

7

How many miles to Babylon?
Three score and ten.
Can I get there by candlelight?
Aye, and back again.
If your feet are nimble and light,
You'll get there by candlelight.

I NEEDED HELP. But not from Nahadoth or Yeine; I dared not chance their tempers. Not until I knew more.

Who could I trust among my siblings? Zhakkarn, of course, but she was never subtle and would be no help in uncovering a conspiracy. The rest—hells. Most of them I had not spoken to in two thousand years. Before that I had tried to kill some of them. Bridges burned, ashes scattered, ground strewn with salt.

And there was the small problem of my inability to return to the gods' realm in my current state. That was less of a problem than it seemed, because fortunately the city beneath Sky was teeming with my youngest siblings, those for whom the novelty of the mortal realm had not yet worn off. If I could convince one of them to help me…But which one?

I turned from the window, frustrated, to pace. The walls of Sky had begun to glow again, and I hated them, for they were more proof of my impotence; once upon a time, they would have dimmed, just a bit, in my presence. I was no Nahadoth, but there was more than a little of his darkness in me. Now, as if to mock me, the walls stayed bright, diffusing every shadow—

—shadow.

I stopped. There was one of my siblings, just maybe, who would help me. Not because she liked me; quite the opposite. But secrets were her nature, and that was something we shared. It was always easier to relate to those of my siblings with whom I had something in common. If I appealed to that, would she listen? Or would she kill me?

"No reward without risk," I murmured to myself, and headed for the apartment door.

I took the lift down to the penultimate level of the underpalace. The corridors here were as quiet as always— and dim, compared to the brighter glow of all the other levels. Yes, this was the place.

For nostalgia's sake, I touched each door as I passed it, remembering. Here were my sisters' rooms: Zhakkarn's with cannon shot embedded in the floor and the walls hung with shields; her hammock of blood-soaked slings and whips. (Very comfortable, I knew from experience, though a little scratchy.) Dear traitor Kurue's, with pearls and coins scattered over nearly every surface, and books stolen from the library stacked atop the rest. The coins would be tarnishing now.

I avoided my own quarters, for fear of how they would make me feel. How long before I ended up living there again? I steered my thoughts off this path with a heavy hand.

This left the fourth chamber, at the center of the level. The one that had been Nahadoth's.

It was pitch-black within, but I could still see a little in the dark even without cat's eyes. The chamber was completely empty. No furnishings, no decorations, no hint that the room had ever been used. Yet every inch of its structure screamed defiance of our onetime jailors: the permanently lightless walls. The ceiling, which dipped toward the center of the room; the floor rose in the same spot, as if some terrible force had sucked the very stone toward itself. The sharp corners, which no other room in Sky had. If I stared hard enough into the dark, I could almost see Nahadoth's silhouette etched against it and hear his soft, deep voice. *Have you come for another story? Greedy child.*

It had been cruel of me to push him away. I would pray an apology to him after this.

Reaching into my shirt, I pulled up the necklace of my own woven hair. Tugging En off the cord, I willed it to hover in the space between the floor and ceiling extrusions. To my relief, this worked; En stayed in the air and began turning at once, happily. This reminded it of the orrery, though it was lonely without planets.

"Sorry," I said, reaching out to stroke its smooth surface with a fingertip. "I'll give you more planets someday. In the meantime, will you give me light?"

In answer, En flared bright yellow-white for me, a gleeful candle. Suddenly Nahadoth's chamber became smaller, stark with shadows. My own loomed behind me, a big-headed apparition that seemed to taunt me with the shape of the child I should have been. I ignored it and focused on the task at hand.

"Lady of Secrets," I said, extending a hand; my shadow did the same. Shaping my fingers just so, I made the profile of a face on the wall and spoke with it. "Shadow in the dark. Nemmer Jru Im, my sister; do you hear me?"

There was a pause. Then, though I did not move, my hand shadow cocked its head.

"Well, this is unexpected," it said in a woman's voice. "Big brother Sieh. It's been some time."

I added my other hand, working the shadow into the shape of a donkey's head. *I've been an ass.* "I hear interesting things about you, Nemmer. Will you speak with me?"

"I answered, didn't I?" The first shadow shifted, impossibly manifesting its own arms and hands, the latter of which were set on its hips. "Though I'll admit that's because I've heard some very interesting things about you, too. I'm *dying* to know if they're true."

Damn. I might have known. "I'll tell you every juicy detail, but I want something in return."

"Do you, now?" I tensed at the wariness in her tone. That she did not trust me was irrelevant; she trusted no one. She did not like me, though, which was another matter entirely. "I'm not certain I'm interested in making any bargains with you, *Trickster.*"

I nodded; no more than I had expected. "I mean no harm to you, Nemmer. Cross my heart and hope to die." I heard the bitterness in my own voice and angled my fingers into the shape of an old man's head. "You did not turn on us in the War. I bear no grudge toward you."

"That I do not believe," she said, folding her arms. "Everyone knows you hate the ones who stood by doing nothing as much as the ones who fought for Itempas."

"*Hate* is a strong word—"

Her silhouette tossed its head in the universal gesture

of rolled eyes. "Resent us, then. *Yearn to kill* us. Is that more accurate?"

I stopped and dropped my hands with a sigh. The talking shadows remained. "You know my nature, Sister. What do you want from me—maturity?" I wanted to laugh, but I was too soul-weary. "Fine, I'll say it: I hate you and I wouldn't have contacted you if I had a choice, and we both know it. Now, will you speak with me, or shall we just tell each other to go to the infinite hells and leave it at that?"

She was silent for a moment. I had time enough to worry: who could I contact if she refused to help me? The other choices were worse. What if—

"All right," she said at last, and the knot that had been tightening in my belly loosened. "I need time to set things up. Come here, a week from today. Noon." The location made itself present in my consciousness, as if I had always known it. A house somewhere in the city below Sky. South Root. "Come alone."

I folded my arms. "Will *you* be alone?"

"Oh, of course."

I made the shape of a cat's head with my hands: ears back, teeth bared. She laughed.

"I don't care if you believe me. You asked for this meeting, not I. Be there in a week, or not at all." With that, her shadow leaned down and blew hard. With a surprised flare, En went dark and dropped to the floor. Then Nemmer was gone.

In the dark, I retrieved En, who was quite put out. I murmured soothing words and tucked it back into my shirt, all the while thinking.

If Nemmer knew what had happened to me—and it was her nature to know such things; not even the Three could keep her out of their business, though she wasn't foolish enough to flaunt that—then when I arrived in a week, I might find her and a group of my least-favorite siblings, some of whom had been waiting for a chance to repay me for the Gods' War for two thousand years.

But Nemmer had never been one to play the games of our family. I didn't know why she'd sat out the war. Had she been torn, like so many of our siblings, between our fathers? Had she been one of those working to save the mortal realm, which had nearly been destroyed by our battling? I sighed in frustration, realizing that *this* was the sort of thing I should have occupied myself with as eldest, not our parents' sordid dramas. If I had bothered to reconcile with my siblings, perhaps tried to understand their reasons for betraying Nahadoth—

"If I had done that, I would not be who I am." I sighed into the dark.

Which, ultimately, was why I would risk trusting Nemmer. She, too, was only what her nature made her. She kept her own counsel, gathering secrets and doling out knowledge where she deemed best and making alliances only as it suited her—briefly, if at all. If nothing else, that meant she was not my enemy. Whether she became my friend would be up to me.

On returning to Deka's room, I was surprised to find that I had visitors again: Morad, the ample-haired palace steward, and another servant, who was busy making the bed and tidying up. Both bowed to me at once, as they would to any Arameri highblood. Then the servant promptly resumed his cleaning duties while Morad looked me up and down with an expression of unconcealed distaste.

Frowning at her scrutiny, I looked at myself—and

then, belatedly, realized why the servants had all stared at me on my way to the underpalace. I still wore the clothing I had conjured for myself two days before. It had been nondescript then, but it was filthy now, after all my scrabbling through dusty corridors and Tree-choked dead spaces. And...I sniffed one of my armpits and wrinkled my nose, appalled that I had not noticed. I had not bathed since my return to this world, and apparently my adolescent body had a greater capacity for generating reek than I had done as a child.

"Oh," I said, smiling sheepishly at Morad. She sighed, though I thought I saw a hint of amusement on her face.

"I'll run you a bath," she said, and paused, looking particularly at my head. "And summon a stylist. And the tailor. And a manicurist."

I touched my stringy, gritty hair with a weak laugh. "I suppose I deserve that."

"As you like, my lord." Morad touched the servant, who had almost finished the bed, and murmured something. He nodded and exited the apartment at once. To my surprise, Morad then rolled up her sleeves and finished tucking the sheets. When that was done, she went into the bathroom; a moment later, I heard water run.

Curious, I followed her into the room and watched while she sat on the tub's edge, testing the water with her fingers. It was even more noticeable with her back turned and all that hair of hers visible in full riot. It was clear that she was not fully Amn; her hair had the kind of tight, small coils that wealthy Amn spent hours and fortunes to achieve, and it was as black as my father's soul. Her skin was pale enough, but the marks of *other* were in her features, plain to anyone who looked. It was also plain that she was not ashamed of her mixed blood; she sat as straight and graceful as a queen. She could not have been raised in Sky or any Amn territory; they would have beaten her spirit down with cruel words long before now.

"Maroneh?" I guessed. "You must've gotten the hair from them, at least. The rest... Teman, maybe? Uthre, a bit of Ken?"

Morad turned to me, lifting one elegant eyebrow. "Two of my grandparents were part Maroneh, yes. One was Teman, another Min, and there are rumors that my father was actually a half-Tok who pretended to be Senmite to get into the Hunthou Legions. My mother was Amn."

More proof of the Arameri's desperation. In the old days, they would barely have acknowledged a woman with such jumbled bloodlines, let alone make her Steward. "Then how..."

She smiled wryly, as if she got such rude questions all the time. "I grew up in southern Senm. When I came of age, I petitioned to come here on the strength of my fourth grandparent—an Arameri highblood." At my grimace, she nodded. It was an old story. "Grandmama Atri never knew my grandfather's name. He was passing through town on a journey. Her family had no powerful friends, and she was a pretty girl." She shrugged, though her smile had faded.

"So you decided to come find Grandpapa the rapist and say hello?"

"He died years ago." She checked the water once more and stopped the taps. "It was Grandmama's idea that I come here, actually. There's not much work in that part of Senm, and if nothing else, her suffering could bring me a better life." She rose and went to stand pointedly beside the washing area's bench, picking up the flask that held shampoo.

I got up and undressed, pleased that my nudity didn't

seem to bother her. When I sat down, before I could warn
her, she lifted the cord that held En from around my neck
and set it on a counter. I was relieved that En tolerated this
without protest. It must have been tired after its earlier
exertion. Plus, it had always had odd taste in mortals.

"You didn't have to come *here* for a better life," I said,
yawning as she wet my hair and began washing it. Sending the message to Nemmer had left me tired, too, and
Morad's fingers were skillful and soothing. "There must
be a thousand other places in the world where you
could've made a living and where you wouldn't have had
to deal with this family's madness."

"There were no other places that paid as much," she
said.

I swung around to stare at her. "They *pay* you?"

She nodded, amused at my reaction, and gently pushed
my head back into place so that she could resume work.
"Yes. Old Lord T'vril's doing, actually. As a quarterblood,
I can retire in five more years with enough money to take
care of my whole family for the rest of my life. I'd say
that's worth dabbling in madness, wouldn't you?"

I frowned, trying to understand. "They are your family," I said. "The ones you left behind, in the south. The
Arameri are just employers to you?"

Her hands paused. "Well. I've been here fifteen years
at this point; it's home now. Some aspects of life in Sky
aren't so terrible, Lord Sieh. I suspect you know that.
And . . . well, there are people I love here, too."

I knew then. She resumed work in silence, pouring
warm water over me and then lathering again, and when
she leaned past me to pick up the flask of shampoo, I got a
good mouthful of her scent. Daystone and paper and
patience, the scents of efficient bureaucracy, and one

thing more. A complex scent, layered, familiar, with each element supporting and enriching the other. Dreams. Pragmatism. Discretion. Love.

Remath.

It was my nature to use the keys to a mortal's soul whenever they fell into my hands. If I had still been myself, the child or the cat, I would have found some way to torment Morad with my knowledge. I might even have made a song of it and sung it everywhere until even her friends found themselves humming the tune. The refrain would have been *see wow, you silly cow, how dare you lose your heart.*

But though I would always be the child, and the child was a bully, I could not bring myself to do this to her. I was going soft, I supposed, or growing up. So I kept silent.

Presently Morad finished with my hair, whereupon she handed me a soapy sponge and stepped back, plainly unwilling to wash the rest of my body. She had wrapped my hair in a damp towel that was tied like a beehive atop my head, which made me giggle when I finished and stood and caught a glimpse of myself in the mirror. Then my eyes drifted down. I saw the rest of me and fell silent.

It was the same body I had shaped for myself countless times, sometimes deliberately, sometimes in helpless response to moments of weakness. Short for "my age"; I would grow another two or three inches but would never be tall by Amn standards. Thinner than I usually made myself, perhaps from years of not eating while I gradually became mortal within Nahadoth. Long-limbed. Beneath my brown skin, there were bones poking out at every juncture, like blemishes. The muscles that lined them were attenuated and not very strong.

I leaned closer to the mirror, peering at the lines of my

face critically. Not very attractive, either, though I knew that would improve. Too disproportionate for now. Too tired-eyed. Shahar was much prettier. And yet she had kissed me, hadn't she? I traced the outline of my lips with a finger, remembering the feel of her mouth. What had she thought of mine, on hers?

Morad cleared her throat.

Did Shahar ever think of—

"The water will get cold," Morad said gently. I blinked, blushing, and was abruptly glad I hadn't made fun of her. I got into the tub, and Morad exited the bathroom to go speak with the tailor, who'd just arrived and announced himself.

When I emerged in a fluffy robe—I looked ridiculous—the tailor measured me, murmuring to himself that I would need looser clothing to conceal my thinness. Then came the manicurist, and the shoemaker, and one or two others whom Morad had somehow summoned, though I hadn't seen her use magic. By the time it was done, I was exhausted—which Morad thankfully noticed. She dismissed all the craft servants and turned to head for the door herself.

Belatedly it occurred to me that she'd been unbelievably helpful. Who knew how many duties she had as steward, and how many of those had she neglected to see to my comfort? "Thank you," I blurted as she opened the door.

She paused and looked back at me in surprise, then smiled in such a genuine, generous way that I suddenly knew what Remath saw in her.

Then she was gone. I sat down to eat the meal the servants had left. Afterward, I sprawled naked across Deka's bed, for once looking forward to sleep so that I could perhaps dream of love and

forget

* * *

I stood upon a plain like a vast glass mirror. Mirrors again. I had seen them in Nahadoth's realm, too. Perhaps there was meaning in this? I would ponder it some other time.

Above me arced the vault of the heavens: an endlessly turning cylinder of clouds and sky, vast and limitless and yet somehow enclosed. Clouds drifted across it from left to right, although the light—from no source I could ascertain—shifted in the opposite direction, waxing light and waning dark in a slow and steady gradient.

The gods' realm, or a dream manifestation of it. It was an approximation, of course. All my mortal mind could comprehend.

Before me, rising from the plain, a palace lay impossibly on its side. It was silver and black, built in no recognizable mortal architectural style and yet suggesting all of them, a thing of lines and shadow without dimension or definition. An impression, not reality. Below, instead of a reflection, its opposite shone in the mirror: white and gold, more realistic but less imaginative, the same yet different. There was meaning in this, too, but it was obvious: the black palace ascendant, the white palace nothing but an image. The silvery plain reflecting, balancing, and separating both. I sighed, annoyed. Had I already become as tiresomely literal as most mortals? How humiliating.

"Are you afraid?" asked a voice behind me.

I started and began to turn. "No," the speaker snapped, and such was the force of his command—commanding reality, commanding my flesh—that I froze. *Now* I was afraid.

"Who are you?" I asked. I didn't recognize his voice, but that meant nothing. I had dozens of brothers and they could take any shape they chose, especially in this realm.

"Why does that matter?"

"Because I want to know, duh."

"Why?"

I frowned. "What kind of question is that? We're family; I want to know which one of my brothers is trying to scare the hells out of me." And succeeding, though I would never admit such a thing.

"I'm not one of your brothers."

At this, I frowned in confusion. Only gods could enter the gods' realm. Was he lying? Or was I simply too mortal to understand what he really meant?

"Should I kill you?" the stranger asked. He was young, I decided, though such judgments meant little in the grand scale of things. He was oddly soft-spoken, too, his voice mild even as he delivered these peculiar not-quite-threats. Was he angry? I thought so, but couldn't be sure. His tone was all flat emotionlessness edged in cold.

"I don't know. Should you?" I retorted.

"I've been contemplating the matter for most of my life."

"Ah," I said. "I suppose you and I must have gotten off on the wrong foot from the beginning, then." That happened sometimes. I'd tried to be a good elder brother for a long time, visiting each of my younger siblings as they were born and helping them through those first, difficult centuries. Some of them I was still friends with. Some of them I'd loathed the instant I'd laid eyes on them, and vice versa.

"From the very beginning, yes."

I sighed, slipping my hands into my pockets. "Must be a difficult decision, then, or you'd have done it already. Whatever I did to make you angry, either it can't have been all that bad, or it's unforgivable."

"Oh?"

I shrugged. "If it was really bad, you wouldn't be waffling about whether to kill me. If it was unforgivable, you'd be too angry for revenge to make any difference. There'd be no *point* in killing me. So which is it?"

"There's a third option," he said. "It was unforgivable, but there *is* a point in killing you."

"Interesting." In spite of my unease, I grinned at the conundrum. "And that point is?"

"I don't simply *want* vengeance. I require and embody and evolve through it."

I blinked, sobering, because if vengeance was his nature, then that was another matter entirely. But I did not remember a sibling who was god of vengeance.

"What have I done to earn your wrath?" I asked, troubled now. "And why are you even asking the question? You have to serve your nature."

"Are you offering to die for me?"

"No, demons take you. If you try to kill me, I'll try to kill you back. Suicide isn't *my* nature. But I want to understand this."

He sighed and shifted, the movement drawing my eye toward the mirror below our feet. It didn't help much. The angle of the reflection was such that I could see little beyond feet and legs and a hint of elbow. His hands were in his pockets, too.

"What you have done is unforgivable," he said, "and yet I *must* forgive it, because you did not know."

I frowned, confused. "What does my knowledge have to do with anything? Harm committed unknowingly is still harm."

"True. But if you had known, Sieh, I'm not certain you would have done it."

At his use of my name, I grew more confused, because his tone had changed. For an instant, the coldness had broken, and I heard stranger things underneath. Sorrow. Wistfulness? Perhaps a hint of affection. But I did not know this god; I was certain of it.

"Irrelevant," I said finally, turning my head as much as I could. Beyond a certain point, my neck simply would not bend; it was like trying to turn with two pillows braced on either side of my head. Pillows formed of nothing but solid, unyielding will. I tried to relax. "You can't base decisions on hypotheticals. It doesn't matter what I *would have* done. You know only what I *did*." I paused meaningfully. "Perhaps you could tell me." For once I wasn't in the mood for games.

Unfortunately, my companion was. "You chose to serve your nature," he said, ignoring my hint. "Why?"

I wished I could look at him. Sometimes a look is more eloquent than any words. "*Why?* What the hells—are you kidding?"

"You are the oldest of us and must pretend to be the youngest."

"I don't pretend anything. I am what I must be, and I'm damn good at it, thanks."

"So we are weaker than the mortals, then." His voice grew soft, almost sad. "Slaves to fate, never to be freed."

"Shut the hells up," I snapped. "You don't know slavery if you think *this* is the same thing."

"Isn't it? Having no choice—"

"You have a choice." I lifted my gaze to the shifting firmament above. The gradient—night to day, day to night—did not change at a constant rate. Only mortals thought of the sky as a reliable, predictable thing. We gods had to live with Nahadoth and Itempas; we knew better. "You can accept yourself, take control of your nature, make it what you *want* it to be. Just because you're the god of vengeance doesn't mean you have to be some brooding cliché, forever cackling to yourself and totting up what you owe to whom. Choose how your nature shapes you. Embrace it. Find the strength in it. Or fight yourself and remain forever incomplete."

My companion fell silent, perhaps digesting my advice. That was good, because it was clear that I'd done him a disservice, besides whatever wrong he felt I'd committed. I did not remember him; that meant I hadn't bothered to find him, guide him, after his birth. And he'd needed such guidance, because it was painfully clear that he did not like the hand fate, or the Maelstrom, had dealt him. I didn't blame him for that; I wouldn't have wanted to be god of vengeance, either. But he was, and he was going to have to find a way to live with that.

In the mirror, I saw the man behind me step closer, raising a hand. I braced myself to fight—purely on principle, since I already knew there was nothing I could do. It was clear his power superseded what little god-magic I had left, or I would have been able to break his compulsion and turn around.

But his hand touched my hair, to my utter shock. Lingered there a moment, as if memorizing the texture. Then fingers grazed the back of my neck, and I jumped. Was this some kind of threat? But he made no attempt to harm me. His finger traced the knots of spine along the back of my neck, stopping only when my clothing interfered. Then—reluctantly, I thought—his hand pulled away.

"Thank you," he said at last. "That was something I needed to hear."

"Sorry I didn't say it sooner." I paused. "So are you going to kill me now?"

"Soon."

"Ah. Good vengeance takes time?"

"Yes." The coldness had returned to his voice, and this time I recognized it for what it was. Not anger. Resolve.

I sighed. "Sorry, too, to hear that. I think I might've liked you."

"Yes. And I you."

There was that, at least. "Well, don't dither too long about it. I've only got a few decades left."

I thought he smiled, which I counted as a victory. "I have already begun."

"Good for you." I hoped he didn't think I was mocking him. It always made me feel good to see the young ones do well, even if that meant they would inevitably threaten me. That was the way of things, after all. Children had to grow up. They did not always become what others wanted. "Do me a favor, though?"

He said nothing, in keeping with his newfound resolve. That was all right. I could be his enemy, if that was what he needed from me. I just didn't see any point in being an ass about it.

"I don't belong here anymore." I gestured around us at the mirrored plain, the palaces, the sky. "Not even in this watered-down dream of reality. Wake me up, will you?"

"All right."

And suddenly a hand ripped through me from behind. I cried out in surprise and agony, looking down to see my mortal heart clenched in a sharp-nailed hand—

I jerked awake to the sound of my own cry, echoing from the vaulted ceiling.

Glowing vaulted ceiling. It was night. Above me loomed Shahar, who had a hand on my chest and a worried look on her face. I was still sleepy, disoriented. A quick check of my chest verified that my heart was still there. Inadvertently, I looked at Shahar's chest, thinking muzzily that my dream-enemy might have tried to harm her, too. Her dress lay in cut strips down to her waist, half undone, and she held a loose sleep shift over her breasts with her free arm, which she must have grabbed to cover herself when she'd come into my room. This did nothing to hide the other beautiful parts of her: the gentle sweep of neck into shoulder, the slight curve of her waist. Of her breasts, I could still see one rounded shadow near her elbow.

I reached up to pull her arm out of the way and stopped with my fingers two inches from her arm. It took her a moment to realize. She stared at my reaching hand uncomprehendingly; then her eyes widened and she jerked away.

I lowered my hand. "Sorry," I muttered.

She glared at me. "You started screaming so loud I could hear you through the adjoining door. I thought something was *wrong* with you."

"A dream."

"Not a pleasant one, obviously."

"Actually, it wasn't so bad, 'til the end." The fear was fading quickly. My dream-companion hadn't been gentle about it, but he'd chosen an excellent way to send me back to the mortal realm. I felt none of the heartrending sorrow that I might have on realizing that the gods' realm was now forbidden to me. Instead I was just annoyed. "Little mortalfucking bastard. If I ever get my magic back, I'm going to break every bone in whatever body he manifests. Let him avenge *that*."

I paused then, because Shahar was looking at me oddly. "What in every god's name are you talking about?"

"Nothing. I'm babbling." I yawned, my jaw cracking with the effort. "Sleep makes me stupid. Never liked it."

"Mortalfuck," she said, looking thoughtful. "Is that—" She paused, grimacing, too refined to say the word beyond repeating my term. "*Being with* a mortal. Is it such an anathema among gods that you use it as a curse?"

I blushed, though it bothered me that I did. I had nothing to be ashamed of. Pushing myself up on my elbows, I said, "No, it's not anathema at all. Far from it."

"What, then?"

I tried to seem nonchalant. "It's just that mortals are dangerous to love. They break easily. In time, they die. It hurts." I shrugged. "It's easier, safer, to just use them for pleasure. But that's hard, too, because it's impossible for us to take pleasure without giving back something of ourselves. We are not..." I groped for the words in Senmite. "We do not...It isn't our way. No, it isn't *natural* to do things that way, to be nothing but body, contained only within ourselves, so when we are with another, we reach out and the mortal gets inside us—we cannot help it—and then it hurts to push them out, too..." I trailed off, because Shahar was staring at me. I'd been talking faster and faster, the words tumbling together in my effort to convey how it felt. I sighed and forced myself back to human speed. "*Being with* mortals isn't anathema, but it's not good, either. It never ends well. Any god with sense avoids it."

"I see." I wasn't sure I believed that, but she sighed. "Well. Give me a moment." She stepped back into her room, not shutting the door, and I heard her wrestle with the cloth of her dress for a few moments. Then she returned, wearing the sleep shift instead of holding it in front of herself this time. By this point I had sat up, rubbing my face to try and banish the dregs of sleep and the memory of my bloody, torn-out heart. When Shahar sat down on the bed, she did so gingerly, at its edge, out of my arms' reach. I didn't blame her for that or the fact that she seemed more relaxed after my speech about avoiding sex.

Still, there was something odd about her manner, something I couldn't put my finger on. She seemed jittery, tense. I wondered why she hadn't just stayed in her room and gone to bed, once she'd seen that I wasn't dying.

"How did your meeting with, ah…" I waved a hand vaguely. Some noble.

She chuckled. "It went well, though that depends on your definition of *well*." She sobered, her eyes darkening with a hint of her earlier anger. "You'll be pleased to know that I did not follow through on my plan to challenge the resistance, per your advice. The message I sent instead—I hope, if I'm right about Lady Hynno—was that I would like to negotiate. Find out more about their demands and determine whether there's some way that we might meet them. Without throwing the world into chaos, that is." She glanced at me warily.

"I'm impressed," I said truthfully. "And surprised. Negotiation—compromise—is usually anathema to Itempans. And you changed your mind because of me?" I laughed a little. There were some good things about being older. People listened to me more.

Shahar sighed, looking away. "We'll see what happens when my mother hears of it. She already thinks I'm weak; after this, I may not be heir for much longer." With a heavy sigh, she lay back on the bed, stretching out her arms over her head. I could not help myself; my eyes settled on the very noticeable contrast of her areolae under the sheer shift. They were surprisingly dark, given her pale coloring. Perfect brown circles, with soft little cylinders at their centers—

Useless stupid animal mortaling body. My penis had reacted before I could stop it, jabbing me in the belly and forcing me to sit up from my usual slouch. It hurt, and I felt hot all over, as if I'd come down sick. (I had. It was called *adolescence*, an evil, evil disease.) But it was not just her flesh that drew me. I could barely see it with my withering senses, but her soul gleamed and whispered like rubbed silk. We have always been vulnerable to true beauty.

I dragged my eyes away from her breasts to find her watching me—watching me watch her? I did not know, but the hunger in me sharpened at the unalarmed, contemplative look in her eyes. I fought the reaction back, but it was difficult. Another symptom of the disease.

"Don't be stupid," I said, focusing on mundanities. "It takes great strength to compromise, Shahar. More than it does to threaten and destroy, since you must fight your own pride as well as the enemy. You Arameri have never understood this—and you didn't have to, when you had us at your beck and call. Now, perhaps, you can learn to be true rulers and not merely bullies."

She rolled onto her belly, which brought her to lie between my legs, propped on her elbows. At this I frowned, growing suspicious, and then wondering at my own unease. She was just a girl testing the waters of womanhood. An older version of *I'll show you mine if you show me yours*. She wanted to know if I found her desirable. Did I not owe her the courtesy of an honest response? I lowered my knees and sat back on my elbows so that she could see the evidence of my admiration in the tented sheet and the heat of my gaze. She immediately blushed, averting her eyes. Then she looked at me again, and away again, and eventually looked down at her folded arms, which were fidgeting on the covers.

"I think Mother wants me to marry Canru," she said. Her words had an air of effort. "The Teman heir I told you about. I think that's why she's let me be friends with him. She's never let anyone else close to me."

I shrugged. "So marry him."

She glared at me, forgetting her prudishness. "I don't want to."

"Then *don't*. Shahar, for the gods' sakes. You're the Arameri heir. Do what you damn well please."

"I can't. If Mother wants this—" She bit her lower lip and looked away. "We have never sold our sons or daughters into marriage before now, Sieh. We didn't have to, because we didn't have anything to gain. We didn't need alliances or money or land. But now...I think...I think Mother understands that the Temans might prove pivotal, given High North's increasing restlessness. I think that's why she's letting me handle things with Lady Hynno. She's putting me on display."

All at once she looked up at me, and there was such ferocity in her expression that it struck me like a blow. Why?

"I want to succeed Mother, Sieh," she said. "I want to be head after her. Not just because I want power; I know the evil our family's done to you and to the world. But we've done good, too, great good, and I want *that* to be our legacy. I will do whatever it takes to achieve that."

I stared at her, taken aback. And mourning. Because what she wanted was impossible. Her childhood promise, to be both a good person and an Arameri, to use her family's power to make the world better—it was naïveté of the highest order. I had seen others like her, a few, one every handful of generations within Itempas's chosen family. They were always the brightest lights, the most glorious souls of the whole grimy bunch. The ones I could not hate, because they were special.

But it never lasted, once they gained power. They streaked through life like falling stars across the heavens, brilliant but ephemeral. The power killed the glory, dulled the specialness into despair. It hurt so much to watch their hopes die.

I could say nothing. To let her see my sorrow would start the process early. So I sighed and turned onto my side, pretending boredom, when in fact I was trying hard not to cry.

Her frustration flared like a struck match. She got up on her hands and knees and crawled over to me, bracing her arms on either side of my body so she could glare into my face. "*Help* me, damn you! You're supposed to be my friend!"

I stifled a yawn. "What do you want me to do? Tell you to marry a man you don't love? Tell you *not* to marry him? This isn't a bedtime tale, Shahar. People marry people they don't love all the time, and it isn't always terrible. He's already your friend; you could do worse. And if it's something your mother wants, you don't have a choice, anyway."

Her hand, braced on the covers in front of me, trembled. My senses throbbed with the waver of her conflicting yearnings. The child in her wanted to do as she pleased, cling to impossible hopes. The woman in her wanted to make sound decisions, succeed even if it meant sacrifice. The woman would win; that was inevitable. But the child would not go quietly.

With that same trembling hand, she touched my shoulder, pushing until I twisted my torso to face her. Then she leaned down and kissed me.

I permitted it, more out of curiosity than anything else. It was clumsy this time and did not last long. She was off the center of my mouth, covering mostly the bottom lip. I did not share myself with her, and she sat up, frowning.

"Does that make you feel better?" I asked. I honestly wanted to know. Shahar's expression crumpled. She turned away and lay down behind me, her back to mine. I felt her fighting tears.

Troubled, and worried that I had somehow harmed her, I turned to her and sat up. "What is it that you want?"

"My mother to love me. My brother back. The world not to hate us. Everything."

I considered this. "Shall I fetch him for you? Deka?"

She tensed, turning over. "Could you do that?"

"I don't know." I could not change my shape anymore. Traveling across distances was not so very different, save that it involved changing the shape of reality to make the world smaller. If I could not do one, I might not be able to do the other.

As I watched, however, the eagerness faded from her expression. "No. Deka may not love me anymore."

I blinked in surprise. "Of course he does."

"Don't patronize me, Sieh."

"I'm not," I snapped. "I can feel the bond between us, Shahar, as clear as this." I took a curl of her hair in my fingers and pulled on it, gentle but steady. She made a sound of surprise and I let the curl go; it bounced back prettily. "You both pull at me and at each other. Neither of you likes me very much now, but otherwise nothing has changed between the two of you since those days in the underpalace, years ago. You still love him, and he still loves you just as much. I'm a god, all right? I know."

I was not strictly telling the truth. It was true that Shahar's feelings toward me had waned, though they grew stronger with every hour I spent in her presence. Deka's, however, had grown stronger, too, even with no contact between us for half his lifetime. I didn't quite know how to interpret that, so I didn't mention it.

Her eyes went wide at my words—and then welled with tears. She made a quick, abortive sound: *buh*. As soon as she uttered it, she clapped a hand to her mouth, but her hand was trembling.

I sighed and pulled her against me, her face against my chest. It was only when I did this—only when she felt safe from eyes that might look upon her humanity and judge it a weakness—that she let herself break into deep, racking sobs so loud that they echoed from the walls of the apartment. Her tears were hot, though they cooled rapidly on my skin and as they pattered onto the sheets. Her shoulders heaved against my arms, and as the sobs grew worse, her arms went hard around me, squeezing me as if her life depended on my solidity and stillness. So I gave her both, stroking her hair and murmuring soothing things in the language of creation, letting her know that I loved her, too. For I did, fool that I was.

When her tears finally stopped, I kept stroking her, liking the way her curls went flat and sprang up again as my hand passed, and thinking of nothing. I barely noticed when her arms loosened, her hands coming to stroke my sides and back and hip. I kept thinking of nothing when she eased my shirt up and laid the lightest of kisses on my belly. It tickled; I smiled. Then she sat up to look at me, her eyes red-rimmed but dry, a peculiar intent in her eyes.

When she kissed me this time, it was wholly different. She nudged my lips apart and touched my tongue with her own, sweet and wet and sour. When I did not react, she slid her hands under my shirt, exploring the flat strangeness of a body that was not her own. I liked this until one of her hands went farther down, her fingers tickling hair and cloth at the edge of my pants, and then I caught her wrist. "No," I said.

She closed her eyes and I felt her aching emptiness. It was not lust. Missing her brother had made her feel alone. "I love you," she said. Not even an admission, this; it was simply a statement of fact, like *the moon is pretty* or *you're going to die*. "I've always loved you, since we were children. I tried not to."

I nodded, stroking her hand. "I know."

"I want to choose. If I have to sell myself for power, I want to give myself first. For love. For a friend."

I sighed, closing my eyes. "Shahar, I told you, it's not good—"

She scowled and lunged forward and kissed me again. I was stunned silent, the objection dying in my throat. Because this time it was like kissing a god. The quintessence of her came through the opening of my lips and drove itself into my soul before I could stop it. I gasped and inhaled a white shivering sun that pulsed strong and weak but never went out and never blew up. A rocky determination, jumbled but sharp-edged, with the potential to become as solid as bedrock. When I opened my eyes, I was lying back and she was above me, still kissing me, her hands coaxing sighs from me despite my reluctance. I did not stop her because I am supposed to be a child but really I am not and my body was too old to provide me with a child's defenses against reality. Children do not think about how magnificent it would be to become one with another person. They do not yearn to lose themselves in force and sensation and panting. Children think about consequences, if only to try and avoid them. It takes an adult to abandon such thoughts entirely.

So when her hand slipped into my pants this time, I did not stop her. And I did not protest while she explored me, first with her fingers and then, oh gods, oh yes, her mouth, her mortal husband could have the rest but I would marry her mouth and fingertips. I murmured without thinking and the walls went dark because there was mischief in what we were doing and that gave me strength. Despite this, I lay there helpless in the dark as she learned to make me whimper. She tormented me with this, tasting every part of my body. She even licked En, where it lay on my chest. Greedy thing, it rolled so that she might try its other side, too, but she didn't notice.

I touched her, too. She liked that lots.

Then she straddled me. There came a moment of lucidity in which I caught her hips and looked up at her and said, "Are you sure—" but she pushed herself down and I cried out because it was so wonderful that it hurt, flesh is not at all a terrible thing, I had forgotten that it could feel good and not just grotesque, it was so nice not to be used. She felt the same as a goddess inside. I whispered this to her and she smiled, rising and falling above me, her mouth open and teeth reflecting the moon, her hair a pale moving shadow. Then we shifted and I was on her, not out of any paltry mortal need on my part to dominate but simply because I liked the sweet mewling sounds she made as I angled my way into her, and also because I was still a god and even a weak god is dangerous to mortals. Matter is such tenuous stuff. So I controlled myself by focusing on her flesh, on her hands stroking my back (inadvertently I purred), on my own clenching tightening quickening excitement, on carrying her only into the good parts of existence and none of the bad ones.

And when she could bear no more, when I knew it was safe to bring her back to herself, when I was sure I could stay corporeal...only then did I let her go, and myself as well.

She fainted. That is normal when one of us mates with a mortal. Only the very extraordinary can touch the divine without being overwhelmed by it. I fetched a damp towel from the bathroom and mopped up the sweat and saliva and so forth, then tucked her against me under the covers so that I could breathe the scent of her hair.

I felt no regret, but I was sad. She was farther from me now, and I was the one who had sent her away.

8

Tell me a story
Fast as you can
Make the world and break it
And catch it in your hand

I SLEPT AGAIN. This time, though, since Shahar had renewed my godly strength—experimentation and abandon are close enough to childish impulses to suit me—I was able to sleep as gods do, and keep the dreams at bay.

When I woke, Shahar was not beside me, and it was noon. I sat up to find her near the window, wrapped in one of the sheets, her slim form still and shadowed against the bright blue sky.

I hopped up, assessed myself to see whether I needed to piss or shit—not yet, though clearly I needed to brush my teeth—and then went over to her. (I was cold again. Damnation.) When she did not move at my approach, lost in thought, I grinned and leaned close and licked a bare spot on the back of her neck, where her hair had not come completely undone during the previous night.

She jumped and whirled and frowned at me, at which

point I belatedly realized that perhaps she was not in a playful mood.

"Hello," I said, feeling suddenly awkward.

Shahar sighed and relaxed. "Hello." Then she lowered her eyes and turned back to the window.

I felt very stupid. "Oh, demons. Did I hurt you? That was the first time...I tried to be careful, but—"

She shook her head. "There was no pain. I...could tell you were being careful."

If she wasn't hurt, then why did she radiate such an ugly, clotted mix of emotions? I struggled to remember my handful of experiences with mortal women from before the War. Was this sort of behavior normal? I thought it might be. What, then, should a lover say at a time like this? Gods, it had been easier when I was a slave; my rapists had never expected me to give a damn about them afterward.

I sighed and shifted from foot to foot and folded my arms so I would not be so cold. "So...I take it you don't like what we did."

She sighed, and if anything, her mood turned darker. "I loved what we did, Sieh."

I was beginning to feel very tired, and it had nothing to do with my mortality affliction. Something had gone wrong; that was obvious. Would she have liked it better if I had become female for her? I wasn't sure I could do that anymore, but it was such a small change. I would try, for her sake, if that would help. "What, then? Why do you look like you just lost your best friend?"

"I may have," she whispered.

I stared at her as she turned back to me. The sheet had slipped off one of her shoulders, and most of her hair was a fright. She looked out of control and out of her element and lost. I remembered her wildness the night before. She had discarded all thought of propriety or position or dignity, and flung herself into the moment with perfect zeal. It had been glorious, but clearly such abandon had cost her something.

Then I noticed, below the hand that held the sheet about herself, her free hand. She held it over her belly, fingering the skin there as if measuring its strength. I had seen ten thousand mortal women make the same gesture, and still I almost missed its meaning. Such things are not normally within my demesne.

Pleased to have finally figured out the problem, I smiled and stepped closer, taking her hand off her belly and coaxing her to open the sheet so that I could step into it. She did so, clumsily adjusting the sheet so that she could hold it around both of us, and I sighed in grateful pleasure at the warmth of her nearness. Then I addressed the unease in her eyes that I thought I understood. Because I was who I was, and I am not always wise, I made it a tease. "Are you planning to kill me?"

She frowned in confusion. I realized for the first time that she was as tall as I was, growing long and lean like a good Amn girl. I slid an arm around her waist and pulled her close, noting that she did not fully relax.

"A child," I said. I put a hand on her belly as she had done, rubbing circles to tease her. "It would kill me, you know." Then I remembered my current condition and my amusement faded a little. "Kill me faster, anyway."

She stiffened, staring at me. "What?"

"I told you already." Her skin felt good beneath my hands. I bent and kissed her smooth shoulder right on the divot of bone and thought of biting her there as I rode her like a cat. Would she yowl for me? "Childhood cannot survive some things. Sex is fine, between friends." I smiled on her skin. "Done without consequences. But consequences—like making a child—change everything."

"Oh, gods. It's your antithesis."

I hated that word. Scriveners had come up with it. The word was like them, cold and passionless and precise and overly logical, capturing nothing of what truly made us what we were. "It corrupts my nature, yes. Many things can harm me—I'm just a godling, alas, not a god—but that one is the most sure." I licked at her neck again, really trying this time, though not holding any great hope of success. Nahadoth had never managed to teach me how to seduce with any real degree of mastery.

"Sieh!" She pushed at me, and when I lifted my head, I saw the horror in her eyes. "I didn't use any... preventative... when we were together last night. I..." She looked away, trembling. I regretted my teasing when I realized she was genuinely upset, but it made me happy that she cared so much.

I laughed gently, relenting. "It's all right. My mother Enefa realized the danger long ago. She changed me. Do you understand? No children."

She did not look reassured—did not *feel* reassured, her anguish tainting the very air around us. I have siblings who cannot endure mortal emotions. They are sad creatures who haunt the gods' realm, devouring tales of mortal life and pretending they are not jealous of the rest of us. Shahar would have killed half of them by now.

"Enefa is dead," she said.

That was more than enough to sober me. "Yes. But not all her works died with her, Shahar, or neither you nor I would be standing here."

She looked up at me, tense and afraid. "You're different now, Sieh. You're not really a god anymore, and mortals—" Her face softened so beautifully. It made me smile, despite the conversation. "*Mortals grow up.* Sieh, I want you to be sure there's no child. Can you check somehow? Because…because…" She lowered her eyes, and suddenly it was shame that she felt, sour and bitter on the back of my tongue. Shame, and fear.

"What?"

She drew a deep breath. "I didn't try to prevent a baby. In fact"—her jaw flexed— "I've been to the scriveners. They used a script." She blushed, but forged ahead. "To make it easier, more likely, for three or four days. And once I, with you, I, I'm supposed to go to them. They have other scripts that they say…Even with a god, fertility magic works the same way."

Her stammering embarrassment confused me; I couldn't figure out what she was trying to say at first. And then, like a comet's icy plume, understanding slashed through me.

"You *wanted* a child?"

She laughed once, bitter. When she turned back to the window, her eyes were hard and older than they should be, and so perfectly Arameri. Then I knew.

"Your mother."

Shahar nodded, still not meeting my eyes. " 'If we cannot *own* gods, then perhaps we can *become* gods,' she said. The demons of old had great magic despite their mortality. Or, at the very least, we can gain the greatest demon magic: the power to *kill* gods."

I stared at her, feeling sick, because I should have known. The Arameri had been trying to get their hands on a demon for decades. I should have seen it in Remath's quest for a godly lover; I should have realized why she'd been so pleased to have me in Sky. Why she'd tried to give me her daughter.

I shrugged off the sheet and walked away from Shahar, manifesting clothing about myself. Black this time, like my fur when I was a cat. Like my father's wrath.

"Sieh?" Shahar blurted the words, cursed, dropped the sheet and grabbed for a robe. "Sieh, what are you—"

I stopped and turned back to her, and she froze at the look in my eyes. Or perhaps at my eyes themselves, because I could not become this angry, even in my weakened half-mortal state, without a little of the cat showing.

I would save the claws, however, for Remath.

"Why did you tell me?" I asked, and she went pale. "Did you wait until now for a reason?" Some of my magic had come back to me. I touched the world, found Remath within it. Her audience chamber, surrounded by courtiers and petitioners. "Were you hoping I would kill her in front of witnesses so the other highbloods would think you weren't involved? Was that what you told yourself so it wouldn't feel like matricide?"

Her lips turned white as she pressed them together. "How dare you—"

"Because this wasn't necessary." I rode over her words with my own, with my grief, and that drove the anger from her face in an instant. "I told you I would kill her for you, if you asked. All I ever wanted was to be able to trust you. If you had given me that, I would have done anything for you."

She flinched as if I'd struck her. Her eyes welled with tears, but this was not like last night. She stood in the slanting afternoon light of Itempas's sun, proud despite her nakedness, and the tears did not fall, because

Arameri do not cry. Not even when they have broken a god's heart.

"Deka," she said at last.

I shook my head, mute, too consumed with my own nature to follow her insane mortal reasoning.

She drew another breath. "I agreed to do this because of Deka. We made a bargain, Mother and I: one night with you, in exchange for him. The scriveners would take care of the rest. But when you said that a child would kill you…" She faltered.

I wanted to believe she had betrayed her mother for my sake. But if that was true, then it meant she had also agreed to sacrifice my love in exchange for her brother.

I remembered the look in her eyes when she'd said she loved me. I remembered the feel of her body, the sound of her sighs. I had tasted her soul and found it sweeter than I could ever have imagined. Nothing in what she'd done with me had been false. But would she have followed through on her desire now, so soon, if not for her mother's bargain? Would she have done it at all if she hadn't wanted someone else more than she wanted me?

I turned my back on her.

"Remath has perverted something that should have been pure," I said. For the first time since I'd joined hands with two bright-eyed mortal children, something of my true self had slipped through the space between worlds to fill me. My voice grew deeper, becoming the man's tenor that I had not quite achieved physically yet. I could have taken any shape I wanted in that moment; it was not beyond me anymore. But the part of me that hurt was the man, not the child or the cat, and it was the man whose pain needed assuaging. The man was the weakest part of me, but it would do for this purpose.

"Sieh," she whispered, and then fell silent. Just as well. I was in no mood to listen.

"I cannot protect children from all the evils of the world," I said. "Suffering is part of childhood, too. But this..." It came out more sibilant than it should have. I fought the change back with a soft snarl. "This, Shahar, is *my* sin. I should have protected you, from your own nature if nothing else. I have betrayed myself, and someone will die for that."

With that, I left. Her apartment door shivered into dust before me. When I stepped into the corridor, the daystone groaned and cracked beneath my feet, sending branching faults up the walls. The handful of guards and servants who stood unobtrusively about the corridor tensed in alarm as I strode toward them. Four of them stopped, sensing with whatever rudimentary awareness mortals have that I was not to be trifled with. The fourth, a guard, stepped into my path. I have no idea whether he meant to stop me or whether he was just moving to the other side of the corridor, where there was more room. I do not think at such times; I do what feels good. So I slashed my will across him like claws and he fell in six or seven bloody pieces to the floor. Someone screamed; someone else slipped in the blood; they did not get in my way again. I walked on.

The floors opened and bent around me, forming steps, slopes, a new path. I stepped into the midday brilliance of the corridor that led to Remath's audience chamber. I walked toward the ornate double doors at the end of the corridor, in front of which stood two Darren women. The warriors of Darr are famous for their skill and wits, which they use to make up for their lack of physical strength. Since the time of our escape, they had been tasked with protecting the Arameri family head, even from other Arameri. But as I came down the hall, spiderwebbing the windows with every step, they looked at each other. There was pride to consider, but stupid Darre do not last long in their culture, and they knew there was no way they could fight me. They could, however, attempt to appease me, which they did by kneeling before the door, heads bowed, praying for my mercy. I showed it by sweeping them off to either side, probably bruising them a little against the walls but not killing them. Then I tore apart the doors and went in.

The room was full of courtiers, more guards, servants, clerks, scriveners. And Remath. She, on her cold stone throne, folded her hands and waited as if she'd been expecting me. The rest stared at me, stunned and silent.

I pulled En loose from its cord. "Kill for me, beloved," I murmured, and dropped it to the floor. It bounced, then shot around the room, ricocheting off walls and windows and the stone of Remath's chair. It did not bounce off mortal flesh. When En had punched holes in enough of them and the screaming stopped, it came back to me, flaring hot to cook off the blood and then dropping cool and satisfied into my hand. I slipped it into my pocket.

Remath had not been touched; En knew my heart well. She had not moved throughout the slaughter and showed no hint of concern that I had just killed thirty or so of her relatives.

"I take it you're unhappy about something," she said.

I smiled and saw her eyes flicker for an instant as she registered my sharp teeth. "Yes," I said, raising my hand. In it, conjured out of possibility, lay ten thick, silver knitting needles. Each was longer than my hand. "But I will feel better in a moment. Cross your heart and hope to die, Remath. Here are my needles for your eyes."

To her credit, she kept her voice even. "I kept my promise. I've done you no harm."

I shook my head. "Shahar was my friend, and you have taken her from me."

"A minor harm," she said, and then she surprised me with a small smile. "But you are a trickster, and I know better than to try and argue with you."

"Yes," I agreed. And then I stepped forward, plucking the first of the needles from my palm and rolling it between my fingers in anticipation, because I am a bully, too, when all is said and done.

I heard Shahar's cry before she ran in, though I ignored it. She gasped as she reached the chamber and saw blood and bodies everywhere, but then she ran forward—slipping once in someone's viscera—and grabbed my arm. This did nothing to slow my advance, since for the moment I was much stronger than any mortal, and after being dragged forward a step or two, she abandoned that effort. But then she ran around me and put herself in my path, just as I put my foot on the first step of the dais that held Remath's throne. "Sieh, don't do this."

I sighed and pushed her aside as gently as I could. This made her stumble off the steps, and she fell into the blood of some cousin or another of hers. I could smell the Arameri in him. Or not *in* him, not anymore; I laughed at my own joke.

As I stopped in front of Remath—who remained where she was, calm as death loomed—Shahar appeared again, this time flinging herself directly in front of her mother's throne. Her gold satin robe was drenched with blood down one side of her body, and somehow she'd gotten it on the side of her face as well. Half her hair hung limp and dripping with it. I laughed again and tried to think up a rhyme that would properly make fun of her. But what rhymed with *horror*? I would ponder it later.

I stopped, however, because Shahar was in the way. "Move," I said.

"No."

"You wanted her dead, anyway."

"Not like *this*, damn you!"

"Poor Shahar." I made a singsong of it. *"Poor little princess, how is she to see? With her fingers and her toes, once her eyes are with me."* I held the needle forward so that she could see it. "You have betrayed me, sweet Shahar. It is nothing to me to kill you, too."

Her jaw tightened. "I thought you loved me."

"I thought you loved *me*."

"You swore not to harm me!"

She was right. Her failure to keep her word did not mean I should stoop to the same level. "Very well. I won't kill you—just her."

"She's my mother," she snapped. "How much do you think it will harm me if you kill her right before my eyes?"

As much as she'd harmed me by betraying my trust. Maybe a bit more. "I'm not interested in bargains right now, Shahar. Move, or I'll move you. I won't be gentle this time."

"Please," she said, which ordinarily would only have goaded me further—bully—but this time it did not. This time, to my own great surprise, the churning vortex of my rage slowed, then went still. In the sudden storm-calm, I gazed at her and realized another truth that she had hidden from me all this time. And perhaps not just from me. I glanced at Remath, who was staring at Shahar, surprised into an expression of astonishment at last. Yes.

"You love her," I said.

And because Shahar was Arameri, she flinched as if struck and looked away in shame. But she did not move out of my way.

I let out a long, heavy sigh, and with it my power began to fade. I couldn't have kept it up much longer anyhow; I was too old for tantrums.

Shaking my head, I let the needles drop to the floor. They scattered over the steps with tinny metal sounds, loud in the chamber's silence. Listening to the nearby world, I could hear shouts and running feet—Captain Wrath and his men racing to save Remath and die in the trying because they were not sensible like Darre. Even the scriveners were marshaling, bringing their most powerful scripts, though they were disorganized because Shevir was here, his corpse cooling among the others I'd killed. I turned and looked at him, his face frozen in a look of surprise beneath the gaping hole in his forehead, and felt regret. He hadn't been a bad man as First Scriveners went. And I had been a very bad boy.

On the strength of that, I took myself away from Sky, not really caring where I went instead, just wanting comfort and silence and a place to be miserable in peace.

I would not see Shahar again for two years.

BOOK TWO

Two Legs at Noon

I AM A FLY ON THE WALL, *or a spider in a bush. Same difference, except that the spider is a predator and suits my nature better.*

I sit in a web that would give me away in an instant if he saw it, because I have woven a smiling face into the tiny dewdrop-beaded strands. It has never been his nature to notice the minutia of his surroundings, however, and the web is half hidden by leaves anyhow. With my many eyes, I observe as Itempas, the Bright Sky, Daybringer, sits on a whitebaked clay rooftop waiting for the sun to rise. It surprises me that he sits to observe this, but then many things have surprised me today. Like the fact that the rooftop is part of a mortal dwelling, and inside it are the mortal woman he loves and the mortal—but halfgod—child she has borne him.

I knew something was wrong. There had been a day of change in the gods' realm not long before. The hurricane that was Nahadoth met the earthquake that was Enefa, and they found stillness in each other. A beautiful, holy thing—I know, I watched. But in the distance, the immovable white-capped mountain that was Item-

pas shimmered and went away. He has been gone ever since.

Ten years, in mortal reckoning. An eyeblink for us, but still unusual for him. He does not sulk. More commonly he confronts a source of disruption, attacks it, destroys it if he can, or settles into some equilibrium with it if he cannot—but he has done neither this time. Instead he has fled to this realm with its fragile creatures and tried to hide himself among them, as if a sun can fit in among match flames. Except he isn't hiding, not exactly. He's just... living. Being ordinary. And not coming home.

The rooftop door opens, and the child comes out. Strange-looking creature, disproportionate with his big head and long legs. (Do I look like that in my mortal form? I resolve to make my head smaller.) He is brown-skinned and blond, freckled. From here, I can see his eyes, as green as the leaves that hide me. He is eight or nine years old now—a good age, my favorite age, old enough to know the world yet young enough to still delight in it. I have heard his name, Shinda, whispered by the other children of this dusty little village; they are frightened of him. They can tell, as I can with just a glance, that he might be mortal, but he will never be one of them.

He comes to stand behind Itempas and wraps his arms around Itempas's shoulders, resting his cheek against his father's densely curled hair. Itempas does not turn to him, but I see him reach up to touch the boy's arms. They watch the sun rise together, never saying a word.

When the day is well begun, there is another movement at the rooftop door; a woman comes to stand there. She is Remath's age, similarly blonde, similarly beautiful. In two thousand years, I will join hands with her descendant and namesake and become mortal. They look much alike, this Shahar, that Shahar, except for the eyes. This Shahar watches Itempas with an unblinking steadiness that I would find frightening if I had not seen it in the eyes of my own worshippers. When her son straightens and comes over to greet her, she does not look at him, though she absently touches his shoulder and says something. He goes inside and she remains there, watching her lover with a high priestess's fanaticism. But he does not turn to her.

I leave, and report back to Nahadoth and Enefa as I have been bidden. Parents often send children as spies and peacemakers when there is trouble between them. I tell them that Itempas is not angry, if anything he seems sad and a bit lonely, and, yes, they should go and bring him home because he has been away too long. And if I do not tell them of his mortal woman, his mortal son, what of it? Why should it matter that the woman loves him, needs him, will probably go mad without him? Why should we care that his return means the destruction of that family and the peace he seems to have found with them? We are gods and they are nothing. I am a far better son than some half-breed demon boy. I will show him, as soon as he comes home.

9

I FELL.

It happens like that sometimes, when one travels through life without a plan. In this case I was traveling through space, motion, conceptualization—same difference, except that mortals cannot survive it. Half mortal that I was, I shouldn't have. But I did, possibly because I did not care.

So it was that I drifted through Sky's white layers, passing through some of the Tree's wooden flesh in the process, down, down, down. Past the lowest layer of clouds, damp and cold. Because I was incorporeal, I saw the city with both mortal and godly eyes: humped silhouettes of buildings and streets aglow with flickers of mortal light, interspersed now and again by the brighter, colored plumes of my brothers and sisters. They could not see me because I had not lost all sense of self-preservation and because even when I am not sulking, my soul's colors are shadowy. That is my father's legacy and a bit of my mother's as well. I am good at sneaking about because of it. Or hiding, when I do not wish to be found.

Down. Past a ring of mansions attached to the World

Tree's trunk, devastatingly expensive tree houses, these, without even ladders or GIRLZ KEEP OWT signs to make them interesting. Below this was another layer of city, this one new: houses and workshops and businesses built atop the Tree's very roots, perched precariously on wildly sloping streets and braced platforms. Ah, of course; the esteemed personages of the mansions above could not be left without servants and chefs and nannies and tailors, could they? I witnessed bizarre contraptions, gouting steam and smoke and metallic groans, connecting this halfway city to the elegant platforms above. People rode up and down in them, trusting these dangerous-looking things to convey them safely. For a moment, admiration for mortal ingenuity nearly distracted me from my misery. But I kept going, because this place did not suit me. I had heard Shahar refer to it, and understood its name now: the Gray. Halfway between the bright of Sky and the darkness below.

Down. And now I blended with the shadows, because there were so many here between the Tree's roots and beneath its vast green canopy. Yes, this suited me better: Shadow, the city that had once been called Sky, before the Tree grew and made a joke of that name. It was here at last that I felt some sense of belonging—though only a little. I did not belong anywhere in the mortal realm, really.

I should have remembered that, I thought in bitterness as I came to rest and turned to flesh again. *I should never have tried to live in Sky.*

Well. Adolescence is all about making mistakes.

I landed in a stinking, debris-strewn alley, in what I would later learn was South Root, considered to be the most violent and depraved part of the city. Because it was so violent and depraved, no one bothered me for the better part of three days while I sat amid the trash. This was good, because I wouldn't have had the strength to defend myself. My paroxysm of rage in Sky and subsequent magical transit had left me too weak to do much but lie there. As I'd been hungry before leaving Sky, I ate: there were some moldy fruit rinds in the bin nearest me, and a rat came near to offer me its flesh. It was an old creature, blind and dying, and its meat was rank, but I have never been so churlish as to disrespect a sacred act.

It rained, and I drank, tilting my head back for hours to get a few mouthfuls. And then, adding the ultimate insult to injury, my bowels moved for the first time in a century. I had enough strength to get my pants down, but not enough to move away from the resulting mess, so I sat there beside it and wept awhile, and just generally hated everything.

Then on the third day, because three is a number of power, things finally changed.

"Get up," said the girl who'd entered the alley. She kicked me to get my attention. "You're in the way."

I blinked up at her to see a small figure, clad in bulky, ugly clothing and a truly stupid hat, glaring down at me. The hat was a thing of beauty. It looked like a drunken cone on top of her head and had long flaps to cover her ears. The flaps could be buttoned under her chin, though she hadn't done so, perhaps because it was late spring and as hot as the Dayfather's temper, even in this city of noon-time shadows.

With a sigh, I pulled myself laboriously to my feet, then stepped aside. The girl nodded too curtly for thanks, then brushed past me and began rummaging through the pile of garbage I'd sat beside. I started to warn her about my small addition to the refuse, but she avoided it without

looking. Deftly plucking two halves of a broken plate
out of the trash, she made a sound of pleasure and stuck
them into the satchel hanging off her shoulder, then
moved on. As she shuffled away, I saw one of her feet
scrape the ground even though she'd lifted it; it was larger
than the other and misshapen, and she'd made it larger
still by bundling rags about the ankle.

I followed her down the alley as she poked through the
piles, picking up the oddest of items: a handleless clay
pot, a rusted metal canister, a chunk of broken window-
pane. This last seemed to please her the most, by the look
of delight on her face.

I leaned in to peer over her shoulder. "What will you
do with it?"

She whipped about and I froze, as she had placed the
tip of a long and wickedly sharp glass dagger at my throat.

"This," she said. "Back off."

I did so quickly, raising my hands to make it clear that I
meant no harm, and she put the knife away, resuming her
work.

"Glass," she said. "Grind it down for knives, use the
leftovers to grind other things. Get it?"

I was fascinated by her manner of speaking. Shadow
dwellers' Senmite was rougher than that of the people in
Sky, and quicker spoken. They had less patience for long,
flowery verbal constructions, and their new, briefer constructions contained additional layers of attitude. I began
adjusting my own speech to suit.

"Got it," I said. "Then?"

She shrugged. "I sell them at the Sun Market. Or give
'em away, if people can't pay." She glanced at me, looking
me up and down, and then snorted. "You could pay."

I looked down at myself. The black clothing I had manifested back in Sky was filthy and stank, but it was made of fine-quality cloth, and the shirt and pants and shoes all matched, unlike her clothes. I supposed I did look wealthy. "But I don't have any money."

"So get a job," she replied, and resumed work.

I sighed and moved to sit down on a closed muckbin, which squelched when my weight bore down on it. "Guess I'll have to. Know anyone who might need"—I considered what skills I had that might be valuable to mortals. "Hmm. A thief, a juggler, or a killer?"

The girl stopped again, looking hard at me, and then folded her arms. "You a godling?"

I blinked in surprise. "Yes, actually. How did you know?"

"Only they ask those kinds of crazy questions."

"Oh. Have you met many godlings?"

She shrugged. "A few. You going to eat me?"

I frowned, blinking. "Of course not."

"Fight me? Steal something? Turn me into something else? Torture me to death?"

"Dear gods, why would I—" But then it occurred to me that some of my siblings were capable of all that and worse. We were not the gentlest of families. "None of those things are my nature, don't worry."

"All right." She turned back to examine something she'd found, which I thought might be an old roof shingle. With an annoyed sigh, she tossed it aside. "You're not going to get many worshippers, though, just sitting there like that. You should do something more interesting."

I sighed and drew my legs up, wrapping arms around them. "I don't have a lot of interesting left in me."

"Hmm." Straightening, the girl pulled off her stupid hat and mopped her brow. Without it, I saw that she was Amn, her white-blonde curls cropped short and held back with cheap-looking barrettes. She looked ten or eleven, though I saw more years than that in her eyes. Fourteen, maybe. She hadn't eaten enough in those years, and it showed, but I could still feel the childhood in her.

"Hymn," she said. A name. My skepticism must have shown, because she rolled her eyes. "Short for Hymnesamina."

"I like the longer name, actually."

"I don't." She looked me up and down perfunctorily. "You're not bad-looking, you know. Skinny, but you can fix that."

I blinked again, wondering if this was some sort of flirtation. "Yes, I know."

"Then you've got another skill besides thieving, juggling, and killing."

I sighed, feeling very tired. "No whoring."

"You sure? You'd make a lot more money than with the rest, except killing, and you don't look very tough."

"Looks mean nothing for a god."

"But they do mean something to mortals. You want to make money as a killer, you need to look like one." She folded her arms. "I know a place where they'd let you pick your clients, you being what you are. If you can make yourself look Amn, you'd make even more." She cocked her head, considering this. "Or maybe the foreign look is better. I don't know. Not my thing."

"I just need enough to buy food." But I would need more mortal things as I grew older, wouldn't I? There would come a time—soon, probably—when I would no longer be able to conjure clothing or necessities, and someday shelter would be more than just a pleasant accessory. Winters in central Senm could kill mortals. I sighed again, resting my cheek on my knees.

Hymn sighed, too. "Whatever. Well…see you." She turned and headed toward the mouth of the alley—then froze, her gaze going sharp and alarmed. Her tension thickened the already-ripe air further when she stepped back, out of the alley's entrance and into the shadows.

This was just enough to pull me out of my mood. I uncurled and watched her. "Muggers, bullies, or parents?"

"Muckrakers," she said, so softly that no mortal would have heard her, but she knew I could.

By the way she said it, I realized she expected me to know what muckrakers were. I could guess, though. There was money to be made from any city's refuse, from charging to get rid of it to selling its useful bits. Curious, I hopped up and came over to where she was standing, out of the slanting light from the torchlamps. When I peeked around her at the street beyond, I saw a group of men near an old mulecart, on the other side of the potholed street. Two of them were laughing and hefting muckbins, dumping them into the cart; two more stood idle, talking, while a fifth was in the cart with a pitchfork and a mask over his face, stirring something that steamed.

I glanced down at the junk in Hymn's bag. "Would they really begrudge you a few small things?"

She glared at me. "The muckrakers don't care if it's just a little bit; it's *theirs*. They pay the Order for the rights, and they don't like it when anybody messes with what's theirs. They warned me once already." Despite her show of anger, I could smell the fear underneath. She looked past me, around the alley, but there was no way out. It stood at the intersection of three buildings, and the nearest window was twenty feet up. She could try to sneak out of the alley, and there was a chance the men wouldn't see her. They were preoccupied with their work and chatter. But if they spotted her, she would not get far with her misshapen foot.

The men were a rough-smelling crew, even without the stench of refuse, and had the unmistakable look of people who have no qualms against harming a child. I bared my teeth at them, for I had always hated such mortals.

At this stirring of my old self, I began to grin.

"Hey!" I shouted. Beside me, Hymn jumped and gasped, whirling to try and escape. I caught her arm and held her in place so they would see her. Sure enough, when the muckrakers looked around, they spotted me— but it was the sight of Hymn that made them scowl.

"What the hells are you doing?" she cried, trying to jerk free.

"It's all right," I murmured. "I won't let them hurt you." The men near the wagon were turning now, heading toward us with purposeful strides and dire intent. Only three of them, though; the two who'd been working had stopped to watch. I grinned at them and raised my voice again. "Hey, you like shit, right? Have some!" And I turned and yanked my pants down to flash my backside. Hymn moaned.

The muckrakers shouted, and even the two who'd been watching ran around the wagons, the whole lot charging toward our little alley. Laughing, I pulled my pants up and grabbed Hymn's arm again. "Come on!" I said, and hauled her toward the back of the alley.

"Where—" She couldn't get out more than that, stumbling over a pile of fungus-covered firewood that someone had dumped between the muckbins. I helped her stay upright, then hauled her back until we were pressed against the alley's rear wall. A moment later, the alley, already dim, went darker still as the men's silhouettes blocked the torchlamps.

"What the hells is this?" one of the men asked Hymn. "We warn you not to steal our stuff, and you not only come back but also bring a friend? Huh?" He stepped over the funguswood, clenching his fists; the others closed in behind him.

"I didn't mean..." Hymn's voice trembled as she started to speak to the men.

"This girl is under my protection," I said, stepping in front of her. I was grinning like a madman; I felt power around me like a wafting shroud. Mischief is a heady thing, sweeter than any wine. "Never touch her again."

The lead man stopped, staring at me in disbelief. "And who in demons are you, brat?"

I closed my eyes and inhaled in pleasure. How long had it been since anyone had called me a brat? I laughed and let go of Hymn and spread my arms, and at the touch of my will, the lids blasted off every bin and crate in the alley. The men cried out, but it was too late; they were mine to toy with.

"I am the son of chaos and death," I said. They all heard me, as intimately as if I'd spoken into their ears, despite the noise of their startled cries and the falling lids. A brisk wind had begun to blow through the alley, stirring the looser refuse and blowing dust into all our eyes. I squinted and grinned. "I know all the rules in the games of pain. But I will be merciful now, because it pleases me. Consider this a warning."

And I curled my fingers into claws. The bins exploded, the refuse contained in each rising into the air and swirling and churning in a circle, a hurricane of debris and foulness that surrounded the five men and herded them together. When I brought my hands together in a clap, all of it sucked inward—plastering them from head to toe with every disgusting substance mortalkind has ever produced. I made sure a bit of my own ordure was in there, too.

I could have been truly cruel. They'd meant to hurt Hymn, after all. I could have shattered the fungus log and speared them with spore-covered splinters. I could have broken their bodies into pieces and stuffed the whole mess back into the bins, muck and all. But I was having fun. I let them live.

They screamed—though some of them had the wit to keep their mouths closed for fear of what the scream would let in—and flailed at themselves with remarkable vigor given what their jobs entailed. But I supposed it was one thing to shovel and haul shit; quite another to bathe in it. I had made certain the stuff went into their clothes and various crevices of their bodies. A good trick is all about the details.

"Remember," I said, stalking forward. Those who could see me, because they had managed to get the muck out of their eyes, yelled and grabbed their still-blind companions and stumbled back. I let them go and grinned, and made a chunk of wood spin like a top on one of my fingertips. A waste of magic, yes, but I wanted to enjoy being strong for however long it lasted. "Never touch her again, or I will find you. Now go!" I stomped at them, mock-threatening, but they were horrified and wise enough to scream and turn and run out of the alley, some of them tripping and slipping in the slime. They fled down the street, leaving behind their wagon and mule. I heard them yelling in the distance.

I fell to the ground—we were still at the back of the alley, where the ground was relatively clean—and laughed and laughed, until my sides ached. Hymn, however, began picking her way over the tumbled debris, trying to find a way out of the alley that would not require her to walk through a layer of filth.

Surprised at being abandoned, I stopped laughing and sat up on one elbow to watch her. "Where are you going?"

"Away from you," she said. Only then did I realize she was furious.

Blinking, I got to my feet and went to her. Strong as I was feeling after that trick, it was nothing to grab her about the waist and leap over the front half of the alley, landing in the brighter-lit, fresher air of the street. There were a few people about, standing and murmuring in the wake of the muckrakers' spectacle, but there was a collective gasp as I landed on the cobblestones. Quickly— hurriedly, in some cases—all of the onlookers turned and left, some of them glancing back as if in fear that I would follow.

Puzzled by this, I set Hymn down, whereupon she immediately began hurrying away, too. "Hey!"

She stopped, and turned back to me with a look of such wariness that I flinched. "What?"

I put my hands on my hips. "I saved you. What, not even a thanks?"

"Thank you," she said tightly, "though I wouldn't have been in danger if you hadn't called out to them."

This was true. But... "They won't bother you again," I said. "Isn't that what you wanted?"

"What I *wanted*," she said, turning red in the face now, "was to do my business in peace. Should've left when I figured out you were a godling! And you're worse somehow. You seemed so sad, I thought for a moment that you were more"—she spluttered, too apoplectic to speak for a moment—"*human*. But you're just like the rest of them, screwing up mortal lives and thinking you're doing us a favor." She turned away, walking briskly enough that the limp made her gait into an ugly sort of half hop. I'd been wrong; the bad foot didn't slow her down at all.

I stared in the direction she had gone until it became clear she would not stop, and then finally I sighed and trotted after her.

I had nearly caught up when Hymn heard my footsteps and stopped, rounding on me. *"What?"*

I stopped, too, putting my hands in my pockets and trying not to hunch my shoulders. "I need to make it up to you." I sighed, wishing I could just leave. "Is there something you want? I can't fix your foot, but...I don't know. Whatever."

I could almost hear her teeth grinding together, though she did not speak for a moment. Perhaps she needed to master her rage before she started shouting at a god.

"I don't want my foot fixed," she said with remarkable calm. "I don't want anything from you. But if it's your nature that you're trying to serve, and you won't leave me alone until you've done it, then here's what I need: money."

I blinked. "Money? But—"

"You're a god. You should be able to make money."

I tried to think of a game or toy that might allow me to produce money. Gambling was an adult game; it did not suit my nature at all. Perhaps I could act out a children's tale or lullaby, that one about the golden ropes and the pearl lanterns..."Would you take jewelry instead?"

She made a sound of utter disgust and turned to leave. I groaned and trotted after her. "Listen, I said I could make things that are valuable, and you can sell them! What's wrong with that?"

"I *can't* sell them," she snapped, still walking. I hurried to keep up. "Trying to sell something valuable would get me killed. If I took it to a pawnbroker, everyone in South Root would know I had money before I left the shop. My house would get robbed, or my relatives would be kidnapped, or something. I don't know anyone in the merchant cartels who could fence it for me, and even if I did, they'd take half or more in 'fees.' And I don't have the status to impress the Order of Itempas, so they'd take the rest in tithes. I could go to one of the godlings around town, maybe, but then I'd have to deal with *more* of you." She threw me a scathing look. "My parents are old, and I'm the only child. What I need is money for food and rent and to get the roof fixed and maybe to buy my father a bottle of wine now and again so he can stop worrying so much about how we're going to survive. Can you give me any of that?"

I stumbled after this litany, a little stunned. "I...no."

Hymn stared at me for a long moment, then sighed and stopped, reaching up to rub her forehead as if it pained her. "Look, which one are you?"

"Sieh."

She looked surprised, which was a welcome change from contempt and exasperation. "I don't recognize your name."

"No. I used to live here"—I hesitated—"a long time ago. But I only came back to the mortal realm a few days ago."

"Gods, no wonder you're such a horror. You're new in town." This seemed to ease some of her anger, and she looked me up and down. "All right, what's your nature?"

"Tricks. Mischief." These were always easier to explain to mortals. They found "childhood" difficult to grasp as a specific concept. Hymn nodded, though, so I took a chance and added, "Innocence."

She looked thoughtful. "You must be one of the older ones. The younger ones are simpler."

"They're not simpler. Their natures are just more attuned to mortal life, since they were born after mortals were created—"

"I know that," she said, looking annoyed again. "Look, people in this city have lived with your kind for a long time now. We get how you work; you don't need to lecture." She sighed again and shook her head. "I know you need to serve your nature, all right? But I don't need tricks; I need money. If you want to conjure something, sell it yourself, and bring me that later, that would be fine. Just try and be discreet, will you? And leave me alone until then. *Please*."

With this, Hymn turned to walk away, slower this time as she had calmed somewhat. I watched her go, feeling altogether out of sorts and wondering how in the infinite hells I was going to get money for her. Because she was right; *playing fair* was as fundamental to my nature as being a child, and if I allowed the wrong I had done her to stand, it would erode a little more of whatever childhood she had remaining. Doing that prior to my transformation would've made me ill. Doing it now? I had no idea what would happen, but it would not be pleasant.

I would have to obtain money by mortal means, then. But if there were jobs to be had, would Hymn have been digging through muckbins and making knives from broken crockery? Worse, I had no knowledge of the city in its current incarnation, and no inkling of where to begin my search for employment.

So I began walking after Hymn again.

The streets were quiet and empty as I walked, taking on a dim, twilightish aspect as the morning progressed. Dawn had come and gone while I tormented the muckrakers, and all around me I could feel the city awakening, its pulse quickening with the start of day. Ghostly white buildings, long unpainted but soundly made and still beautiful in a run-down way, loomed out of the dark on either side of the street. I saw faces peering through the windows, half hidden by the curtains. Through gaps in the buildings I could see the mountainous black silhouette of a Tree root. Roots hemmed in this part of the city, while the Tree itself loomed above all to the north. There would be no sunlight here, no matter how bright the day grew.

Then I turned another corner and stopped, for Hymn stood there glaring at me.

I sighed. "I'm sorry. I really am! But I need your help."

We sat in the small common room of her family's home. An old inn, she explained, though they hardly ever had travelers through anymore and survived by taking in long-term boarders when they could. For the time being, there were none.

"It's the only way," I said, having reached this conclusion by my second cup of tea. Hymn's mother had served it to me, her hand shaking as she poured, though I'd tried my best to put her at ease. When Hymn murmured something to her, she'd withdrawn into another room, though I could hear her still lurking near the door, listening. Her heartbeat was very loud.

Hymn shrugged, toying with the plate of dry cheese and stale bread her mother had insisted upon serving. She ate only a little of it, and I ate none, for it was easy to see this family had almost nothing. Fortunately this behavior was considered polite for a godling, since most of us didn't need to eat.

"Your choice, of course," she said.

I did not like the choices laid before me. Hymn had confirmed my guess that there was little in the way of work, as the city's economy had lost ground in recent years to innovations coming out of the north. (In the old days, the Arameri would have unleashed a plague or two to kill off commoners and increase the demand for labor. Unemployment, frustrating as it was, represented progress.) There was still money to be made from serving the mortals who came to the city on pilgrimage, to pray for one of any dozen gods' blessing, but not many employers would be pleased to hire a godling. "Bad for business," Hymn explained. "Too easy to offend someone by your existence."

"Of course," I sighed.

Since the city's legitimate business was closed to me, my only hope was its illegitimate side. For that, at least, I had a possible way in: Nemmer. I was to meet her in three more days, according to our agreement. I no longer cared that some sibling of ours was targeting the Arameri. Let them all die, except perhaps Deka, whom I would geld and put on a leash to keep him sweet. But the conspiracy against our parents meant I should still see her. I could ask her help in finding work then.

If I could stomach the shame. Which I could not. So I had decided to try another way into the city's shadier side. Hymn's way: the Arms of Night. The brothel she had already tried to convince me to join.

"A friend of mine went to work there a couple of years ago," she said. "Not as a prostitute! She's not their type. But they need servants and such, and they pay a good wage." She shrugged. "If you don't want to do the one thing, you could always do the other. Especially if you can cook and clean."

I was not fond of that idea, either. Enough of my mortal years in Sky had been spent serving one way or another. "I don't suppose any of their customers would like a nice game of tag?" Hymn only looked at me. I sighed. "Right."

"We should go now, if you want to talk to them," she said. "They get busy at night." She spoke with remarkable compassion given how tired she already was of me. I supposed the misery in my expression had managed to penetrate even her cynical armor. Which might have been why she tried again to dissuade me. "I don't care, you know. If you make up for nearly getting me killed. I told you that."

I nodded heavily. "I know. This isn't really about you, though."

She sighed. "I know, I know. You must be what you are." I looked up in surprise, and she smiled. "I told you. Everyone here understands gods."

So we left the inn and headed up the street, which was bustling now that I'd been out of sight for a while. Carters rattled past with their rickety old wagons while vendors pushed along rolling stands to sell their fruit and fried meat. An old man sat on a blanket on one corner, calling out that he could repair shoes. A middle-aged man in stained laborer's clothes went over to him, and they crouched to dicker.

Hymn limped easily through this chaos, waving cheerfully to this or that person as we passed, altogether more comfortable amid her fellow mortals than she'd been in my company. I watched her as we walked, fascinated. I could taste a solid core of innocence underneath her cynical pragmatism, and just the faintest dollop of wonder, because not even the most jaded mortal could spend time in a god's presence without feeling *something*. And she was amused by me, despite her apparent annoyance. That made me grin—which she caught when she looked around and caught a glimpse of my face. "What?" she asked.

"You," I said, grinning.

"What about me?"

"You're one of mine. Or you could be, if you wanted." That thought made me cock my head in consideration. "Unless you've pledged yourself to another god?"

She shook her head, though she said nothing, and I thought that I sensed tension in her. Not fear. Something else. Embarrassment?

I remembered Shevir's term. "Are you a primortalist?"

She rolled her eyes. "Do you ever stop talking?"

"It's very hard for me to be quiet and well behaved," I said honestly, and she snorted.

The road we were on went uphill for a ways. I guessed there might be a root of the Tree underground somewhere, close to the surface. As we went up, we passed gradually into a zone of relative brightness, which would probably receive direct sunlight at least once a day, whenever the sun sank below the Tree's canopy. The buildings grew taller and better maintained; the streets grew busier, too, possibly because we were traveling inward toward the city's heart. Hymn and I now had to shift to the sidewalk to avoid coaches and the occasional finely made palanquin borne along by sweating men.

At last we reached a large house that occupied the majority of a bizarrely triangular block, near the intersection of two brisk-moving streets. The house was triangular as well, a stately six-story wedge, but that was not what made it so striking. What made me stop, half in the street, and stare was the fact that someone had had the audacity to paint it *black*. Aside from wooden lintels and white accents, the whole structure from roof edge to foundation was stark, unrelenting, unabashed blackness.

Hymn grinned at my openmouthed expression and pulled me forward so I wouldn't get run over by a human-drawn carriage. "Amazing, isn't it? I don't know how they get away with breaking the White Law. My papa says the Order-Keepers used to kill homeowners as heretics if they refused to paint their houses white. They still issue fines sometimes—but nobody bothers the Arms of Night." She poked me in the shoulder, making me look at her in surprise. "You be polite, if you really care about making it up to me. These people are into more than whorehouses. No one crosses them."

I smiled weakly, though my stomach had tightened in unease. Had I fled Sky only to put myself in the hands of other mortals with power? But I owed Hymn, so I sighed and said, "I'll be good."

She nodded, then led me through the house's gate and up to its wide, plain double doors.

A servant—conservatively dressed—opened the door at her knock. "Hello," said Hymn, inclining her head in a polite bow. (She glared at me, and I hastily did the same.) "My friend here has business with the proprietor."

The servant, a stocky Amn woman, swept a quick assessing glance over me and apparently decided I was worthy of further attention. Given that I wore three days' worth of alley filth, this made me feel quite proud of my looks. "Your name?"

I considered half a dozen, then decided there was no point in hiding. "Sieh."

She nodded and glanced at Hymn, who introduced herself as well. "I'll let him know you're here," the woman said. "Please, wait in the parlor."

She led us to a small, stuffy little room with wood-paneled walls and an elaborately patterned Mencheyev carpet on the floor. It had no chairs, so we stood while the woman closed the door behind us and left.

"This place doesn't feel much like a whorehouse," I said, going to the window to peer out at the bustling street. I tasted the air and found nothing I would have expected—no lust, though that could only have been because there were no clients present. No misery either, though, or bitterness or pain. I could smell women, and men, and sex, but also incense and paper and ink, and fine food. Far more businesslike than sordid.

"They don't like that word," Hymn murmured, coming near so that we could speak. "And I told you, the people who work here aren't whores—not people who will do anything for money, I mean. Some of the ones here don't work for money at all."

"What?"

"That's what I've heard. And more, the people who run this place are taking over all the brothels in the city and making them work the same way. I hear that's why the Order-Keepers give them so much leeway. Darkwalker tithe money is just as shiny as anyone else's, when it comes down to it."

"Darkwalkers?" My mouth fell open. "I don't believe it. These people—the proprietors or whatever—they worship *Nahadoth*?" I could not help thinking of Naha's worshippers of old, in the days before the Gods' War. They had been revelers and dreamers and rebels, as resistant to the idea of organization as cats to obedience. But times had changed, and two thousand years of Itempas's influence had left a mark. Now the followers of Nahadoth opened businesses and paid taxes.

"Yes, they worship Nahadoth," said Hymn, throwing me a look of such challenge that I instantly understood. "Does that bother you?"

I put my hand on her bony shoulder. If I could have, I would have blessed her, now that I knew who she belonged to. "Why would it? He's my father."

She blinked but remained wary, her tension shifting from one shoulder to the other. "He's the father of most godlings, isn't he? But not all of them seem to like him."

I shrugged. "He's hard to like sometimes. I get that from him." I grinned, which pulled a smile from her, too. "But anyone who honors him is a friend of mine."

"That's good to know," said a voice behind me, and I went stiff because it was a voice that I had never, ever expected to hear again. Male, baritone-deep, careless, cruel. The cruelty was most prominent now, mingled with amusement, because here I was in his parlor, helpless, mortal, and that made him the spider to my fly.

I turned slowly, my hands clenching into fists. He smiled with almost-perfect lips and gazed at me with eyes that weren't quite dark enough. "*You*," I breathed.

My father's living prison. My tormentor. My victim.

"Hello, Sieh," he said. "Nice to see you again."

10

It should never have happened.

Itempas's madness, Enefa's death, Nahadoth's defeat. The War. The sundering of our family.

But it had, and I had been chained within a sack of meat that slurped and leaked and thumped about, clumsy as a cudgel, more helpless than I had been even as a newborn. Because newborn gods were free, and I? I was nothing. Less than nothing. A slave.

We had sworn from the beginning to look out for one another, as slaves must. The first few weeks were the worst. Our new masters worked us to the bone repairing their broken world—which, in all honesty, we had helped to break. Zhakkarn went forth and rescued all the survivors, even the ones buried under rubble or half crisped by lava or lightning. I, better than anyone at clearing up messes, rebuilt one village in every land for the survivors' housing. Meanwhile, Kurue made the seas live and the soils fruitful again.

(They had ripped off her wings to force her to do it. It was too complex a task to be commanded, and she was too wise; she could easily find the loopholes in it. The wings grew back and they tore them away again, but she bore the pain in cold silence. Only when they'd driven heated spikes into her skull, threatening to damage her now-vulnerable brain, had she capitulated. She could not bear to be without her thoughts, for those were all she had left.)

Nahadoth, that awful first year, was left alone. This was partly necessity, as Itempas's betrayal had left him silent and broken. Nothing stirred him; not words, not whippings. When the Arameri commanded, he would move and do as he was told—no more, no less. Then he would sit back down. This stillness was not his nature, you understand. There was something so obviously wrong with it that even the Arameri let him be.

But the other problem was Naha's unreliability. By night he had power, but send him to the other side of the world, past the dawnline of the sun, and he turned to drooling, senseless meat. He had no power at all in that form—could not even manifest his own personality. The meat's mind was as empty as a newborn babe's. Still dangerous, though, especially when sunset came.

Because it was, in its own way, a child, I was given charge of it.

From the first I hated this. It shat itself every day, sometimes more than once. (One of the mortal women tried to show me how to use a diaper; I never bothered. Just left the creature on the ground to do its business.) It moaned and grunted and screamed, incessantly. It bit me bloody when I tried to feed it—newborn or not, it had a man's flesh, and that man had a full set of strong, sharp teeth. The first time it did this, I knocked several of those teeth out. They grew back the next night. It didn't bite me again.

Gradually, though, I came to be more accepting of my duty, and as I warmed toward the meat, so it regarded me with its own simple species of affection. When it began to walk, it followed me everywhere. Once Zhakka and Rue and I had built the first White Hall—the Arameri still pretended to be priests back then—the creature filled the shining corridors with jabbering as it learned to talk. Its first word was my name. When I grew weak and lapsed into the horrifying state that mortals called *sleep*, the meat creature snuggled against me. I tolerated this because sometimes, when dusk fell and it became my father again, I could snuggle back and close my eyes and imagine that the War had never happened. That all was as it should be.

But those dreams never lasted. The thin, lifeless dawn, and my mindless charge, always returned.

If only it had stayed mindless. But it did not; it began to think. When the others and I probed inside it, we found that it had begun, like any thinking, feeling being, to grow a soul. Worst of all, it—he—began to love me.

And I, as I should never, ever have done, began to love him back.

Hymn and I stood now in the creature's large, handsomely furnished office, wreathed in disgusting smoke.

"I'd ask you to sit," he said, pausing to take another long drag on the burning thing in his mouth, exhaling the smoke with a languid air, "but I doubt you would." He gestured at the equally handsome leather chairs that faced his desk. He sat in a fine chair across from these.

Hymn, who had been glancing uneasily at me since we'd come upstairs from the parlor, sat. I did not.

"My lord—" she began.

"*Lord?*" I spat this, folding my arms.

He looked at me with amusement. "Nobility these days has less to do with bloodlines and friendships with the Arameri, and more to do with money. I have plenty of that, so yes, that makes me a lord." He paused. "And I go by the name 'Ahad' now. Do you like it?"

I sneered. "You can't even bother to be original."

"I have only the name you gave me, lovely Sieh." He hadn't changed. His words were still velvet over razors. I ground my teeth, bracing for cuts. "Speaking of loveliness, though, you're rather lacking at the moment. Did you piss off Zhakkarn again? How is she, by the way? Always liked her."

"What in the fifty million hells are you doing alive?" I demanded. This earned a little gasp from Hymn, but I ignored her.

Ahad's smile never flagged. "You know precisely why I'm alive, Sieh. You were there, remember? At the moment of my birth." I stiffened at this. There was too much knowing in his eyes. He saw my fear. "'Live,' she said. She was newborn herself; maybe she didn't know a goddess's word is law. But I suspect she did."

I relaxed, realizing that he referred to his rebirth as a whole and separate being. But how many years had passed since then? Ahad should have grown old and died years before, yet here he was, as hale and healthy as he'd been on that day. Better, in fact. He was smug and well dressed now, his fingers heavy with silver rings, his hair long and straight and partially braided like a barbarian's. I blinked. No, like a Darre's, which was what he looked like now: a mortal, Darren man. Yeine had remade him to suit her then-tastes.

Remade him. "What are you?" I asked, suspicious.

He shrugged, setting that shining black hair a-ripple

over his shoulders. (Something about this movement nagged me with its familiarity.) Then he lifted a hand, casually, and turned it into black mist. My mouth fell open; his smile widened just a touch. His hand returned, still holding the smelly cheroot, which he raised for another long inhalation.

I went forward so swiftly and intently that he rose to face me. An instant later, I stopped against a radiant cushion of his power. It was not a shield; nothing so specific. Just *his will* given force. He did not want me near him and this became reality. Along with the scent that I'd drawn near him to try and detect, this confirmed my suspicions. To my horror.

"You're a godling," I whispered. "She made you a *godling*."

Ahad, no longer smiling, said nothing, and I realized I was still closer than he wanted me. His distaste washed against me in little sour-tasting tides. I stepped back, and he relaxed.

I did not understand, you see. What it meant to be mortal—relentlessly, constantly, without recourse to the soothing aethers and rarefied dimensions that are the proper housing for my kind. Years passed before I realized that to be bound to mortal flesh is more than just magical or physical weakness; it is a degradation of the mind and soul. And I did not handle it well, those first few centuries.

So easy to endure pain and pass on in turn to those weaker than oneself. So easy to look into the eyes of someone who trusted me to protect him—and hate him, because I could not.

What he has become is my fault. I have sinned against myself, and there is no redeeming that.

*   *   *

"So it appears," Ahad said. "I have such peculiar abilities now. And as you've noticed, I grow no older." He paused, looking me up and down. "Which is more than I can say for you. You smell like Sky, Sieh, and you look like some Arameri have been torturing you again. But"—he paused, his eyes narrowing—"it's more than that, isn't it? You feel...wrong."

Even if he had not become a god, he was the last person to whom I would have willingly revealed my condition. Yet there was no hiding it, now that he'd seen me. He knew me better than anyone else in this realm, and he would be that much more vicious if I tried to hide it.

I sighed and waved a hand to clear some of the drifting smoke from my vicinity. It came right back. "Something has happened," I said. "I was in Sky, yes, for a few days. The Arameri heir—" No. I didn't want to talk about that. Better to get to the worst of it. "I seem to be"—I shifted, put my hands into my pockets, and tried to seem nonchalant—"dying."

Hymn's eyes widened. Ahad—I hated that stupid name of his already—looked skeptical.

"Nothing can kill a godling but demons and gods," he said, "and the world's fresh out of demons, last I heard. Has Naha finally grown tired of his little favorite?"

I clenched my fists. "He will love me until time ends."

"Yeine, then." To my surprise, the skepticism cleared from Ahad's face. "Yes, she is wise and good-hearted, but she didn't know you back then; you played the innocent boy so well. She could make you mortal, couldn't she? If so, I commend her for giving you a slow, cruel death."

I would have gotten angrier, if my own cruel streak hadn't come to the fore. "What's this? Have you got a baby-god crush on Yeine? It's hopeless, you know. Nahadoth's the one she loves; you're just his leftovers."

Ahad kept smiling, but his eyes went black and cold. He had more than a little of my father still in him; that much was obvious.

"You're just mad neither of them wants *you*," he said.

The room went gray and red. With a wordless cry of rage, I went for him—meaning, I think, to rip him open with my claws, and forgetting for the moment that I had none. And forgetting, far more stupidly, that he was a god and I was not.

He could have killed me. He could have done it by accident; newborn godlings don't know their own strength. Instead he simply caught me by the throat, lifted me bodily, and slammed me onto the top of his desk so hard that the wood cracked.

While I groaned, dazed by the blow and the agony of landing on two paperweights, he sighed and sucked more smoke from the cheroot with his free hand. He kept me pinned, easily, with the other.

"What does he want?" he asked Hymn.

As my vision cleared, I saw she had gotten to her feet and was half ducked behind her chair. At his question, she straightened warily.

"Money," she said. "He got me into trouble earlier today. Said he needed to make it up to me, but I don't need any of his tricks."

Ahad laughed, in the humorless way he had done for the last dozen centuries. I couldn't remember the last time I'd felt true amusement from him. "Isn't that just like him?" He smiled down at me, then lifted a hand. A purse appeared in it; I heard heavy coins jingle within. Without looking at Hymn, he tossed it. Without blinking she caught it.

"That enough?" he asked when she tugged open the pouch's string to look inside. Her eyes widened, and she nodded. "Good. You can go now."

She swallowed. "Am I in trouble for this?" She glanced at me as I struggled to breathe around Ahad's tightening hand.

"No, of course not. How could you have known I knew him?" He threw her a significant look. "Though you still don't know anything, you understand. About me being what I am, him being what he is. You never met him, and you never came here. Spend your money slowly if you want to keep it."

"I know that." Scowling, Hymn made the pouch disappear. Then to my surprise, she glanced at me again. "What are you going to do with him?"

I had begun to wonder that myself. His hand was tight enough to feel the pounding of my pulse. I reached up and scrabbled at his wrist, trying to loosen it, but it was like trying to loosen the roots of the Tree.

Ahad watched my efforts with lazy cruelty. "I haven't decided yet," he said. "Does it matter?"

Hymn licked her lips. "I don't do blood money."

He looked up at her and let the silence grow long and still before he finally spoke. His words were kinder than his eyes. "Don't worry," he said. "This one is a favorite of two of the Three. I'm not stupid enough to kill him."

Hymn took a quick, deep breath—for strength, I thought. "Look, I don't know what's happened between you two, and I don't care. I never would have...I didn't mean to—" She stopped, took a deep breath. "I'll give you back the money. Just let him come with me."

Ahad's hand tightened until I saw stars at the edges of my vision. "Don't," he said, sounding far too much like my father in that instant, "*ever* command me."

Hymn looked confused, but of course mortals do not realize how often they speak in imperatives—that is, ordinary mortals do not. Arameri long ago learned that lesson when we killed them for forgetting.

I fought back fear so that I could concentrate. *Leave her alone, damn you! Play your games with me, not her!*

Ahad actually started, throwing a sharp glance at me. I had no idea why—until I remembered just how young he was, in our terms. And that reminded me of my one advantage over him.

Closing my eyes, I fixed my thoughts on Hymn. She was a hot bright point on the darkening map of my awareness. I had found the power to protect her when the muckrakers came. Could I now protect her from one of my own?

Wind shot through the hollows of my soul, cold and electric. Not much; not nearly as much as there should have been. But enough. I smiled.

And reached up to grip Ahad's hand. "Brother," I murmured in our tongue, and he blinked, surprised that I could talk. "Share yourself with me."

Then I took him into my self. We blazed, white green gold, through a firmament of purest ebony, down, down, down. This was not the core of me, for I would never trust him in that sweet, sharp place, but it was close enough. I felt him struggle, frightened, as all that I was—a torrent, a current—threatened to devour him. But that was not my intention. As we swirled downward, I dragged him closer to me. Here without flesh, I was the elder and the stronger. He did not know himself and I overpowered him easily. Gripping the front of his shirt, I grinned into his wide, panicked eyes.

"Let's see *you* now," I said, and thrust my hand into his mouth.

He screamed—a stupid thing to do under the circumstances. That just made it easier. I compacted myself into a single curved claw and plunged into the core of him. There was an instant of resistance, and pain for both of us, because he was not me and all gods are antithetical to each other on some level. Then there was the briefest plume of strangeness as I tasted his nature, dark but not, rich in memory yet raw with his newness, craving, desperate for something that he did not want and did not know that he needed—but it latched on to me with a ferocity I had not expected. Young gods are not usually so savage. Then I was the one being devoured—

I came out of him with a cry and twisted away, curling in on myself in agony while Ahad stumbled and fell across the empty chair. I heard him utter a sound like a sob, once. Then he drew deep breaths, controlling himself.

Yes, I had forgotten. He was not truly new. He wasn't even young, like Yeine. As a mortal, he had seen thousands of years before his effective rebirth. And he had endured hells in that time that would have broken most mortals. It had broken *him*, but he'd put himself back together, stronger. I laughed to myself as the pain of nearly becoming something else finally began to recede.

"You never change, do you?" My voice was a rasp. He'd left finger marks in the flesh of my neck. "Always so difficult."

His reply was a curse in a dead language, though I was gratified to hear weariness in his voice as well.

I pushed myself up, slowly. Every muscle in my body ached, along with the bump to the back of the head I'd taken. At the corner of my vision there was movement: Hymn. Coming back into the room, after quite sensibly vacating it while two godlings fought. I was surprised, given her knowledge of us, that she hadn't vacated the house and neighborhood, too.

"You done?" she asked.

"Very," I said, pulling myself to sit on the edge of the desk. I would need to sleep again soon. But first I had to make my peace with Ahad, if he would allow that.

He was glaring at me now, from the chair. Nearly recovered already, though his hair was mussed and he had lost his cheroot. I hated him more for a moment, and then sighed and let that go. Let it all go. Mortal life was too short.

"We are no longer slaves," I said softly. "We need no longer be enemies."

"We weren't enemies because of the Arameri," he snapped.

"Yes, we were." I smiled, which made him blink. "You wouldn't have even existed if not for them. And I—" If I allowed it, the shame would come. I had never allowed it before, but so much had changed since those days. Our positions had reversed: he wàs a god; I wasn't. I needed him; he didn't need me. "I would have at least... would have tried to be a better..."

But then he surprised me. He had always been good at that.

"Shut up, you fool," he said, getting to his feet with a sigh. "Don't be any more of an ass than you usually are."

I blinked. "What?"

Ahad stalked over to me, surprising me further. He hadn't liked being near me for centuries. Planting his hands on the desk on either side of my hips, he leaned down to glare into my face. "Do you really think me so petty that I would still be angry after all this time? Ah, no—that isn't it at all." His smile flickered, and perhaps it was my imagination that his teeth grew sharper for a moment. I *hoped* it was, because the last thing he needed was an animal nature. "No, I think you're just so gods-damned certain of your own importance that you haven't figured it out. So let me make this clear: *I don't care about you*. You're irrelevant. It's a waste of my energy even to hate you!"

I stared back at him, stunned by his vehemence and, I will admit, hurt. And yet.

"I don't believe you," I murmured. He blinked.

Then he pushed away from the desk with such force that it scooched back a little, nearly jostling me off. I stared as he went over to Hymn, grabbed her by the scruff of her shirt, and half dragged her to the door, opening it.

"I'm not going to kill him," he said, shoving her through hard enough that she stumbled when he let her go. "I'm not going to do a damned thing other than gloat over his prolonged, humiliating death, which I have no reason whatsoever to hasten. So your money's clean and you can wash your hands of him in good conscience. Be glad you escaped before he could ruin your life. Now get out!" And he slammed the door in her face.

I stared at him as he turned to regard me, taking a long, slow breath to compose himself. Because I knew his soul, I felt the moment that he made a decision. Perhaps he had already guessed at mine.

"Would you like a drink?" he asked at last, with brittle politeness.

"Children shouldn't drink," I said automatically.

"How fortunate that you're not a child anymore."

I winced. "I, ah, haven't had alcohol in a few centuries." I said it carefully, testing this new, fragile peace beneath us. It was as thin as the tension on a puddle's surface, but if we tread delicately, we might manage. "Do you have anything, er..."

"For the pathetic?" He snorted and went over to a handsome wood cabinet, which turned out to hold a dozen or so bottles. All of them were full of strong, richly colored liquids. Stuff for men, not boys. "No. You'll have to sink or swim, I'm afraid."

Most likely I would sink. I looked at the bottles and committed myself to the path of truce with a heavy sigh.

"Pour on, then," I said, and he did.

Some while later, after I had unfortunately remembered too late that vomiting is far, far more unpleasant than defecating, I sat on the floor where Ahad had left me and took a long, hard look at him. "You want something from me," I said. I believe I said it clearly, though my thoughts were slurred.

He lifted an eyebrow in genteel fashion, not even tipsy. A servant had already taken away the wastebasket splattered with my folly. Even with the windows open, the stench of Ahad's cheroot was better than the alternative, so I did not mind it this time.

"So do you," he said.

"Yes," I said, "but my wants are always simple things. In this case I want money, and since I really wanted it for Hymn and you've already given it to her, that essentially solves the problem. *Your* wants are never simple."

"Hmm." I didn't think this statement pleased him. "And yet you're still here, which implies you want something more."

"Care during my feeble senescence. It will take me another fifty or sixty years to die, during which I will require increasing amounts of food and shelter and"—I looked at the bottle on the desk between us, considering—"and other things. Mortals use money to obtain these things; I am becoming mortal; therefore, I will need a regular source of money."

"A job." Ahad laughed. "My housekeeper thought you might make a good courtesan, if you cleaned up a little."

Affront penetrated the alcohol haze. "I'm a god!"

"Nearly a third of our courtesans are godlings, Sieh. Didn't you feel the presence of family when you came in?" He gestured around the building, his hand settling on himself, and I flushed because in fact, I had not sensed him or anyone else. More evidence of my weakness. "A goodly number of our clients are, too—godlings who are curious about mortals but afraid or too proud to admit it. Or who simply want the release of meaningless, undemanding intercourse. We aren't so different from them, you know, when it comes to that sort of thing."

I reached out to touch the world around me as best I could, my senses numbed and unsteady as they were. I could feel a few of my siblings then. Mostly the very youngest. I remembered the days when I had been fascinated by mortalkind—especially children, with whom I had loved to play. But some of my kind were drawn to adults, and with that came adult cravings.

Like the taste of Shahar's skin.

I shook my head—a mistake, as the nausea was not quite done with me. I said something to distract myself. "We've never needed such things, Ahad. If we want a mortal, we appear somewhere and point at one, and the mortal gives us what we want."

"You know, Sieh, it's all right that you haven't paid attention to the world. But you really shouldn't *talk* as though you have."

"What?"

"Times have changed." Ahad paused to sip from a square glass of fiery red liquid. I had stopped drinking that one after the first taste because mortals could die of alcohol poisoning. Ahad held it in his mouth a moment, savoring the burn, before continuing. "Mortalkind, heretics excepted, spent centuries believing in Itempas and nothing else. They don't know what happened to him—the Arameri keep a tight grip on that information, and so do we godlings—but they know *something* has changed. They aren't gods, but they can still see the new colors of existence. And now they understand that our kind are powerful, admirable, but fallible." He shrugged. "A godling who wants to be worshipped can still find adherents, of course. But not many—and really, Sieh, most of us don't *want* to be worshipped. Do you?"

I blinked in surprise, and considered it. "I don't know."

"You could be, you know. The street children swear by you when they speak any god's name at all. Some of them even pray to you."

Yes, I had heard them, though I'd never done anything to encourage their interest. I'd had thousands of followers once, but these days it always surprised me that they remembered. I drew up my knees and wrapped my arms around them, understanding finally what Ahad meant.

Nodding as if I'd spoken my thoughts aloud, Ahad continued. "The rest of our clients are nobles, wealthy merchants, very lucky commoners—anyone who's ever yearned to visit the heavens before death. Even our mortal courtesans have been with gods enough to have acquired a certain ethereal technique." He smiled a salesman's smile, though it never once touched his eyes.

"That's what you're selling. Not sex, but divinity." I frowned. "Gods, Ahad, at least worship is *free*."

"It was never free." His smile vanished. It hadn't been real, anyway. "Every mortal who offered a god devotion wanted *something* in exchange for it—blessings, a guaranteed place in the heavens, status. And every god who demanded worship expected loyalty and more, in exchange. So why shouldn't we be honest about what we're doing? At least here, no god lies."

I flinched, as he had meant me to. Razors. Then he went on.

"As for our residents, as we call them, there is no rape here, no coercion. No pain, unless that's mutually agreed upon by both client and resident. No judgments, either." He paused, looking me up and down. "The housekeeper usually has a good eye for new talent. It will be a shame to tell her that she was so far off in your case."

It was not entirely due to the alcohol that I straightened in wounded pride. "I could be a *marvelous* whore." Gods knew I had enough practice.

"Ah, but I think you would be unable to keep yourself from contemplating the violent murder of any client who claimed you. Which, given your nature and the unpredictability of magic, might actually cause such death to occur. That's not good for business." He paused, and I did not imagine the cold edge to his smile. "I have the same problem, as I discovered quite by accident."

There was a long silence that fell between us. This was not recriminating. It was simply that such statements stirred up sediment of the past, and it was natural to wait for that to settle before we moved on.

Changing the subject helped, too. "We can discuss the matter of my employment later." Because I was almost certain he would hire me. Unreasoning optimism is a fundamental element of childishness. "So what is it, then, that you want?"

Ahad steepled his fingers, propping his elbows on the arms of the handsome leather chair. I wondered whether this was a sign of nerves. "I should think you'd have guessed. Considering how easily you defeated me in—" He paused, frowning, and then I finally did catch on.

"No mortal tongue has words for it," I said softly. I would have to speak diplomatically, and that was never easy for me. "In our realm there is no need for words. Naturally you will have picked up some of our tongue over the centuries...." I let the question ask itself, and he grimaced.

"Not much of it. I couldn't hear...feel..." He struggled to say it in Senmite, probably out of stubbornness. "I was like any other mortal before Yeine did this to me. I tried speaking your words a few times, died a few times, and stopped trying."

"*Your* words now." I watched Ahad absorb this, his expression going unreadably blank. "I can teach you the language, if you want."

"There are several dozen godlings living in Shadow," he replied stiffly. "If and when I deem it valuable, I can learn from them."

Idiot, I thought, but kept it behind my teeth, nodding as if I thought deliberate ignorance was a good idea. "You have a bigger problem, anyway."

He said nothing, watching me. He could do that for hours, I knew; something he'd learned during his years in Sky. I had no idea whether he knew what I was about to say.

"You don't know your nature." That was how I'd known I could best him, or at least get him off me, in the contest of our wills. His reaction to the touch of my thoughts had given it away: I had seen mortal newborns do the same at the brush of a fingertip. A quick, startled jerk, a flailing look to determine *what and how and why*, and *will it hurt me?* Only learning oneself better, and understanding one's place in the world, made the touch of another mundane.

After a moment, Ahad nodded. This, too, was a gesture of trust between us. In the old days he would never have revealed so much weakness to me.

I sighed and got up, swaying only a little as I gained my feet, and went over to his chair. He did not rise this time, but he grew palpably less relaxed as I got closer, until I stopped.

"I will do you no harm," I said, scowling at his skittishness. Why couldn't he just be a coldhearted bastard all the time? I could never truly hate him, for pity. "The Arameri hurt you worse than I ever did."

Very, very quietly he replied, "*You let them.*"

There was nothing I could say to that, because it was true. So I just stood there. This would never work if we began to rehash old hurts. He knew it, too. Finally he relaxed, and I stepped closer.

"All gods must learn who and what they are for themselves," I said. As gently as I could—my hands were rough and dirty from my days in the alley—I cupped his face and held it. "Only you can define the meaning and limit of your existence. But sometimes, those of us who have already found ourselves can give the new ones a clue."

I had already gained that clue during our brief metaphysical struggle. That fierce, devouring need of his. For what? I looked into his strangely mortalish eyes—strange because he had never really been mortal, yet mortality

was all he knew—and tried to understand him. Which I
should have been able to do because I had been there at
the moment of his birth. I had seen his first steps and
heard his first words. I had loved him, even if—

The nausea struck faster than ever before, because the
alcohol had already made me ill. I barely managed to
whirl away and collapse onto the floor before I was retching, screaming through the heaves, wobbling because my
legs were trying to jerk and my spine was trying to bow
backward even as my stomach sought to cast out the poison I had taken in. But this poison was not physical.

"Still a child after all." Ahad sighed into my ear, his
voice a low murmur that easily got through my strangled
cries. "Shall I call you big brother or little brother? I suppose it doesn't matter. You will never grow up fully, no
matter how old you look. Brother."

Brother. Brother. Not child, not
forget
Ahad was not my son, not even figuratively, because
forget
Because a god of childhood could not be a father, not if
he wanted to *be* at all, and
forgetforgetforget
Brother. Ahad was my brother. My new little brother,
Yeine's first child. Nahadoth would be . . . well, not proud,
probably. But amused.

My body unknotted. The agony receded enough that I
stopped screaming, stopped spasming. There was nothing
in my stomach anyhow. I lay there, returning gradually to
myself as the horror faded, then drew one cautious breath.
Then another.

"Thank you," I whispered.

Ahad, crouching over me, sighed. He did not say *you're*

welcome, because I was not welcome and we both knew it. But he had done me a kindness when he hadn't had to, and that deserved acknowledgment.

"You smell," he said, "and you're filthy, and you look like horseshit. Since you're too useless to take yourself out of here as you should, I have no choice but to put you up for the night. But don't get used to it; I want you living somewhere else after this." He got up and went away, I assume to find a servant and make arrangements for my stay.

When he came back, I had managed—barely—to sit on my knees. I was still shaky. Insanely, my stomach now insisted that it needed to be filled again. *In or out*, I told it, but it did not listen.

Ahad crouched in front of me again. "Interesting."

I managed to lift my eyes to him. His expression betrayed nothing, but he lifted a hand and conjured a small hand mirror. I was too tired even for envy. He lifted the mirror to show me my face.

I had grown older. The face that gazed back at me was longer, leaner, with a stronger jawline. The hair on my chin was no longer downy and barely visible; it had grown darker, longer, the wispy precursors of a beard. Late adolescence, rather than the middling stage of it I'd been in. Two years of my life gone? Three? Gone, regardless.

"I should be flattered, perhaps," Ahad said. "That you remember the old days with such fondness." His words skirted the edge of danger, but I was too tired for true fear. He could kill me anytime he wanted, and would've done it by now if he'd really meant to. He just liked flaunting his power.

Suddenly this seemed monumentally unfair. "I hate this," I whispered, not caring if he heard me. "I hate that I'm nothing now."

Ahad shook his head, less annoyed than unsurprised. His hand seized the back of my shirt and pulled me to my feet. "You're not 'nothing.' You're mortal, which is far from nothing. The sooner you accept that, the better off you'll be." He took one of my arms, holding it up, and made a sound of disgust. "You need to *eat*. Start taking care of your body if you want it to last for the few years you have left. Or would you rather die now?"

I closed my eyes, letting myself dangle from his grasp. "I don't want to be mortal." I was whining. It felt good to realize I still could, however much I'd grown up. "Mortals lie when they say they love you. They wait until you trust them, then shove the knife in, and then they work it around to make sure it kills you."

There was a moment of silence, during which I closed my eyes and honestly contemplated having a good cry. It ended when the office door opened and two servants came in, and when Ahad gave me a slap on the cheek that was not *quite* gently chiding.

"Gods do that, too," he snapped, "so you're damned whichever way you turn. Shut up and deal with it."

Then he shoved me into the servants' waiting arms and they hauled me away.

11

I L-O-V-E, love you
I'll K-I-S-S, kiss you
Then I pushed him in a lake
And he swallowed a snake
And ended up with a tummy ache

THE SERVANTS TOOK ME to a large sumptuous bathchamber with lovely benches that reeked of sex despite their freshly laundered cushions. They stripped me, throwing my old clothes into a pile to be burned, and scrubbed me with careless efficiency, rinsing me in perfumed water. Then they put me into a robe and took me to a room and let me sleep the whole day and well into the night. I did not dream.

I woke up thinking that my sister Zhakkarn was using my head as a pike target, though she would never do such a thing. When I managed to sit upright, which took doing, I contemplated nausea again. A long-cold meal and a pitcher of room-temperature water sat on a sideboard of the room, so I decided on ingestion rather than ejection and applied myself grimly. It helped that the food tasted good. Beside this sat a small dish holding a dab of thick white paste and a paper card, on which elegant blocky letters had been written: EAT IT. The hand was familiar, so I sighed and tasted the paste. The alley rat had been more rancid but not by much. Still, as I was a guest in Ahad's home, I held my breath and gulped the rest down, then quickly ate more food in an attempt to disguise the bitter taste. This did not work. However, I began to feel better, so I was pleased to confirm it was medicine, not poison.

Fresh clothing had been set out for me, too. Pleasantly nondescript: loose gray pants, a beige shirt, a brown jacket, brown boots. Servant attire, most likely, since I suspected that would suit Ahad's sense of cruelty. Thus arrayed, I opened the door of the room.

And promptly stopped, as the sounds of laughter and music drifted up from downstairs. Nighttime. For a moment the urge to play a dozen bawdy, vicious tricks was almost overwhelming, and I felt a tickle of power at the thought. It would be so easy to change all the house's sensual oils into hot chili oil or make the beds smell of mildew rather than lust and perfume. But I was older now, more mature, and the urge passed. I felt a fleeting sadness in its wake.

Before I could close the door, however, two people came up the steps, giggling together with the careless intimacy of old friends or new lovers. One of them turned her head, and I froze as our eyes met. Egan, one of my sisters—with her arm around the waist of some mortal. I assessed and dismissed him in a glance: richly dressed, middle-aged, drunk. I turned back to meet Egan's frowning gaze.

"Sieh." She looked me up and down and smirked. "So the rumors are true; you're back. Two thousand years wasn't enough mortal flesh to satisfy you?"

Once upon a time, Egan had been worshipped by a

desert tribe in eastern Senm. She had taught them to play music that could bring rain, and they had sculpted a mountain face to make a statue of her in return. Those people were gone now, absorbed into the Amn during one of that tribe's endless campaigns of conquest before the War. After the War, I had destroyed Egan's statue myself, under orders from the Arameri to eliminate anything that blasphemed against Itempas, no matter how beautiful. And here stood the original in mortal flesh, with an Amn man's hand on her breast.

"I'm here by accident," I said. "What's your excuse?"

She lifted a graceful eyebrow, set into a beautiful Amn face. It was a new face, of course. Before the War, she had looked more like the people of the desert tribe. Both of us ignored the mortal, who had by now begun trying to nibble at her neck.

"Boredom," she said. "Experience. The usual. During the War, it was the ones who'd spent the most time among mortalkind, defining their natures, who survived best." Her eyes narrowed. "Not that you helped."

"I fought the madman who destroyed our family," I said wearily. "And yes, I fought anyone who helped him. I don't understand why everyone acts like I did a horrible thing."

"Because you—all of you who fought for Naha—lost yourselves in it," Egan snapped, her body tensing so with fury that her paramour lifted his head to blink at her in surprise. "He infected you with his fury. You didn't just kill those who fought; you killed anyone who tried to stop you. Anyone who pleaded for calm, if you thought they should've been fighting. Mortals, if they had the temerity to ask you for help. In the Maelstrom's name, you act like Tempa was the only one who went mad that day!"

I stared at her, fury ratcheting higher in me, and then,

suddenly, it died. I couldn't sustain it. Not while I stood there with my head still aching from alcohol and Ahad's beating the day before, and my skin crawling as infinitesimal flecks of it died—some renewed, some lost forever, all of it slowly becoming dryer and less elastic until one day it would be nothing but wrinkles and liver spots. Egan's lover touched her shoulder to try and soothe her, a pathetic gesture, but it seemed to have some effect, because she relaxed just a little and smiled ruefully at him, as if to apologize for destroying the mood. That made me think of Shahar, and how lonely I was, and how lonely I would be for the rest of my mercilessly brief life.

It is very, very hard to sustain a two-thousand-year-old grudge amid all that.

I shook my head and turned to go back into my room. But just before I could close the door, I heard Egan. "Sieh. Wait."

Warily I opened the door again. She was frowning at me. "Something's different about you. What is it?"

I shook my head again. "Nothing that should matter to you. Look…" It occurred to me suddenly that I would never have a chance to say this to her or to any of my siblings. I would die with so much unfinished business. It wasn't fair. "I'm sorry, Egan. I know that means nothing after everything that's happened. I wish…" So many wishes. I laughed a little. "Never mind."

"Are you going to be working here?" She smoothed a hand over her mortal man's back; he sighed and leaned against her, happy again.

"No." Then I remembered Ahad's plans. "Not…like this." I gestured toward her with my chin. "No offense, but I'm not overly fond of mortals right now."

"Understandable, after all you've been through." I

blinked in surprise, and she smiled thinly. "None of us liked what Itempas did, Sieh. But by then, imprisoning you seemed the only sane choice he'd made, after so much insanity." She sighed. "We all had a long time to think about how wrong that decision was. And then...well, you know how he is about changing his mind."

By which she meant *he didn't*. "I know."

Egan glanced at her mortal, thoughtful, and then at me. Then at the mortal again. "What do you think?"

The man looked surprised but pleased. He looked at me, and abruptly I realized what they were considering. I couldn't help blushing, which made the man smile. "I think it would be nice," he said.

"No," I said quickly. "I—er—thank you. I can see you mean well...but no."

Egan smiled then, surprising me, because there was more compassion in it than I'd ever expected to see. "How long since you've been with your own?" she asked, and it threw me. I couldn't answer, because I couldn't remember the last time I'd made love to another god. Nahadoth, but that was not the same. He'd been diminished, stuffed into mortal flesh, desperate in his loneliness. That hadn't been lovemaking; it had been pity. Before that, I thought it might have been—

forget

Zhakka, maybe? Selforine? Elishad—no, that had been ages ago, back when he'd still liked me. Gwn?

It would be good, perhaps, to lose myself in another for a while. To let one of my kind take my soul where she would and give it comfort. Wouldn't it?

As I had done for Shahar.

"No," I said again, more softly. "Not now...not yet. Thank you."

She eyed me for a long moment, perhaps seeing more than I wanted her to see. Could she tell I was becoming mortal? Another reason not to accept her offer; she would know then. But I thought maybe that wasn't the reason for her look. I wondered if maybe, just maybe, she still cared.

"The offer stands for whenever you change your mind," she said, and then flashed me a smile. "You might have to share, though." Turning her smile on the mortal, she and he moved on, heading up to the next floor.

My stirrings had been noticed. When I turned from watching Egan leave, the servant man who had quietly come upstairs bowed to me. "Lord Sieh? Lord Ahad has asked that you come to his office, when you're ready."

I put a hand on my hip. "I know full well he didn't *ask*."

The servant paused, then looked amused. "You probably don't want to know the word he actually used in place of your name, either."

I followed the servant downstairs. During these evening hours, he explained quietly, only the courtesans were to be visible; this was necessary to maintain the illusion that the house contained nothing but beautiful creatures offering guiltless pleasure. The sight of servants reminded the clientele that the Arms of Night was a business. The sight of people like me—servants of a different kind, he did not say, but I could guess—reminded them that the business was one of many, whose collective owners had fingers in many pots.

So he took me into what looked like a closet, which proved to lead into a dimly lit, wide back stairwell. Other servants and the occasional mortal courtesan moved back and forth along this, all of them smiling or greeting each other amiably in passing. (So different from servants in

Sky.) When we reached the ground floor, the servant led me through a short convoluted passage that reminded me a bit of my dead spaces, and then opened a door that appeared to have been cut from the bare wooden wall. "In here, Lord Sieh." Unsurprisingly, we were back in Ahad's office. Surprisingly, he was not alone.

The young woman who sat in the chair across from him would have been striking even if she hadn't been beautiful. This was partly because she was Maroneh and partly because she was very tall for a woman, even sitting down. The roiling nimbus of black hair about her head only added to the inches by which she topped the chair's high back. But she was also elegant of form and bearing, her presence accented by the faint fragrance of hiras-flower perfume. She had dressed herself like a nobody, in a nondescript long skirt and jacket with worn old boots, but she carried herself like a queen.

She had been smiling at something Ahad said when I entered. As I stepped into the room, her eyes settled on me with a disconcertingly intent gaze, and her smile faded to something cooler and more guarded. I had the sudden acute feeling of being sized up, and found wanting.

The servant bowed and closed the door behind me. I folded my arms and watched her, waiting. I was not so far gone that I didn't know power when I smelled it.

"What are you?" I asked. "Arameri by-blow? Scriv-ener? Noblewoman in disguise so you can visit a brothel in peace?"

She did not respond. Ahad sighed and pinched the bridge of his nose.

"Glee is part of the group that owns and supports the Arms of Night, Sieh," he said. "She's come to see you, in fact—to make certain you won't jeopardize the investment she and her partners have already made. If she doesn't like you, you ridiculous ass, you don't stay."

This made me frown in confusion. "Since when does a godling do a mortal's bidding? Willingly, that is."

"Since godlings and mortals began to have mutual goals," said the woman. Her voice was low and rolling, like warm ocean waves, yet her words were so precisely enunciated that I could have cut paper with them. Her smile was just as sharp when I turned to her. "I imagine such arrangements were quite common before the Gods' War. In this case, the relationship is less supervisory and more…partnership." She glanced at Ahad. "Partners should agree on important decisions."

He nodded back, with only a hint of his usual sardonic smile. Did she know he would gut-knife her in a moment if it benefitted him more than cooperation did? I hoped so and held out my hands to let her get a good look at me. "Well? *Do* you like me?"

"If it were a matter of looks, the answer would be no." I dropped my arms in annoyance and she smiled, though I didn't think she'd been kidding. "You don't suit my tastes at all. Fortunately, looks are not the means by which I judge value."

"She has a job for you," Ahad said. He swiveled in his chair to face me and leaned back, propping one foot on the desk. "A test, of sorts. To see if your unique talents can be put to some use."

"What the hells kind of test?" I was affronted by the very idea.

The woman—Glee? oddly cheerful for a Maroneh woman's name—lifted one perfectly arched eyebrow in a way that felt inexplicably familiar. "I would like to send you to meet Usein Darr, scion of the current baron. Are you, perhaps, familiar with recent political events in the North?"

I tried to remember the things I'd overheard or been told while in Sky. But then, the image of Nevra and Criscina Arameri's bodies came to mind.

"You want me to find out what this new magic is all about," I said. "These masks."

"No. We know what they are."

"You do?"

Glee folded her hands, and the sense of familiarity grew. I had never met her before; I was certain of it. Very strange.

"The masks are art," she said. "Specifically derived from a Mencheyev-Darren method of prayer that long predates the Bright, which they kept up in secret to avoid persecution. Once, they danced their exhortations to and praises of the gods, with each dancer donning a mask in order to act out specific, contextualized roles. Each dance required certain interactions of these roles and a common understanding of the archetypes represented. The Mother, for example, symbolized love, but also justice; it was actually a representation of death. The Sorrowful was worn by an angry, prideful person, who would eventually commit great wrongs and come to regret what they had done. Do you understand?"

I fought to stifle a yawn. "Yeah, I get the idea. Someone takes an archetype, mixes it with common symbology, carves it out of wood from the World Tree using the blood of a slaughtered infant or something—"

"The blood of a godling, actually."

I fell silent in surprise. Glee smiled.

"We don't know whose. Perhaps just godsblood bought off the street; the specific originator of the blood may not matter, just its inherent power. We're looking into that as well. And I don't know about wood from the Tree, but I wouldn't be surprised." She sobered. "Finding out how the masks work isn't what I want you to do in Darr. We're less concerned with the tool, more concerned with the wielder. I would like you to approach Usein Darr with an offer from our group."

I could not help perking up. There was great potential for mischief in any negotiation. "You want their magic?"

"No. We want peace."

I started. *"Peace?"*

"Peace serves the interests of both mortals and gods," Ahad said when I looked at him to see if this Glee was a madwoman.

"I have to agree." I frowned at him. "But I didn't think *you* did."

"I have always done whatever makes my life easier, Sieh." He folded his hands calmly. "I am not Nahadoth, as you're so fond of pointing out. I'm rather fond of predictability and routine."

"Yes. Well." I shook my head and sighed. "But *mortals* are part Nahadoth, and it sounds like the ones up north would rather live in chaos than endure the Arameri's world order any longer. It's not our place to tell this woman she's wrong, if she's the head of it."

"Usein Darr is not the sole force behind the northern rebellion," Glee said. "And it must be called a rebellion at this point. Darr is now one of five northern nations that have ceased to tithe to the White Halls within its borders, though they instead offer schooling, care for the elderly, and so forth to their citizens directly. That keeps the Nobles' Consortium from censuring them for failure to govern—though since no High Northern noble has attended a Consortium session in over a year, it hardly matters. The whole of High North has, effectively, refused to recognize the Consortium's authority." She sighed. "The only thing they haven't done is raise an army, probably because that would bring the Arameri's wrath down on them. Everything but open defiance—but still, defiance. And Darr is, if not its head, most certainly its heart."

"So what am I to offer *this* Darre, then, if her heart's set on freeing the world from Arameri tyranny? A goal I don't at all disagree with, mind you." I considered. "I suppose I could kill her."

"No, you could not." Glee did not raise her voice, but then she didn't have to. Those paper-cutting words suddenly became knives, sharp enough to flense. "As I said, Usein Darr is not the sole motivator of these rebels. Killing her would only martyr her and encourage the rest."

"Besides that," said Ahad, "those godlings who dwell in the mortal realm do so on the sufferance of Lady Yeine. She has made it clear that she values mortal independence and is watching closely to see whether our presence proves detrimental. And please remember that *she* was once Darre. For all we know, Usein is some relative of hers."

I shook my head. "She's not mortal anymore. Such considerations are meaningless to her now."

"Are you sure?"

I paused, suddenly uncertain.

"Well, then." Ahad steepled his fingers. "Let's kill Usein and see. Should be a delight, pissing off someone who had an infamous temper *before* she became the goddess of death."

I rolled my eyes at him but did not protest. "Fine, then," I said. "What *is* my goal in Darr?"

Glee shrugged, which obliquely surprised me because she hadn't seemed like the kind to be that casual. "Find out what Usein wants. If it's within our power, offer it."

"How the hells do I know what's within you people's power?"

Ahad made a sound of exasperation. "Just assume anything and promise nothing. And lie, if you must. You're good at that, aren't you?"

Mortalfucking son of a demon. "Fine," I said, slipping my hands into my pockets. "When do I go?"

I should have known better than to say that, because Ahad sat a little straighter, and his eyes turned completely black. Then he smiled with more than a bit of his old cruelty and said, "You realize I've never done this before."

I tried not to show my alarm. "It's not much different from any other magic. A matter of will." But if his will faltered...

"Ah, but, Sieh, I would so happily will you out of existence."

Better to let him see my fear. He had always cultivated that in the old days; he liked to feel powerful. So I licked my lips and met his eyes. "I thought you didn't care about me. Didn't hate me, didn't love me."

"Which compounds the problem. Perhaps I don't care enough to make sure I do this right."

I took a deep breath, glancing at Glee. *See what you're dealing with?* But she showed no reaction, her beautiful face as serene as before. She would have made a good Arameri.

"Perhaps not," I said, "but if you do care at all about... craftsmanship, or whatever, then could you please be sure to just wipe me out of existence? And not, instead, spread my innards thinly across the face of reality? I've seen that happen before; it looks painful."

Ahad laughed, but a feeling that had been in the air—an extra measure of heaviness and danger that had been thickening around us—eased. "I'll take care, then. I do like being neat."

There was a flicker. I felt myself disassembled and pushed out of the world. Despite Ahad's threats, he was actually quite gentle about it. Then a new setting melted together around me.

Arrebaia, the largest city amid the collection of squabbling tribes that had grown together and decided to fight others instead of each other. I could remember when they had not been Darre, just Somem and Lapri and Ztoric, and even further back when they had been families, and before that when they had been wandering bands lacking names of any kind. No more, however. I stood atop a wall near the city's heart and privately marveled at how much they'd grown. The immense, tangled jungle that dominated this part of High North shone on the distant horizon, as green as the dragons that flew through other realms and the color of my mother's eyes when she was angry. I could smell its humidity and violent, fragile life on the wind. Around me spread a maze of streets and temples and statues and gardens, all rising in stony tiers toward the city's center, all carpeted in the paler green of the ornamental grass that the Darre cultivated. It made their city glow like an emerald in the slanting afternoon light.

Before me, in the near distance, loomed the hulking, squared-off pyramid of Sar-enna-nem. My destination, I guessed, since Ahad did not strike me as the subtle type.

My arrival had not gone unnoticed, however. I glanced down from the wall on which I stood to find an old woman and a boychild of four or five years staring up at me. Amid the crowded street, they alone had stopped; between them was a rickety-looking cart bearing a few tired-looking vegetables and fruits. Ah, yes, the end of the market day. I sat down on the wall, dangling my feet over it and wondering how the hell I was supposed to get down, since it was a good ten feet high and I now had to worry about breaking bones. Damn Ahad.

"Hey, there," I said in Senmite. "You know whether this wall runs all the way to Sar-enna-nem?"

The boy frowned, but the old woman merely looked thoughtful. "All things in Arrebaia lead to Sar-enna-nem," she said. "But you may have trouble getting in. Foreigners are more welcome in the city than they used to be, but they are barred from the temple by declaration of our *ennu*."

"Temple?"

"Sar-enna-nem," said the boy, his expression suddenly scornful. "You don't know anything, do you?"

He spoke with the thickest accent I'd heard in centuries, his Senmite inflected by the gulping river flow of the Darren tongue. The woman's Senmite bore only a trace of this. She had learned Senmite early, probably before she'd learned Darre. The boy had done it the other way around. I glanced up as a pack of children near the boy's age ran past, shrieking as children always seem to. They were shrieking in Darre.

"I know a lot of things," I said to the boy, "but not everything. I know Sar-enna-nem *used to be* a temple, long ago, back before the Arameri made the world over. So it's a temple again?" I grinned, delighted. "Whose?"

"All the gods', of course!" The boy put his hands on his hips, having clearly decided I was an idiot. "If you don't like that, you can leave!"

The old woman sighed. "Hush, boy. I didn't raise you to be rude to guests."

"He's a Teman, Beba! Wigyi from school says you can't trust those eyes of theirs."

Before I could retort, the old woman's hand shot out and cuffed the boy. I winced in sympathy at his yelp, but really, a smart child would've known better.

"We will discuss proper comportment for a young man when we get home," she added, and the boy looked chastened at last. Then she focused on me again. "If you didn't know the temple is a temple again, then I doubt you've come looking to pray. What is it that you really want here, stranger?"

"Well, I was looking for your *ennu*—or his daughter Usein, rather." I had vague memories of someone mentioning a Baron Darr. "Where might she be found?"

The old woman narrowed her eyes at me for a long moment before answering. There was an attentiveness in her posture, and I noted the way she shifted her stance back, just a little. She moved her right hand to her hip, too, for easy access to the knife that was almost surely sheathed at the small of her back. Not all of Darr's women were warriors, but this one had been, no doubt about it.

I flashed her my broadest, most innocent smile, hoping she would dismiss me as harmless. She didn't relax—my smile didn't work as well as it had when I'd been a boy—but her lips did twitch in an almost-smile.

"You want the Raringa," she said, nodding westward. The word meant something like "seat of warriors" in one of the older High Northern trade tongues. Where the warriors' council met, no doubt, to advise the young ennu-to-be on her dangerous course of action. I looked around and spotted a low, dome-shaped building not far from Sar-enna-nem. Not nearly so majestic, but then the Darre were not much like the Amn. They judged their leaders by standards other than appearance.

"Anything else?" the old woman asked. "The size and armament of her guard contingent, maybe?"

I rolled my eyes at this, but then paused as a new thought occurred to me. "Yes," I said. "Say something in Darre for me."

Her eyebrows shot toward her hairline, but she said in that tongue, "It's a shame you're mad, pretty foreign boy, because otherwise you might sire interesting daughters. Though perhaps you're just a very stupid assassin, in which case it's better if someone kills you before you breed."

I grinned, climbing to my feet and dusting grass off my pants. "Thanks much, Auntie," I said in Darre, which made both her and the boy gape. The language had changed some since I'd last spoken it; it sounded more like Mencheyev now, and they'd lengthened their vowels and fricatives. I probably still sounded a little strange to them, and I would definitely have to watch my slang, but already I could do a passable imitation of a native speaker. I gave them both a flourishing bow that was probably long out of fashion, then winked and sauntered off toward the Raringa.

I was not the only foreigner about, I saw as I came onto the wide paved plaza that led into the building. Knots of people milled about the area: some locals, others wearing fancy attire from their own lands. Diplomats, perhaps— ah, yes, come a-courting the new power in the region, feeling out the woman who would soon hold its reins. Maybe they were even coming to probe the possibility of an alliance—discreetly, of course. Darr was still very small, and the Arameri were still the Arameri. But it had escaped no one's notice that the world was changing, and this was one of the epicenters of transformation.

Luck favored me as I approached the gates, for the

guards there were men. Doubtless because so many of the foreigners hailed from lands ruled by men; a bit of unspoken diplomacy to make them more comfortable. But in Darr, men became guards if they were not handsome enough to marry well or clever enough to serve in some more respected profession, like hunting or forestry. So the pair who watched the Raringa's gates did not notice what smarter men might have, such as my Teman face but lack of Teman hair cabling or the fact that I wore plain clothing. They simply looked me over to be certain I had no obvious weapons, then nodded me onward.

Mortals notice that which stands out, so I didn't. It was simple enough to match my gait and posture to that of other foreigners heading toward this or that meeting, or aides moving in and out of the Raringa's vaulted main doors. The place was not large and had clearly been designed in days when Darr had been a simpler society and its people could just walk in and talk to their leaders. So I found the main council chamber through the biggest set of doors. And I figured out which one of the women seated on the council dais was Usein Darr by the simple fact that her presence practically filled the building.

Not that she was a large woman, even by Darren standards. She sat cross-legged on a low, unadorned divan at the farthest end of the council circle, her head above theirs as they all slouched or reclined on piles of cushioning. If not for that, she would not have been visible at all, hidden by their taller frames. Several feet of long, defiantly straight hair draped her shoulders, night-black, some of it gathered atop her head in an elaborate series of looped and knotted braids; the rest hung free. Her face was a thing of high umber planes and glacial, unadorned slopes: beautiful by any standard, though no Amn would ever have admitted it. And strong, which meant that she was beautiful by Darren standards as well.

The council dais had a gallery of curved benches around it, for the comfort of any spectators who chose to sit through the proceedings. A handful of others, mostly Darre, sat here. I chose an unoccupied bench and settled onto it, watching for a while. Usein said little but nodded now and again as the members of the council each took their turn to talk. She'd propped her hands on her knees in such a way that her elbows jutted out, which I thought was an overly aggressive posture until I belatedly noticed the swell of her belly above her folded legs: she was well into a pregnancy.

I quickly grew bored as I realized that the matter Usein and her councillors were discussing so intently was whether to clear a section of forest to allow coffee growing. Thrilling. I supposed it had been too much to hope that they would discuss their war plans in public. Since I was still tired and just a little hungover, I fell asleep.

Someone shook me an uncountable time later, pulling me from a hazy dream dominated by a woman's bulging belly. Naturally I thought I was still dreaming when I opened my eyes to find another belly hovering in front of me, and naturally I put out a hand to stroke it. I have always found pregnancy fascinating. When mortal women permit, I hover near them, listening for the moment when the child's soul ignites out of nothingness and begins to resonate with mine. The creation of souls is a mystery that we gods endlessly debate. When Nahadoth was born, his soul was fully formed even though no mother ever carried him within her body. Did the Maelstrom give it to him? But only things with souls can bestow souls, or so we have come to believe over the aeons. Does this mean It has a soul? And if so, where did Its soul come from?

All irrelevant questions, because an instant after my hand touched Usein Darr's belly, her knife touched the skin beneath my eye. I came very much awake.

"My apologies, Usein-*ennu*," I said, lifting my hand very carefully. I tried to lift my eyes, too, to focus on her, but it was the knife that dominated my attention. She had been much faster than Hymn, which I supposed was not surprising. I seemed to attract women who were good with a blade.

"Just Usein," she said in Darre. A rude thing to do to an obvious foreigner, and unnecessary, since her knife made its own silent point. "My father is in poor health, but he may live years more, despite the ill wishes of others." Her eyes narrowed. "I imagine women in Tema are no happier to have strangers pawing them, so I see no reason to excuse your behavior."

Swallowing, I finally forced my gaze upward to her face. "My apologies," I said again, also in Darre. One of her eyebrows lifted. "Would you excuse me if I said I'd been dreaming about a woman like you?"

Her lips twitched, considering a smile. "Are you a father already, little boy? You should be at home knitting blankets to warm your babies, if so."

"Not a father and never a father, actually, not that any woman would want children who took after me." (My own smile faltered as I remembered Shahar; then I pushed her out of my mind.) "Congratulations on your conception. May your delivery be swift and your daughter strong."

She shrugged, after a moment taking her knife from my skin. She did not sheathe it, however—a warning. "This babe will be what it is. Probably another son, given that my husband seems to produce nothing else." With a sigh, she put her free hand on her hip. "I noticed you during our council session, pretty boy, and came over to find out more about you. Especially as Temans don't bother coming here anymore; they've made their allegiance to the Arameri clear. So, are you a spy?"

Casting an uneasy glance at her still-naked blade, I considered several lies—then decided the truth was so outrageous that she might believe it more readily. "I'm a godling, sent by an organization of godlings based in Shadow. We think you might be trying to destroy the world. Could you, perhaps, stop?"

She did not react quite as I'd expected. Instead of gaping at me, or laughing, she gazed at me in solemn silence for a long, taut moment. I couldn't read her face at all.

Then she sheathed her knife. "Come with me."

We went to Sar-enna-nem.

Night had fallen while I napped, the moon rising high and full over the branching stone streets. I had only a few moments to glimpse this before Usein Darr and I— accompanied by two sharp-eyed women and a handsome young man who'd greeted Usein with a kiss and me with a threatening look—stepped inside the temple. One of the guardswomen was pregnant, too, though not overtly so because she was stocky and heavyset. Her child's soul had grown, though, so I knew.

The instant I crossed the threshold, I knew why Usein had brought me here. Magic and faith danced along my skin like raindrops on a pond's surface. I closed my eyes and reveled in it, soaking it in as I walked over the glimmering mosaic stones, letting my reawakened sense of the world steer my feet. It had been months since I'd last felt the world fully. Listening now, I heard songs that had last been sung before the Gods' War, echoing from Sar-enna-nem's ceiling arches. I licked my lips and tasted the spiced wine that had once been used for offerings, tinged with occasional drops of blood. I put out my hands, stroking the air of the place, and shivered as it returned the caress.

Illusions and memories; all I had left. I savored them as best I could.

There had been only a few people in the temple when we'd entered: a man in priest garb, a portly woman carrying two fretting babes, a few worshippers kneeling in a prayer area, and a few unobtrusive guards. I navigated around these and between the small marble statues that stood on plinths all about the chamber, letting resonance guide me. When I opened my eyes, the statue at which I'd stopped gazed back at me with uncharacteristic solemnity on its finely wrought features. I reached up to touch its small, cheeky face, and sighed for my lost beauty.

There was no surprise in Usein Darr's voice. "I thought so. Welcome to Darr, Lord Sieh. Though I heard you stopped involving yourself in mortal affairs after T'vril Arameri's death."

"I had, yes." I turned away from the statue of myself and put one hand on my hip, adopting the same pose. "Circumstances have forced my hand, however."

"And now you help the Arameri who once enslaved you?" She did not, to her credit, laugh.

"No. I'm not doing this for them."

"For the Dark Lord, then? Or my exalted predecessor, Yeine-*ennu*?"

I shook my head and sighed. "No, just me. And a few other godlings and mortals who would rather not see a return to the chaos of the time before the Gods' War."

"Some would call that time 'freedom.' I would think *you* would call it so, given what happened after."

I nodded slowly and sighed. This was a mistake. Glee should never have sent me on a mission like this. I wasn't going to be able to do a very good job of negotiating with Usein, because I didn't really disagree with her goals. I didn't care if the mortal realm descended back into strife and struggle. All I cared about was—

Shahar, her eyes soft and full of a tenderness I'd never expected to see as I taught her everything I knew of pleasure. Deka, still a child, blushing shyly and moving close to me whenever he could—

Distraction. A reminder. I had sworn an oath.

"I remember what your world was like then," I said softly. "I remember when Darre infants starved in their cribs because enemies burned your forests. I remember rivers with water tinted red, fields that bloomed greener and richer because the soil had soaked up so much blood. Is that really what you want to return to?"

She came over, gazing up at the statue's face rather than at me. "Were you the one who made the Walking Death?"

I twitched in surprise and sudden unease.

"It seems like the sort of disease you would create," she said with brutal softness. "Tricksy. There hasn't been an outbreak since Yeine-*ennu*'s day, but I've read the accounts. It lurks for weeks before the symptoms appear, spreading far and wide in the meantime. At its height, the victims of the disease seem more alive than ever, but their minds are dead, burned away by the fever. They walk, but only to carry death to new victims."

I could not look at her, for shame. But when she spoke again, I was surprised to hear compassion in her voice.

"No mortals should have as much power as the Arameri had when they owned you," she said. "No mortals should have as much power as they have *now*: the laws, the scriveners, their army, all their pet nobles, the wealth they've claimed from peoples destroyed or exploited. Even the history taught to our children in the White Hall schools glorifies them and denigrates everyone else. *All civilization*, every bit of it, is made to keep the Arameri strong. That is how they've survived after losing you. That is why the only solution is to destroy everything they've built. Good and bad, all of it is tainted. Only by starting fresh can we truly be free again."

At this, however, I could only smile.

"Start fresh?" I asked. I looked up at the statue of myself. Its blank eyes. I imagined them green, like my own. Like those of Shinda, Itempas's dead demon son.

"For that," I said, "you would have to go further back than the Bright. Remember what caused it, after all—the Gods' War, which was what put me and the other Enefadeh under the Arameri's control in the first place. And remember what caused that: our bickering. Our love affairs gone horribly, horribly wrong." Usein grew silent behind me, in surprise. "To really start fresh, you need to get rid of the gods, not just the Arameri. Then burn every book that mentions us. Smash every statue, including this pretty one here. Raise your children to be ignorant of the world's creation or our existence; let them come up with stories of their own to explain it all. For that matter, kill any child who even *thinks* about magic—because that is how deeply we have tainted mortalkind, Usein Darr." I turned to her and reached out. This time when I put my hand on her swollen belly, she did not draw her knife; she flinched. I smiled. "We're in your blood. Because of us, you know all the wonders and horrors of possibility. And someday, if you don't kill yourselves, if we don't kill you, you might *become* us. So how fresh of a start do you really want?"

Her jaw twitched, the muscles flexing once. I felt her fight for something—courage, maybe. Resolve. Beneath my fingers, her child shifted, pressing briefly against my hand. I felt its shiny new soul thrum in concert with my own for a moment. *His* soul, alas for her poor husband.

After a moment, Usein drew a deep breath. "You wish to know our plans."

"Among other things, yes."

She nodded. "Come, then. I'll show you."

Sar-enna-nem is a pyramid; only the topmost hall of it held prayer space and statues. The next levels down held much more interesting things.

Like masks.

We stood in a gallery of sorts. Our escort had left us at Usein's unseen signal, though her glowering husband had brought an oddly shaped stool so that she could sit. She watched while I strolled about, looking at each mask in turn. The masks lined every shelf; they were set into the walls between the shelves; they were artfully positioned on display tables in front of the shelves. I even glimpsed a few attached to the ceiling. Dozens of them, maybe hundreds, every size and color and configuration, though they had some commonalities. All of them were oval shaped, as a base. All had open eyeholes and sealed mouths. All of them were beautiful, and powerful in ways that had nothing to do with magic.

I stopped at one of the tables, gazing down at a mask that made something inside me sing in response. There, on the table, was Childhood: smooth, fat cheeks; a mischievously grinning mouth; great wide eyes; broad forehead waiting to be filled with knowledge. Subtle inlays and painting around the mouth had been applied, some of it realistic and some pure abstraction. Geometric designs and laugh lines. Somehow, it hinted that the mask's grin could have been simple joy or sadistic cruelty, or joy in cruelty. The eyes could have been alight with the pleasure of learning or aghast at all the evils mortals inflict on their young. I touched its stiff lips. Just wood and paint. And yet.

"Your artist is a master," I said.

"Artists. The art of making these masks isn't purely a Darre thing. The Mencheyev make them, too, and the Tok—and all of our lands got the seed of it from a race called the Ginij. You may remember them."

I did. It had been a standard Arameri extermination. Zhakkarn, via her many selves, had hunted down every last mortal of the race. Kurue erased all mention of them from books, scrolls, stories, and songs, attributing their accomplishments to others. And I? I had set the whole thing in motion by tricking the Ginij king into offending the Arameri so that they had a pretext to attack.

She nodded. "They called this art *dimyi*. I don't know what the word means in their tongue. We call it *dimming*." She shifted to Senmite to make the pun. The word was meaningless in itself, though its root suggested the mask's purpose: to diminish its wearer, reduce them to nothing more than the archetype that the mask represented.

And if that archetype was *Death*...I thought of Nevra and Criscina Arameri, and understood.

"It started as a joke," she continued, "but over time the word has stuck. We lost many of the Ginij techniques when they were destroyed, but I think our dimmers—the artists who make the masks—have done a good job of making up the difference."

I nodded, still staring at Childhood. "There are many of these artists?"

"Enough." She shrugged. Not wholly forthcoming, then.

"Perhaps you should call these artists *assassins* instead." I turned to look at Usein as I said this.

Usein regarded me steadily. "If I wanted to kill Arameri," she said, slowly and precisely, "I wouldn't kill just one, or even a few. And I wouldn't take my time about it."

She wasn't lying. I lowered my hands and frowned, trying to understand. How could she not be lying? "But you *can* do magic with these things." I nodded toward Childhood. "Somehow."

She lifted an eyebrow. "I don't know these people you work for, Lord Sieh. I don't know your aims. Why should I share my secrets with you?"

"We can make it worth your while."

The look she threw me was scornful. I had to admit, it had been a bit clichéd.

"There is nothing you can offer me," she said, getting to her feet with pregnant-woman awkwardness. "Nothing I want or need from anyone, god or mortal—"

"Usein."

A man's voice. I turned, startled. The gallery's open doorway framed a man, standing between the flickering torch sconces. How long had he been there? My sense of the world was fading already. I thought at first it was a trick of the light that he seemed to waver; then I realized what I was seeing: a godling, in the last stages of configuring his form for the mortal realm. But when his face had taken its final shape—

I blinked. Frowned.

He stepped farther into the light. The features he'd chosen certainly hadn't been meant to help him blend in. He was short, about my height. Brown skin, brown eyes, deep brown lips—these were the only things about him that fit any mortal mold. The rest was a jumble. Teman sharpfolds with orangey red islander hair and high, angular High Northern cheekbones. Was he an idiot? None of those things fit together. Just because we could look like anything didn't mean we *should*.

But that was not the biggest problem.

"Hail, Brother," I said uncertainly.

"Do you know me?" He stopped, slipping his hands into his pockets.

"No…" I licked my lips, confused by the niggling sense that I *did* know him, somehow. His face was unfamiliar, but that meant nothing; none of us took our true shape in the mortal realm. His stance, though, and his voice…

Then I remembered. The dream I'd had a few nights before. I'd forgotten it thanks to Shahar's betrayal. *Are you afraid?* he'd asked me.

"Yes," I amended, and he inclined his head.

Usein folded her arms. "Why are you here, Kahl?"

Kahl. The name wasn't familiar, either.

"I won't be staying long, Usein. I came only to suggest that you show Sieh the most interesting of your masks, since he's so curious." His eyes never left mine as he spoke to her.

From the corner of my eye, I saw a muscle in Usein's jaw flex. "That mask isn't complete."

"He asked you how far you were willing to go. Let him see."

She shook her head sharply. "How far *you* are willing to go, Kahl. We have nothing to do with your schemes."

"Oh, I wouldn't call it nothing, Usein. Your people were eager enough for my help when I offered it, and some of you likely guessed what that help would cost. I never deceived you. *You* were the one who chose to renege on our agreement."

There was a curious shiver to the air, and something about Kahl wavered again, not quite visibly. Some aspect of his nature? Ah, but of course; if Usein had indeed reneged on some deal with him, he would consider her a target for vengeance, too. I looked at her, wondering if she knew just how dangerous it was to cultivate a godly enemy. Her lips were tight and her face sheened lightly with sweat as she watched him, her knife hand twitching. Yes. She knew.

"You used us," she said.

"As you used me." He lifted his chin, still watching me. "But that's beside the point. Don't you want your gods to see how powerful you've become, Usein? Show him."

Usein made a frustrated sound, part fear and part annoyance. But she went to one of the wall shelves and pushed aside a book, exposing a previously hidden hole. She reached into it and pulled something. There was a low clack from somewhere behind the shelves, as of an unseen latch opening, and then the whole wall swung outward.

The power that flooded forth staggered me. I gasped and tried to stumble back from it, but I had forgotten the new size of my feet. I tripped and fell against a nearby table, which was the only thing that kept me upright. The radiating waves felt like . . . like Nahadoth at his worst. No, worse. Like all the weight of every realm pressing down, not on my flesh but on my mind.

And as I panted there, sweat dropping onto my fore-arms where they trembled on the table, I realized: I had felt this horror before.

There is a resonance, Nahadoth had said.

I managed to force my head upright. My flesh wanted to let go of itself. I fought to remain corporeal, since I wasn't sure I'd be able to re-form if I didn't. Across the room I saw that Kahl had stepped back, too, bracing his hand against the door frame; his expression was unsur-prised, grimly enduring. But elated, too.

"What...?" I tried to focus on Usein, but my sight blurred. "What is..."

She stepped into the hidden alcove that had been revealed by the opened wall. There, on a darkwood plinth, sat another mask—one that was nothing like the others. It seemed to be made of frosted glass. Its shape was more elaborate than an oval, the edges fluted and geometric. I thought it might hurt the face of whoever donned it. It was larger than a standard mask, too, bearing flanges and extensions at jawline and forehead that reminded me, somehow, of wings. Of flight. Of falling, down, down, through a vortex whose walls churned with a roar that could shatter the mortal realm—

Usein picked it up, apparently heedless of its power. Couldn't she feel it? How could she bring her child near something so terrible? There were no torches in the alcove; the thing glowed with its own soft, shifting light. Where Usein's fingers touched it, I saw a hint of move-ment, just for an instant. The glass turned to smooth brown flesh like the hand that held it, then faded back to glass.

"This mask—or so Kahl tells me—has a special power," she said, glancing at me. Then she narrowed her eyes at Kahl, who nodded in return, though he was looking decidedly uncomfortable, too. Hard to tell anything, looking at that stoic face of his. "When it's complete, if it works as predicted, it will confer godhood upon its wearer."

I stiffened. Looked at Kahl, who merely smiled at me. "That's not possible."

"Of course it is," he said. "Yeine is the proof of that."

I shook my head. "She was special. Unique. Her soul—"

"Yes, I know." His gaze was glacially cold, and I remembered the moment he'd committed himself to being my enemy. Had the same expression been on his face then? If so, I would have tried harder to earn his forgiveness. "The conjunction of many elements, all in just the right proportion and strength, all at just the right time. Of such a recipe is divinity made." He gestured toward the mask; his hand shook and grew blurry before he lowered it. "Godsblood and mortal life, magic and art and the vagaries of chance. And more, all bound into that mask, all to impress upon those who view it, an *idea*."

Usein set the thing down on the carved wooden face that served as its stand. "Yes. And the first mortal who put it on burned to death from the inside out. It took three days; she screamed the whole time. The fire was so hot that we couldn't get near enough to end her misery." She turned a hard look on Kahl. "That thing is evil."

"Merely incomplete. The raw energy of creation is neither good nor evil. But when that mask is ready, it will churn forth something new . . . and wondrous." He paused, his expression turning inward for a moment; he spoke softer, as if to himself, but I realized that his words were actually aimed at me. "I will not be a slave to fate. I will embrace it, control it. I will be what I *wish* to be."

"You're mad." Usein shook her head. "You expect us to

put this kind of power into your hands, for demons know what purpose? No. Leave this place, Kahl. We've had enough of your kind of help."

I hurt. The incomplete mask. It was like the Maelstrom: potential gone mad, creation feeding upon itself. I was not mortal enough to be immune to it. Yet that was not the sole source of my discomfort; something else beat against me like an oncoming tide, trying to drive me to my knees. The mask had heightened my god-senses, allowing me to feel it, but my flesh was only mortal, too weak to endure so much power in one place.

"What are you?" I asked Kahl in our words, between gasps. "Elontid? Imbalance..." That was the only explanation for the seesaw flux I felt from him. Resolve and sorrow, hatred and longing, ambition and loneliness. But how could there be another elontid in the world? He could not have been born during the time of my incarceration, not with Enefa dead and all gods rendered sterile for that time. And who were his parents? Itempas was the only one of the Three who could have made him, but Itempas did not mate with godlings.

Kahl smiled. To my surprise, there was no hint of cruelty in it—only that curious, resolute sorrow I'd heard in my dream.

"Enefa is dead, Sieh." His voice was soft now. "Not all her works vanished with her, but some did. *I* remembered. You will, too, eventually."

Remember what?

forget

Forget what?

Kahl staggered suddenly, bracing himself against the door and sighing. "Enough. We'll finish this later. In the meantime, a word of advice, Sieh: find Itempas. Only his

power can save you; you know this. Find him, and live for
as long as you can." When he pushed himself upright, his
teeth were a carnivore's, needle-sharp. "Then if you must
die, die like a god. At my hands, in battle."

Then he vanished. And I was alone, helpless, being
churned to pieces by the mask's power. My flesh tried,
again, to fragment; it *hurt*, the way disintegration should.
I screamed, reaching out for someone, anyone, to save
me. Nahadoth— No, I didn't want him or Yeine anywhere
near that mask, no telling what it would do to them. But I
was so afraid. I did not want to die, not yet.

The world twisted around me. I slid through it, gasping—

Rough hands grasped me, hauled me over onto my
back. Above me, Ahad's face. Not Nahadoth but close
enough. He was frowning, examining me with hands and
other senses, actually looking concerned.

"You care," I said dizzily, and stopped thinking for a
while.

12

Wʜᴇɴ I ᴡᴏᴋᴇ, I told Ahad what I had seen in Darr, and he got a very odd look on his face. "That was not at all what we suspected," he muttered to himself. He looked over at Glee, who stood by the window, her hands clasped behind her back, as she gazed out over the quiet streets. It was nearly dawn in this part of the world. The end of the working day for the Arms of Night.

"Call the others," she said. "We'll meet tomorrow night."

So Ahad dismissed me for the day, ordering the servants to give me food and money and new clothing, because the old set no longer fit well. I had aged again, you see—perhaps five years this time, passing through my final growth spurt in the process. I was two inches taller and even thinner than before, unpleasantly close to skeletal. My body had reconfigured its existing substance to forge my new shape, and I hadn't had much substance to go around. I was well into my twenties now, with no hint of childhood remaining. Nothing but human left.

I went back to Hymn's house. Her family ran an inn, after all, and I had money now, so it made sense. Hymn was relieved to see me, though she puzzled over my changed appearance and pretended to be annoyed. Her parents were not at all pleased, but I promised to perform no impossible feats on their premises, which was easy because I couldn't. They put me in the attic room.

There, I ate the entire basket of food Ahad's servants had packed for me. I was still hungry when the food was gone—though the basket had been generously packed—but had sated myself enough that I could attend to other needs. So I curled up on the bed, which was hard but clean, and watched the sun rise beyond my lone window. Eventually I considered the topic of death.

I could kill myself now, probably. This was not normally an easy thing for any god to do, as we are remarkably resilient beings. Even willing ourselves into nonexistence did not work for long; eventually we would forget that we were supposed to be dead and start thinking again. Yeine could kill me, but I would never ask it of her. Some of my siblings, and Naha, could and would do it, because they understood that sometimes life is too much to bear. But I did not need them anymore. The past two nights' events had verified what I'd already suspected: those things that had once merely weakened me before could kill me now. So if I could steel myself to the pain of it, I could die whenever I wished simply by continuing to contemplate antithetical thoughts until I became an old man, and then a corpse.

And perhaps it was even simpler than that. I needed to eat and drink and pass waste now. That meant I could starve and thirst, and that my intestines and other organs were actually necessary. If I damaged them, they might not grow back.

What would be the most exciting way to commit suicide?

Because I did not want to die an old man. Kahl had gotten that much right. If I had to die, I would die as myself—as Sieh, the Trickster, if not the child. I had blazed bright in my life. What was wrong with blazing in death, too?

Before I reached middle age, I decided. Surely I could think of something interesting by then.

On that heartening note, I finally slept.

I stood on a cliff outside the city, gazing upon the wonder that was Sky-in-Shadow and the looming, spreading green of the World Tree.

"Hello, Brother."

I turned, blinking, though I was not really surprised. When the first mortal creatures grew the first brains that did more than pump hearts and think of meat, my brother Nsana had found fulfillment in the random, spitting interstices of their sleeping thoughts. He had been a wanderer before that, my closest playmate, wild and free like me. But sad, somehow. Empty. Until the dreams of mortals filled his soul.

I smiled at him, understanding at last the sorrow he must have felt in those long empty years before the settling of his nature.

"So this is the proof of it," I said. I had pockets for the moment, so I slipped my hands into them. My voice was higher pitched; I was a boy again. In dreams, at least, I was still myself.

Nsana smiled, strolling toward me along a path of flowers that stirred without wind. For a moment his truest shape flickered before me: faceless, the color of glass, reflecting our surroundings through the distorting lenses of limbs and belly and the gentle featureless curve of his face. Then he filled in with detail and colors, though not those of a mortal. He did nothing like mortals if he could help it. So he had chosen skin like fine fabric, unbleached damask in swirling raised patterns, with hair like the darkest of red wine frozen in midsplash. His irises were the banded amber of polished, petrified wood—beautiful, but unnerving, like the eyes of a serpent.

"The proof of what?" he asked, stopping before me. His voice was light, teasing, as if it had been only a day since we'd seen each other and not an aeon.

"My mortality," I said. "I wouldn't have seen you otherwise." I smiled, but I knew he would hear the truth in my voice. He had abandoned me for mortalkind, after all. I'd gotten over it; I was a big boy. But I would not pretend it hadn't happened.

Nsana let out a little sigh and walked past me, stopping on the edge of a cliff. "Gods can dream, too, Sieh. You could have found me here anytime."

"I hate dreaming." I scuffed the ground with a foot.

"I know." He put his hands on his hips, his expression frankly admiring as he gazed over the dreamscape I'd created. This one was not merely a memory, as my dream of the gods' realm had been. "A shame, too. You do it so well."

"I don't *do* anything. It's a dream."

"Of course you do. It comes from you, after all. All of this"—he gestured expansively around us, and the dreamscape rippled with the passage of his hands—"is you. Even the fact that you let me come here is your doing, because you certainly never allowed it before." He lowered his arms and looked at me. "Not even during the years you spent as an Arameri slave."

I sighed, tired, even asleep. "I don't want to think right now, Nsa. Please."

"You never want to think, you silly boy." Nsana came over, wrapping an arm around my shoulders and pulling me close. I put up a token resistance, but he knew it was token, and after a moment I sighed and let my head rest on his chest. Then it was not his chest—it was his shoulder—because suddenly I was taller than him and not a child anymore. When I lifted my head in surprise, Nsana let out a long sigh and cupped my face in his hands so that he could kiss me. He did not share himself with me that way because there was no point; I already stood encompassed within him, and he within me. But I did remember other kisses, and other existences, when innocence and dreams had been two halves of the same coin. Back then, I'd thought we would spend the rest of eternity together.

The dreamscape changed around us. When we parted, Nsana sighed, the fabric patterns of his face shifting into new lines. They hinted at words, but meant nothing.

"You're not a child anymore, Sieh," he said. "Time to grow up now."

We stood on the streets of the First City. Everything that mortals will or might become is foreshadowed in the gods' realm, where time is an accessory rather than a given, and the essences of the Three mingle in a different balance depending on their whims and moods. Because Itempas had been banished and diminished, only the barest remnant of his order held sway now. The city, which had been recognizable just a few years before, was only barely so now, and it shifted every few moments in some cycle we could not fathom. Or perhaps that was because this was a dream? With Nsana, there was no telling.

So he and I walked along cobblestoned streets that turned into smoothly paved sidewalks, stepping onto moving metal pathways now and again as they grew from the cobblestones and then melted away, as if tired. Pathways of mushrooms grew and withered in our wake. Each block, some of which were circular, held squat buildings of painted wood, and stately domes of hewn marble, and the occasional thatched hut. Curious, I peered into one of these buildings through its slanted window. It was dim, full of hulking shapes too distorted and uncomfortable-looking to be furniture, its walls decorated with blank paintings. Something within moved toward the window, and I backed up quickly. I wasn't a god anymore. Had to be careful.

We were shadowed now and again by great towers of glass and steel that floated, cloudlike, a few meters off the ground. One of them followed us for two blocks, like a lonely puppy, before it finally turned with a foggy groan and drifted down another avenue. No one walked with us, though we felt the presence of others of our brethren, some watching, some uncaring. The City attracted them because it was beautiful, but I could not understand how they endured it. What was a city without inhabitants? It was like life without breathing, or friendship without love; what was the point?

But there was something in the distance that caught my attention, and Nsana's, too. Deep in the City's heart, taller and more still than the floating skyscrapers: a smooth, shining white tower without windows or doors. Even amid the jumbled, clashing architecture of that place, it was clear: this tower did not belong.

I stopped and frowned up at it, as a mushroom taller than Nsa spread its ribbed canopy over our heads. "What is that?"

Nsana willed us closer, folding the city until we stood at the tower's feet. This confirmed there were no doors, and I curled my lip as I realized the thing was made of daystone. A little piece of Sky amid the dreams of gods: an abomination.

"You have brought this here," said Nsana.

"The hells I did."

"Who else would have, Sieh? I touch the mortal realm only through its dreams, and it does not touch me. It has never marked me."

I threw a sharp look at him. "Marked? Is that how you think of me?"

"Of course, Sieh. You *are*." I stared at him, wondering whether to feel hurt or angry or something else entirely, and Nsana sighed. "As I am marked by your abandonment. As we are all marked by the War. Did you think the horrors you've endured would simply slough away when you became a free god? They have become part of you." But before I could muster a furious retort, Nsana frowned up at the tower again. "There is more to this, though, than just bad experiences."

"What?"

Nsana reached out, laying a hand on the surface of the white tower. It glowed like Sky at night beneath his touch, becoming translucent—and within the tower, suddenly, I could see the shadow of some vast, twisting shape. It filled the tower, brown and indistinct, like ordure. Or a cancer.

"There's a secret here," said Nsana.

"What, in my dreams?"

"In your soul." He looked at me, thoughtful. "It must be old, to have grown so powerful. Important."

I shook my head, but even as I did so, I doubted.

"My secrets are small, silly things," I said, trying to ignore that worm of doubt. "I kept the bones of the Arameri I killed in a stash beneath the family head's bedroom. I piss in the punch bowl at weddings. I change directions on maps so they make no sense. I stole some of Nahadoth's hair once, just to see if I could, and it almost ate me alive—"

He looked hard at me. "You have childish secrets and adult ones, Sieh, because you have never been as simple as you claim or wish to be. And this one—" He slapped the tower, making a sound that echoed from the empty streets around us. "This one is something you've kept even from yourself."

I laughed, but it was uneasy. "I can't keep a secret from myself. That doesn't make any sense."

"When have you ever made sense? It's something you've forgotten."

"But I—"

forget

I faltered, silent. It was cold all of a sudden. I began shivering, though Nsana—who wore only his hair—was fine. But his eyes had narrowed suddenly, and abruptly I realized he'd heard that odd little burp of my thoughts.

"That was Enefa's voice," he said.

"I don't..." But it had been. It had always been Mother whispering in my soul, nudging my thoughts away from this place when they got too close. Her voice: *forget*.

"Something you've forgotten," Nsana said softly, "but perhaps not by your own will."

I frowned, torn between confusion and alarm and fear. And above us, in the white tower, the dark thing shifted with a low rumbling groan. There was the faintest sound of stone shifting, and when I looked up at the tower, I spied a series of fine, barely noticeable cracks in its day-stone surface.

Something I had forgotten. Something Enefa had *made*

me forget. But Enefa was gone now, and whatever she had done to me was beginning to wear off.

"Gods and mortals and demons in between." I rubbed my face. "I don't want to deal with this, Nsa. My life is hard enough right now."

Nsana sighed, and his sigh transformed the City into a playground of delights and horrors. A high, steep slide ended in a pit of chewing, flensing, disembodied teeth. The chains on a nearby swing set were wet with oil and blood. I could not see the trap in the seesaw, but I was certain there was one. It was too innocent-looking—like me, when I am up to something.

"Time for you to grow up," he said again. "You ran away from me rather than do it before. Now you have no choice."

"I had no choice before!" I rounded on him. "Growing old will kill me!"

"I didn't say grow old, you fool. I said grow *up*." Nsana leaned close, his breath redolent of honey and poisonous flowers. "Just because you're a child doesn't mean you have to be immature, for the Maelstrom's sake! I have known you long and well, my brother, and there's another secret you hide from yourself, only you do a terrible job so everyone knows: you're lonely. You're always lonely, even though you've left more lovers in your wake than you can count. You never want what you have, only what you can't!"

"That's not—"

He cut me off ruthlessly. "You loved me before I learned my nature. While I needed you. Then when I found my strength and became whole, when I no longer *needed* you but still *wanted* you—" He paused suddenly, his jaw flexing as he choked back words too painful to speak. I stared back at him, rendered speechless. Had he really felt this way, all this time? Was that how he'd seen it? I had always thought *he* had left *me*. I shook my head in wonder, in denial.

"You cannot be one of the Three," he whispered. I flinched. "It's long past time you accepted that. You want someone you can never leave behind. But *think*, Sieh. Not even the Three are like that. Itempas betrayed all of us and himself. Enefa grew selfish, and Nahadoth has always been fickle. This new one, Yeine, she'll break your heart, too. Because you want something that she can never give you. You want perfection."

"Not perfection," I blurted, and then felt ill as I realized I had confirmed everything else he'd said. "Not... perfection. Just..." I licked my lips, ran my hands through my hair. "I want someone who is *mine*. I...I don't even know..." I sighed. "The Three, Nsana, they are *the Three*. Three facets of the same diamond, whole even when separate. No matter how far apart they drift, they always, always, come back together eventually. That closeness..."

It was what Shahar had with Deka, I realized: a closeness that few outsiders would ever comprehend or penetrate. More than blood-deep—soul-deep. She hadn't seen him for half her life and she'd still betrayed me for him.

What would it be like to have that kind of love for myself?

I wanted it, yes. Gods, yes. And I did not really want it from Yeine or Nahadoth or Itempas, because they had each other and it would have been wrong to interfere with that. But I wanted something like it.

Nsana sighed. Here in my dream, he was supreme; he could know my every thought and whim if he wanted, without even trying. So of course he knew now that he had never been enough for me.

"I'm sorry," I said, very softly.

"You certainly are." Looking sour, Nsana turned away for a moment, contemplating his own thoughts. Then he sighed and faced me again.

"Fine," he said. "You need help, and I'm not so churlish that I'd ignore your need. So I'll try to find out more about this secret of yours. At the rate you're going, you'll be dead before you figure it out."

I lowered my eyes. "Thank you."

"Don't thank me, Sieh." He gestured, and I followed this movement to see a little patch of flowers on one side of the playground. Amid dozens of black daisies that bobbed and swayed in the cool breeze, a single white-petaled flower stood utterly still. It was not a daisy. I had seen such a flower before: an altarskirt rose, one of a rare variety bred in High North. The white tower of my secret, repeating itself across theme and form.

"This secret will hurt when it is finally revealed," he said.

I nodded slowly, my eyes on that single frightening flower. "Yes. I can see that."

The hand on my shoulder caught me by surprise, and I turned to see that Nsana's mood had changed again: he was no longer exasperated with me, but something closer to pitying. "So many troubles," he said. "Impending death, our parents' madness, and I see someone has broken your heart recently, too."

I looked away at this. "It's no one. Just a mortal."

"Love levels the ground between us and them. When they break our hearts, it hurts the same as if the deed were done by one of our own." He cupped the back of my head, ruffling my hair companionably, and I smiled weakly and tried not to show how much I really wanted a kiss instead. "Ah, my brother. Do stop being stupid, will you?"

"Nsana, I—"

He put a finger over my lips, and I fell silent.

"Hush," he murmured, then leaned close. I closed my eyes, waiting for the touch of his lips, but they came where I had not been expecting them: on my forehead. When I blinked at him, he smiled, and it was full of sorrow.

"I'm a god, not a stone," he said. I flushed in shame. He stroked my cheek. "But I will love you always, Sieh."

I woke in the dark and cried myself back to sleep. If I dreamt again before morning, I did not remember it. Nsa was kind like that.

My hair had grown again, though not as much as before. Only a couple of feet. Nails, too, this time; the longest was four inches, jagged and beginning to curl. I begged scissors from Hymn and chopped off both as best I could. I had to get Hymn's father to teach me how to shave. This so amused him that he forgot to be afraid of me for a few minutes, and we actually shared a laugh when I cut myself and yelled out a very bad word. Then he started to worry that I would cut myself and blow up the house someday. We don't read minds, but some things are easy for anyone to guess. I excused myself then and went off to work.

I offended the Arms of Night's housemistress immediately by coming in through the main door. She took me back out and showed me the servants' door, an unobtrusive entrance at the house's side, leading to its basement level. It was a better door, quite frankly; I have always preferred back entrances. Good for sneaking. But my pride was stung enough that I complained, anyway. "What, I'm not good enough to come in the front?"

"Not if you're not paying," she snapped.

Inside, another servant greeted me and let me know that Ahad had left instructions in case of my arrival. So I followed him through the basement into what appeared to be a rather mundane meeting room. There were stiff-backed chairs that looked as though they had absorbed years' worth of boredom, and a wide, square table on which sat an untouched platter of meats and fruits. I barely noticed all this, however, for I had stopped, my blood going cold as I registered who sat at the room's wide table with Ahad. Nemmer.

And Kitr. And Eyem-sutah. And Glee, the only mortal. And, of all the insanities, Lil.

Five of my siblings, sitting about a meeting table as though they had never spun through the vortices of the outermost cosmos as laughing sparkles. Three of the five hated me. The fourth might; no way of knowing with Eyem-sutah. The fifth had tried to eat me more than once. She would very likely try again, now that I was mortal.

If there's anything edible left when the others get done with me, that is. I set my jaw to hide my fear, which probably telegraphed it clearly.

"About time," said Ahad. He nodded to the servant, who closed the door to leave us alone. "Please, Sieh, sit down."

I did not move, hating him more than ever. I should have known better than to trust him.

With a sigh of mild annoyance, Ahad added, "None of us are stupid, Sieh. Harming you means incurring Yeine's and Nahadoth's displeasure. Do you honestly think we would do that?"

"I don't know, Ahad," said Kitr, who was smiling viciously at me. "I might."

Ahad rolled his eyes. "You won't, so be silent. Sieh, sit *down*. We have business to discuss."

I was so startled by Ahad's shutdown of Kitr that I forgot my fear. Kitr, too, looked more astonished than affronted. Any fool could tell that Ahad was the youngest of us, and inexperience meant weakness among our kind. He *was* weak, lacking the crucial means of making himself stronger. Yet there was no hint of fear in his eyes as he met her glare, and to my amazement—and everyone else's, to judge by their expressions—Kitr said nothing in reply.

Feeling vaguely unimportant in the wake of this, I came to the table and sat down.

"So what the hells is this?" I asked, choosing a chair with no one on either side of me. "The weekly meeting of the Godlings' Auxiliary, Lower Shadow Chapter?"

They all glowered. Except Lil, who laughed. Good old Lil. I had always liked her, when she wasn't asking for my limbs as snacks. She leaned forward. "We are *conspiring*," she said. Her raspy voice was filled with such childlike glee that I grinned back.

"This is about Darr, then." I looked at Ahad, wondering if he had told them about the mask already.

"This is about many things," he replied. He alone had a comfortable chair; someone had carted in the big leather chair from his office. "All of which may fit into a larger picture."

"Not just the pieces you've discovered." Nemmer smiled sweetly. "Isn't that why you contacted me, Brother? You're turning mortal, and it's making you pay attention to more than your own ass for a change. But I thought you were staying in Sky. Did the Arameri throw you out?"

Kitr laughed hard enough to make the hairs on the back of my neck bristle. "Gods, Ahad, you said he was powerless, but I never dreamt it would be this bad. You're *mortal*, Sieh. What good can you do in all this? Nothing but run to Daddy and Mommy—who aren't here now to protect you." Her eyes fixed on me, her smile fading, and I knew she was remembering the War. I was remembering it, too. Beneath the table, my hands clenched into fists and I wished I had my claws.

Eyem-sutah, who had not fought because he'd loved a mortal and had nearly killed himself protecting her, let out a long, weary sigh. "Please," he said. "Please. This helps nothing."

"Indeed, it does not," said Ahad, looking at all of us with contempt. "So if we are agreed that no one is a child here, not even the one who should be, can we then please focus on events of *this* millennium?"

"I don't like your tone—" began Kitr, but then to my greater surprise, Glee cut her off.

"I have limited time," she said. She seemed so completely at ease in a room full of godlings that I wondered again if she might be Arameri. It was far back in her lineage if so; she looked to be pure-blooded Maroneh.

To my surprise, all my siblings fell silent at her words, looking at her with a combination of consternation and unease. This made me even more curious—so Ahad was not the only one who deferred to her?—but that curiosity would have to remain unsatisfied for the moment.

"All right, then," I said, addressing Ahad because he seemed to be at least trying to stay focused. "Who's going to go take that mask and destroy it?"

"No one." Ahad steepled his fingers.

"Excuse me?" Kitr spoke before I could. "Based on

what you've told us, Ahad, nothing so powerful should be left in mortal hands."

"And what better hands are there for it?" He looked around the table, and I flinched as I realized what he meant. Nemmer, too, sighed and sat back. "One of us? Nahadoth? Yeine?"

"It would make more sense—" Kitr began.

"No," said Nemmer. "No. Remember what happened the last time a god got hold of a powerful mortal weapon." At this, Eyem-sutah, who had chosen to resemble an Amn, went pale.

Kitr's face tightened. "You don't know that this mask is even dangerous to us. It hurt *him*." She jabbed a thumb at me, her lip curling. "But harsh language could hurt him now."

"It hurt Kahl, too," I said, scowling. "The thing is broken, incomplete. Whatever it's supposed to do, it's doing it wrong. But as powerful as it is now, I see no reason why we should wait for the mortals to *complete* it before we act." I glared at Ahad, and at Glee, too. "You know what mortals are capable of."

"Yes, the same things as gods, on a smaller scale," Ahad replied, his voice bland.

Glee glanced at him, but I could not read the look on her face before she turned to me. "There is more to this than you know."

"So tell me!" Ahad I was used to. He kept secrets like I kept toys, and he did it mostly out of spite. Glee hadn't seemed the type, however.

"You aren't a child anymore, Sieh. You should learn patience," Ahad drawled. His smirk faded. "But you're right; an explanation may be in order since you're new, both to our organization and to Shadow. This group's original purpose was merely to police our own behavior and prevent another Interdiction. To a degree, that is still our purpose. Things changed, however, when a few mortals used demons' blood to express their displeasure at our arrival." He sighed, crossing his legs and leaning back in his chair. "This was a few years back. You may recall the time."

Of course I did. A handful of my siblings had been killed, and Nahadoth had come very close to turning Sky-in-Shadow into a large smoking crater. "Hard to forget."

He nodded. "This group had already organized in order to protect *them* from *us*. After that incident, it became clear that we should also work to protect *us* from *them* as well."

"That's stupid," I said, frowning around the table. Glee lifted an eyebrow, and I grimaced but ignored her. "The demon was taken care of; the menace has ended. What is there to fear? Any one of you could smash this city, melt down the surrounding mountains, make the Eyeglass's water burn—"

"No," said Eyem-sutah. "We cannot. If we do, Yeine will revoke our right to dwell here. You don't understand, Sieh; you didn't *want* to come back after your incarceration ended. I don't blame you, given circumstances. But would you truly prefer never to visit the mortal realm again?"

"That's beside the—"

Eyem-sutah shook his head and leaned forward, cutting me off. "Tell me you have never nestled into some mortal woman's breast to be held, Sieh, and loved unconditionally. Or felt adoration when some mortal man tousles your hair. Tell me they mean nothing to you. Look into my eyes and say it, and I will believe you."

I could have done it. I am a trickster. I can look into

anyone's eyes and say anything I need to say and be completely believable in the process. Only Nahadoth, who knows me better than any other, and Itempas, who always knows falsehood, have ever been able to catch me out when I truly want to lie.

But even tricksters are not without honor, as Eyemsutah well knew. He was right, and it would have been wrong of me not to acknowledge that. So I lowered my eyes, and he sat back.

"Out of such debate was this organization born," Ahad said, with only a hint of dryness. "Not all godlings have chosen to participate, but most adhere to the rules we set, out of mutual self-interest." He shrugged. "Those who do not, we deal with."

I propped my chin on my fist, pretending boredom to hide the unease Eyem-sutah's questions had left in me. "Fine. But how'd you end up in charge? You're an infant."

Ahad smiled by curling his upper lip. "No one else wanted the task, after Madding died. Lately, however, our structure has changed. Now I'm merely the organizer, at least until such time as our actual leader chooses to take a more active role."

"And your leader is...?" Not that I thought he'd tell me.

"Does it matter?"

I considered. "I guess not. But this is all awfully... *mortal*, don't you think?" I gestured around at the meeting room, the table and chairs, the tray of bland finger foods. (I restrained my urge to reach for a piece of cheese, out of pride.) "Why not come up with some sinister-sounding name, too, if you're going to go this far? 'The Organization' or something original like that. Whatever, if we're going to act like a bunch of mortals."

"We have no need of a name." Ahad shrugged, then glanced pointedly at Glee. "And our group consists of more than just gods, which requires some concession to mortal convention." Glee inclined her head to him in silent thanks. "In any case, we dwell in the mortal realm. Should we not at least attempt to think like mortals from time to time, in order to anticipate our adversaries more easily?"

"And then do nothing when we actually discover a threat?" Kitr clenched a fist on the table.

Ahad's expression went Arameri-neutral. "What, precisely, would you have us do, Kitr? Go and take this mask? We don't know who created it, or how; they could simply make another. We don't know what it does. Sieh said this Kahl seemed to be using the Darre to create it. Doesn't that imply it's something mortals can touch but that might strike a god dead?"

I frowned, unwilling to concede the point. "We have to do *something*. The thing is dangerous."

"Very well. Shall we capture Usein Darr, torture her to learn her secrets? We could threaten to give her unborn child to Lil, perhaps." Lil, who had been staring at the plate of food, smiled and said "Mmmmm" without taking her eyes away from it. "Or shall we dispense with subtlety and smite Darr with fire and pestilence and erasure, until its cities are in ruins and its people forgotten? Does that sound at all familiar to you, *Enefadeh*?"

Every voluntary muscle in my body locked in fury. En pulsed once, questioningly, against my chest—did I want it to kill someone again? It was still tired from my rage at Remath, but it would try.

That, and that alone, calmed me. I put my hand over En, stroking it through my shirt. No more killing now, but it was a good little star for wanting to help. With another pulse of pleasure, En cooled back into sleep.

"We are not the Arameri," Ahad said, speaking softly, though his eyes stayed on me. Demanding my acknowledgment. "We are not Itempas. We cannot repeat the mistakes of the past. Again and again our kind have tried to dominate mortalkind and have harmed ourselves in the doing. This time, if we choose to dwell among mortals, then we must share the risks of mortality. We must *live* in this world, not merely visit it. Do you understand?"

Of course I did. *Mortals are as much Enefa's creations as we ourselves.* I had argued this with my fellow prisoners a century ago as we contemplated using a mortal girl's life to achieve our freedom. We'd done it anyway, and the plan had been successful—more in spite of our efforts than because of them—but I had felt the guilt keenly back then. And the fear: for if we did as Itempas and his pet Arameri had done, did we not risk becoming just like them?

"I understand," I said, very softly.

Ahad watched me a moment longer, then nodded.

Glee sighed. "I'm more concerned about this Kahl than any mortal magic. No godling by that name is on any city registry. What do the rest of you know of him?" She looked around the table.

No one responded. Kitr and Nemmer looked at each other, and at Eyem-sutah, who shrugged. Then they all looked at me. My mouth fell open. "*None* of you knows him?"

"We thought you would," Eyem-sutah said. "You're the only one who was around when all of us were born."

"No." I chewed my lip in consternation. "I could swear I've heard the name before, but..." The memory danced on the edge of my consciousness, closer than ever before.

forget, whispered Enefa's voice. I sighed in frustration.

"He's elontid," I said, staring at my own clenched fist. "I'm sure of that. And he's young—I think. Maybe a little older than the War." But Madding had been the last godling born before the War. Even before him, Enefa had made few children in the last aeon or so—certainly no elontid. She had lost the heart for childbearing after seeing so many of her sons and daughters murdered in the battle against the demons.

Would that you were a true child, she would say to me sometimes while stroking my hair. I lived for such moments. She was not much given to affection. *Would that you could stay with me forever.*

But I can, I would always point out, and the look in her eyes would turn inward and sad in a way that I did not understand. *I will never grow old, never grow up. I can be your little boy forever.*

Would that this were true, she would say.

I blinked, frowning. I had forgotten that conversation. What had she meant by—

"Elontid," said Ahad, almost to himself. "The ones borne of god and godling, or Nahadoth and Itempas." He turned a speculative look on Lil. She had begun to stroke one of the strawberries on the platter, her bony, jagged-nailed finger trailing back and forth over its curve in a way that would have been sensual in anyone else. She finally looked away from the platter but kept fingering the strawberry.

"I do not know a Kahl," she said, and smiled. "But we do not always wish to be known."

Glee frowned. "What?"

Lil shrugged. "We elontid are feared by mortals and gods alike. Not without reason." She threw me a glance that was pure lasciviousness. "You smell delicious now, Sieh."

I flushed and deliberately took something off the platter. Cucumber slathered with maash paste and comry eggs. I made a show of stuffing it into my mouth and swallowing it barely chewed. She pouted; I ignored her and turned to Glee.

"What Lil means," I said, "is that the elontid are different. They aren't quite godlings, aren't quite gods. They're"—I thought a moment—"more like the Maelstrom than the rest of us. They flux and wane, create and devour, each in their own way. It makes them…hard to grasp." I glanced at Lil, and when I did, she scooped up a cucumber slice and downed it in a blur, then stuck her tongue out at me. I laughed in spite of myself. "If any god could conceal his presence in the world, it would be an elontid."

Glee tapped a finger on the table, thoughtful. "Could they hide even from the Three?"

"No. Not if they united. But the Three have had their own problems to worry about for some time now. They are incomplete." I blinked then, as something new occurred to me. "And the Three could be *why* none of us remembers this Kahl. Enefa, I mean. She might have made all of us—"

forget

Shut up, Mother, I thought irritably.

"—forget."

"Why would she do that?" Eyem-sutah looked around, his eyes widening. "That makes no sense."

"No," said Nemmer softly. She met my eyes, and I nodded. She was one of the older ones among us—nowhere near my age, but she had been around to see the war against the demons. She knew the many strange configurations that could result among the children of the Three. "It makes perfect sense. Enefa—" She grimaced. "She had no problem killing us. And she would do it, if any of her children were a threat to the rest. After the demons, she wasn't willing to take more risks. But if a child *could* survive without harming others, and if that child's survival depended for some reason on others not knowing of its existence…" She shook her head. "It's possible. She might have even created some new realm to house him, apart from the rest of us. And when she died, she took the knowledge of that child with her."

I thought of Kahl's intimation. *Enefa is dead now. I remembered.* Nemmer's theory fit, but for one thing.

"Where's this elontid's other parent? Most of us wouldn't just leave a child to rot in some heaven or hell forever. New life among our kind is too precious."

"It has to be a godling," Ahad mused. "If it were Itempas or Nahadoth, this Kahl would just be"—his mouth began to shape the word *normal*, but then Lil turned a glare on him to make Itempas proud, and he amended himself—"niwwah, like the rest of you."

"I am mnasat," Kitr snapped, glaring herself.

"Whatever," Ahad replied, and I was suddenly glad the platter's paring knife was out of Kitr's reach. Hopefully Ahad would find his nature soon; he wasn't going to last long among us otherwise.

"Many godlings died in the War," said Glee, and we all sobered as we realized what she meant.

"Gods," murmured Kitr, looking horrified. "To be raised in exile, forgotten, orphaned…Did this Kahl even know how to find us? How long was he alone? I can't imagine it."

I could. The universe had been much emptier once. There had been no word for *loneliness* back then, in my true childhood, but all three of my parents—Nahadoth in particular—had worked hard to protect me from it. If Kahl had lacked the same... I could not help but pity him.

"This complicates things to an unpleasant degree," said Ahad, sighing and rubbing his eyes. I felt the same. "From what you reported, Sieh, it sounds as though the High Northers and Kahl are working at cross-purposes. He's using their dimmers to create a mask that turns mortals into gods, for some reason I can't fathom. And they are using the same art to create masks that somehow kill Arameri."

"Or else *Kahl* has been killing the Arameri, using the masks, and doing it to cast suspicion on the northerners," I said, remembering the dream conversation I'd had with him. *I have already begun*, he had said then. It was the oldest of tricks, to sow dissension between groups that had common interests. Good for deflecting attention from greater mischief, too. I contemplated it more and scowled. "And there's another thing. The Arameri destroy any land that injures them—which guarantees that their enemies will strike decisively, if and when they ever do." I thought of Usein Darr, proudly stating that she would never kill just *a few* Arameri. "The High Northers wouldn't bother with assassins and a lowblood here, a highblood there. They'd bring an army and try to destroy the whole family at once."

"There's no evidence that they're building an army at all," said Nemmer.

There was, but it was subtle. I thought of Usein Darr's pregnancy and that of her guardswoman, and the woman in Sar-enna-nem who'd had two babies with her, both too young to be eating solid food yet. I thought of the children

I'd seen there—belligerent, xenophobic, barely multilingual, and every one of them four or five years old at the most. Darr was famous for its contraceptive arts. Even before scrivening, the women there had long ago learned to time childbearing to suit their constant raiding and intertribal wars. Their war crop, they called it, making a joke of other lands' reliance on agriculture. In the years preceding a war, every woman under thirty tried her best to make a child or two. The warriors would nurse the babes for a few days, then hand them over to the nonwarriors in the family—who, having also recently borne children, would simply nurse two or three, until all the children could be weaned and handed over to grandmothers or menfolk. Thus the warriors could go off to fight knowing that their replacements were growing up safe, should they fall in battle.

It was a bad sign to see so many Darre breeding. It was a worse sign that the children hated foreigners and weren't even trying to ape Senmite customs. They certainly weren't preparing those children for *peace*.

"Even if they were building an army," said Ahad, "there would be no reason for us to interfere. What mortals do to each other is their business. Our concern lies solely with this godling Kahl and the strange mask Sieh saw."

At this, Glee's already-grim look grew positively forbidding. "So you will do nothing if war breaks out?"

"Mortals have warred with one another since their creation," Eyem-sutah said with a soft sigh. "The best we can do is try to prevent it . . . and protect the ones we love, if we fail. It is their nature."

"Because it is *our* nature," snapped Nemmer. "And because of us, they now have magic as a weapon for their warring. They'll use soldiers and swords like before the

Gods' War, but also scriveners and these masks, and demons know what else. Do you have any idea how many could die?"

It would be worse than that, I knew. Most of mortal-kind had no idea what war really meant anymore. They could not imagine the famine and rapine and disease, not on such a scale. Oh, they feared it of old, and the memory of the ultimate war—*our* War—had burned itself into the souls of every race. But that would not stop them from unleashing its full fury again and learning too late what they had done.

"This will do more than kill," I murmured. "These people have forgotten what humanity can be like at its worst. Rediscovering this will shock them; it will wound their souls. I have seen it happen before, here and on other worlds." I met Ahad's eyes, and he frowned, just a little, at the look on my face. "They'll burn their histories and slaughter their artists. They'll enslave their women and devour their children, and they'll do it in the gods' names. Shahar was right; the end of the Arameri means the end of the Bright."

Ahad spoke with brutal softness. "It will be worse if we get involved."

He was right. I hated him more than ever for that.

In the silence that fell, Glee sighed. "I've stayed too long." She rose to leave. "Keep me informed of anything else you discover or decide."

I waited for one of the gods at the table to chastise her for giving them orders. Then I realized none of them were planning to. Lil had begun to lean toward the platter, her eyes gleaming. Kitr had taken the small paring knife and was spinning it on her fingertip, an old habit that meant she was thinking. Nemmer rose to leave as well, nodding casually to Ahad, and suddenly I couldn't stand it any-more. I shoved back my chair and marched around the table and got to the door just as Glee started to open it. I slammed it shut.

"Who in the suppurating bright hells are you?" I demanded.

Ahad groaned. "Sieh, gods damn it—"

"No, I need to know this. I swore I'd never take orders from a mortal again." I glared up at Glee, who didn't look nearly as alarmed by my tantrum as I wanted her to be. What ignominy; I couldn't even make mortals fear me anymore. "This doesn't make sense! Why are all of you *listening* to her?"

The woman lifted an eyebrow, then let out a long, heavy sigh. "My full name is Glee Shoth. I speak for, and assist, Itempas."

The words struck me like a slap—as did the name, and the odd familiarity of her manner, and her Maroneh heri-tage, and the way my siblings all seemed uneasy in her presence. I should have seen it at once. Kitr was right; I really was losing my touch.

"You're his daughter." I whispered it. I could barely make my mouth form the words. Glee Shoth—daughter of Oree Shoth, the first and, as far as I knew, only mortal friend Itempas had ever had. Clearly they had gone beyond friendship. "His...dear gods, his *demon* daughter."

Glee did not smile, but her eyes warmed in amusement—and now that I knew, all those tiny niggling familiarities were as obvious as slaps to the face. She didn't look like him; in features, she'd taken more after her mother. But her mannerisms, the air of stillness that she wore like a cloak...It was all there, as plain as the risen sun.

Then I registered the implications of her existence. A demon. A demon *made by Itempas*—he who had declared the demons forbidden in the first place and led the hunt to wipe them out. A daughter, allied to him, *helping* him.

I considered what it meant, that he loved her.

I considered his reconciliation with Yeine.

I considered the terms of his imprisonment.

"It's him," I whispered. I nearly staggered, and would have if I had not leaned on the door for support. I focused on Ahad to marshal my shaken thoughts. "*He's* the leader of this crazy group of yours. *Itempas*."

Ahad opened his mouth, then closed it. "'You will right all the wrongs inflicted in your name,'" he said at last, and I twitched as I remembered the words. I had been there, the first time they'd been spoken, and Ahad's voice was deep enough, had just the right timbre, to imitate the original speaker perfectly. He shrugged at my stare and finally flashed his usual humorless smile. "I'd say the Arameri, and all they've done to the world, count as one great whopping wrong, wouldn't you?"

"And it is his nature." Glee threw Ahad an arch look before returning her attention to me. "Even without magic, he will fight the encroachment of disorder in whatever way he can. Is that so surprising?"

I resisted out of stubbornness. "Yeine said she couldn't find him lately."

Glee's smile was paper-thin. "I regret concealing him from Lady Yeine, but it's necessary. For his protection."

I shook my head. "Protection? From— Gods, this makes no sense. A mortal can't hide from a god."

"A demon can," she said. I blinked, surprised, but I shouldn't have been. I'd already known that some demons had survived their holocaust. Now I knew how. Glee continued. "And fortunately, some of us can hide others when we need to. Now, if you'll excuse me..." She looked pointedly at my hand on the door, which I let fall.

Ahad had taken out a cheroot and was rummaging absently in his pockets. He threw a lazy glance at Glee, and there was a hint of the old evil in his eyes. "Tell the old man I said hi."

"I will not," she replied promptly. "He hates you."

Ahad laughed, then finally remembered he was a god and lit the cheroot with a moment's concentration. Sitting back in his chair, he regarded Glee with steady lasciviousness as she opened the door. "But you don't, at least?"

Glee paused on the threshold, and the look in her eyes was suddenly as familiar as her not-quite-smile had been a moment before. Of course it was. I had seen that same easy, possessive arrogance all my life. The absolute assurance that all was as it should be in the universe, because all of it was hers—if not now, then eventually.

"Not yet," she said, and not-smiled again before leaving the room.

Ahad sat forward as soon as the door shut, his eyes fixed on the door in such obvious interest that Lil began staring at him, finally distracted from the food. Kitr made a sound of exasperation and reached for the platter, probably out of irritation rather than any actual hunger.

"I'll see if I can get one of my people into Darr," said Nemmer, getting to her feet. "They're suspicious of strangers, though... might have to do it myself. Busy, busy, busy."

"I will listen harder to the sailors' and traders' talk," said Eyem-sutah. He was the god of commerce, to whom the Ken had once dedicated their magnificent sailing vessels. "War means shipments of steel and leather and march-bread, back and forth and back and forth…" His eyelids fluttered shut; he let out a soft sigh. "Such things have their own music."

Ahad nodded. "I'll see all of you next week, then." With that, Nemmer, Kitr, and Eyem-sutah disappeared. Lil rose and leaned over the table for a moment; the platter of food vanished. So did the platter, though Ahad's table remained untouched. Ahad sighed.

"You have become interesting, Sieh," Lil said to me, grinning beneath her swirling, mottled eyes. "You want so many things, so badly. Usually you taste only of the one endless, unfulfillable longing."

I sighed and wished she would go away, though that was pointless. Lil came and went as she pleased, and nothing short of a war could dislodge her when she took an interest in something. "What are you doing here?" I asked. "I didn't think you cared about anything but food, Lil."

She shrugged with one painfully bony shoulder, her ragged hair brushing the cloth of her gown with a sound like dry grass. "This realm changed while we were away. Its taste has grown richer, its flavors more complex. I find myself changing to suit." Then to my surprise, she came around the table and put her hand on mine. "You were always kind to me, Sieh. Be well, if you can."

She vanished as well, leaving me even more perplexed than before. I shook my head to myself, not really noticing that I was alone with Ahad until he spoke.

"Questions?" he asked. The cheroot hung between his fingers, on the brink of dropping a column of ash onto the carpet.

I considered all the swirling winds that blew around me and shook my head.

"Good," he said, and waved a hand. (This flung ash

everywhere.) Another pouch appeared on the table. Frowning, I picked it up and found it heavy with coins.

"You gave me money yesterday."

He shrugged. "Funny thing, employment. If you keep doing it, you keep getting paid."

I glowered at him. "I take it I passed Glee's test, then."

"Yes. So pay that mortal girl's family for room and board, buy some decent clothing, and for demons' sake, eat and sleep so you stop looking like all hells. I need you to be able to blend in, or at least not frighten people." He paused, leaning back in his chair and taking a deep draw from the cheroot. "Given the quality of your work today, I can see that I'll be making good use of you in the future. That is, by the way, the standard salary we offer to the Arms of Night's top performers." He gave me a small, malicious smile.

If the day hadn't already been so strange, I would have marveled at his praise, laced with insults as it was. Instead I merely nodded and slipped the pouch into my shirt, where pickpockets wouldn't be able to get at it easily.

"Well, get out, then," he said, and I left.

I was five years older, several centuries chastened, and more hated than ever by my siblings, including the one I'd apparently forgotten. As first days on the job went . . . well. I was still alive. It remained to be seen whether this was a good thing.

BOOK THREE

Three Legs in the Afternoon

I DRIFT THROUGH DREAMING. *Since I am not mortal, there are no nightmares. I never find myself naked in front of a crowd, because that would never bother me. (I would waggle my genitals at them, just to see the shock on their faces.) Most of what I dream is memory, probably because I have so many of them.*

Images of parents and children. Nahadoth, shaped like some sort of great star-flecked beast, lies curled in a nest of ebon sparks. This is in the days before mortals. I am a tiny thing half hidden in the nest's glimmers. An infant. I huddle against her for comfort and protection, mewling like a new kitten, and she strokes me and whispers my name possessively—

Shahar again. The Matriarch, not the girl I know. She is younger than in my last dream, in her twenties perhaps, and she sits in a window with an infant at her breast. Her chin is propped on her fist; she pays little attention to the babe as it sucks. Mortal, this child. Fully human. Another human child sits in a basket behind her—twins—tended by a girl in priest's robes. Shahar wears robes, too, though hers are finer. She is high ranking. She has borne children as her faith demands, but soon she will abandon them, when her lord needs her. Her eyes are ever on the horizon, waiting for dawn—

Enefa, in the fullest glory of her power. All her experiments, all the tests and failures, have reached the pinnacle of success at last. Merging life and death, light and dark, order and chaos, she brings mortal life to the universe, transforming it forever. She has been giving birth for the past billion years. Her belly is an earth of endless vastness and fecundity, rippling as it churns forth life after life after life. We who have already been born gaze upon this geysering wonder in worshipful adoration. I come to her, bringing an offering of love, because life needs that to thrive. She devours it greedily and arches, crying out in agony and triumph as another species bursts forth. Magnificent. She gropes for my hand because her brothers have gone off somewhere, probably together, but that's all right. I am the oldest of her godchildren, a man grown. I am there for her when she needs me. Even if she does not need me very often—

Myself. How strange. I sit on a bed in the first Sky, in mortal flesh, confined to it by mad Itempas and my dead mother's power. This is in the early years, I can tell, when I fought my chains at every turn. My flesh still bears the red weals of a whip, and I am older than I like, weakened by the damage. A young man. Yet I sit beside a longer, larger form whose back is to me. Male, adult, naked. Mortal: black hair a tangled mass. Sickly white skin. Ahad, who had no name back then. He is weeping, I know the way shoulders shake during sobs, and I—I do not remember what I have done to him, but there is guilt as well as despair in my eyes—

Yeine. Who has never borne a child as mortal or goddess, yet who became my mother the instant she met me.

She has the nurturing instincts of a predator: choose the most brutal of mates, destroy anything that threatens the young, raise them to be good killers. Yet compared to Enefa, she is a fountain of tenderness, and I drink her love so thirstily that I worry she will run out. (She never has.) In mortal flesh we curl on the floor of the Wind Harp chamber, laughing, terrified of the dawn and the doom thatseemsinevitable,yetwhichis,infact,onlythebeginning—

Enefa, again. The great quickening is long done. These days she makes few new children, preferring to observe and prune and transplant the ones she already has, on the nonillion worlds where they grow. She turns to me and I shiver and become a man by her will, though by this point I have realized that child *is the most fundamental manifestation of my nature. "Don't be afraid," she says when I dare to protest. She comes to me, touches me gently; my body yields and my heart soars. I have yearned for this, so long, but—*

I am dying, this love will kill me, get it away oh gods I have never been so afraid—

Forget.

13

One for sorrow
Two for joy
Three for a girl
Four for a boy
Five for silver
Six for gold
Seven for a secret
Never to be told.

MORTAL LIFE IS CYCLES. Day and night. Seasons. Waking and sleep. This cyclical nature was built into all mortal creatures by Enefa, and the humans have refined it further by building their cultures to suit. Work, home. Months become years, years shift from past to future. They count endlessly, these creatures. It is this which marks the difference between them and us, I think, far more than magic and death.

For two years, three months, and six days, I lived as ordinary a life as I could. I ate. I slept. I grew healthier, taking pains to make myself sleek and strong, and dressed better. I contemplated asking Glee Shoth to arrange a meeting between myself and Itempas. I chose not to, because I hated him and would rather die. Perfectly ordinary.

The work was ordinary, too, in its way. Each week I traveled wherever Ahad chose to send me, observing what I could, interfering where I was bidden. Compared to the life of a god...well. It was not boring, at least. It kept me busy. When I worked hard, I thought less. That was a good and necessary thing.

The world was not ordinary, either. Six months after I'd met her, and three months after the birth of her latest lamented son, Usein Darr's father died of the lingering illness that had incapacitated him for some while. Immediately afterward, Usein Darr got herself elected as one of the High North delegates. She traveled to Shadow in time for the Consortium's voting season, whereupon her first act was to give a fiery speech openly challenging the existence of Shadow's delegate. No other single city had a delegate on the Consortium. "And everyone knows why," Usein declared, then dramatically (according to the news scrolls) turned to glare into the eyes of Remath Arameri, who sat in the family box above the Consortium floor. Remath said nothing in reply—probably because everyone *did* know why, and there was no point in her confirming the obvious. Shadow's delegate was in fact Sky's delegate, little more than another mouthpiece through which the Arameri could make their wishes known. This was nothing new.

What *was* new was that Usein's protest was not struck down by the Consortium Overseer; and that several other nobles—*not* all northerners—rose to voice agreement with her; and that in the subsequent secret vote, nearly a third of the Consortium agreed that Shadow's delegate should be abolished. A loss, and yet a victory. Once upon a time, such a proposal would never have even made it to vote.

It was not a victory so much as a shot across the bow. Yet the Arameri did not respond in kind, as the whispers predicted in the Arms of Night's parlor and the back of the bakery and even at the dinner table with Hymn's family each evening. No one tried to kill Usein Darr. No mysterious plagues swept through the stone-maze streets of Arrebaia. Darren blackwood and herbal rarities continued to fetch high prices on the open and smugglers' markets.

I knew what this meant, of course. Remath had drawn a line somewhere, and Usein simply had yet to cross it. When she did, Remath would bring such horrors to Darr as the land had never seen. Unless Usein's mysterious plans reached fruition first.

Politics would never be interesting enough to occupy the whole of my attention, however, and as the days became months and years, I felt ever more the weight of unfinished, childishly avoided business upon my soul. Eventually one particular urge became overwhelming, and on a slow day, I begged a favor of Ahad. Surprisingly, he obliged me.

Deka was still at the Litaria. That I hadn't expected. After Shahar's betrayal, I had braced myself to find him in Sky somewhere. She had done it to get him back, hadn't she? Yet when Ahad's magic settled, I found myself in the middle of a classroom. The chamber was circular—a remnant of the Litaria's time as part of the Order of Itempas—and the walls were lined by slate covered in chalk renderings: pieces of sigils with each stroke carefully numbered,

whole sigils lacking only a stroke or two, and strange
numerical calculations that apparently had something to
do with how scriveners learned our tongue.

I turned and blinked as I realized I was surrounded by
white-clad children. Most were Amn, ten or eleven years
old; all sat cross-legged on the floor, with their own slates
or pieces of reed paper in their laps. All of them gaped
at me.

I put my hands on my hips and grinned back. "What?
Your teacher didn't tell you a godling was dropping by?"

An adult voice made me turn, and then I, too, gaped as
the children did.

"No," drawled Dekarta from the lectern. "We're doing
show-and-tell *next* week. Hello, Sieh."

Deka wore black now.

I had been surprised by this, but that was not the only
shock. I stole little looks up at him—he was much taller
than me now—as we walked through a brightly lit, carpeted corridor lined with the busts of dead scriveners. His
stride was easy, unhurried, confident. He did not look at
me, though he must have noticed me watching him. I tried
to read his expression and could not. Despite his exile
from Sky, he had still mastered the classic Arameri
detachment. Blood told.

Oh, yes, it did. He looked like Ahad.

Demonshitting, hells-spawned, Yeine-loving ratbas-
tard *Ahad*.

So many things made sense now; so many more did
not. The resemblance was so strong as to be undeniable.
Deka was an inch or two shorter than Ahad, leaner and
somewhat unfinished in the manner of young men. He
wore his hair short and plain, where Ahad's was long and

elaborate. Deka looked more Amn, too; Ahad's features leaned more toward the High Norther template. But in every other way, and particularly in this new aura of easy, dangerous strength, Deka might as well have been made as Ahad had: sprung to life full grown from his progenitor, with no mother in the way to gum things up.

Yet that could not be. Because if Ahad was some recent ancestor of Dekarta's, then that meant Dekarta, and Shahar, and whichever of their parents carried Ahad's blood, were demons. Demons' blood should have killed me the day we'd made the oath of friendship.

And not like this, slowly, cruelly. I had seen what demons' blood did to gods. It should have snuffed out the light of my soul like water on a candleflame. Why was I still alive at all, much less in this hobbled form?

I groaned softly, and at last Deka glanced over at me. "Nothing," I said, rubbing my forehead, which felt as though it *should* ache. "Just...nothing."

He uttered a low chuckle of amusement. My sweet little Deka was a baritone now, and not at all little anymore. Was he still sweet? That was something only time could tell.

"Where are we going?" I asked.

"My laboratory."

"Oh, so they let you use one by yourself?"

He had not stopped smiling; now he developed a smug air. "Of course. All teachers have their own."

I slowed, frowning up at him. "You mean you're a full scrivener? Already?"

"Shouldn't I be? The course of study isn't that difficult. I finished it a few years back."

I remembered the wistful, shy child he had been—so unsure of himself, so quick to let his sister take the lead. Could it be that here, beyond the shadow of his family's disapproval, he had unleashed that wild cleverness of his? I smiled. "Still the arrogant Arameri, in spite of everything."

Deka glanced at me, his smile fading just a little. "I'm not Arameri, Sieh. They threw me out, remember?"

I shook my head. "The only way to truly leave the Arameri is to die. They'll always come back for you, otherwise—if not for you, for your children."

"Hmm. True enough."

We had turned a corner in the meantime and headed down another carpeted corridor, and now Deka led me up a wide, banistered stairwell. Three girls carrying reed pens and scrolls bobbed in polite greeting as they came down the stairs and passed us. All three blushed or batted their eyes at Deka. He nodded back regally. As soon as they were out of sight around the corner, I heard their burst of excited giggling and felt a flicker of my old nature respond. Crushes: like butterfly wings against the soul.

At the top of the stairs, Deka unlocked and opened a pair of handsome wooden doors. Inside, the room was not what I expected. I had seen the First Scrivener's laboratory in Sky: a stark, forbidding place of white gleaming surfaces that held only ephemeral touches of color, like black ink or red blood. Deka's lab was Darrwood, deep and brown, and gold Chellin marble. Octagonal in shape, four of its walls were nothing but books—floor-to-ceiling shelves, each stacked two or three deep with tomes and scrolls and even a few stone or wooden tablets. Wide flat worktables dominated the center of the room, and something odd, a sort of glass-enclosed booth, stood on the room's edge at the juncture of two walls. Yet there were no tools or implements in sight, other than those used for writing. No cages along the wall, filled with specimens for experiments. No lingering scent of pain.

I looked around the room in wonder and confusion. "What the hells kind of scrivener are you?"

Deka closed the door behind me. "My specialty is god-ling lore," he said. "I wrote my concluding thesis on you."

I turned to him. He stood against the closed doors, watching me. For an instant, in his stillness, he reminded me of Nahadoth as much as Ahad. All three had that same habit of unblinking intensity, which in Ahad covered nihilism and in Nahadoth covered madness. In Deka, I had no idea what it meant. Yet.

"You don't think I tried to kill you, then," I said.

"No. It was obvious something went wrong with the oath."

One knot of tension eased inside me; the rest stayed taut. "You don't seem surprised to see me."

He shrugged, ducking his eyes, and for a moment I saw a hint of the boy he'd been. "I still have friends in Sky. They keep me informed of events that matter."

Very much still the Arameri, whatever his protestations to the contrary. "You knew I would be coming, then."

"I guessed. Especially when I heard about your leaving, two years ago. I expected you then, actually." He looked up, his expression suddenly unreadable. "You killed First Scrivener Shevir."

I shifted from one foot to another, slipping my hands into my pockets. "I didn't mean to. He was just in the way."

"Yes. You do that a lot, I've realized from studying your history. Typical of a child, to act first and deal with the consequences later. You're careful to do that—act impulsively—even though you're experienced and wise enough to know better. This is what it means to live true to your nature."

I stared at him, flummoxed.

"My contacts told me you were angry with Shahar," he said. "Why?"

I set my jaw. "I don't want to talk about it."

"You didn't kill her, I see."

I scowled. "What do you care? You haven't spoken to her for years."

Deka shook his head. "I still love her. But I've been used as a weapon against her once already. I will not let that happen again." He pushed away from the door abruptly and came toward me, and so flustered was I by his manner that I took a step back before I caught myself.

"*I will be her weapon instead*," he said.

It took me a shamefully long time, all things considered, to realize that he had spoken to me in the First Tongue.

"What the hells are you doing?" I demanded, clenching my fists to keep from clapping a hand over his mouth. "Shut up before you kill us both!"

To my shock, he smiled and began to unfasten his overshirt. "I've been speaking magic for years, Sieh," he said. "I can hear the world and the stars as gods do. I know when reality listens closest, when even the softest word will awaken its wrath or coax it into obedience. I don't know how I know these things, but I do."

Because you are one of us, I almost said, but how could I be sure of that? His blood hadn't killed me. I tried to understand even as he continued undressing in front of me.

Then he got his overshirt open. I knew before he'd unlaced the white shirt underneath; the characters glowed dark through the fabric. Black markings, dozens of them, marched along most of his upper torso and shoulders, beginning to make their way down the flat planes of his abdomen. I stared, confused. Scriveners marked themselves whenever they mastered a new activation; it was the way of their art. They put our powerful words on their fragile mortal skin, using will and skill alone to keep the magic from devouring them. But they used ordinary ink to do it, and they washed the marks off once the ritual was done. Deka's marks, I saw at once, were like Arameri blood sigils. Permanent. Deadly.

And they were not scrivening marks. The style was all wrong. These lines had none of the spidery jaggedness I was used to seeing in scrivener work: ugly, but effective. These marks were smooth and almost geometric in their cleanliness. I had never seen anything like them. Yet they had power, whatever they were; I could read that in the swirling interstices of their shapes. There was meaning in this, as multilayered as poetry and as clear as metaphor. Magic is merely communication, after all.

Communication, and conduits.

This is something we have never told mortals. Paper and ink are weak structures on which to build the framework of magic. Breath and sound aren't much better, yet we godlings willingly confine ourselves to those methods because the mortal realm is such a fragile place. And because mortals are such dangerously fast learners.

But flesh makes for an excellent conduit. This was something the Arameri had learned by trial and error, though they'd never fully understood it. They wrote contracts with us onto their foreheads for protection, calling them blood sigils as if that was all they were, and *we could not kill them*, no matter how badly worded they were. Now Deka had written demands for power into his own skin, and his flesh gave the words meaning. He had written it in a script of his own devising, more flexible and beautiful than the rough speech of his fellow scriveners, and *the universe would not deny him.*

He had made himself not quite as powerful as a god—his flesh was still mortal, and the marks had only limited meaning—but surely more powerful than any scrivener who had ever lived. I had an inkling that his markings would be more effective than even the northerners' masks; those were only wood and godsblood, after all. Deka was more than that.

My mouth fell open, and Deka smiled. Then he closed his undershirt.

"H-how...?" I asked. But I could guess. Demon and scrivener. A combination we had already learned to fear, channeled here toward a new purpose. *"Why?"*

"You," he said, very softly. "I was planning to go find you."

There was, fortunately, a small couch nearby. I sat down on it, dazed.

We exchanged stories. This was what Deka told me.

Shahar had been the one to suggest his exile. In the tense days after our oath and the children's injury, the clamors for Deka's execution had run loud in the halls of Sky. There were still a dozen or so fullbloods and twenty or thirty highbloods altogether. In the old days, they had not mattered because the family head's rule had been absolute. These days, however, the highbloods had power of their own. Some of them had their own pet scriveners, their own pet assassins. A few had their own pet armies. If enough of them banded together and acted against Remath, she could be overthrown. This had never happened in all the two-millennia history of the Arameri, but it could happen now.

But when they had demanded Deka's death, Shahar had spoken for him, as soon as she was well enough to talk. She had gone toe-to-toe with Remath—an epic debate, Deka called it, all the more impressive because one of its combatants was eight years old—and gotten her to acknowledge that exile was a more suitable punishment than death. Deka could never win enough support to become heir now, even if his looks could somehow be overcome. He would be forever branded by the stigma of failure. And Shahar needed him alive, she had argued, so as to have one advisor whose prospects were so truncated, so hopeless, that he would have no choice but to serve her faithfully in order to survive. Remath had agreed.

"I imagine dear Sister will fill this in when I go back," Deka said then, touching his semisigil with a soft sigh. I nodded slowly. He was probably right.

So Deka had left Sky for the Litaria. The first few months of his exile had been misery, for with a child's eyes, he had seen only his mother's rejection and his sister's betrayal. He had not reckoned, however, on one crucial thing.

"I am happy here," he said simply. "It isn't perfect; there are cliques and bullies, politics, unfairness, like anywhere. But compared to Sky, this is the gentlest of heavens."

I nodded again. Happiness has healing power. Between that and the wisdom brought by maturity, Deka had come to realize what Shahar had done for him, and why. By then, however, several years had passed during which he'd returned all her letters, until she'd finally stopped sending them. It would have been dangerous in the extreme to resume communication at that point, because any of Shahar's rivals—who were surely watching her mailings—would know that Deka was once again her weakness. There was strength in the fact that she could pretend not to love him and point to her hand in his exile as proof. And as long as Deka pretended not to love her back, they were both safe.

I shook my head slowly, though, troubled by his plan. Love could not be conditional. I had seen the danger of that too often. Conditions created a chink in otherwise unbreakable armor, left a fatal flaw in the perfect weapon. Then the armor broke, at precisely the wrong time. The weapon turned against its wielder. Deka and Shahar's game could so easily turn real.

But it was not my place to say that, because they were still children enough to learn best through experience. I could only pray to Nahadoth and Yeine that they would not learn this lesson in the most painful way.

After our talk, Deka rose. An hour or so had passed. Beyond the laboratory windows, the sun had moved through noon into afternoon. I was hungry again, damn it, but no one had brought food. Perhaps there were no servants in this place where learning created its own hierarchy.

As if guessing my thought (though my stomach had also rumbled loudly), Deka went to a cabinet and opened a drawer, taking out several flat loaves of bread and a chub of dry sausage. He began slicing this on a board. "So why have you come? It can't just have been to see an old friend."

He still thought of me as a friend. I tried not to let him see how this affected me. "I did just want to see you, believe it or not. I wondered how you'd turned out."

"You can't have wondered all that hard, since it took you two years to come."

I winced. "After Shahar, what happened with her, I mean...I didn't want to see you, because I was afraid that you would be...like her." Deka said nothing, still working on the food. "I thought you would be back in Sky by now, though."

"Why?"

"Shahar. She made a deal with your mother to bring you home."

"And you thought I would go as soon as my sister snapped her fingers?"

I faltered silent, confused. As I sat there, Deka turned back to me and brought the sausage and bread over, setting it before me as if he were a servant and not an Arameri. No poor man's gristle-and-scraps here, I found when I took a slice. The sausage was sweet and redolent of cinnamon, bright yellow in color per the local style. The Litaria might make Remath Arameri's son serve his own food, but the food was at least suited to his station. He'd brought a flask of wine, too, light and strong, of equal quality.

"Mother sent a letter shortly after you left Sky, inquiring as to when I might return," Deka said, sitting in the chair across from me and taking a slice of meat for himself. He swallowed and uttered a short, sour laugh. "I responded with a letter of my own, explaining that I intended to remain until I'd completed my research."

I burst out laughing at his audacity. "You told her you'd come back when you were good and ready, is that it? And she didn't force you home?"

"No." Deka's expression darkened further. "But she had Shahar write to me, asking the same question."

"And you said?"

"Nothing."

"Nothing?"

He sat back in his chair, crossing his legs and toying with the glass of wine in his fingers. I didn't like that pose for him; it reminded me too much of Ahad. "There was no need. It was a warning. Shahar's letter said, 'I am told the standard course of study at the Litaria is ten years. Surely you can finish your research within that time?'"

"A deadline."

He nodded. "Two years to wrap up my affairs here and go back to Sky—or, no doubt, Mother's willingness to let me return would expire." He spread his hands. "This is my tenth year."

I thought of what he'd told me and shown me. The strange new magic he'd developed, his vow to become Shahar's weapon. "You're going back, then."

"I leave in a month." He shrugged. "I should arrive by midsummer."

"Two months' traveling time?" I frowned. The Litaria was a sovereign territory within the sleepy agrarian land of Wiru, in southern Senm. (That way only a few farmers would die if the place ever blew to the heavens.) Sky was not that far. "You're a scrivener. Draw a gate sigil."

"I don't actually need to; the Litaria has a permanent gate that can be configured to Sky's. But to travel that way would make it seem as though I was afraid of assault. There is the family pride to consider. And more importantly, I will not slink to Sky quietly, like a bad dog finally allowed back into the house." He sipped from his glass of wine. Over the rim, his eyes were dark and colder than I'd ever expected to see. "Let Mother and the rest of them see what they have chosen to create by sending me here. If they will not love me, fear is an acceptable substitute."

For a moment I was stunned. This was not at all the

Deka I remembered, but then, he was no longer a child, and he had never been a fool. He knew as well as I did what he was going back to in Sky. I could not blame him for hardening himself to prepare for it. But I did mourn, just a little, for the sweet boy I'd first known.

At least he had not become what I'd feared, though: a monster, worthy only of death.

Yet.

At my silence, Deka glanced up, gazing at me just a moment too long. Did he sense my unease? Did he *want* me to feel uneasy?

"So...what will you do?" I asked. I fought the urge to stammer.

He shrugged. "I informed Mother that I would be traveling overland and made note of the route. Then I sent it by standard courier, with only the usual privacy sigils in the seal."

I whistled with a lightheartedness that I didn't feel. "Every highblood in Sky will have seen it, then." I frowned. "These mask-wielding assassins, though... And gods, Deka, if any of *your relatives* want you dead, you've given them a map for the best places to ambush you!"

"And if Mother stints me on an appropriate guard complement, that's precisely what will happen." He shrugged. "As head, she must be seen to at least *try* to protect the Central Family, the Matriarch's bloodline. To do any less would make her unfit to lead. So she'll likely send a whole legion to escort me—thus the two months of travel."

"Caught in your own trap. Poor Deka." He smiled, and I grinned back. Yet I found myself sobering. "What if there *is* an attack, though? Assassins, regardless who sends them? A legion of enemy soldiers?"

"I'll be fine."

There was arrogance, and there was stupidity. "You should be afraid, Deka, no matter how powerful you've become. I've seen this mask magic. It's like nothing the Litaria has prepared you for."

"I've seen Shevir's notes, and the Litaria has been closely involved in the investigation into this new magical form. The masks are like scrivening, like the gods' language: merely a symbolic representation of a concept. Once one understands this, it is possible to develop a countermeasure." He shrugged. "And these mask makers don't know anything about *my* new magical form. No one does but me. And now you."

"Um. Oh." I fell silent again, awkwardly.

Abruptly, Deka smiled. "I like this," he said, nodding toward me. "You're different now, not just physically. Not so much the brat. Now you're more..." He thought a moment.

"Heartless bastard?" I smiled. "Obnoxious ass?"

"Tired," he said, and I sobered. "Unsure of yourself. The old you is still there, but it's almost buried under other things. Fear, most noticeably."

Inexplicably, the words stung. I stared back at him, wondering why.

His expression softened, a tacit apology. "It must be hard for you. Facing death, when you're a creature of so much life."

I looked away. "If mortals can do it, I can."

"Not all mortals do, Sieh. You haven't drunk yourself to death yet, or flung yourself into dangerous situations, or killed yourself in any of a hundred other ways. Considering that death is a new reality for you, you're handling it remarkably well." He leaned forward, resting his elbows on his knees, his eyes boring into my own. "But the biggest change is that you're not happy anymore. You were always lonely; I saw that even as a child. But the loneliness wasn't destroying you back then. It is now."

I flinched back from him, my thoughts moving from stunned toward affronted, but they lacked the strength to go all the way there, instead flopping somewhere in between. A lie came to my lips, and died. All that remained was silence.

A hint of the old self-deprecation crossed Deka's face; he smiled ruefully. "I still want to help you, but I'm not sure if I can. You aren't sure you like me anymore, for one thing."

"I—" I blurted. Then I got up and walked away from him, over to one of the windows. I had to. I didn't know what to say or how to act, and I didn't want him to say anything else. If I'd still had my power, I would have simply left the Litaria. Maybe the mortal realm entirely. As it was, the best I could do was flee across the room.

His sigh followed me, but he said nothing for a long while. In that silence, I began to calm down. Why was I so agitated? I felt like a child again, one with jittery buttons dancing on his skin, like in an old Teman tale I'd heard. By the time Deka spoke, I was almost myself again. Well, not *myself*. But human, at least.

"You came to us all those years ago because you needed something, Sieh."

"Not two little mortal brats," I snapped.

"Maybe not. But we gave you something that you needed, and you came back for it twice more. And in the end, I was right. You *did* want our friendship. I've never forgotten what you said that day: '*Friendships can transcend childhood, if the friends continue to trust each other as they grow older and change.*' " I heard him shift in his chair, facing my back. "It was a warning."

I sighed, rubbing my eyes. The meat and bread sat uneasily in my belly. "It was sentimental rambling."

"Sieh." How could he know so much, so young? "You were planning to kill us. If we became the kind of Arameri who once made your life hell—if we betrayed your trust—you knew you would *have* to kill us. The oath, and your nature, would have required it. You told us that because you didn't want to. You wanted real friends. Friends who would last."

Had that been it? I laughed hopelessly. "And now I'm the one who won't last much longer."

"Sieh—"

"If it was like you say, I would have killed Shahar, Deka. Because she betrayed me. She knew I loved her, and she used me. She…" I paused, then looked up at the reflection in the window. My own face in the foreground, pinched and tired, too big as always, shaped wrong, old. I had never understood why so many mortals found me attractive in this shape. In the background, watching me from the couch on which he sat, Deka. His eyes met mine in the glass.

"I slept with her," I said, to hurt him. To shut him up. "I was her first, in fact. Little Lady Shar, so perfect, so cute. You should have heard her moan, Deka; it was like hearing the Maelstrom itself sing."

Deka only smiled, though it seemed forced. "I heard about Mother's plan." He paused. "Is that why you didn't kill Shahar? Because it was Mother's plan and not hers?"

I shook my head. "I don't know why I didn't kill her. There was no why. I do what feels good." I rubbed my temples, where a headache had begun.

"And you didn't feel like murdering the girl you loved."

"Gods, Deka!" I rounded on him, clenching my fists. "Why are we talking about this?"

"So it was just lust? The god of childhood leaps on the first half-grown woman he meets who's willing?"

"No, of course not!"

He sighed and got to his feet. "She was just another Arameri, then, forcing you into her bed?" The look on his face showed that he didn't remotely believe that. "You wanted her. You loved her. She broke your heart. And you didn't kill her because you love her still. Why does that trouble you so?"

"It doesn't," I said. But it did. It shouldn't have. Why did it matter to me that some mortal had done precisely what I'd expected her to do? A god should not care about such things. A god...

...should not need a mortal to be happy.

Gods. Gods. What was wrong with me? Gods.

Deka sighed and came over to me. There were many things in his eyes: compassion. Sorrow. Anger, though not at me. Exasperation. And something more. He stopped in front of me, and I was not as surprised as I should have been that he lifted a hand to cup my cheek. I did not pull away, either. As I should have.

"*I* will not betray you," he murmured, much too softly. This was not the way a friend spoke to a friend. His fingertips rasped along the edge of my jaw. This was not the touch of a friend. But—I did not think—Oh, gods, was he...

"I'm not going anywhere, either. I have waited so long for you, Sieh."

I started, confused, remembering. "Wait, where did you hear—"

Then he kissed me, and I fell.

Into him. Or he enveloped me. There are no words for such things, not in any mortal language, but I will try, I will try to encapsulate it, confine it, define it, because my mind does not work the way it once did and I want to understand, too. I want to remember. I want to taste again his mouth, spicy and meaty and a little sweet. He had always been sweet, especially that first day, when he'd looked into my eyes and begged me to help them. I craved his sweetness. His mouth opened and I delved into it, meeting him halfway. I had blessed him that day, hadn't I? Perhaps that was why, now, the purest of magic surged through him and down my throat, flooding my belly, overflowing my nerves until I gasped and tried to cry out, but he would not let my mouth go. I tried to back away but the window was there. We could not travel to other realms safely. My only choice was to release the magic or be destroyed. So I opened my eyes.

Every lantern in the room flared like a bonfire, then burst in a cloud of sparks. The walls shook, the floor heaved. One of the shelves on a nearby bookcase collapsed, spilling thick tomes to the floor. I heard the window frame rattle ominously at my back, and someone on the floor above cried out in alarm. Then Deka ended the kiss, and the world was still again.

Darkness and damnation and eighth-blooded unknowing Arameri *demons*.

Deka blinked twice, licked his lips, then flashed me the sort of elated, look-what-I-did grin I'd once been famous for. "That went better than expected."

I nodded beyond him. "You were expecting this?"

He turned, and his eyes widened at the fallen shelf, the now-smoldering lanterns. One lay on the floor, its glass shattered. As he stared, a scroll that had not dropped with the others fluttered to the shelf below, forlorn.

I touched his shoulder. "You need to send me back to

Shadow." This made him turn around, a protest already on his lips. I gripped his shoulder to make him listen. "No. I won't do this again, Deka. I can't. You were right about Shahar. But that's why...I, with you, I—" I sighed, inexpressibly weary. Why did mortal troubles never wait for convenient times? "Gods, I can't do this right now."

I saw Deka struggle for a mature response, which heartened me because it meant that he had not somehow outgrown me at a mere eighteen years. He took a deep breath and moved away from me, running a hand through his hair. Finally he turned to one of the tables in the room and pulled out a large sheet of the thick, bleached paper that scriveners used for their work. He took a brush, inkstone and stick, and reservoir from a nearby table, and said with his back to me, "The way you appeared was gods' magic."

"One of my siblings." *Your great-grandfather.* Ahad was going to love this.

"Ah." He prepared the ink, his fingers grinding the sigil-marked inkstone back and forth slowly, meditatively. "Do you think, next time, I'll be able to summon you to me the way Shahar did?"

He was too tense to even attempt subtlety. I sighed and gave him what he wanted. "There's only one way to find out, I suppose."

"May I attempt it? At an appropriate time, of course."

I leaned against the window again. "Yes."

"Good." The tension in his broad shoulders eased, just a touch. He began to sketch the sigil for a gate with quick, decisive movements—stunningly fast, compared to most scriveners I had seen. Every line was perfect. I felt the power of it the instant he drew the final line.

"I may be able to help you." He said this briskly, with a

scrivener's matter-of-fact detachment. "I can't promise anything, of course, but the magic I've been designing—my body-marking—accesses the potential hidden within an individual. Whatever's happening to you, you're still a god. That should give me something to work with."

"Fine."

Deka set the sigil on the floor and stepped back. When I went to stand beside it, his expression was as carefully blank as if he stood before Remath. I could not leave things that way between us.

So I took his hand, the one I'd held ten years before, when his demon blood had mingled with mine and failed to kill me. His palm was unmarked, but I remembered where the cut had been. I traced a line across it with a fingertip, and his hand twitched in response.

"I'm glad I came to see you," I said.

He did not smile. But he did fold his hand around mine for a moment.

"I'm not Shahar, Sieh," he said. "Don't punish me for what she did."

I nodded wearily. Then I let go of him, stepped onto the sigil, and thought of South Root. The world blurred around me, leaping to obey Deka's command and my will. I savored the momentary illusion of control. Then, when the walls of my room at Hymn's snapped into place around me, I lay down on the bed, threw an arm over my eyes, and thought of nothing but Deka's kiss for the rest of the night.

14

It felt good to run up sand dunes. I put my head down and took care to churn the sand behind me and scuff up the perfect wave patterns the wind had etched around the sparse grasses. By the time I reached the top of the dune, I was out of breath, and my heart was pumping steadily within its cage of bones and muscle. I stopped there, putting my hands on my hips, and grinned at the beach and the spreading expanse of the Repentance Sea. I felt young and strong and invincible, even though I really wasn't any of those things. I didn't care. It was just nice to feel good.

"Hello, Sieh!" cried my sister Spider. She was down at the water's edge, dancing in the surf. Her voice carried up to me on the salty ocean breeze, as clear as if I stood beside her.

"Hello, there." I grinned at her, too, and spread my arms. "All the oceans in the world, and you had to pick the *boiled* one?" One of my siblings, the Fireling, had fought a legendary battle here during the Gods' War. She'd won, but not before the Repentance was a bubbling stewpot filled with the corpses of a billion sea creatures.

"It has nice rhythms." She was doing something strange in her dance, squatting and hopping from one foot to another with no recognizable semblance of rhythm. But that was Spider; she made her own music if she needed to. So many of Nahadoth's children were like her, just a little mad but beautiful in their madness. Such a proud legacy our father had given us.

"All the dead things here scream in time with each other," she said. "Can't you hear them?"

"No, alas." It almost didn't hurt anymore, acknowledging that my childhood was gone and would never return. Mortals are resilient creatures.

"A shame. Can you still dance?"

In answer, I ran down the dune, side-sliding so that I wouldn't overbalance. When I reached level ground, I altered my steps into a side-to-side sort of hop that had been popular in upper Rue once, centuries before the Gods' War. Spider giggled and immediately came out of the water to join my dance, her steps alternating to complement mine. We met at the tideline, where dry sand turned to hard-packed wet. There she grabbed my hands and pulled me into a new dance, formal and revolving and slow. Something Amn, or possibly just something she'd made up on the spot. It never mattered with her.

I grinned, taking the lead and turning us in a looping circle, toward the water and away. "I can always dance for you."

"Not so well anymore. You have no rhythm." We were in northern Tema, the land whose people we had both watched over long ago. She had taken the shape of a local girl, small and lithe, though her hair was bound up in a bun at the back of her head as no self-respecting Teman would have done. "You can't hear the music at all?"

"Not a note." I pulled her hand close and kissed the back of it. "But I can hear my heart beating, and the waves coming in, and the wind blowing. I may not be exactly on the beat, but you know, I don't have to be a *good* dancer to love dancing."

She beamed, delighted, and then spun us both, taking control of the dance so deftly that I could not mind. "I've missed you, Sieh. None of the others ever loved to move like you do."

I twirled her once more so that my arms could settle around her from behind. She smelled of sweat and salt and joy. I pressed my face into her soft hair and felt a whisper of the old magic. She was not a child, but she had never forgotten how to play.

"Oh—" She stopped, her whole body going taut with attention, and I looked up to see what had interested her so. A few dozen feet away on the beach, lurking near a dune as if ready to duck back behind it: a young man, slim and brown and handsome, fascinating in his shy eagerness. He wore no shirt or shoes, and his pants were rolled up to his knees. In one hand he carried a bucket full of sandy clams.

"One of your worshippers?" I murmured in her ear, and then I kissed it.

Spider giggled, though her expression was greedy. "Perhaps. Move away from me, Brother. He's shy enough as it is, and you're not a little boy anymore."

"They're so beautiful when they love us," I whispered. I pressed against her, hungry, and thought for the umpteenth time of Deka.

"Yes," she said, reaching back to cup my cheek. "But I don't share, Sieh, and I'm not the one you want anyway. Let go now."

Reluctantly I did so and stepped back, bowing extravagantly to the young man so that he would know he was welcome. He blushed and ducked his head, the long cabled locks of his hair falling forward. Because he was poor, he had wrapped the locks with some sort of threadlike seaweed and ornamented them with seashells and bits of bright coral, rather than the metal bands and gemstones most Temans preferred. He did begin to walk closer at our tacit invitation, holding the bucket in both hands with an air of offering. His whole day's income, most likely—a sincere mark of devotion.

While he approached, Spider glanced back at me, her eyes gleaming. "You want to know about Kahl, don't you?"

I blinked in surprise. "How did you know?"

She smiled. "*I* can hear the world just fine, Brother. The wind says you're playing errand boy for Ahad, the new one. Everyone knows who *he* works for."

"I didn't." I could not keep the sourness out of my voice.

"That's because you're selfish and flighty. Anyhow, of course that's why you came. There's nothing else in Tema that could be of interest to you."

"Maybe I just wanted to see you."

She laughed, high and bright, and I grinned, too. We had always understood each other, she and I.

"For the past, then," she said. "Only for you, Sieh."

Then, turning a little pirouette that marked a strange and powerful pattern into the sand, Spider stopped on one toe and dipped toward me, her other leg extending gracefully above her in a perfect arabesque. Her eyes, which had been brown and ordinary until then, suddenly glimmered and became different. Six additional tiny-pupilled irises swirled out of nowhere and settled into place around her existing irises, which shrank a bit to make room for them. The clam boy stopped where he was a few feet away, his eyes widening at the sight. I didn't blame him; she was magnificent.

"Time has never been as straightforward as Itempas wished," she said, stroking my cheek. "It is a web, and we all dance along its threads. You know that."

I nodded, settling cross-legged in front of her. "No one dances like you, Sister. Tell me what you can."

She nodded and fell silent for a moment. "A plains fire has been lit." For an instant as she spoke, I glimpsed fingerlike palps wiggling behind her human teeth. She used magic to speak when she was in this state, or else she would have lisped badly. She had always been vain.

"A fire?" I prompted when she fell silent. Her eyes flickered, searching realms I had never been able to visit, even as a god. This was what I had come for. It was difficult to convince Spider to scry the past or future, because she didn't like dancing those paths. They made her strange and dangerous, when all she really wanted to do was spin and mate and eat. She was like me; once, we had both had other shapes and explored our natures in other ways. We liked the new ways better, but one could never leave the past entirely behind.

"The Darre's new ennu, I think, is the kindling. But this fire will burn far, far beyond this realm."

I frowned at this. "How can mortal machinations affect anything more than mortal life?" But that was a foolish question. I had spent two thousand years suffering because of one mortal's evil.

She shivered, her eyes glazing, though she never once lost her balance on that single toe. The clam boy frowned from where he knelt on the sand, his bucket set before him. When this was done, I knew, Spider would demand a dance with him. If he pleased her, and was lucky, she would make love with him for a few hours and then send him on his way. If he was not lucky...well. The clams would make a fine appetizer. Those mortals who choose to love us know the risks.

"A seashell." Her voice dropped to a murmur, flat and

inflectionless. "It floats on green wood and shining white bones. Inside is betrayal, love, years, and more betrayal. Ah, Sieh. All your old mistakes are coming back to haunt you."

I sighed, thinking of Shahar and Deka and Itempas, to name a few. "I know."

"No. You don't. Or rather, you do, but the knowledge is buried deep. Or rather, it was." She cocked her head, and all her dozen pupils expanded at once. Her eyes, speckled with holes, pulled at me. I looked into them and glimpsed deep chasms bridged by gossamer webs. Quickly I leaned back, averting my eyes. Anyone drawn into Spider's world became hers, and she did not always let them go. Not even if she loved them.

"The wind blows louder by the moment," she whispered. "*Sieh, Sieh, Sieh*, it whispers, in the halls of the unknowable. Something stirs in those halls, for the first time since Enefa's birth. *It is alive. It thinks. It considers you.*"

This nonsense was not at all what I had expected, and not really what I wanted to hear. I frowned and licked my lips, wondering how to steer her back toward the knowledge I needed. "What of Kahl, Sister? The Arameri's enemy?"

She shook her head suddenly, vehemently, closing her eyes. "He is *your* enemy, Sieh, not theirs. They are irrelevant. Innocent—ha!—bystanders." She shuddered, and to my surprise she abruptly tottered on her toe, nearly losing her balance. The clam boy looked up suddenly, his face taut with fervor; I heard him utter a low, intent prayer. We have never needed prayers, but we do like them. They feel much like...hmm. Like a push, or a supporting hand on the back. Even gods need encouragement sometimes. After a moment, Spider steadied.

"Itempas," she said at last, sounding abruptly weary. "He is the key. Stop being stubborn, Sieh; just talk to him."

"But—" I clamped my teeth down on what I would have said. This was what I'd asked her to give me. I had no right to complain just because it wasn't what I wanted to hear. "Fine."

With a sigh she opened her eyes, which were human again. When she straightened and stepped off the pattern, carefully removing her toe from its center without disturbing it, I saw the lingering sheen of magic within its lines.

"Go away now, Brother," she said. "Come back in a million years, or whenever you think of me again."

"I won't be able to," I said softly. In a million years I would be less than dust.

She glanced at me, and for just an instant her eyes flickered strange again. "No. I suppose you won't, will you? But don't forget me, Brother, amid all the new mysteries you'll have to explore. I'll miss you."

With that, she turned to her clam boy and offered him her hand. He came and took it, rising, his face alight even as she suddenly grew four additional arms and wrapped all six of them about him tightly. She would probably let him live, given that he had helped her. Probably.

I turned and headed back over the dunes, leaving my sister to her dance.

It had been a busy month since my trip to see Deka. A week later had come the expected announcement: Remath Arameri was bringing her beloved son home at last. Dekarta had begun his journey toward Sky amid great fanfare and three whole legions of soldier escorts. They would make a tour of the procession, visiting a dozen of the southern Senm kingdoms before reaching Sky-in-Shadow on the auspicious summer solstice. I had laughed on hearing about the tour. Three legions? That went beyond any need to protect Deka. Remath was showing off. Her message was clear: if she could spare three legions just to protect a less-favored son, imagine how many she could bring to bear for something that mattered?

So Ahad had kept me on the move visiting this noble or that merchant, spending a night on the streets in a few cities to hear what the commonfolk thought, sowing rumors and then listening to see what truths sprang up as a result. There had been more meetings, too, though Ahad invited me only when he had to. Nemmer and Kitr had complained after I loosened the legs of their chairs one time. I couldn't see what they were so upset about; neither had actually fallen. *That* would have been worth the broken collarbone Kitr gave me in recompense. (Ahad sent me to a bonebender for healing and told me not to speak to him for a week.)

So, left to my own devices, I'd spent the last few days tooling about Tema. Beyond the beach dunes stood a city, shimmering through the heat haze: Antema, capital city of the Protectorate. It had been the greatest city in the world before the Gods' War and was one of the few cities that had managed to survive that horror mostly unscathed. These days it was not quite as impressive as Sky—the World Tree and the palace were just too stunning for any other city to top—but what it lacked in grandeur it made up in character.

I admired the view again, then sighed and finally fished in my pocket for the messaging sphere Ahad had given me.

"What," he said, when the sphere's soft thrum had finally gotten his attention. He knew exactly how long to keep me waiting; an instant longer and I would've stilled the activation.

I had already decided not to tell him about my visit with Spider, and I was still considering whether to request a meeting with Itempas. So I said, "It's been a week. I'm getting bored. Send me somewhere."

"All right," he said. "Go to Sky and talk to the Arameri."

I stiffened, furious. He knew full well that I didn't want to go there, and why. "Talk to them about what, for demons' sake?"

"Wedding gifts," he said. "Shahar Arameri is getting married."

It was the talk of the town, I discovered, when I got to Antema and found a tavern in which to get very, very drunk.

Teman taverns are not made for solitary drunkenness. The Teman people are one of the oldest mortal races, and they have dealt with the peculiar isolation of life in cities for longer than the Amn have even had permanent houses. Thus the walls of the tavern I'd fallen into were covered in murals of people paying attention to me—or so it seemed, as each painted figure sat facing strategic points where viewers might sit. They leaned forward and stared as if intent upon anything I might say. One got used to this.

One also got used to the carefully rude way in which the taverns were furnished, so as to force strangers together. As I sat on a long couch nursing a hornlike cup of honey beer, two men joined me because there were only couches to sit on and I was not churl enough to claim one alone. Naturally they began talking to me, because the tavern's musician—an elderly twin-ojo player—kept taking long breaks to nap. Talking filled the silence. And then two women joined us, because I was young and handsome and the other two men weren't bad-looking themselves. Before long, I was sitting among a laughing, raucous group of utter strangers who treated me like their best friend.

"She doesn't love him," said one of the men, who was well into his own honey horn and growing progressively more slurred in his speech because of it. Temans mixed it with something, aromatic sea grass seed I thought, that made it a fearsomely strong drink. "Probably doesn't even like him. An Amn, Arameri no less, marrying a Temaboy? You just know she looks down her pointy white nose at all of us."

"I heard they were childhood friends," said a woman, whose name was Reck or Rook or possibly Rock. Ruck? "Datennay Canru passed all the exams with top marks; the Triadice wouldn't have confirmed him as a *pymexe* if he wasn't brilliant. It's an honor to the Protectorate, the Arameri wanting him." She lifted her Amn-style glass, which contained something bright green, and out of custom, all of us raised our drinks to answer her toast.

But as soon as our arms came down, her female companion scowled and leaned forward, her locks swinging for emphasis. "It's an insult, not an honor. If the damned Arameri thought so much of our Triadice, they would've deigned to marry in before now. All they want's our navy to guard against the crazy High Northers—"

"It's an insult only if you make it one," said one of the men, who spoke rather hotly because there were three men and two women and he was the homeliest of the group, and he knew that he was most likely to go home alone. "They're still Arameri. They don't need us. And she genuinely likes him!"

This triggered a chorus of agreement and protest from the whole group, during which I alternated my attention between them and a set of peculiar masks hanging on one of the tavern's walls. They reminded me a bit of the masks I'd seen in Darr, though these were more elaborately styled and decorated, in the Teman fashion. They all had hair locks and jolly faces, yet somehow they were even more distracting than the staring mural people. Or perhaps I was just drunk.

After the argument had gone back and forth a few times, one of the women noticed that I had been quiet. "What do you think?" she asked, smiling at me. She was a bit older, relatively speaking, and seemed to think I needed the encouragement.

I finished the last of my horn, gave a discreet nod to the waiter for more, and sat back, grinning at the woman. She was pretty, small and dark and wiry as Teman women tended to be, with the most beautiful black eyes. I wondered if I was still god enough to make her faint.

"Me?" I asked, and licked spoiled honey from my lips. "I think Shahar Arameri is a whore."

There was a collective gasp—and not just from my couch, because my voice had carried. I looked around and saw shocked stares from half the tavern. I laughed at all of them, then focused on my own group.

"You shouldn't say that," said one of the men, who had also been giving me the eye—though now, I suspected, he was rethinking that. "The Order doesn't care what you say about the gods anymore, except Itempas, but the Arameri..." He darted a look around, as if afraid Order-Keepers would appear out of nowhere to beat me senseless. In the old days they would have. Lazy sots. "You shouldn't say that."

I shrugged. "It's true. Not her fault, of course. Her mother's the problem, see. She gave the girl to a god once, as a broodmare, hoping to make a demon-child. Probably let your *pymexe* have a free ride, too, to seal the deal. You say he's a smart man. I'm sure he wouldn't mind treading in the footsteps of gods."

The waiter, who had been on his way to me with

another horn, stopped just beyond the couch, his eyes wide and horrified. The man who had been thinking about me stood up, quickly, almost but not quite before his third companion, who'd ignored me entirely up to that point, leapt to his feet. "Canru is my second cousin, you green-eyed half-breed nobody—"

"Who's a half-breed?" I drew myself up to my full sitting height, which made me nowhere near as tall as he was. "There's not a drop of mortal in me, damn it, no matter how old I look!"

The man, already opening his mouth to roar at me, faltered to silence, staring at me in confusion. One of the women leaned away, the other closer; both had wide, wondering eyes. "What did you say?" asked the closer-leaner. "Are you a godling?"

"I am," I said gravely, and belched. "Pardon me."

"You're as godly as my left testicle," snapped the furious man.

"Is that very godly?" I laughed again, feeling full of mischief and rage and joy. The rage was strongest, so before the man could react, I shot out my free hand and grabbed at his crotch, correctly guessing precisely where his left testicle would be. It was child's play—for a mean child, anyway—to grasp the thing and give it a sharp, expert twist. He screamed and doubled over, his face purpling with shock and agony as he grabbed at my arm, but dislodging me would've necessitated a harder pull on his tender bits. With his face inches from mine, I flashed my teeth and hissed at him, tightening my fingers just enough for warning. His eyes went wide and terrified for some reason, which I could tell had nothing to do with the threat to his manhood. I doubted that my eyes had changed; there wasn't enough magic left in me for that. Something else, maybe.

"These don't seem very godly to me," I said, giving his balls another jiggle. "What do you think?"

He gaped like a fish. I laughed again, loving the flavor of his terror, the thrill of even this paltry, pointless sort of power—

"Let him go."

The voice was familiar, and female. I craned my neck back, blinking in surprise to see that Glee Shoth stood behind my couch. She stood with her hands on her hips, tall and imposing and so very Maroneh in that room full of Temans. The look on her face was somehow disapproving and serene at once. If I hadn't spent several billion years trying to provoke that precise expression on another's face, I would have found it wholly disconcerting.

I beamed at her upside down and let the man go. "Oh, you are *so* his child."

She lifted an eyebrow, proving my point. "Would you care to join me outside?" Without waiting to see if I agreed, she turned and walked out.

Pouting, I got to my feet and swayed a bit. My companions were still there, to my surprise, but they were silent, all of them regarding me with a mixture of fear and distaste. Ah, well.

"May both my fathers smile upon you," I said to them, gesturing expansively and making a genuine effort to bless them, though nothing happened. "If you can manage to get a smile out of them, anyway, the ill-tempered bastards. And may my mother kill you all gently in your sleep, at the end of a long and healthy span. Farewell!"

The whole tavern was silent as I stumbled out after Glee.

She turned to walk with me as I reached the foot of the steps. I had not drunk so much that I couldn't walk, but steadiness was another matter. As I had expected, Glee made no compensation for my weaving and stumbling, and for the first block or so, I lagged about three paces behind her. "Your legs are very long," I complained. She was almost a foot taller than me.

"Make yours longer."

"I can't. My magic is gone."

"Then move them faster."

I sighed and did so. Gradually I drew alongside her. "Did you inherit anything from your mother? Or are you just him done over with breasts?"

"I have my mother's sense of humor." She glanced at me, contempt clear in her face. "I expected rather more of *you*, though."

I sighed. "I've had a hard day."

"Yes. When you cut off the messaging sphere, Ahad asked me to find you. He suggested I search the gutters. I suppose I should be glad he was wrong about that."

I laughed, though a moment later my laughter faltered silent and I glared at her, affronted. "Why are you doing his bidding? Aren't you his boss? And what does it matter if I relax a little? I've spent the past two years running that bastard's errands, trying to help that pathetic little group of his keep this world from falling apart. Don't I deserve a night off?"

She stopped. By this point we stood on a quiet street corner in a residential neighborhood. It was late enough that no one was about. Which is perhaps why, for just an instant, her eyes seemed to flare red-gold like a struck match. I started, but then they were brown again, and more than a little angry.

"I have spent nearly this past *century* trying to keep this world from falling apart," she snapped. I blinked in surprise; she looked no older than thirty. I had forgotten that demons usually lived longer than humans, though both were mortal. "I'm not a god. I have no choice but to live in this realm, unlike you. I will do whatever I must to save it—including working with godlings like you who claim to despise Itempas, though in reality you're just as selfish and arrogant as him at his worst!"

She resumed walking, leaving me behind because I was too stunned to follow. By the time I recovered, she had disappeared around a corner. Furious, I ran after her, only to nearly trip when I rounded the corner and found her there, waiting.

"How dare you!" I hissed the words. "I am nothing like him!"

She sighed, shaking her head, and to my greater fury she decided not to argue with me. That sort of thing has always driven me mad. "Has it even occurred to you to ask why I came? Or are you too inebriated to think that far?"

"I don't—" I blinked. "Why are you here?"

"Because, as Ahad would have told you if you'd given him the chance to finish, we have work to do. Dekarta Arameri is altering and accelerating his route to proceed directly to Shadow in light of the engagement. When he and his escort arrive at Shadow—*tomorrow*, to foil potential troublemakers—there will be a grand procession through the city. Shahar Arameri is scheduled to appear publicly, on the steps of the Salon, for the first time since she gained her majority. The official announcement of the engagement will be made then, before the Nobles' Consortium and half the city, and Dekarta will be officially welcomed home at the same time. It should be quite the event."

Despite Glee's needling, I was not, in fact, too inebriated to think. The Arameri were not given to public spectacle—or at least they hadn't been during my time of servitude—mainly because it hadn't been necessary. What could top the glory of their unstated, rarely seen, utterly devastating power? And Sky was symbol enough of who they were. But times had changed, and their power now derived at least partially from their ability to awe the masses who had once been beneath their notice.

And . . . I shivered as I realized it. What better opportunity could there be for the Arameri's enemies to strike?

Glee nodded as she saw that I understood at last. "We will need everyone in the city, to watch for trouble."

I licked my lips, which were suddenly dry. "I don't have any magic left," I said. "Not a drop. I can do a few tricks, things maybe scriveners can do, but that's nothing much. I'm just a mortal now."

"Mortals have their uses." She said this with such delicate irony that I grimaced. "And you love them, don't you? Shahar and Dekarta."

I remembered the mask-decayed bodies I had seen two years before, during my disastrous few days in Sky. I tried to imagine Shahar's and Dekarta's corpses laid out in the same way, their faces obscured by burned masks and their flesh too destroyed even to rot.

"Take me there," I said softly. "Wherever you're going. I want to help."

She inclined her head and extended a hand to me. I took it before it occurred to me to wonder what she could do. She wasn't a godling, just a demon. A mortal.

Then her power clamped down on the world around us, taking us in and out of reality with a god's deft strength. I could not help admiration; she had our father's touch.

Glee had rented an inn room in the northern Easha section of Shadow, a thriving business district near the city's center. I realized at once that it was one of the nicer inns—the kind of place I couldn't afford even on the salary Ahad gave me, and especially not before a major event in the city. It sounded as though there was a large and raucous crowd in the common room downstairs. Every inn in the city was probably filling up as people from the surrounding lands poured in to see the spectacle. Even Hymn's place would be getting some business amid this; I was glad, if so. Though hopefully they wouldn't be so crass as to rent out *my* room.

Glee went to the window and opened the shutters, revealing the reason she'd brought us here. I went to stand beside her and saw that the window overlooked the Avenue of Nobles, at the distant end of which stood the imposing white bulk of the Salon. We had a good view: I could see the tiny figures of people milling about the avenue near the Salon's wide steps and Order-Keepers in their conspicuously white uniforms setting up barriers to keep the onlookers back. Arameri did not appear in public often, though their faces were known thanks to the Order's news scrolls and the currency. Everyone in a hundred-mile radius had probably traveled to the city, or was on their way, to catch a once-in-a-lifetime glimpse.

Glee pointed along the avenue in the opposite direction, since it ran past the building we were in. "Dekarta's procession will enter the city from there. The route hasn't been published, but it will be in the news scrolls tomorrow morning. That makes it difficult for assassins to plan. But the procession will have to travel along the avenue this far; there's no other way for a large party to reach the Salon."

"Which means they might strike anywhere along this street?" I shook my head, incredulous. Even if I'd still had magic, it was an impossible scenario to try and plan for. In the morning, the dozens of mortals around the Salon would have grown to hundreds; by afternoon, when the event was to take place, there would be thousands. How to find just one amid the morass? "Do you know how the assassins get their victims to don the masks?"

"No." She sighed, and for an instant her stoic face slipped. I realized she was very tired, and troubled. Was Itempas doing nothing, fobbing all the work of protecting the world off on her? Bastard.

Turning from the window, Glee went to the room's handsome leather chair and sat down. I turned to sit on the windowsill, because I have always been more comfortable on such perches than in any conventional seat.

"So, we stay here until tomorrow, and then... what?" I asked.

"Nemmer has a plan in place," she said. "Her people have done such things before. She knows how best to utilize the strengths of both godlings and mortals. But since you and I are neither, she's suggested that perhaps we could contribute most usefully by circulating through the crowd and keeping watch for anything unusual."

I shifted to prop one leg against the window frame, sighing at her characterization of me. "I still *think* like a godling, you know. I've tried to adjust, be more mortal, but—" I spread my hands. "I have been the Trickster for more years than most mortals know how to count. I'm not sure I'll live long enough to become anything else, in my head."

She rested her head on the chair back and closed her eyes, evidently planning to sleep there. "Even gods have limits; yours are just different. Do what you can within them."

Silence fell between us, but for the soft stir of a night breeze through the open window and the mortals in the common room below, who were singing some sort of song in lusty and off-beat cadence. I listened to them for a while, smiling as I recognized the song as a variation on one I'd taught their ancestors. I hummed the tune along with them until I grew bored, and then I glanced at Glee to see if she was asleep—to find her eyes open, watching me.

So I sighed and decided to address the matter directly. "So, little sister." She lifted an eyebrow at this, and I smiled. "How old are you?"

"Older than I look, like you."

Nearly a century, she'd said. "You're Oree Shoth's daughter." I vaguely remembered her. A beautiful mortal girl, blind and brave. She had loved one of my younger brothers, who'd died. And she'd loved Itempas, too, apparently. I couldn't see him coupling with her otherwise. Ephemeral intimacy offended him.

"Yes."

"She still call him 'Shiny'?"

"Oree Shoth is dead."

"Oh." I frowned. Something about her phrasing was odd, but I couldn't figure out what. "I'm sorry."

Glee was silent for a moment, her gaze disconcertingly direct. Another thing she'd gotten from him. "Are you really?"

"What?"

She crossed her legs primly. "I was always told that you were one of mortalkind's champions, in the old days. But now you don't seem to like mortals much." She shrugged as I scowled. "Understandably. But given that, I can't see you getting especially upset about one more death."

"Well, that would mean you don't know me very well, wouldn't it?"

To my surprise, she nodded. "That's precisely what it means. Which is why I asked: are you sorry for my mother's death? Honestly."

Surprised, I closed my mouth and considered my answer. "I am," I said at last. "I liked her. She had the kind of personality that I think I could've gotten along with, if she hadn't been so devoted to Itempas." I paused, considering. "Even so, I never would've expected him to *respond* to that devotion. Oree Shoth must've been pretty special to make him take a chance on a mortal woman again..."

"He left my mother before I was born."

"He—" Now I stared at her, flummoxed, because that was not at all like him. His heart did not change. But then I remembered another mortal lover and child he'd left behind, centuries ago. It was not his nature to leave, but he could be persuaded to do so, if it was in the best interests of those he cared for.

"Lord Nahadoth and Lady Enefa demanded it," Glee said, reading my face. "He left only to save her—our—lives. So, later, when I was old enough, I went looking for him. Eventually I found him. I've traveled with him ever since."

"I see." A tale worthy of the gods, though she wasn't one of us. And then, because it was in my mind and she knew it was there and there was no point in my trying to conceal the obvious, I asked the question that had hovered between us for the whole two years since we'd met. "What is he like now?"

She took her time answering, appearing to consider her words carefully. "I don't know what he was like before the War," she said, "or even during the years of your... incarceration. I don't know if he's the same as he was then, or different."

"He doesn't change."

Another of those odd silences. "I think he may have."

"He *can't* change. It's anathema to him."

She shook her head, with familiar stubbornness. "He

can. He did when he killed Enefa, and I believe he's changed again since. He's *always* been able to change, and he's always done it, however slowly or reluctantly, because he's a living being and change is part of life. Enefa didn't make it that way; she just took the common qualities her brothers already possessed and put those into the godlings and mortals she created."

I wondered if she'd had this conversation with Itempas. "Except she made mortalkind complete, unlike us."

She shook her head again, the soft curls of her hair wafting gently as if in a breeze. "Gods are just as complete as mortals. Nahadoth isn't wholly dark. Father isn't wholly light." She paused, her eyes narrowing at me. "*You* haven't been a true child since the universe was young. And for that matter, the War in part began because Enefa—the preserver of balance—*lost* her balance. She loved one of her brothers more than the other, and that broke them all."

I stiffened. "How *dare* you blame her! You don't know anything about it—"

"I know what he told me. I know what I've learned, from books and legends and conversations with godlings who were there when the whole mess began, who watched from the sidelines and tried to think how to stop it, and wept as they realized they could not. You were too close, Sieh; you were hip-deep in the carnage. You decided Itempas was to blame without ever asking *why*."

"He killed my mother! Who cares why?"

"His siblings abandoned him. Only for a brief time, but solitude is his antithesis; it weakened him. Then Shahar Arameri murdered his son, and that drove him over the edge. In this case, the 'why' matters a great deal, I think."

I laughed, bitter, sick with guilt and trying to hide my

shock. Solitude? *Solitude?* I had never known that— No, none of that mattered. It could not matter. "A mortal! Why in the Maelstrom's name would he mourn a single mortal so powerfully?"

"Because he loves his children." I flinched. Glee was glaring at me, her eyes plainly visible in the dim room. Neither of us had bothered to put on a light, because the light from the street lanterns was more than enough to see by. "Because he's a good father, and good fathers do not stop loving if their children are merely mortal. Or if those children hate them."

I stared at her and found myself trembling. "He didn't love us when he fought us in the War."

Glee folded her hands in front of her, steepling her fingers. She'd been spending too much time with Ahad. "From what I understand, your side was winning until Shahar Arameri used the Stone of Earth. Weren't you?"

"What the hells does that matter?"

"You tell me."

And of course I thought back to the worst days of my life. Shahar had not been the first to use the Stone. I had sensed a godling's controlling hand first, sending searing power—the power of life and death itself—in a terrible wave across the battlefield of earth. Dozens of my siblings had fallen in that attack. It had nearly caught me, too. That had been the first warning that the tide was turning. Until then, the taste of triumph had been thick in my mouth. Who had that godling been? One of Tempa's loyalists; he'd had his own, same as Nahadoth. Whoever it was had died trying to wield the power of Enefa.

Then Shahar had gotten the Stone, and she hadn't bothered attacking mere godlings. She went straight for Nahadoth, whom she hated most because he had taken Itempas from her. I remembered watching him fall. I had screamed and wept and known then that it was my fault. All of it.

"He...didn't have to..." I whispered. "Itempas. If he was so sorry, he could have just—"

"That isn't his nature. Order is cause and effect, action and reaction. When attacked, he fights back."

I heard her shift to get comfortable in the chair. I heard this, because I could not look at her anymore, with her fine dark skin and too-keen eyes. She was not as obviously alien as Shinda had been, all those centuries ago. She could hide among mortalkind more easily because her peculiar heritage did not immediately announce itself and because the last thing anyone noticed about a six-foot-tall black woman was the aura of magic. There was something about her that made me think she was quite capable of defending herself, too—and I sensed Itempas's hand in that. Action and reaction. *This* mortal child would not die so easily; her father had made sure of that.

Our father.

"Many things triggered the War," said Glee, speaking softly. "Shahar Arameri's madness, Itempas's grief, Enefa's jealousy, Nahadoth's carelessness. No one person is to blame." She lifted her chin belligerently. "However much you might like to believe otherwise."

I stayed silent.

Itempas had never been like Nahadoth. Naha plucked lovers from the mass of mortality like flowers from a meadow, and he discarded them as easily when they wilted or a more interesting flower came along. Oh, he loved them, in his own erratic way, but steadfastness was not his nature.

Not so Itempas. He did not love easily—but when he did, he loved forever. He had turned to Shahar Arameri, his high priestess, when Nahadoth and Enefa stopped wanting him. They'd never stopped loving him, of course; they'd just loved each other a little more. But to Itempas, it must have felt like the darkest of hells. Shahar had offered her love, and he had accepted it, because he was a creature of logic, and *something* was better than *nothing*. And because he had chosen to love her and please her, he had bent his own rules enough to give her a son. Then he'd loved that son and stayed with his mortal family for ten years. He could have easily been content with them for the remainder of their mortal lives. An eyeblink in a god's eternity. No great matter.

He had left them only because Naha and Nefa had convinced him that the mortals would be better off without him. And Naha and Nefa had done that only because someone had lied to them.

Just a harmless trick, I had thought then. It harmed only the mortals, and then only a little. Shahar had status and wealth, and mortals were adaptable. They did not need him.

Just a harmless trick.

No one person is to blame, Itempas's daughter had said. I closed my mouth against the taste of old, ground-in guilt.

In my silence, Glee spoke again. "As for what kind of man he is now..." I thought she shrugged. "He's stubborn, and proud, and infuriating. The kind of man who will move the earth and skies to get what he wants. Or to protect those he cares for."

Yes. I remembered that man. How minute of a change was sanity to insanity and back? Not much, across the expanse of time.

"I want to see him," I whispered.

She was silent for a moment. "I will not allow you to harm him."

"I don't want to harm him, damn it—" Though I had, I remembered, on one of the last occasions I'd seen him. She must have heard about that. I grimaced. "I won't do anything this time, I promise."

"The promise of a trickster."

I forced myself to take a deep breath against my own temper, releasing that held breath rather than the furious words in my thoughts. It was not right, the way I thought of her. Mortal. Inferior. It was not right that I struggled to respect her. She was as much a child of the Three as I.

"There's no promise I can offer that you'll trust," I said, and was relieved that my voice stayed soft. "You shouldn't, really. I only *have* to keep promises to children. And honestly, I don't know if even that applies anymore. Everything I am has changed." I leaned my head back on the window and gazed out at the night-lit city below.

Nahadoth could hear any words spoken at night, if he wanted.

"Please let me see him," I said again.

She watched me steadily. "You should know that his magic works only in certain circumstances. It's not powerful enough to stop whatever's happened to you—not in his current form."

"I know. And I know you have to keep him safe. Do what you have to do. But if it's possible..."

I could see her, very faintly, beyond my reflection. She nodded to herself slowly, as if I'd passed some sort of test. "It's possible. I can't promise anything, of course; he may not want to see *you*. But I'll speak to him." She paused. "I'd appreciate it if you didn't tell Ahad."

Surprised, I glanced at her. My senses were not so dull that I couldn't still distinguish scents, and the faint whiff of Ahad—cheroots and bitterness and emotions like long-clotted blood—clung to her like stale perfume. It was a few days old, but she had been in his presence, close to him, touching him. "I thought you had a thing with him."

She had the grace to look abashed. "I find him attractive, I suppose. That's not 'a thing.'"

I shook my head, bemused. "I'm still amazed that he had enough of a soul to be made into a complete and separate being. I don't know what you see in him."

"You don't know him," she said, with a hint of sharpness that told me there was more to the "thing" than she was letting on. "He does not reveal himself to you. He loved you once; you can hurt him as no one else can. What you think of him, and what he truly is, are very different things."

I rocked back a little, surprised at her vehemence. "Well, clearly you don't trust him—"

She flicked a hand impatiently, dismissively. Gods, she was so much like Itempas that it hurt. "I'm not a fool. It may be a long time before he sheds the habits of his former life. Until then, I'm cautious with him."

I was tempted to warn her further: she needed to be more than cautious with Ahad. He had been created from the substance of Nahadoth in his darkest hour, nurtured on suffering and refined by hate. He liked to hurt people. I don't think even he realized what a monster he was.

But that impatient little flick had been a warning for *me*. She wasn't interested in whatever I had to say about Ahad. Clearly she intended to judge him for herself. I couldn't really blame her; I wasn't exactly unbiased.

I wasn't tired, but clearly Glee was. She fell silent after that, and I turned back to the window to let her sleep. Presently her breathing evened out, providing a slow and curiously soothing background noise for my thoughts.

The people in the common room had finally shut up. There was no one but me and the city.

And Nahadoth, appearing silently in the window reflection behind me.

I was not surprised to see him. I smiled at the pale glimmer of his face, not turning from the window. "It's been a while."

The change to his face was minute; a slight drawing together of those fine, perfect brows. I chuckled, guessing his thoughts. A while; two years. Barely noticeable, to a god. I'd taken longer naps. "Every passing moment shortens my life, Naha. Of course I feel it more now."

"Yes." He fell silent again, thinking his unfathomable thoughts. He didn't look well, I decided, though this had nothing to do with his actual appearance, which was magnificent. But that was just his usual mask. Beneath that mask, which I could just barely perceive, he felt...strange. Off. A storm whose winds had faltered at the touch of colder, quelling air. He was unhappy—very much so.

"When you see Itempas," he said at last, "ask him to help you."

At this I swung around on the windowsill, frowning. "You're not serious."

"Yeine can do nothing to erase your mortality. I can neither cure nor preserve you. I meant it, Sieh, when I said I would not lose you."

"There's nothing he can *do*, Naha. He's got less magic than me!"

"Yeine and I have discussed the matter. We will grant him a single day's parole if he will agree to help you."

My mouth fell open. It took me several tries to speak. "He's endured barely a century of mortality. Do you really think we can trust him?"

"If he attempts to escape or attack us, I will kill his demon."

I flinched. "Glee?" I glanced at her. She had fallen asleep in the chair, her head slumped to one side. Either she was a heavy sleeper, an excellent faker, or Naha was keeping her asleep. Most likely the latter, given the subject of our conversation.

She had tried to help me.

"Are we Arameri now?" I asked. My voice was harsher than usual in the dimness, deep and rough. I kept forgetting that it was not a child's voice. "Are we willing to pervert love itself to get what we want?"

"Yes." I knew he meant it by the fact that the room's temperature suddenly dropped ten degrees. "The Arameri are wise in one respect, Sieh: they show no mercy to their enemies. I will not risk unleashing Itempas's madness again. He lives only because the mortal realm cannot exist without him and because Yeine has pleaded for his life. I permitted him to keep his daughter only for this purpose. Demon, beloved... she is a weapon, and I mean to use her."

I shook my head in disbelief. "You regretted what you did to the demons, Naha. Have you forgotten that? They are our children, too, you said—"

He stepped closer, reaching for my face. "You are the only child who matters to me now."

I recoiled and struck his hand away. His eyes widened in surprise. "What the hells kind of father are you? You always say things like that, treat some of us better than others. Gods, Naha! How twisted is that?"

Silence fell, and in it my soul shriveled. Not in fear. It was simply that I knew, or had known, precisely why he did not love all his children equally. Differentiation, variation, appreciation of the unique: this was part of what he was. His children were not the same, so his feelings toward each were not the same. He loved us all, but differently. And because he did this, because he did not pretend that love was fair or equal, mortals could mate for an afternoon or for the rest of their lives. Mothers could tell their twins or triplets apart. Children could have crushes and outgrow them; elders could remain devoted to their spouses long after beauty had gone. The mortal heart was fickle. Naha made it so. And because of this, they were free to love as they wished, and not solely by the dictates of instinct or power or tradition.

I had understood this once. All gods did.

My hand dropped into my lap. It was shaking. "I'm sorry," I whispered.

He lowered his hand, too, saying nothing for a long, bruised moment.

"You cannot remain in mortal flesh much longer," he said at last. "It's changing you."

I lowered my head and nodded once. He was my father, and he knew best. I had been wrong not to listen.

With a night-breeze sigh, Nahadoth turned away, his substance beginning to blend into the room's shadows. Sudden, irrational panic seized me. I sprang to my feet, my throat knotting in fear and anguish. "Naha—please. Will you..." Mortal, mortal, I was truly mortal now. I was his favorite, he was my dark father, his love was fickle, and I had changed almost beyond recognition. "Please don't leave yet."

He turned back and swept forward all in one motion, and all at once I was adrift and cradled in the soft dark of his innermost self, with hands I could not see stroking my hair.

"You will always be mine, Sieh." His voice was

everywhere. He had never let anyone but me and his siblings into this part of himself. It was the core of him, vulnerable, pure. "Even if you love him again. Even if you grow old. I am not wholly dark, Itempas is not wholly light, and there are some things about me that will never change, not even if the walls of the Maelstrom should fall."

Then he was gone. I lay on the patterned rug, shivering as the inn room began to warm up in Nahadoth's wake, watching the silver curls of my own breath. I was too cold to cry, so I tried to remember a lullaby that Nahadoth had once sung to me, so that I could sing myself to sleep. But the words would not come. The memory was gone.

In the morning I woke to find Glee standing over me with a mixture of confusion and contempt on her face. But she offered me a hand to help me up from the floor.

A new little sister. And Ahad was a new sibling, too. I vowed to try and be a better brother to them both.

Dekarta's procession was spotted on the outskirts of the city around midmorning. At the rate they were wending their way through the streets—passing through South Root, of all things; Hymn's parents would make a killing—they would reach the Avenue of Nobles at twilight.

Auspicious timing, I decided. Then I followed Glee out of the inn and we slipped into the crowd to try and keep Shahar and Dekarta alive for a few paltry years more.

15

The soldiers go a-marching
pomp pomp pomp
The catapults are flinging
whomp whomp whomp
The horses come a-trotting
clomp clomp clomp
And down falls the enemy
stomp stomp stomp!

THE STEPS OF THE SALON were impressive on their own: white marble, wide and colonnaded, gently curving around the building's girth. Clearly they were not impressive enough for Arameri tastes, however, and so the steps had been embellished. Two additional stairwells—immense and unsupported—curved off the Salon's steps to the left and right like wings poised in flight. They were made of daystone so that they glowed faintly; only a scrivener could have built them. They were magnificent even against the looming backdrop of the Tree, which tended to diminish any mortal effort at grandeur to pointlessness. In fact, the twin stairwells seemed to come from the Tree itself, suggesting a divine connection for the people who descended them. Which was probably the point.

I could not see the platforms at the tops of the daystone stairways, but it was not hard to guess that the scriveners had etched gates into each. Shahar, Remath, and perhaps a few others of the Central Family would arrive by this means, then descend to the Salon's actual steps. Revoltingly predictable, but they were Itempans; I couldn't expect better.

Sighing, I craned my neck again from my vantage point: the lid of a muckbin at the corner of a dead-end street, about a block away from the Salon building. The Avenue of Nobles was a sea of mortal heads, thousands of people standing about or walking, laughing, talking, the aura of excitement wafting off them like a warm summer breeze. The city's street artists had taken shameless advantage of the opportunity to make festive ribbon pennants, dancing puppets with the faces of famous folk, and small contraptions that blatted out a few flakes of sparkling white confetti when blown hard. Already the air was thick with the glittering motes, which did a marvelous job of capturing the thin, dappled light that passed for daytime in Shadow. Adults and children alike seemed to love the things. I shivered now and again as their pleasure in the toys stirred whatever was left of the god in me.

Hard to focus, amid so many distractions. (My hands itched to play with one of the puppets. It had been so long since I'd had a new toy.) But I had a job to do, so I kept scanning the crowd, holding on to a gutter pipe as I leaned this way and that. I would know when I found what I was looking for. It was only a matter of time.

Then, just as I had begun to worry, I spotted my quarry. Moving past a tightly packed group of middle-aged women who looked both thrilled and terrified to be among such a crowd: a boy of nine or ten years old. Amn, wearing old clothing that had the look of garments taken from a White Hall tithe pile, with unkempt hair that hadn't seen a comb in days. He passed one of the women and stumbled, bracing one hand on her back to right himself and apologizing quickly. It was nicely done; he had bowed himself away and into the current of foot traffic almost before the woman realized he'd touched her.

I grinned, delighted. Then I hopped down from the bin lid (another man immediately claimed my place atop it, throwing a belligerent look at my back) and hurried after him.

Took half a block to catch up with him; he was small and wove among the members of the crowd as deftly as a river snake among reeds. I was a grown-up and had to be polite. But I'd guessed his destination—a pack of children milling about a stall that sold tamarind-lime juice—and that made it easy to head him off a few feet before he reached them. I caught his thin, wiry arm and stayed ready, because boys his age were not defenseless. They had no compunctions against biting, and they tended to run in packs.

The boy swore at me in polyglot profanity, immediately trying to pull free. "Leggo!"

"What'd you take?" I asked, genuinely curious. The woman hadn't had a purse visible, probably fearing exactly what had happened to her, but there could have been one beneath her clothing. "Jewelry? A shawl or something? Or did you actually manage to get into her pocket?" If the latter, he was a master of his craft and would be perfect for my needs.

His eyes grew wide. "'In't take nothin'! Who th' hells—" He jumped suddenly and grabbed at my wrist, which was already emerging from *his* pocket. I'd gotten only one coin; my hands were too damned big now for proper pocket-picking. But his face turned purple with fury and consternation, and I grinned.

I lifted the hand that held the coin and closed my fingers around it. Didn't even need magic for this trick: when I opened my hand again, two coins lay there, his and one from my own pocket.

The boy froze, staring at this. He did not take either coin, turning a suddenly shrewd and wary look on me. "Wh'you want?"

I let him go, now that I'd gotten his attention. "To hire you, and any friends you've got with similar inclinations."

"We don't want trouble." The slangy, contracted Senmite he'd been using vanished as swiftly as he had, after lifting the woman's purse. "Keepers don't bother us as long as we stick to pockets and wallets. Anything more and they'll hunt us down."

I nodded, wishing I could bless him with safety. "All I want you to do is look," I said. "Move through the crowd, see what you usually see, do what you usually do. But if you let me, I can look through your eyes."

He caught his breath, and for a moment I couldn't read his face. He was astonished and skeptical and hopeful and frightened, all at once. But he searched my face with such sudden intensity that I realized, far later than I should have, what he was thinking. When I did, I started to grin, and that did it: his eyes got as big as twenty-meri coins.

"Trickster, trickster," he whispered. "Stole the sun for a prank." En pulsed on my breast, pleased to be mentioned.

"No prayers, now," I said, cupping his cheek with one hand. Mine. "I'm not a god today, just a man who needs your help. Will you give it?"

He inclined his head just a hair more formally than he needed to. Ah, he was marvelous. "Your hand," I said, and he offered it to me at once.

I still had a few ways of using magic, though they were crude and weak and a betrayal of my pride to employ. The universe did not listen to me the way it once had, but as long as I kept the requests simple, it would grudgingly obey. "Look," I said in our tongue, and the air shivered around us as I traced the shape of an eye into the boy's palm with my fingertip. "Hear. Share."

The outline flickered briefly, a silver flash like drifting confetti, and then the boy's flesh was just flesh again. He peered at it, fascinated.

"Find your friends," I said. "Touch as many of them as you can with this hand, and send them out among the crowd. The magic will end when the Arameri family head returns to Sky." Then I closed my free hand and opened it again. This time a single coin sat in my palm: a hundred-meri piece, more than the boy could have stolen in a week, unless he'd gotten very bold or very lucky.

The boy's eyes fixed on it, but he did not reach for it, swallowing. "I can't take money from you."

"Don't be stupid," I said, and tucked the coin into his pocket before I let him go. "No follower of mine should ever do something for nothing. If you need to change it safely, go to the Arms of Night in South Root and tell Ahad I sent you. He'll be an ass about it, but he won't cheat you. Now go." And because he was staring at me, awe stunting his wits, I winked at him and then stepped back, letting myself vanish amid the crowd. There was no magic to this. It just took an understanding of how mortals moved when they gathered together in great herds like this. The boy did the same thing as part of his pickpocketing, but I had several thousand years' experience on him. From his perspective, I seemed to disappear. I caught a final glimpse of his mouth falling open, and then I let the traffic carry me elsewhere.

"Smoothly done," said Glee when I found her again. She had been waiting in front of a small café, standing as still and striking as a pillar amid the flow of babbling mostly Amn.

"You were watching?" The café had a bench, which was packed; I didn't even try to sit. Instead I leaned against a wall, half in Glee's shadow. Though neither of us were Amn, I was betting no one would notice me with her there. After five minutes I knew I was right; half the people who had passed us glanced at her, and the other half ignored us altogether.

"Some," she replied. "I'm not a god. I can't see without my eyes like you do. But I can see magic, even in a crowd."

"Oh." Demon magic was always strange. I slipped my hands into my pockets and yawned loudly, not bothering to cover my mouth despite the disgusted glances of a passing couple. "So, Itempas around here somewhere, too?"

"No."

I snorted. "What exactly is it that you're protecting him *from*? Nothing short of demons' blood can kill him, and who would do that, given the consequences?"

She said nothing for a long moment, and I thought she would ignore me. Then she said, "How much do you know about godsblood?"

"I know the mortals drink it, when they can, for a taste of magic." My lip curled. During my first few decades in Sky, some of the Arameri had taken blood from me. It had done nothing for them, since my flesh then was more or less mortal, but that hadn't stopped them from trying. "I know some of my siblings sell it to them, gods know why."

Glee shrugged. "Our organization, via Kitr's group, keeps an eye on such sales. A few months ago, Kitr received a request for some very unusual godsblood. More unusual, anyway, than the standard requests for menstrual flow or heart blood."

Now it was my turn to be surprised, mostly because I hadn't realized any of my sisters bothered menstruating. Why in darkness— Well, it didn't matter. "Itempas is mortal now. His flesh is, anyway. His blood would only sour some poor mortal's stomach."

"He's still one of the Three, Sieh. Even without magic, his blood has value. And who's to say that these mask users can't find a way to eke magic out of Father's blood even in his current state? Remember that there is godsblood in the northerners' masks... and remember that Kahl's mask is yet incomplete."

I cursed as I understood. I did this strictly in Senmite— too dangerous to speak our tongue under these conditions. No way to know who was listening or what strange magics slept nearby. "*This* is what comes of gods selling pieces of themselves to mortals." My stupid, stupid younger siblings! Hadn't they seen, again and again, that mortals would always find a way to use gods, hurt us, control us, if they could? I slammed a fist against the unyielding stone of the wall behind me and gasped as, instead of cracking the wall, my hand reminded me of its fragility with a white, breathtaking flash of pain.

Glee sighed. "Stop that." Coming over, she took my hand and lifted it, turning it this way and that to see whether I'd broken the bone. I hissed and tried to pull away, but she threw me such a quelling glare at me that I stopped squirming and meekly held still. She would be a terrifying mother someday, if she ever had children.

"For what it's worth, I agree with you," she said quietly. "Though I don't limit my condemnation to mortals. Remember what gods have done with the blood of demons, after all."

I flinched at this, my anger evaporating into shame.

"Not broken," she pronounced, and let me go. I cradled my hand to my chest since it still hurt, and sulking made me feel better.

"Gods are not truly creatures of flesh," Glee continued, nodding toward my injured hand. "I understand this. But the vessels that you wear in this realm contain something of the real you—enough to access the greater whole." She let out a long, heavy breath. "The Arameri had Nahadoth in their possession for centuries. You know, better than I, how much of his body they might have taken in that time. And while I doubt they have anything of Yeine, they *did* have a piece of Enefa in their keeping."

I inhaled. The Stone of Earth. The last remnant of my mother's flesh, taken from the corporeal form that had died when Itempas poisoned her with demons' blood. It was gone now, because Yeine had incorporated it into herself. But for two thousand years it had been a physical object, kept in the exclusive possession of mortals who had already developed a taste for the power of gods.

"A pound of the Nightlord's flesh," Glee said, "and perhaps nothing more than a speck of the Gray Lady's. Add to that some portion of the Dayfather, and use mortal magic to stir the mix..." She shrugged. "I cannot imagine what would result from such a recipe. Can you?"

Nothing good. Nothing *sane*. To mingle the essences of the Three was to invoke a level of power that no mortal, and few godlings, could handle safely. The crater that

would be left by such an attempt would be immense—
and it would be a crater not on the face of the world but on
reality itself.

"No god would do this," I murmured, shaken. "This
Kahl...he has to know how dangerous this is. He can't be
planning what we think he's planning." Vengeance was
his nature, but this went beyond vengeance. This was
madness.

"Nevertheless," Glee said. "The worst case is what we
must prepare for. And this is why I don't intend to let anyone have my father." The familiar look was there again, in
the cold implacability of her voice and the stubborn
set of her shoulders. For a moment I imagined a circle of
light revolving about her, a white sword in her hands...
but no.

"You're mortal," I said softly. "Even if you can somehow keep Itempas hidden from a god, you won't be able to
do it forever. If nothing else, Kahl can wait you out."

She looked at me, and for an instant I was painfully
aware that only the fragile shield of her skin stood
between me and her deadly, demonic blood.

"Kahl will die before I do," she said. "I'll make certain
of that." With that, she turned and walked into the crowd,
leaving me alone with my wonder and fear.

I bought a tamarind juice to console myself.

After a while, I decided to see whether the seed I'd
planted had borne any fruit. Closing my eyes and sitting
down on the steps of a closed bookstore, I sought out the
boy who bore my mark. It took only a moment, and to my
delight I found that he had spread the mark to eight others
already, all of whom were now roving through the crowd
on both sides of the barricaded street. I could hear through
them, too—mostly the ever-present murmur of the crowd,

punctuated by the occasional variance: horse hooves as a mounted Order-Keeper passed on the street, music as a busker plied his trade. All of the sights were from a child's point of view. I sighed in longing and settled in to wait for the festivities to begin.

Two hours passed. Glee eventually came back and reported that Nemmer—who hadn't bothered to speak to me—had sent a message that there was no sign of trouble thus far. Better still, Glee handed me a cup of savory ice flavored with rosemary and serry flowers that she'd bought from some vendor; for that alone I would love her forever.

As I licked my fingers, the crowd abruptly grew tense, and their noise trebled all at once. I had to keep my eyes closed in order to focus on the children's vision, but through their eyes I saw the first white, waving banners of Dekarta's procession, which had reached the Avenue of Nobles at last. There came a marching column of soldiers first, several hundred deep. In their midst rode a massive palanquin, gliding smoothly along on the shoulders of dozens of men. Mounted soldiers and Order-Keepers flanked this, some with an air that made me suspect they were scriveners, and more soldiers followed behind. The palanquin was simple and graceful in its design, little more than a railed platform, but it had been constructed of daystone, too, and shone like noonday in this perpetually twilit city.

And atop this, stunning and stark in black, stood Dekarta. He'd added a heavy mantle to his outfit, which suited his broad shoulders perfectly, and he stood with legs apart and his hands gripping the forward rail as if it were the yoke of the world. No detached gaze for him; his eyes scanned the crowd as the procession traveled, his expression as cool and challenging as I'd ever seen. When the palanquin stopped and the men lowered it to the ground, he did not wait for it to touch the street stones before he stepped off its side and strode forward, purposeful and swift. The soldiers parted clumsily, and his guards scrambled to follow. Deka stopped, however, on reaching the foot of the steps. There he flicked back his cloak and waited, his eyes trained on the World Tree—or perhaps he was gazing at the palace nestled in the lowest fork of its trunk. It was his first sight of home in ten years, after all. If he still considered Sky home.

The crowd, meanwhile, had gone mad for him. People on either side of the street barriers cheered, shouted, and waved their white pennants. Through one of my spy-children's eyes, I saw a gaggle of well-dressed merchant girls scream and point at Deka and scream again, clutching each other and jumping up and down. It was more than his beauty, I realized. It was everything: his hauteur, the implied defiance of his clothing, the confidence that seemed to issue from his very pores. Everyone knew his story—born an outsider, the spare who could never be heir. That was part of it, too. He was more like them than a true Arameri, and he was stronger, not weaker, for his difference. They certainly seemed to love him for it.

But then there was a stir at the other end of the avenue. From somewhere within the Salon, two people emerged. Ramina Arameri, magnificent in a white uniform with the full sigil stark on his brow, and another man I didn't recognize. Well dressed, Teman, tall for one of that race, with waist-length locks wrapped in silver cuffs and studded with what had to be diamonds. He wore white, too, though not completely. The centerline of his uniform, which otherwise matched Ramina's, had been accented by a double line of green fabric edged in gold. The colors of the Teman Protectorate. Datennay Canru, Shahar's husband-to-be.

They moved to the center of the steps and then stood waiting, their presence enough of a warning that no one missed what followed.

There was a flicker atop both sets of daystone steps, and in the same instant two women appeared. To the right was Remath, clad in a deceptively simple white satin gown, carrying an object that made my belly clench: a glass scepter, tipped with a spadelike sharp blade. To the left...

In spite of everything that had happened, in spite of my resolve to be a man and not a boy about it, I had to open my own eyes to see her for myself. Shahar.

It was clear that Remath intended for her daughter to be the center of attention. This was not difficult, as like Dekarta, Shahar had only grown in beauty over the years. Her figure had filled out, her hair was longer, and the lines of her face seemed more settled and mature—the face of a woman, at last, rather than a girl. The dress she wore seemed barely attached to her flesh. The base garment was a translucent tube, thin enough that all of Shadow could see her pale skin through its fabric—but at her breasts and hips, enormous silvery flower petals, loose and curling and long as a man's arm, had been adhered to the material. They drifted behind her like clouds as she came down the steps. There was a collective gasp from the crowd as everyone realized: the petals were real and taken from the World Tree's flowers. Given the size, however, they could only have been blossoms from very high on the Tree, where the Tree pierced the world's envelope. No mortal flower collector could climb to such airless heights, and the Arameri no longer had god-slaves. How had they gotten them? Regardless, the effect was perfect: Shahar had become a mortal woman swathed in the divine.

Shahar's expression, unlike Remath's, was everything an Arameri heir's should be: proud, arrogant, superior. But when she turned to face her mother and they walked toward each other, she lowered her gaze with just the perfect touch of humility. The world was not hers, not yet, not quite. Mother and daughter met between the steps, and Remath took Shahar's left hand in her right. Then—with such casual grace that they had to have practiced it dozens of times—both women turned toward the Avenue of Nobles and raised their free hands toward Dekarta, in clear welcome.

Showing no hint of the reticence or resentment that I suspected he felt, Dekarta climbed the steps to reach them, then knelt at their feet. Both women bent, offering him their hands, each of which he took in his own. Then he rose, moving to Remath's left, and all three turned to face the waiting masses, raising their joined hands for the world to see.

The crowd was a many-headed beast, screaming, stamping, cheering. The air was so full of glittering confetti that the city seemed to have been struck by a silver snowstorm. And as this little show took place, I redoubled my concentration and straightened from my slouch against the wall. I caught a glimpse of Glee, not far off: she stood tense, scanning the street with whatever peculiar senses a demon could bring to bear. This was the moment, I felt with certainty. If Usein Darr or Kahl or some ambitious Arameri rival meant to strike, they would do it now.

Sure enough, one of my spy-children saw something.

It might have been nothing. The busker I had noticed

earlier near the public well had stopped playing a battered old brass lunla to peer at something. I would have dismissed the image if it had not come from my clever one, the pickpocket I'd marked. If he was paying such sudden and close attention to the busker, then there was something about the busker worth seeing.

I noticed the busker's open lunla case, which he'd set out before him as a silent appeal to passersby. Atop the layer of coins and notes scattered on the worn velvet, someone had tossed a larger object. I saw the busker pick it up, frowning in puzzlement. I saw the eyeholes and caught a quick glimpse of lacing lines on the inside of the thing before the busker turned it around, trying to figure out what it was.

A mask.

I was moving before I opened my eyes. Glee was beside me, both of us rudely shoving our way through the crowd as needed. She had taken out the small messaging sphere again, and this time it glowed red instead of white, sending some wordless signal. For an instant my god-senses actually worked, and in that span, I felt the faint tremor of my siblings' movements, folding and unfolding the world as they converged on the area.

Through the eyes of my boy, I saw the busker's face go suddenly slack, as though a brain fit had seized him. Instead of twitching or slumping, however, he moved the mask forward, like a man moving in a dream. He put it over his face. As he tied it at the back, I caught a glimpse of white lacquer and starkly drawn shade lines. The suggestion of an entirely different face: implacable, serene, frightening. I had no idea what archetype it had been meant to symbolize. Through the eyeholes of this, the busker blinked once, sudden awareness and confusion coming into them as though he couldn't fathom why he'd put the demonshitting thing on. He reached up to pull it off.

The designs of the mask flickered, as if they'd caught the light for a moment. A breath later, the man's eyes went dead. Not closed, not dazed. I am a son of Enefa; I know death when I see it.

Yet the busker got to his feet and looked around, pausing as his white-masked face oriented on the top of the Salon steps. I expected him to begin walking in that direction. Instead he charged toward the steps, running faster than any mortal should have been able, plowing down or flinging aside—*far* aside—anyone unfortunate enough to get in his way.

I also did not expect the cobblestones that edged the Salon steps to suddenly flare white, revealing themselves to be bricks of daystone that someone had painted gray to match the surrounding granite. Through this translucent layer of paint, I could see the darker, starker lines of an etched sigil, the characters on each stone together commanding immobility in the harshest gods' pidgin and addressed to any living thing that tried to cross it. A shield, of sorts, and it should have worked. The Arameri on the steps had no fear of knives or arrows; their blood sigils could deflect such things easily. All they needed to fear were the mask-wielding assassins, whose strange magic could somehow circumvent their sigils. Keep them out of reach and the Arameri would be safe— so the scrivener corps had reasoned.

The busker staggered, then stopped as he reached the ring of stones. The mask swung from side to side, not in negation, and not with any movement that could be interpreted as human. I had seen gravel lizards do the same, swaying back and forth over a carcass.

Too late I remembered the simplistic literalness of

scrivening magic. Any *living* thing, the stones commanded. But even if the busker's heart still beat and his
limbs still moved, that alone did not qualify as life. The
mask had dimmed his soul to nothingness.

The busker stopped swaying, the rounded eyeholes fixed
on a target. I followed its gaze and saw Shahar frozen at the
top of the steps, her eyes wide and her expression still.

"Oh, demons," I groaned, and ran for the steps as fast
as I could.

The busker stepped closer to the sigil-stones.

"There!" cried Glee, pointing.

She could not have been talking to me. As the crowd's
cheers turned to screams and stamping became stampeding,
Kitr appeared at the foot of the steps, just in front of the
Arameri guard. A line of twelve glowing red knives
appeared in the air before her, hovering and ready. I had
seen her fling those knives through armies, leaving fallen
mortals like scythed wheat. She could have done that
here, risking the crowd to get her target, but like most of
the godlings of the city, she would not. They had all taken
an oath to respect mortal life. So she waited for the fleeing mortals to scatter more, giving her a clear shot.

I saw the danger before she did, for she had ignored the
Arameri's guards behind her. Faced with a strange godling and a mad mortal, they reacted to both. Half of them
fired crossbows at the masked man; the other half fired at
Kitr. This could not do her any lasting harm, but it did
throw her off balance as her body jerked with the impact
of the bolts. She recovered in an instant, shouting at them
in fury—and as she did so, the masked man pushed past
the barrier, as if the air had turned fleetingly to butter.
Slowed, but not stopped.

I thought Kitr would miss her chance, distracted by the

mortals. Instead she hissed, her form flickering for just an instant. In her place curled an enormous red-brown snake, its cobralike hood flared. Then she was a woman again, and the knives streaked at the man with the speed of spat poison, all twelve of them thudding into his body with such force that he should have been flung halfway to the city limits.

Instead he merely stopped for a moment, rocking back on his heels. That was the first evidence that the mask had its own protective magic. I saw a glimmer around the edges of his mask, against his skin, underneath. What was it doing? Strengthening his flesh, certainly, or Kitr's knives would've torn it apart. Displacing the force of the blows. Before I could fathom it, the busker started forward again, running slower because of the knives in his thighs. But running.

And in that instant, a second masked man, this one bigger and heavier, raced out of the crowd and plowed into the guards from the side.

Two of them. *Two* of them.

Glee cursed. We were too far from the madness, going too slow as we fought our way through the panicked crowd. She grabbed my shoulder. "Get them to Sky!" she said, and flung me through the ether. Startled, I materialized atop the Salon steps, in front of an equally stunned cluster of Arameri and soon-to-be-Arameri eyes.

"Sieh," said Shahar. She stared at me, oblivious to the chaos twenty steps away, and I knew in that instant that she still loved me.

"Get the hells out of here," I snapped at her, stifling my fury at Glee. Why in heavens had she sent me? What could I do, with no useful magic? "Why are you just standing here? Go back to Sky, damn it!"

There was a crackle, and lightning arced up from somewhere within the crowd, twisting back down to strike the second masker and a handful of guards, who were flung away screaming. Idiot scriveners. Like the first masker, this one stumbled. Stopped. A moment later he lurched forward, his hands scrabbling for purchase on the steps until he could manage to run upright again.

The guards had had enough time to recoup, however. Wrath Arameri, a naked sword in his hand, swept past us at the head of twin lines of soldiers. One line split and converged around us to protect Remath and the rest of us. The other line Wrath directed to assist the guards at the foot of the steps. Wrath fell in at Remath's side, daring to put a hand on her shoulder as he urged her back toward the daystone steps. Both maskers ran right into a thicket of pikes and swords. From the men's reactions, however—or lack thereof—it was already clear the blows would only slow them down, not stop them or kill them. They were already dead.

"What in demons?" murmured Datennay Canru. I followed his gaze, and my mouth went dry: a third masker had appeared, this one on the steps of the nearby Itempan White Hall. He wore the uniform of an Order-Keeper, but unlike the first two, his mask was the deep splashy crimson of blood, with stylized white and gold designs and an open mouth that suggested a roar of vengeful fury. This man, too, began to run toward us—and with the crowd thinning and the guards occupied, nothing stood in his way.

Nothing but me.

"Oh gods, no," I whispered. What could I do? En pulsed hot against the skin of my chest. I grabbed for it; then I remembered. En's power was mine; when I was strong, so was it. But I was only mortal now. If I used En, drained the last of its strength…

No. I would not kill my oldest friend, not for this. And I would not let my new friends, even if one of them had betrayed me, die. I was still a god, damn it, even without magic. I was still the wind and caprice, even bound into dying flesh. I would fear no mere mortal, no matter how powerful.

So I bared my teeth and lashed the tail I no longer possessed. Shouting a challenge, I ran down the steps to meet the crimson masker.

My words had been in the First Tongue, a command, though I hadn't expected the man to listen. But to my shock, the crimson masker stopped and turned toward me.

This mask was beautiful and horrid, the runnels and paint suggesting fouled rivers, the strange-angled eyes like crooked mountains. Its mouth—a stylized thing of lips and teeth with a dark pit of an opening beyond which I could not see its wearer's face—was twisted, a wail of utmost despair. *Murderer*, its markings whispered to me, and suddenly I thought of all the evils I'd done during the Gods' War. I thought of the evils I'd done since— sometimes at the Arameri's bidding, sometimes out of my own rage or cruelty. Forgetting my own challenge amid crushing guilt, I stumbled to a halt.

I felt a jolt. Sudden restriction and pain. Blinking, I looked down and found that the man had made a blade of his hand and had thrust it into my body at the midriff, nearly up to the wrist.

I was still staring down at this when Dekarta reached me. He grabbed my arm and spoke without words, whipping his head in a wide, vicious arc. Sound and force flooded from his throat, a roar of denial powered by the living energy of his skin and blood and bone. Better than many gods could have done. Where the power struck the crimson-masked man, I saw it cancel the mask's message. The mask split down the center with a faint crack, and an instant later he flew backward a good fifty feet, vanishing amid the fleeing crowd. I could not see precisely where he landed because then Deka's power struck the steps of the Salon, which erupted, shattering into rubble and bursting upward in an arcing spray.

There could be no precision to such a strike. Guards and soldiers went flying, screaming, along with the enemy. Through all this I saw another white-masked man, one I hadn't noticed, run into the barrier of broken, flying stone and tumble back. But as the dust and rubble returned to earth, he sat up.

Nemmer appeared swathed in shadows, facing me. I saw her eyes widen at the sight of my wound. Beyond her, I saw the fallen white-masked man get to his feet and come charging again, this time leaping with godlike strength over the channel of rubble that Deka had created. I willed a warning, since I could not muster the breath, and to my astonishment Nemmer seemed to hear me. She turned and met the man as he struck.

Then I was in Deka's arms, being carried like a child, *bump te bump te bump*. It was nice that he was so much bigger than me. He ran up the steps to the rest of the Arameri party, who had finally—finally!—begun to hurry up the curving steps toward the nearer gate. From Deka's embrace, I tried to shout at them to go faster, but I couldn't lift my head. So strange. It was like my first day as a mortal, when Shahar had summoned me to this realm as the cat, or the day two thousand years before that, when Itempas had thrown me down in chains of flesh and given my leash to a woman, one of Shahar's daughters, who looked equal parts horrified and elated at the power she held.

Then we reached the top of the steps, and the world folded into a blur, and I passed out in its rippling crease.

16

I SEE SOMETHING I should not.

I see as gods do, absorbing all the world around us whether we have eyes to see it or ears to hear it or a body at all present. I know things because they happen. This is not a mortal thing, and it should not happen while I am in the mortal realm, but I suppose it is proof that I am not completely mortal yet.

We have reached Sky. The forecourt is chaos. The captain of the guard is shouting and gesturing at a gaggle of men who crossed the gate with us. Soldiers and scriveners are running, the former to surround the Vertical Gate with spears and swords in case the maskers follow, the latter bringing brushes and inkpots so that they can seal it off before that happens. While this occurs, Wrath and Ramina try to pull Remath into the palace, but she shakes them off. "I will not retreat in my own home," she says, so the soldiers and scriveners make ready to defend her with their lives.

Amid all this running and shouting, I flop about in Deka's arms, dying. Dying faster, that is, instead of the decades-long death that aging has imposed on me. The crimson masker has punched a hole through many of my organs and a good chunk of my spine. If I somehow survive, which is highly unlikely, I will never walk again. Yet my heart still beats, and my brain still fires sparks within its wrinkled meat, and as long as those things continue, there is an anchor for my soul to hold on to.

I'm glad it will be like this. I died protecting those I cared for, facing an enemy, like a god.

Deka has carried me off the Vertical Gate, onto the unblemished white daystone of Sky's forecourt. He falls to his knees, shouting for someone to hold me, he can save me if he has help, help him, damn it.

It is Shahar who comes to her brother's call. She kneels at my other side, and their long-awaited reunion is a quick and panicked meeting of eyes across the gore of my open belly. "Get his clothes open," he commands, though she is the heir and he is nothing, just a fancy servant. (I am useless, aside from the part of me that watches. My eyes have rolled back in my head, and my mouth hangs open, ugly and inelegant. Some god.) While she struggles to lift my shirt—she tried to tear it first, thinking that would disturb the wound less, but the cheap material is surprisingly strong—Deka pulls a square of paper and a capped brush from wherever scriveners keep such things, and sketches a mark that means hold. *He means for it to hold in my blood, hold back the filth that is already poisoning my body. That will give him time to write more sigils, which might actually heal me. (Has he only painted offensive magic into his skin? Silly boy.)*

But as he completes the mark and reaches for me, putting his hand on Shahar's to brace himself so that he can lay the sigil in place, something happens.

The universe is a living, breathing thing. Time, too. It moves, though not as mortals imagine. It is restless, twitchy. Mortals don't notice because they're restless and twitchy, too. Gods notice, but we learn to ignore these things early on, the same way mortal newborns eventually ignore the lonely silence of a world without heartbeats. Yet suddenly I notice everything. The slow, aeons-deep inhalation of the stars. The crackle of the sun's power against this planet's veil of life. The minute scratching of mites too small to see on Shahar's pristine white skin. The lazy, buzzy jolt of hours and days and centuries.

And between them, beneath their hands, I open my eyes. My mouth opens. Am I shouting? I cannot hear the words. I reach up, my hands covering Shahar's and Dekarta's, and there is a flicker of something, like lightning, along their skins. Shahar gasps, her eyes going wide. Dekarta stares at her, opening his mouth to cry out.

There is a blurring. White lines, like the streaking of comets, run through the shapes of our flesh. It is like before, the watching-me realizes—like the time of our oath, when we touched and they made me mortal. But this is different. This time, when the power comes, it is not a wild concussion. There is a will at work: two wills, with one purpose. Something bursts within me and is funneled to a fine point.

Then
it
becomes

I flopped about in Deka's arms, pissed. "Put me down, Maelstrom, damn you. I'm a god, not a sack of potatoes—"

He stumbled to a halt just beyond the Vertical Gate. A few paces ahead, Shahar had done the same. Eight of Captain Wrath's men surrounded her, trying to hurry her into the palace as they had already done Remath, but she shook them off. "I will not retreat in my own—"

She paused. Deka did, too. He set me on my feet. I swept marble dust off my clothes and hair and straightened my clothing, and then froze.

Oh.

Oh.

I understood, and did not. Many combinations in existence had meaning, and meaning has always imbued power—whether purely of an existential nature, or materially, or magically. There were the Three, of course, omnipotent on the infinitely rare occasions that they worked together. Twins. Male and female. God and mortal and the demons between.

But there was no reason for this. No precedent. They'd changed the universe. A pair of mortals.

They'd changed the universe *to heal me*.

They had changed the universe.

I stared at them. They stared back. Around us the chaos continued. All the other mortals seemed oblivious to what had happened, which was unsurprising. To them, it *hadn't* happened. There was no blood on the ground where I'd lain. My clothes weren't torn, because there had never been a wound. If I tried to remember, my mind conjured a glimpse of the crimson masker, hand poised before the blow, flying backward as Deka's blast of raw magic struck. But I could also remember the blow happening first.

A moment later Nemmer appeared, dropping something heavy to the ground. A body. I blinked. No, a masker; one of the white ones. Trussed up in what looked like huge writhing snakes formed of translucent shadow. This was Nemmer's magic. The instant she appeared, half of Wrath's soldiers moved to attack, and the other half realized the mistake and tried to stop them. There was a flurry of shouts and aborted lunges and then a great deal of confused milling. I suspected that if Wrath got through this day with his position intact, he would soon put his soldiers through a heavy training course on Gods, the Quick Recognition and Not Attacking Of.

"Got them," she said, putting her hands on her hips. She glanced at me and grinned. "Tell your mortals to stand down, Sieh. The danger has passed."

I stared at her, mute with shock. Her grin faltered. She glared at me, then snapped her fingers at my face. I jumped.

"What the hells is wrong with you?" Her smile turned vicious. "Were you so frightened by your first taste of mortal danger, big brother?"

I felt no real anger at her taunt because I had been in mortal danger a thousand times more than she had ever been. And I had far stranger things to occupy my thoughts.

But I was not the Trickster for nothing, and my mouth moved automatically while my brain continued to churn. "I was frightened by the incompetence I saw down there," I snapped. "Did you *plan* to let them nearly achieve their goal, or were your much-vaunted professionals caught napping?"

Nemmer did not lose her temper, but it was a near thing. At least she stopped smiling. "There were ten of them," she said, which broke some of my shock and brought me back to the present. "Counting the one your pet scrivener killed. All coming from different directions, all unstoppable—unless their bodies are completely destroyed or the masks are broken. You're lucky only one got through. We weren't prepared for a strike of this magnitude."

Ten of them. Ten mortals, tricked into donning the masks and turning themselves into living weapons. I shook my head, sickened.

"All the mortals up here are fine?" She spoke in a neutral tone. We were back to the unspoken truce, then.

I looked around, noting Shahar and Dekarta standing together nearby, listening to our conversation. Not far beyond them was Canru, looking uncomfortable and alone. Across the courtyard, Remath had stopped on the steps and seemed to be arguing with Ramina. Wrath faced us, his hand on his sword hilt, his gaze riveted on the masked creature at Nemmer's feet.

"The mortals who matter are fine," I said, feeling weary and full of grief. Ten who did not matter had died. And how many soldiers and innocents among the crowd? "We are all fine."

She looked uneasy at my wording but nodded, gesturing at the trussed-up man in the white mask. He was not dead; I saw him fighting the bonds, panting with the effort. "This one's for you, then. I figure the scrivener boy might be able to figure out something about this magic. Mortals understand how mortals think better than I ever will." She paused, then lifted her hand; something else appeared in it. "I'll give you this, too. Be careful of the intact masks, but once they're broken, the magic dies."

She held it out: the broken halves of the crimson mask.

I felt hard fingers punch through my flesh.

I took the mask pieces from her.

"Got to go," she said. She sounded just like a common mortal, right down to the Wesha accent. "Things to do, secrets to gather. We'll talk soon." With that, she vanished.

Remath was walking back, unhurried, as if she strolled through the aftermath of an attack on her family every day. While I could speak without her hearing, I went to Shahar and Dekarta, handing the pieces of the mask to Deka. He did not take them with his bare hands, quickly pulling his sleeves down to take the halves, gingerly, by the edges.

"Say nothing of what happened," I said, speaking low and quickly.

"But—" Shahar began, predictably.

"*No one remembers but us*," I said, and she shut up. Not even Nemmer, whose nature it was to sense the presence of secrets, had noticed anything. Dekarta caught his breath; he understood what this meant as well as I had. Shahar flicked a glance at him and at me, and then—as if she had not spent ten years apart from him, and as if she had not once broken my heart—she covered for us both, immediately turning to face her oncoming mother.

"The situation has been controlled," she said as Remath drew to a halt before us. Wrath positioned himself directly between me and Remath, his hard brown gaze fixed on me. (I winked at him. He did not react.) Ramina remained behind her, his arms folded, showing no hint of relief that his son and daughter were alive and well.

"Lady Nemmer reported there were ten assailants in all," Shahar continued. "Her organization captured the rest and will be conducting its own investigation. She would like mortal input, however." With a look of distaste, Shahar glanced at the immobilized masker.

"How considerate of her," said Remath, with only the faintest hint of sarcasm. "Wrath." He flinched and left off glaring at me. "Return to the city and oversee the investigation there. Be certain to find out why so many of these creatures were able to make it through our lines."

"Lady..." Wrath began. He glanced at me.

Remath lifted an eyebrow and faced me as well. "Lord Sieh. Are you planning to try and kill me again?" She paused, and added, "Today?"

"No," I said, letting my voice and face show that I still hated her, because I was not an Arameri and I saw no point in hiding the obvious. "Not today."

"Of course." To my surprise, she smiled. "Do stay awhile, Lord Sieh, since you're here. If I recall, you are prone to boredom, and I have plans of my own to set in motion, now that this unpleasantness has occurred." She glanced at the masker again, and there was an odd sort of sorrow in her expression for the most fleeting of moments. If it had lasted, I might have begun to pity her. But then it vanished and she smiled at me and I hated her again. "I believe you will find the next few days most interesting. As will my children."

While Shahar and I digested this in silence, Remath glanced at Deka, who stood just behind Shahar, his expression so neutral that he reminded me, at once, of Ahad. There was a long, silent moment. I saw Shahar, wearing her own careful mask, glance from one to the other.

"Not the homecoming you were expecting, I imagine." Remath's tone surprised me. She sounded almost affectionate.

Deka almost smiled. "Actually, Mother, I *was* expecting someone to try and murder me the instant I arrived."

The look that crossed Remath's face in that instant would have been difficult for anyone to interpret, mortal or immortal, if they were not familiar with Arameri ways. It was one of the ways they trained themselves to conceal emotion. They smiled when they were angry and showed sorrow when they were overjoyed. Remath looked wryly amused, skeptical of Deka's apparent nonchalance, mildly impressed. To me her feelings might as well have been written into the sigil on her forehead. She was glad to see Deka. She was very impressed. She was troubled—or bitterly empathetic, at least—to see him so cold.

Shahar loved her. I wasn't sure about Deka. Did Remath love either of her children back? That I could not say.

"I'll see both of you tomorrow," she said to Shahar and Dekarta, then turned and walked away. Wrath bowed to her back, then strode off with a final glance at us before raising his voice to call his men. Ramina, however, lingered.

"Interesting stylistic choice," he said to Deka. As if in response to his words, a stray breeze lifted Deka's black cloak behind him like a living shadow.

"It seemed fitting, Uncle," Deka replied. He smiled thinly. "I am something of a black sheep, am I not?"

"Or a wolf, come to feast on tender flesh—unless someone tames you." Ramina's eyes drifted to Deka's forehead, then to Shahar, in clear implication. Shahar's brows drew down in the beginnings of a frown, and Ramina flashed a loving smile at both of them. "But perhaps you're more useful with sharp teeth and killer instincts, hmm? Perhaps the Arameri of the future will need a whole *pack* of wolves." And with this, he glanced at me. I frowned.

With studied boredom in her tone, Shahar said, "Uncle, you're being even more obscure than usual."

"My apologies." He didn't look apologetic at all. "I

merely came to mention a detail about the meeting Sister asked that you attend tomorrow. She's ordered full privacy—no guards, no courtiers beyond the ones invited. Not even servants will be present."

At this, Shahar and Dekarta both looked at each other, and I wondered what in the infinite hells was going on. Remath should never have declared her intention for a private meeting in advance; too easy for other Arameri or interested parties to slip in a listening sphere. Or an assassin. But Ramina was marked with a full sigil; he could not act against his sister even if he wanted to. Which meant that he was speaking on Remath's behalf. But why?

Then I realized Ramina was still looking at me. So it was something Remath wanted *me* to know, in particular. To make sure I'd be there.

"Damned twisty-headed Arameri," I said, scowling at him. "I've had a horrid day. Say what you mean."

He blinked at me with such blatant surprise that he fooled no one. "I should think it would be obvious, Trickster. The Arameri are about to implement a trick that should impress even you. Naturally we would welcome your blessing for such an endeavor." With that, he smiled and strode after his sister.

I stared after him in confusion, as if that would help. It didn't. And now I spied Morad approaching at the head of a phalanx of servants, all of them pausing to bow as Ramina walked past in the palace archway.

Shahar turned to me and Deka, speaking low and quickly. "I must attend to Canru and the Teman party down at the Salon; they'll be very put out about this. Both of you, request quarters that can be reached through the dead spaces. Sieh knows what I mean." With that, she, too, left us, heading over to join her fiancé.

"Are you all right?" I heard Canru ask her. I tightened my jaw against inadvertent approval and turned to Deka.

"I suppose you'll want to settle in, too," I said. "Order the scrivener corps about and start dissecting your new prize, or whatever it is you people do." I looked over at the trussed-up masker.

"I'd much rather go somewhere and have a long talk with you about what just happened," he said, and there was something in his voice, a smoothness, that made me blush inadvertently. He smiled, missing nothing. "But I suppose that will have to wait. I'll be taking one of the spire rooms—Spire Seven, most likely, if it's still available. Where will you be?"

I considered. "The underpalace." There was no place more private in all of Sky. "Deka, the dead spaces—"

"I know what they are," he said, surprising me, "and I can guess which room you'll be in. We'll come around midnight."

Flustered, I watched Deka as he turned to greet Morad. I heard him issue orders as easily as if he had not just returned from a ten-year exile, and I heard Morad answer with, "At once, my lord," as if she had never missed him.

All around the courtyard, everyone spoke with someone else. I stood alone.

Obscurely troubled, I went over to the masker and prodded him with a toe, sighing. He grunted and struggled toward me in response. "Why must all you mortals be so difficult?" I asked. The dead man, predictably, did not answer.

My old room.

I stood in the open doorway, unsurprised to see that it

had not been touched in the century since I'd left. Why would any servant, or steward for that matter, have bothered? No one would ever want to dwell in a chamber that had housed a god. What if he'd left traps behind or woven curses into the walls? Worse, what if he came back?

The reality was that I had never intended to come back, and it had never occurred to me to weave curses into anything. If I had, I would never have burdened the walls with anything so trivial as a curse. I would have created a masterwork of pain and humiliation and despair from my own heart, and I would have forced any mortal who invaded the space to share those horrors. Just for a moment or two, rather than the centuries I endured, but none of it blunted.

An old wooden table stood on one side of the room. On its surface were the small treasures I had always loved to gather, even when they had no life or magic of their own. A perfect dried leaf, now probably too fragile to touch. A key; I did not remember what it opened or if its lock still existed. I just liked keys. A perfectly round pebble that I had always meant to turn into a planet and add to my orrery. I had forgotten about it after I'd gotten free, and now I had no power to correct the error.

Beyond the table was my nest—or so I had styled it, though it had none of the comfort or beauty of my true nest in the gods' realm. This was just a pile of rags, gray and dry-rotted and dusty now, and probably infested with vermin to boot. Some of the rags were things I had stolen from the fullbloods: a favorite scarf, a baby's blanket, a treasured tapestry. I'd always tried to take things they cared about, though they'd punished me for it whenever they'd caught me. Every blow had been worth it—not because the thefts caused them any great hardship, but because I was *not* a mortal, *not* just a slave. I was still

Sieh, the mischievous wind, the playful hunter, and no punishment could ever break me. To remind myself of that, I had been willing to endure anything.

Dust and mite food now. I slid my hands into my pockets, sat down against a wall, and sighed.

I was dozing when they arrived, through the floor. Shahar, to my surprise, was the first one through. I smiled to see that she held a small ceramic tablet, on which had been drawn a single, simple command in our language. *Atadie.* Open. I had shown her the door, and she'd had someone make her a key.

"Have you been wandering the dead spaces by yourself these past few years?" I asked as she climbed out of the hole and dusted herself off. She or Dekarta had made steps out of the reshaped daystone. He came up behind her, looking around in fascination.

She looked at me warily, no doubt remembering that the last time I'd seen her, really spoken to her, had been two years before, the morning after we'd made love.

"Some," she said, after a moment. "It's useful to be able to go where I want with none the wiser."

"Indeed it is," I said, smiling thinly. "But you should be careful, you know. The dead spaces were mine once— and any place that was mine for so long is likely to have taken on some of my nature. Step into the wrong corridor, open the wrong door, and you never know what might jump out and bite you."

She flinched, as I'd meant her to, and not just at my words. *Betrayer,* I let my eyes say, and after a moment she looked away.

Deka looked warily at us both, perhaps only now realizing how bad things were between us. Wisely, he chose not to mention it.

"There's panic in Shadow," he said, "and we're getting reports of unrest from elsewhere in the world. There have been riots, and the Order has instituted extra services at all White Halls to accommodate the Itempans who suddenly feel compelled to pray. Mother's called an emergency session of the Consortium in three days' time, and she's authorized the Litaria to facilitate travel by gate for all the representatives. Rumor has the Arameri all dead and a new Gods' War impending."

I laughed, though I shouldn't have. Fear was like poison to mortals; it killed their rationality. Somewhere, there would be deaths tonight.

"That's Remath's problem, not mine," I said, sitting forward, "or yours. We have a more significant concern."

They looked at each other, then at me, and waited. Belatedly I realized they thought I was about to explain something.

"I haven't got a clue what happened," I said, raising my hands quickly. "Never seen anything like that in my life! But I have no idea why anything happens the way it does around you two."

"It didn't come from us." Shahar spoke softly, with the barest hint of hesitation. I scowled at her and she blanched, but then tightened her jaw and lifted her chin. "We felt it, Deka and I, and this time you did, too. We have felt that power before, Sieh. It was the same as the day the three of us took our oath."

Silence fell, and in it I nodded slowly. Trying not to be afraid. I had already guessed that the power was the same. What frightened me was my growing suspicion as to *why*.

Deka licked his lips. "Sieh. If the three of us touch, and it somehow causes this . . . this *thing* to occur, and if that power can be directed…Sieh, Shahar and I—" He took a deep breath. "We want to try it again. See if we can turn you back into a godling."

I caught my breath, wondering if they had any idea of how much danger we were all in.

"No," I said. I stood and stepped away from the wall, too tense to maintain my pose of indifference.

"Sieh—" Deka began.

"No." Gods. They really had no idea. I turned and began to pace, nibbling a thumbnail. All that happened in darkness. Sky's glowing halls had been designed specifically to thwart Nahadoth's nature, and Itempas was diminished to mortality. Yeine, though…every creature that had ever lived could be her eyes and ears, if she so chose. Was she observing us now? Would she…?

"Sieh." Shahar. She stepped in front of me and I stopped, because it was either that or run into her. I hissed, and she glared back. "You're making no sense. If we can restore your magic—"

"They'll kill you," I said, and she flinched. "Naha, Yeine. If the three of us have that kind of power, they'll kill us all."

They both looked blank. I groaned and rubbed my head. I had to make them understand.

"The demons," I said. More confusion. They did not know they were Ahad's descendants. I cursed in three languages, though I made sure none of them were my own. "The demons, damn it! Why did the gods kill them?"

"Because they were a threat," said Deka.

"No. No. Gods, do both of you only ever listen to teaching poems and priests' tales? You're Arameri; you know that stuff is all lies!" I glared at them.

"But that *was* why." Deka was looking stubborn

again, as he'd done as a child, as he'd probably done in
every Litaria lesson since. "Their blood was poison to
gods—"

"And they could pass for mortals, better than any god
or godling. They could, and did, blend in." I stepped
closer and looked into his eyes. If I wasn't careful, if I did
not work hard to keep the years hidden, mortals were not
fooled by my outward appearance. Now, however, I let
him see all I had experienced. All the aeons of mortal life,
all the aeons before that. I had been there nearly from the
beginning. I understood things Deka would never comprehend, no matter how brilliant he was and no matter
how diminished I became as a mortal. I *remembered*. So I
wanted him to believe my words now, without question,
the way ordinary mortals believed the words of their
gods. Even if that meant making him fear me.

Deka frowned, and I saw the awareness come over him.
And though he loved me and had wanted me since he was
too young to know what desire meant, he stepped back. I
felt a moment's sorrow. But it was probably for the best.

Shahar, sweet, beautiful betrayer that she was, leapt to
my point before her brother did.

"They made *mortalkind* a threat," she said very softly.
"They fit in among us, yes. Interbred with us. Passed on
their magic, and sometimes their poison, to all their mortal descendants."

"Yes," I said. "And though it was the poison that was of
immediate concern—one of my brothers died of demon
poison, which set the whole thing off—there was also the
fear of what would happen to our magic, filtered and distorted through a mortal lens. We saw that some of the
demons were just as powerful as pure godlings." I looked
at Deka as I said it. I couldn't help myself. He stared back

at me, still shaken to discover that his childhood crush was something frightening and strange, oblivious to my real implication. "It wasn't hard to guess that someday, somehow, a mortal might be born with as much power as one of the Three. The power to change reality itself on a fundamental level." I shook my head and gestured around us, at the room, Sky, the world, the universe. "You don't understand how fragile all this is. Losing one of the Three would destroy it. Gaining a Fourth, or even something close to a Fourth, would do the same."

Deka frowned, concern overwhelming shock. "And what we did... you think the Three would see that as the culmination of their fears?"

"But it's not as though we did anything harmful—" Shahar began.

"Changing reality *is* harmful! If you tried it again, even to help me— Deka, you understand how magic works. What happens if you misdraw a sigil or misspeak a godword? If the two of you try to use this power to remake me..." I sighed, and faced the truth I hadn't wanted to admit. "Well, think of what happened last time. You wanted me to be your friend, a true friend— something that I could never have been as a god. You would have grown up and understood how different I was. You would have become proper Arameri and wondered how you could use me." Now I looked at Shahar, whose lips tightened ever so slightly. "If I had stayed a god, our friendship would never have survived this long. So you, some part of you, made me into something that *could* be your friend."

Deka took another step back, horror filling his face. "You're saying *we* did this? The collapse of the Nowhere Stair, your mortality...?"

At this I sighed and went back to the wall, sliding down
to sit against it. "I don't know. This is all guesses and con-
jecture. Your will, if it had this strange magic behind it,
may have focused the magic just enough to cause a
change, but then it backlashed...or something. None of
that answers the fundamental question of *why* you have
this power."

"It isn't just us, Sieh." Shahar again, quiet again. "Deka
and I have touched many times, and nothing came of it.
It's only when we touch *you* that there's any change."

I nodded bleakly. I had figured that out as well.

Silence fell as they digested everything I'd said. It was
broken by the loud grumbling of my empty belly and my
louder yawn. At this, Dekarta shifted uncomfortably.
"Why did you come here, Sieh? There are no servants this
far down, and this room is...foul." He looked around, his
lip curling at the pile of ancient rags.

A foul place for a fouled god, I thought. "I like it here,"
I said. "And I'm too tired to go anywhere else. Go away
now, both of you. I need to rest."

Shahar turned toward the hole in the floor, but Deka
lingered. "Come with us," he said. "Have something to
eat, take a bath. There's a couch in my new quarters."

I looked up at him and saw the bravery of his effort. I
had jarred his fantasies badly, but he would try, even now,
to be the friend he'd promised to be.

You are the one who did this to me, beautiful Deka.

I smiled thinly, and he frowned at the sight.

"I'll be all right," I said. "Go on. Let's all be ready to
face your mother in the morning."

So they left.

As the daystone of the floor resealed itself, I lay down
and curled up to sleep, resigning myself to stiffness by

morning. But as soon as I closed my eyes, I realized I was
no longer alone.

"Are you really afraid of me?" asked Yeine.

I opened my eyes and sat up. She sat cross-legged in
my old nest, dainty as always, beautiful even amid rags.
The rags were no longer dry-rotted, however. I could see
color and definition returning to what had been a gray
mass and could hear the faint tightening of the thread
fibers as they regained cohesion and strength. Along one
of Yeine's thighs, a line of barely visible mites had begun
to crawl, vanishing over the rise of her flesh. Sent packing,
I imagined, or she might be killing them. One never knew
with her.

I said nothing in response to her question, and she
sighed.

"I don't care if mortals grow powerful, Sieh. If they do,
and they threaten us, I'll deal with that then. For now"—
she shrugged—"maybe it's a good thing that some of them
have magic like this. Maybe that's what they really need,
power of their own, so they can stop being jealous of ours."

"Don't tell Naha," I whispered. At this she sobered and
grew silent.

After a moment, she said, "You used to come to me
whenever we were alone."

I looked away. I wanted to. But I knew better.

"Sieh," she said. Hurt.

And because I loved her too much to let her think the
problem was her, I sighed and got up and went over to the
nest. Climbing into it brought back memories, and I
paused for an instant, overwhelmed by them. Holding
Naha on a moonless night—the one time he was safe
from both Itempas and the Arameri—as he wept for the
Three that had been. Endless hours I'd spent weaving new

orbits for my orrery and polishing my Arameri bones.
Grinding my teeth as another guard-captain, this one a
fullblood and cruel, ordered me to turn over for him. (I
had gotten his bones, too, in the end. But they had not
made as good toys as I'd hoped, and eventually I'd tossed
them off the Pier.)

And now Yeine, whose presence burned away the bad
and burnished the good. I wanted to hold her so much, but
I knew what would happen. It amazed me that she didn't.
She was so very young.

She frowned at me in puzzlement, reaching out to cup
my cheek. My self-control broke, and I flung myself against
her as I had done so many times, burying my face in her
breast, gripping the cloth at the back of her vest. It felt so
good, too, at first. I felt warm and safe and young. Her arms
came around me, and her face pressed into my hair. I was
her baby, her son in all but flesh, and the flesh didn't matter.

But there is always a moment when the familiar
becomes strange. It is always there, just a little, between
any two beings who love one another as much as she and
I. The line is so fine. In one moment I was her child, my
head pillowed on her breast in all innocence. In the next I
was a man, lonely and hungry, and her breasts were small
but full. Female. Inviting.

Yeine tensed. It was barely perceptible, but I had been
expecting it. With a long sigh I sat up, letting her go.
When her eyes—troubled, uncertain—met mine, I turned
away. I am not a complete bastard. For her, I would stay
the boy that she needed and not the man I had become.

To my surprise, however, she caught my chin and made
me look at her again.

"There is more to this than you being mortal," she said.
"More than you wanting to protect those two children."

"I want to protect *mortalkind*," I said. "If Naha finds out what those two can do . . ."

Yeine shook her head, and shook mine a little, refusing to be distracted. Then she searched my face so intently that I began to be afraid again. She was not Enefa, but . . .

"You've been with Nahadoth and many of your siblings," she said. Her revulsion crawled along my skin like the evacuating mites. She was trying to resist it, and failing. "I know . . . things are different, for godkind."

If she had only been older. Just a few centuries might have been enough to reduce the memory of her mortal life and her mortal inhibitions. I mourned that I would not have time to see her become a true god.

"I was Enefa's lover, too," I said softly. I did not look at her at first. "Not . . . not often. When Itempas and Nahadoth were off together, mostly. When she needed me."

And because there would be no other time, I looked up at her and let her see the truth. *You might have needed me, too, in time. You're stronger than Naha and Tempa, but you're not immune to loneliness. And I have always loved you.*

To her very great credit, she did not recoil. I loved her more than ever for that. But she did sigh.

"I've felt no urge to have children," she said, grazing her knuckles along my cheek. I leaned into her touch, closing my eyes. "With so many angry, damaged stepchildren already, it seems foolish to complicate matters further. But also . . ." I felt her smile, like starlight on my skin. "You are my son, Sieh. It makes no sense. I should be your daughter. But . . . that's how I feel."

I caught her hand and pulled it against my chest so she could feel my mortal heartbeat. I was dying; it made me bold. "If I can be nothing else to you, I am glad to be your son. Truly."

Her smile turned sad. "But you want more."

"I always want more. From Naha, from Enefa...even from Itempas." I sobered at that, shifting to lie against her side. She permitted this, even though it had gone wrong before. A sign of trust. I did not abuse it. "I want things that are impossible. It's my nature."

"Never to be satisfied?" Her fingers played with my hair gently.

"I suppose." I shrugged. "I've learned to deal with it. What else can I do?"

She fell silent for so long that I grew sleepy, warm and comfortable with her in the softness of the nest. I thought she might sleep with me—just sleep, nothing more—which I wanted desperately and no longer knew how to ask for. But she, goddess that she was, had other things in mind.

"Those children," she said at last. "The mortal twins. They make you happy."

I shook my head. "I barely know them. I befriended them on a whim and fell in love with them by mistake. Those are things children do, but for once I should have thought like a god, not a child."

She kissed my forehead, and I rejoiced that there was no reticence in the gesture. "Your willingness to take risks is one of the most wonderful things about you, Sieh. Where would you and I be, if not for that?"

I smiled in spite of my mood, which I think was what she'd wanted. She stroked my cheek and I felt happier. Such was her power over me, which I had willingly given.

"They are not such terrible people to love," Yeine said, her tone thoughtful.

"Shahar is."

She pulled back a little to look at me. "Hmm. She must have done something terrible to make you so angry."

"I don't want to talk about it."

She nodded, allowing me to sulk for a moment. "Not the boy, though?"

"Dekarta." She groaned, and I chuckled. "I did the same thing! He's nothing like his namesake, though." Then I paused as I considered Deka's body-markings, his determination to be Shahar's weapon, and his relentless pursuit of me. "He's Arameri, though. I can't trust him."

"*I'm* Arameri."

"Not the same. It isn't an inborn thing. You weren't raised in this den of weasels."

"No, I was raised in a different den of weasels." She shrugged, jostling my head a little. "Mortals are the sum of many things, Sieh. They are what circumstance has made them and what they wish to be. If you must hate them, hate them for the latter, not the former. At least they have some say over that part."

I sighed. Of course she was right, and it was nothing more than I had argued with my own siblings over the aeons, as we debated—sometimes more than philosophically—whether mortals deserved to exist.

"They are such fools, Yeine," I whispered. "They squander every gift we give them. I..." I trailed off, trembling inexplicably. My chest ached, as though I might cry. I was a man, and men did not cry—or at least Teman men did not—but I was also a god, and gods cried whenever they felt like it. I wavered on the brink of tears, torn.

"You gave this Shahar your love." Yeine kept stroking my hair with one hand, absently, which did not help matters. "Was she worthy of it?"

I remembered her, young and fierce, kicking me down the stairs because I'd dared to suggest that she could not determine her own fate. I remembered her later, making love to me on her mother's orders—but how hungry she'd looked as she held me down and took pleasure from my body! I had not abandoned myself so completely with a mortal for two thousand years.

And as I remembered these things, I felt the knot of anger in me begin to loosen at last.

With a soft, amused chuckle, Yeine disentangled herself from me and sat up. I watched her do this wistfully. "Be a good boy and rest now. And don't stay up all night thinking. Tomorrow will be interesting. I don't want you to miss any of it."

At this I frowned, pushing myself up on one elbow. She ran fingers through her short hair as if to brush it back into place. A hundred years and still so much the mortal: a proper god would simply have willed her hair perfect. And she did not bother to hide the smug look on her face as she peered at me now.

"You're up to some mischief," I said, narrowing my eyes.

"Indeed I am. Will you bless me?" She got to her feet and stood smirking with one hand on her hip. "Remath Arameri is as interesting as her children, is all I'll say for now."

"Remath Arameri is evil, and I would kill her if Shahar did not love her so." As soon as I said this, however, Yeine raised an eyebrow, and I grimaced as I realized how much I had revealed—not just to her, but also to myself. For if I loved Shahar enough to tolerate her horror of a mother, then I loved Shahar enough to forgive her.

"Silly boy," Yeine said with a sigh. "You never do things the easy way, do you?"

I tried to make a joke of it, though the smile was hard to muster. "Not if the hard way is more fun."

She shook her head. "You almost died today."

"Not really." I flinched as she leveled A Look at me. "Everything turned out all right!"

"No, it didn't. Or rather, it shouldn't have. But you still have a god's luck, however much the rest of you has changed." She sobered suddenly. "A good mother desires not only her children's safety, but also their happiness, Sieh."

"Er…" I could not help tensing a little, wondering what she was going on about. She was not as strange as Naha, but she thought in spirals, and sometimes—locked in a mortal's linear mind as I was—I could not follow her. "That's good, I suppose…."

Yeine nodded, her face still as unfathomable thoughts churned behind it. Then she gave me another Look, and I blinked in surprise, for this one held a ferocity that I hadn't seen from her in a mortal lifetime.

"I will see to it that you know happiness, Sieh," she said. "*We* will do this."

Not she and Naha. I knew what she meant the way I knew the Three merited capital-letter status. And though the Three had never joined in the time since her ascension, she was still one of them. Part of a greater whole— and when all three of them wanted the same thing, each member spoke with the whole's voice.

I bowed my head, honored. But then I frowned as I realized what else she was saying. "Before I die, you mean."

She shook her head, just herself again, then leaned over to put a hand on my chest. I felt the minute vibration of her flesh for just an instant before my dulled senses lost the full awareness of her, but I was glad for that taste. She had no heart, my beautiful Yeine, but she didn't need one.

The pulse and breath and life and death of the whole universe was a more than sufficient substitute.

"We all die," she said softly. "Sooner or later, all of us. Even gods." And then, before her words could bring back the melancholy that I'd almost shed, she winked. "But being my son should get you *some* privileges."

With that she vanished, leaving behind only the cooling tingle of warmth where her fingers had rested on my chest and the renewed, clean rags of my nest. When I lay down, I was glad to find she'd left her scent, too, all mist and hidden colors and a mother's love. And a whiff—no more than that—of a woman's passion.

It was enough. I slept well that night, comforted.

But not before I'd disobediently lain awake for an hour or so, wondering what Yeine was up to. I could not help feeling excited. Every child loves a surprise.

"Thank you all for coming," said Remath. Her eyes touched on each of us in turn: me, Shahar, Dekarta, and, oddly, Wrath and Morad, alone of Remath's full court. The latter two knelt behind Shahar and Deka, conceding right of prominence to the fullbloods. Ramina was present, too, standing behind and to the left of Remath's throne. I leaned against the wall nearby, my arms folded as I pretended boredom.

It was late afternoon. We'd expected Remath's summons earlier in the day—in the morning, when she took her usual audience, or after that. But no one had come to fetch us, so Shahar and Deka had done whatever it was Arameri fullbloods did all day, and meanwhile I had slept until noon, mostly because I could. Morad, bless her, had sent brave servants to beard me in my lair with food and clothing, then bring me to Remath.

From the blocky stone chair that had been an Itempan altar before the Gods' War, and that still smelled faintly of Shinda Arameri's demon blood, Remath smiled at us.

"In light of yesterday's disturbing events," she said, "it seems the time has come to implement a plan that I hoped I would never need. Dekarta." He twitched in surprise and looked up. "Your teachers at the Litaria assure me that you are without doubt the finest young scrivener they have ever graduated, and as my spies at the Litaria confirm your accomplishments, it appears this is not just toadying praise. This pleases me more than you can know."

Dekarta stared at her in obvious surprise for a full second before answering. "Thank you, Mother."

"Do not thank me yet. I have a task for you and Shahar, one that will take substantial time and effort, but upon which the family's future will entirely depend." She folded her legs and glanced at Shahar. "Do you know what that task is, Shahar?"

It had the feel of an old question. Perhaps Remath quizzed Shahar in this manner all the time. Shahar seemed unfazed by it as she lifted her head to reply.

"I'm not certain," she said, "but I have suspicions, as my own sources have informed me of some very curious activities on your part."

"Such as?"

Shahar narrowed her eyes, perhaps considering how much she wanted to divulge in front of the mixed audience. Then, bluntly, she said, "You've had parties examining remote locations around the world, and you've had several of the scriveners—in secret, on pain of death—researching the building techniques used to create Sky."

She glanced at me briefly. "Those that can be replicated with mortal magic."

I blinked in surprise. Now *that* I hadn't been expecting. When I frowned at Remath, I was even more disturbed to find her smiling at me, as if my shock pleased her.

"What in the heavens are you up to, woman?" I asked.

She ducked her eyes almost coyly, reminding me, suddenly, of Yeine. Remath had that same smug look Yeine had worn the evening before. I did not like being reminded that they were relatives.

"The Arameri must change, Lord Sieh," she said. "Is that not what the Nightlord told us, on the day you and the other Enefadeh broke free from your long captivity? We have kept the world still too long, and now it twists and turns, reveling in sudden freedom—and risking its own destruction by changing too far, too fast." She sighed, the smugness fading. "My spies in the north gave me a report last year that I did not understand. Now, having seen the power of these masks, I realize we are in far greater danger than I ever imagined...."

Abruptly she trailed off, falling silent, and for a breath-held moment there were hells in her eyes—fears and weariness that she had not let us see up to now. It was a stunning lapse on her part. It was also, I realized as she lifted her gaze to Shahar, deliberate.

"My spies have seen hundreds of masks," she said softly. "Perhaps *thousands*. In nearly every High North nation there are *dimyi* artists; the northerners have been spreading knowledge of the form and nurturing youngsters with the talent for more than a generation. They sell them to foreigners as souvenirs. They give them to traders as gifts. Most people hang them on their walls as decoration. There is no way to know how many masks exist—in the north, on the islands, throughout Senm. Even in this city, from Sky to the Gray to Shadow beneath. No telling."

I inhaled, realizing the truth of her words. Gods, I had *seen* the masks myself. On the walls of a tavern in Antema. In the Salon once, right below Sky, when I'd pretended to be the page of some noble in order to eavesdrop on a Consortium session. Stern, commanding faces arranged on a wall in the bathroom; they'd drawn my eye while I took a piss. I hadn't known what they were then.

Remath continued. "I have, of course, requested the aid of the Order-Keepers in locating and neutralizing this threat. They have already begun searching homes and removing masks—without touching them," she added, as Deka looked alarmed and had opened his mouth to speak. "We are aware of the danger."

"No," Deka said, and we all blinked in surprise. One did not interrupt the Arameri family head. "No one is aware of the danger, Mother, until we've had a chance to study these masks and understand how they work. They may function through more than contact."

"We must nevertheless try," she said. "If even one of those masks can turn an ordinary mortal into a nigh-unstoppable creature like the ones that attacked us yesterday, then we are *already surrounded* by our enemies. They need not muster soldiers, or train them, or feed them. They can create their army at any time, in any place, through whatever mechanism or spell they use to control the masks. And the defenses our scriveners have devised have proven woefully inadequate."

"The corps have only now obtained examples of these masks in their undamaged state to study," said Shahar. "It would seem too soon—"

"I cannot risk this family's fortunes on uncertainties. We've lost too much already, relying on tradition and our reputation. We believed we were unassailable, even as our enemies winnowed our ranks." She paused for a moment, a muscle flexing in her jaw, her eyes going dark and hard. "You will make stranger choices, Shahar, when the time comes for you to lead. Not for nothing did I give you our Matriarch's name." Her eyes flicked to Deka. "Though I know already that you have the strength to do what's right."

Shahar tensed, her eyes narrowing. In suspicion? Or anger? I cursed my paltry mortal awareness of the world.

Remath took a deep breath. "Shahar. With the aid of Dekarta, and our family's most capable members, you are to oversee the preparation of a new home for the Arameri."

Utter silence fell. I stared along with the rest of them. Unknowable Maelstrom, she'd actually sounded serious.

"A *new palace*?" Shahar did not bother to hide her incredulity. "Mother..." She trailed off, shaking her head. "I don't understand."

Remath extended a graceful hand. "It is very simple, Daughter. A new palace will soon be built for us—in a hidden location, far more defensible and isolated than Sky. Captain Wrath and the White Guard, Steward Morad, and any others whom you trust implicitly will reside in this new palace—alone, until such time as you can make it ready for the whole family. Unlike Sky, the location of this new palace shall be secret. Dekarta, you are to ensure that this remains the case, utilizing whatever magical means are at your disposal. Create new ones if you must. Ramina, you are to advise my children."

I could see which people in the room had known

about this by their reactions. Shahar's eyes were bigger than En; so were Deka's. Wrath's mouth hung open, but Morad continued to watch Remath, impassive. So Remath had told her lover. And Ramina smirked at me; he, too, had known.

But it made no sense. The Arameri had built a new palace before, but only when the old one had been destroyed, thanks to Nahadoth and an especially stupid Arameri family head. The current Sky was fine, and safer than any location in the world, seated as it was within a *giant tree*. There was no need for this.

I stepped away from the wall, putting my hands on my hips. "And what orders do you have for me, Remath? Will you command me to hew the stones and lay the mortar for this new palace? After all, I and my siblings built *this* one."

Remath's gaze settled on me, inscrutable. She was silent for so long that I actually began to wonder if she would try to kill me. It would be utterly stupid on her part; nothing short of the Maelstrom would be able to stop Nahadoth's fury. But I put nothing past her.

Try me, I thought at her, and bared my teeth in a grin. En pulsed on my breast in hot agreement. At my smile, however, Remath nodded slightly, as if I'd confirmed something.

"You, Lord Sieh," she began, "are to look after my children."

I froze. Then, before I could muster a thought, Shahar sprang to her feet, abandoning protocol. Her hands were fists at her sides, her expression suddenly fierce. She rounded on all of us.

"Out," she said. *"Now."*

Wrath alone looked at Remath, who said nothing.

Ramina and Morad held still for a breath, perhaps also waiting to see if Remath would counter Shahar's command, but they carefully did not look at either woman. It was never wise to take sides in a battle between the head and heir. As soon as it was clear that Remath would not intervene, they left. The chamber's heavy doors swung shut with an echoing silence.

Shahar glared at Dekarta, who had gotten to his feet as well but remained where he was, his face set and hard. "No," he said.

"How dare you—"

"Mark me," he snapped, and she flinched, silent. "Put a true sigil on me, geld me like Ramina. Do this if you want me to obey. Otherwise, *no*."

Shahar's lips tightened so much that I saw them turn white under the rouge. She was angry enough to say the words—in front of Remath, who might not let her take them back. Fools, her and Deka both. They were too young to play this game yet.

With a sigh I strode forward, stopping between and to one side of them. "You took the oath to each other as well," I said, and they both glared at me. If Remath had not been there, I would have cuffed them like the squabbling brats they were, but for the sake of their dignity, I merely glared back.

With a dismissive *hmmph*, Shahar turned her back on us, striding up to the foot of the dais that held her mother's chair. She stopped when they were eye to eye.

"You will not do this," she said, her voice low and tight. "You will not make plans for your own death."

Remath sighed. Then, to my surprise, she stood and walked down the steps until she stood before Shahar. They were of a height, I saw. Shahar might never be as full in breast or hip, but she did not turn aside as her mother drew near, her gaze clear and angry. Remath looked her up and down and slowly, smiled.

Then she embraced Shahar.

I gaped. So did Deka. So did Shahar, who stood stiff within her mother's arms, her face a study in shock. Remath's palms pressed flat against Shahar's back. She even rested her cheek on Shahar's shoulder, closing her eyes for just a moment. At last, with a reluctance that could not be feigned, she spoke.

"The Arameri must change," she said again. "This is too little, and perhaps too late—but you have always had my love, Shahar. I am willing to admit that, here, in front of others, because that, too, is part of the change we must make. And because it is true." She pulled back then, her hands lingering on Shahar's arms until distance forced her to let go. I had the sense that she would have preferred not to. Then she glanced at Deka.

Deka's jaw flexed, his hands clenching into fists at his sides, and though I doubt anyone else saw it, the marks on his body, beneath his clothing, flared in black warning. Remath would get no welcome there. She sighed, nodding to herself as if she'd expected nothing more. Her sorrow was so plain that I didn't know what to think. Arameri did not show their feelings so honestly. Was this some sort of trick? But it did not feel like one.

Her eyes fell on me then, and lingered. Uneasily I wondered if she would try to hug me, too. If she did, I decided I would goose her.

"You will not distract me, Mother," Shahar said. "Are you mad? Another *palace*? Why are you sending me away?"

Remath shook off the moment of candor, her face

resuming its usual family head mask. "Sky is an obvious and valuable target. Anyone who wants to damage Arameri influence in the world knows to come here. Just one masked assassin through the Gate would be sufficient; even if no one is harmed, the fact that our privacy can be breached would show our every potential enemy that we are vulnerable." She turned away from us, heading over to the windows, and sighed at the city and mountains beyond. A branch of the Tree arced away, miles long. The blossoms had begun to disintegrate, the Tree's time of flowering having ended. Petals floated away from the branch, dancing along an air current in a winding trail.

"And our enemies include a god," she said. "So we must take radical steps to protect ourselves, for the world still needs us. Even if it thinks otherwise." She glanced back at us over her shoulder. "This *is* a contingency, Shahar. I have no intention of dying anytime soon."

Shahar—stupid, gullible girl—actually looked relieved.

"That's all well and good," I said, rolling my eyes, "but building a secret palace is impossible. You'll need workers, crafters, suppliers, and unless you mean for Shar and Deka to scrub their own toilets, servants. You don't exactly have enough of those to go around here in Sky, so that means hiring locals from wherever your new palace is situated. There's no way to keep a secret with that many people involved, even with magic." Then it occurred to me how she could keep the secret. "And you can't have them *all* murdered."

Remath lifted an eyebrow. "I could, actually, but as you've guessed, that would leave its own trail of questions to be answered. Such crimes are more difficult to hide these days." She nodded sardonically to me, and I smiled bitterly back, because once it had been my job to help erase the evidence of Arameri atrocities.

"In any case," Remath said, "I have found another way."

Beyond the windows, the sun had begun to set. It hadn't touched the horizon yet, and there were still a good twenty minutes or so to go before twilight officially began. This, I would later realize, when I recovered from the shock, was why Remath murmured a soft prayer of apology before she spoke aloud.

"Lady Yeine," she said, "please hear me."

My mouth fell open. Shahar gasped.

"I hear," Yeine said, appearing before us all.

And Remath Arameri—head of the family that had remade the world in Bright Itempas's name, great-granddaughter of a man who had thrown Enefa's worshippers off the Pier for fun, many-times-great-granddaughter of the woman who had brought about Enefa's death—dropped to one knee before Yeine, with her head bowed.

I went over to Remath. My eyes were defective; they had to be. I leaned closer to peer at her but detected no illusion. I hadn't mistaken someone else for her.

I looked up at Yeine, who looked positively gleeful.

"No," I said, stunned.

"Yes," she replied. "A fine trick, wouldn't you say?"

Then she turned to Shahar and Dekarta, who kept looking from her to their mother and back at Yeine. They didn't understand. I didn't want to.

"I will build your new palace," she said to all of us. "In exchange, the Arameri will now worship me."

17

IT WAS SIMPLE, really.

The Arameri had served Itempas for two thousand years. But Itempas was now useless as a patron, and Yeine was family, of a sort. I suppose that was how Remath rationalized it to herself—if she'd needed to. Perhaps it had been nothing more than pragmatism for her. Devout Arameri had always been rare. In the end, all most of them truly believed in was power.

We would travel to the site of the new palace at dawn, Remath told us. There Yeine would build it according to Remath's specifications, and the Arameri would enter a new era in their long and incredible history.

I exited the audience chamber with the rest of them, leaving Remath and Yeine alone to discuss whatever family heads discussed with their new patron goddesses. Wrath, Morad, and Ramina, who had waited in the corridor outside, were called in as Shahar, Deka, and I left, probably to make their obeisance to Yeine as well. No doubt they would have tasks to complete by morning, as they would be traveling to the new palace with us. We would also take a minimal complement of guards, court-iers, and servants, because—according to Remath—we would need no more than that to establish ourselves. Sha-har and Deka, respectively, were to choose those mem-bers of the family and the various corps who would accompany us. Unspoken in all of this was the fact that anyone who traveled to the new palace, for reasons of secrecy, might never be permitted to return.

I informed Shahar that I had business in Shadow for a few hours and left. The Vertical Gate had been reconfig-ured in the days since the attack. Now it was set by default to transport in one direction only—away from the palace—and returning required a password sent via a special messaging sphere, which I was given as I prepared to leave. The scrivener on duty, who stood among the sol-diers guarding the gate, solemnly reminded me not to lose the sphere, because I would be killed by magic the instant I stepped onto the Gate without it, or killed by the soldiers should I survive and somehow manage the transit, any-way. I made sure I didn't lose the sphere.

That done, I traveled to South Root, where I notified first Hymn and then Ahad that I would be staying at Sky for the time being.

Hymn was more subdued about this than I'd expected, though her parents were plainly overjoyed to see the back of me. Hymn said little as she helped me pack my meager belongings; everything I owned fit into a single cloth satchel. But when I turned to go, she caught my hand and pressed two things into it. The first was a glass knife, the same faded-leaves color as my eyes. She had clearly worked on it for some time; the blade had been polished to mirror smoothness, and she'd even managed to fit it with a brass kitchen-knife handle. The other thing she gave me was a handful of tiny beads in different sizes and colors, each made from glass or polished stone, each etched with infinitesimal lines of clouds or continents. They had holes bored through them to go onto my necklace alongside En.

"How did you know?" I asked as she spilled them into my hand.

"Know what?" She looked at me as though I'd gone mad. "I just remembered that old rhyme about you. About how you stole the sun for a prank? I figured, suns need planets, don't they?"

Pathetic, compared to my lost orrery. Magnificent, given the love that had gone into making them. She turned away when I clutched them to my chest, though I managed—just—not to cry in front of her.

Ahad was in an odder state when I found him at the Arms of Night. As it was afternoon at the time, and the house was about to open for its usual leisurely business, I had expected to find him in his offices. He was on the back porch, however, and instead of his usual cheroot, he held a plucked flower, turning it contemplatively in his fingers. By the troubled expression on his face, the contemplations were not going well.

"Good," was all he said when I informed him that I was moving back to Sky, and that the Arameri had become Yeinans instead of Itempans, and that, by the way, there was going to be a new palace somewhere.

"*Good?* That's all you have to say?"

"Yes."

I thought of the half-dozen slurs and insults he should've thrown at me in place of that quiet affirmative, and frowned. Something was wrong. But I could not exactly ask him whether he was all right. He would laugh at my attempted concern.

So I tried a different tack. "They're yours, you know. Shahar, Dekarta. Your grandchildren. Great-grand, actually."

This, at least, drew his attention. He frowned at me. "What?"

I shrugged. "I assume you slept with T'vril Arameri's wife before you left Sky."

"I slept with *half* of Sky before I left. What does that have to do with anything?"

I stared at him. "You really don't know." And here I'd thought he'd done it as part of some scheme. I frowned, putting my hands on my hips. "Why the hells did you leave Sky anyhow? Last I saw, you were on the brink of being adopted into the Central Family, maneuvering your way toward becoming the next family head. A bare century later, you're a whoremonger, living among the commonfolk in the seediest part of town?"

His eyes narrowed. "I got tired of it."

"Got tired of what?"

"All of it." Ahad looked away now, toward the center of town—and the great omnipresent bulk of the World Tree, a brown and green shadow limned by the slanting afternoon sun. Almost hidden in the first crotch of the trunk was a glimmer of pearlescent white: Sky.

"I got tired of the Arameri." Ahad turned the flower again. It looked like something common—a dandelion, one of the few flowers that still bloomed in Shadow's dimness. He'd apparently plucked it from between the walkway stones that led up to the back door. I wondered why he was so fascinated by it. "T'vril married a fullblood to cement his rule. She was his third cousin on his father's side or something. Didn't give a damn about him, and the feeling was mutual. I seduced her on behalf of a branch family from outside Sky; they wanted their own girl married to T'vril instead. I needed the capital to boost my investments. So I took the money that they offered and made sure he found out about the affair. He wasn't even upset." His lip curled.

I nodded, slowly. It amazed me that it had taken so much for him to understand. "Not much different from what you did when we were slaves."

Ahad's glare was sharp and dangerous. "It was by my choice. That makes all the difference in the world."

"Does it?" I leaned against one of the porch columns, folding my arms. "Being used one way or another—does it really feel all that different?"

He fell silent. That, and the fact that he'd left Sky afterward, was answer enough. I sighed.

"T'vril's wife must've been pregnant when you left." I would look up the timing when I got back to Sky, though that was hardly necessary. Deka was all the evidence that mattered.

"I can't have children." He said it wearily, with the air of something often repeated. Did so many women want his bitter, heartless seed? Amazing.

"You *couldn't*," I said, "not while there was no goddess of life and death. Not while you were part of Naha, just a half-time reflection of him. But Yeine made you whole. She gave you the gift that gods lost when Enefa died. We all regained it when Yeine took Enefa's place." Except me, I did not add, but he already knew that.

Ahad frowned at the flower that dangled in his fingers, considering. "A child...?" He let out a soft chuckle. "Well, now."

"A son, I'm told."

"A son." Was there regret in his voice? Or just a different sort of apathy? "Come unknown and gone already."

"A *demon*, you fool," I said. "And Remath, Shahar, and Dekarta are probably demons as well." How far removed from a godly forbear did mortals have to be before their blood lost its deadly potency? Shahar and Dekarta were one-eighth god, and their blood had not killed me. Could only a few generations make such a difference? We had all overestimated the danger of the demons, if that was the case—but then, no god would ever have been stupid enough to sample a possible demon's blood and find out.

Ahad chuckled again. This time it was low and malicious. "Are they, now? From god-enslavers to god-killers. The Arameri are so endlessly interesting."

I stared at him. "I will never understand you."

"No, you won't." He sighed. "Keep me apprised on everything. *Use* the damned messaging sphere I gave you; don't just play with it or whatever it is you do."

As this was positively friendly by his standards, and I was tired of the flower silliness, I finally gave in to my curiosity. "You all right?"

"No. But I'm not interested in talking about it."

Ordinarily I would have left him to his brooding. But there was something about him in that moment—a peculiar sort of weight to his presence, a taste on the air—that intrigued me. Because he wasn't paying any attention to me, I touched him. And because he was so absorbed in whatever he was thinking about, he allowed this.

A lick of something, like fire without pain. The world breathed through both of us, quickening—

At this point, Ahad noticed me and knocked my hand away, glaring. I smiled back. "So you've found your nature?"

His glare became a frown so guarded that I couldn't tell whether he was confused or just annoyed again. Had I guessed correctly, or had he not realized what he was feeling? Or both?

Then something else occurred to me. I opened my mouth to breathe his scent, tasting the familiar disturbed ethers as best I could with my atrophied senses. Particularly around that flower. Yes, I was sure.

"Glee's been here," I said, thoughtful. She had worn the flower in her hair, to judge by the scent. I could tell more than that, actually—such as the fact that she and Ahad had recently made love. Was that what had him in such a mood? I held off on teasing him about this, however, because he already looked ready to smite.

"Weren't you going somewhere?" he asked, pointedly and icily. His eyes turned darker, and the air around us rippled in blatant warning.

"Back to Sky, please," I said, and before I finished the sentence, he'd thrown me across existence. I chuckled as I detached from the world, though he would hear it and my laughter would only piss him off. But Ahad had his revenge. I appeared ten feet above the daystone floor, in one of the most remote areas of the underpalace. The fall broke my wrist, which forced me to walk half an hour for a healing script from the palace scriveners.

There had been no progress on determining who had sent the assassins, the scriveners informed me in terse, monosyllabic responses when I questioned them. (They had not forgotten that I'd killed their previous chief, but there was no point in my apologizing for it.) They were hard at work, however, determining how the masks functioned. In the vast, open laboratory that housed the palace's fifty or so scriveners, I could see that several of the worktables had been allocated to the crimson mask pieces, and an elaborate framework had been set up to house the white mask. I did not see the mortal to whom the white mask had been attached, but it was not difficult to guess his fate. Most likely the scriveners had the corpse somewhere more private, dissecting it for whatever secrets it might hold.

Once my wrist was done, I returned to my quarters and stuffed the clothes and toiletries Morad had given me into Hymn's satchel and was thus packed.

The sun had set while I did my business in Shadow. Night brought forth Sky's glow in unmarked stillness. I left my room, feeling inexplicably restless, and wandered the corridors. I could have opened a wall, gone into the dead spaces, but those weren't wholly mine anymore; I did not want them now. The servants and highbloods I passed in the corridors noticed me, and some recognized me, but I ignored their stares. I was only one murderous god, and a paltry one at that. Once, four had walked the halls. These mortals didn't know how lucky they were.

Eventually I found myself in the solarium, the Arameri's private garden. It was a natural thing to follow the white-pebbled path through the manicured trees. After a time I reached the foot of the narrow white spire that jutted up from the palace's heart. The stairway door was not locked, as it had normally been in the old days, so I climbed the tight, steep twist of steps until I emerged onto the Altar—the flattened, enclosed top of the spire where, for centuries, the Arameri had conducted their Ritual of Succession.

Here I sat on the floor. Countless mortals had died in this chamber, spending their lives to wield the Stone of Earth and transfer the power of gods from one Arameri generation to the next. The spire was empty now, as dusty and disused as the underpalace. I supposed the Arameri did their successions elsewhere. The hollow plinth that had once stood at the center of the room was gone, shattered on the day Yeine and the Stone became one. The crystal walls had been rebuilt, the cracked floors repaired, but there was a still lifelessness to the room that I did not remember feeling during the days of my incarceration.

I pulled En off its chain and set it on the floor before me, rolling it back and forth and remembering what it had felt like to ride a sun. Aside from that, I thought of nothing. Thus I was as ready as I could have been when the daystone floor suddenly changed, brightening just a little. The room felt more alive, too.

He had always had that effect, in the old days.

I looked up. The glow of the daystone made for a nice reflection in the glass, so it was easy to see the two figures behind me: Glee and someone the same height. Broader. Male. Glee nodded to me in the reflection, then vanished, leaving the two of us alone.

"Hi," I said.

"Hello, Sieh," said Itempas.

I waited, then smiled. "No 'It's been a while,' or 'You're looking well'?"

"You aren't looking well." He paused. "Does it seem a long time to you?"

"Yes." It wouldn't have, before I'd turned mortal. He had been mortal for a century himself, though; he understood.

Footsteps, heavy and precise, approached me from behind. Something moved on the periphery of my vision. For an instant I thought he would sit beside me, but that would have been too strange for both of us. He walked past me and stopped at the edge of the Altar, gazing through the glass at the night-dark, branch-shrouded horizon beyond.

I gazed at his back. He wore a long leather coat that had been bleached almost white. His white hair was long, too, twisted into a heavy mane of thick cords, like Teman cable-locks but bare of ornamentation other than a clasp that kept them neat and controlled. White trousers and shirt. *Brown* boots. I found myself perversely pleased that he'd been unable to find boots in white.

"I will, of course, accept Nahadoth's offer," he said. "If it is within my power to heal you, or at least stop your aging, I will do all I can."

I nodded. "Thanks."

He returned the nod. Though he faced the horizon, his eyes were on me in the glass reflection. "You intend to stay with these mortals?"

"I suppose. Ahad wants me to keep him informed of what the Arameri are doing." Then I remembered. "Of course, *you're* Ahad's boss, so . . ."

"You may stay." His gaze was intent, lacking none of its old power despite his mortal condition. "And you *should* stay, to be near the mortals you love."

I frowned at him. His eyes flicked away from mine. "Their lives are too brief," he added. "One should not take that time for granted."

He meant Glee's mother. And perhaps the first Shahar Arameri, too. He had loved her despite her obsessive, destructive madness.

"How do you feel about the Arameri dumping you?" I asked, a bit nastily. I didn't have the energy for real nastiness. I was just trying to change the subject.

I heard the creak of leather and the rasp of hair as he shrugged. "They're mortal."

"No tears shed, hmm?" I sighed, lying back on the stone and stretching my arms above my head. "The whole world will follow them, you know, and turn away from you. It's already happening. Maybe they'll keep calling it the Bright, but it'll really be the Twilight."

"Or the Dawn."

I blinked. Something I hadn't considered. That made me sit up on one elbow and narrow my eyes at him. He stood the way he always had: legs apart, arms folded, motionless. Same old Dayfather, even in mortal flesh. He did not change.

Except.

"Why did you allow Glee Shoth to live?" I asked.

"For the same reason I allowed her mother to live."

I shook my head in confusion. "Oree Shoth? Why would you have killed her?" I scowled. "She wouldn't put up with your shit, is that it?"

If I hadn't been watching him in the glass, I would never have believed what I saw. He *smiled*. "She wouldn't, no. But that wasn't what I meant. She was also a demon."

This rendered me speechless. In the silence that fell, Itempas finally turned to me. I flinched in shock, even though he looked the same as the last time I'd seen him, apart from the hair and the clothes. And yet something about him—something I could not define—was different.

"Do you plan to kill Remath Arameri and her children?" he asked.

I stiffened. He knew. I said nothing, and he nodded, point made.

Suddenly I was full of nervous tension. I got to my feet, shoving En into a pocket. The Altar was too small for real pacing, but I tried anyway, walking over to him—and then I stopped, seeing my own reflection beside his in the glass. He turned, too, following my gaze, and we looked at ourselves. Me, short and wiry and defensive and confused. I had developed a slouch in my manifest maturity, mostly because I did not like being so tall. Him: big and powerful and elegant, as he had always been. Yet his eyes were so full of knowing and yearning that almost, almost, I wanted him to be my father again.

Almost, almost, I forgave him.

But that could not be, either. I hunched and looked away. Itempas lowered his eyes, and a long, solid silence formed in the enclosed space.

"Tell Glee to come back and get you," I said at last, annoyed. "I've said all I'm going to say."

"Glee is mortal, and I have no magic. We cannot speak as gods do; we must use words. And actions."

I frowned. "What, then, you're staying here?"

"And traveling with you to the new palace, yes."

"Yeine will be here, too." At this I clenched my fists and resumed pacing, in tight angry arcs. "Oh, but you must know that. You came here for her." The two of them, entwined, his lips on the nape of her neck. I forced this image from my mind.

"No. I came for you."

Words. Actions.

Both meaningless. They should not have made my throat clench the way they did. I fought them with anger, glaring at his back. "I could call Naha. I could ask him to kill you over and over, until you beg to truly die." And because I was a brat, I added, "He'll do it, too, for me."

"Is that truly what you wish?"

"Yes! I'd do it myself if I could!"

To my surprise, Itempas pivoted and came toward me, opening his coat. When he reached into one of the inner-breast pockets, I tensed, ready to fight. He pulled out a sheathed dagger, and I grabbed for En. But then he handed the dagger to me, hilt-first. It was a small, light thing, I found when I took it; a child's weapon, in those parts of the world where mortals gave their children sharp toys. Not altogether different from the dagger I'd used to damage Shahar's innocence, ten years before—except this dagger was strapped securely into the leather sheath, held in place by a loop about the guardpiece. No one would be able to draw this blade by accident.

As I turned the thing in my fingers, wondering why in his own name Itempas had given it to me, my nose caught the faint whiff of old, dried blood.

"A gift from Glee," he said. "To me. If death ever becomes preferable to living."

I knew what it was, then. *The gift of mortality*, Enefa had called it. Glee's blood was on the knife—her terrifying, poisonous demon blood. She had given Itempas a way out of his imprisonment, if he ever found the courage to take it.

My hand clenched convulsively around the knife's hilt. "If you ever use this, the mortal realm will die."

"Yes."

"*Glee* will die."

"If she hasn't already died by then, yes."

"*Why would she give this to you?*"

"I don't know."

I stared at him. He wasn't being deliberately obtuse. He must have asked her. Either he hadn't believed her answer, or—more likely, given how much she'd taken after him—she hadn't bothered to answer. And he had accepted her silence.

Then he knelt before me, flicking his coat behind himself in the process, so that it spread out gracefully along the white stone floor. He lifted his head, too, partly because he was an arrogant son of a demon and partly to give me easy access to his chest and throat. Such a handsome, proud offering.

"Bastard," I said, clenching my fist around the knife hilt. Death. I held the death of the universe in my fist. "Arrogant, selfish, evil *bastard*."

Itempas merely waited. The knife was small, but I could angle it just so, get it between the ribs easily to prick his heart. Hells, if Oree Shoth had been a demon, too, then her daughter was more than half god. Even a scratch tainted with her blood might do the trick.

I unfastened the loop, but my fingers were shaking. When I took the hilt in my hand to draw it, I couldn't. My hands just wouldn't move. Eventually I let them—and the dagger—drop to my sides.

"If you want me to die—" he began.

"Shut up," I whispered. "Shut up, gods damn you. I hate you."

"If you hate me—"

"Shut up!" He fell silent, and I cursed and threw the dagger to the floor between us. The sound of leather on daystone made an echoing *crack* from the chamber's walls. I had begun to cry. I raked my hands through my hair. "Just shut up, all right? Gods, you're so insufferable! You can't *make me* choose something like that! I'll hate you if I damn well please!"

"All right." His voice was soft, soothing. Against my will, I remembered times—rare but precious—when we had sat together in his placid realm, watching time dance. I had always been conscious of the fact that he and I would never be friends. Lovers was out of the question. But father and son? That much we could do.

"All right, Sieh," he said now, so gently. He did not change. "Hate me if you like."

The urge to love him was so powerful that I shook with it.

I turned and stormed over to the stair entrance, trotting down the steps. When I looked up, just before my head passed beyond the floor's threshold, I saw Itempas watching me. He had not picked up the knife. He had, however, changed: his face was wet with tears.

I ran. I ran. I ran.

The door to Deka's apartment was not locked. No servant would invade his privacy unannounced, and no highblood would come near him as yet. He was an unknown commodity. His family feared him, as he'd wished. I should have, too, because he was more powerful than me, but I had always loved strong people.

He rose from the worktable at which he'd been sitting—not a standard furniture item in Sky. Already he'd made changes. "Who the— Sieh?" He looked exhausted. He'd been up most of the night before, working with the scrivener corps to examine the assassins' masks. Yet here he was, barefoot and tunicless, hair mussed, still awake. I saw sketches on several scrolls and a stack of sheets marked with the Litaria's official sigil. Personnel for the new palace, perhaps. "Sieh, what...?"

"There's no need to fear me," I said, coming around the worktable at him. I held his eyes as I would those of any prey. He stared back. So easy to catch them when they wanted to be caught. "I may be older than the world, but I'm also just a man; no god is ever only one thing. If the whole of me frightens you, love whichever part you like."

He flinched, confusion and desire and guilt all rising

and sinking out of sight in his face. Finally he sighed as I reached him. His shoulders slumped a little in defeat. "Sieh."

So much meaning in that one word. The wind, but also lightning, and need as raw as an open wound. I put my arms around him. The power written into his skin pulsed once, whispering warningly to me of pain and slaughter. I pressed my face to his shoulder and clenched my fists on the back of his shirt, wishing it was gone so I could touch those deadly marks.

"Sieh…" Deka began. He'd gone stiff at my embrace, holding his arms out as if afraid to touch me. "Sieh, gods—"

"Just let me do this," I breathed into his shoulder. "Please, Deka."

His hands landed on my shoulders, too light, hesitant. That wouldn't do. I pulled him harder against me and he made a soft, strained sound. Then his arms slid around me, tightening. I felt the scrape of nails through my shirt. His face pressed into my hair. A hand cupped the back of my neck.

There was a time of stillness. It wasn't long, because nothing in the mortal realm lasts long. It felt long, however, which was all that really mattered.

When I'd finally had enough, I pulled back and waited for the questions. Mortals always asked questions. *Why did you come here?* would be first, I was certain, because he wanted me and probably hoped that I wanted him. That wasn't it at all, but I would tell him what he wanted to hear.

A long, awkward silence fell. Deka fidgeted and said, "I need at least a few hours of sleep."

I nodded, still waiting.

He looked away. "You don't have to leave."

So I didn't.

We lay in his bed, side by side, chaste. I waited, expecting his hands, his mouth, the weight of his body. I would give him what he wanted. Might even enjoy it. Anything not to be alone.

He shifted closer and put his hand over mine. I waited for more, but a long while passed. Eventually, I heard long, even breaths from his side of the bed. Surprised, I turned my head. He was dead asleep.

I gazed at him until I slept, too.

Cycles.

Deka woke some time before dawn and shook me awake. Quite without planning, we did what mortal lovers have done since time immemorial, stumbling blearily around each other as we each prepared for the day. While he spoke to the servants, ordering tea and summoning a clerk to distribute messages to the scriveners, assassins, and courtiers he'd chosen to accompany us, I went into the bathroom and made myself presentable. Then while he did the same, I drank the tea and peeked at his desk, where he'd scribbled notes about defensive magic and begun penning some sort of request to the Litaria. He caught me doing this as he emerged from his bedroom, but he didn't seem to care, walking past me and checking to see how much tea I'd left him. (Not much. This earned me a glower. I shrugged.)

We proceeded to the forecourt. A group of thirty or so scriveners, soldiers, and various highbloods were already there, including Shahar, who stood dressed in a furred traveling cloak against the brisk morning air. She nodded to us as we arrived, and I nodded back, which made her blink. Servants were arriving, too, carrying trunks and satchels that probably contained more of the highbloods' belongings than their own. As the eastern horizon grew more solidly pale with the imminence of dawn, Remath arrived—and with her, to my great surprise, came Itempas and Yeine. I saw many of the other assembled folk peer at the latter in confusion, since they were obviously not of the family. Yeine stopped some ways back, turning toward the distant horizon as if hearing its call; this was her time. Itempas broke off from Remath as they reached the group, coming to stand near the rest of us, though not close enough for conversation. He watched Yeine.

Deka turned, staring at Itempas, and then abruptly his eyes widened. "Sieh, is that—"

"Yes," I snapped. I folded my arms and carefully ignored both of them.

Ramina was there as well, clearly awaiting Remath, as was Morad, who was dressed for travel. That surprised me. Was Remath willing even to give up her lover to this madness? Perhaps they were not so close after all. Morad's face was impassive, but I suspected she was less than happy about it.

"Good morning, my friends," Remath said, though aside from Morad, no one there was her friend. "By now matters have been explained to you. Naturally you will be unhappy at the short notice, but this was necessary for the sake of secrecy and safety. I trust there are no objections."

In any other circumstance, there would have been, but these were Arameri, and particularly ones who had been chosen for their wits and value. Silence greeted her in response.

"Very well. We await one final guest, and then we will proceed."

Abruptly the world gave a faint, and deliciously familiar,

shudder. It was a delicate thing, yet powerful; even the mortals could feel it. The daystone beneath our feet creaked ominously, while the satinbell trees in the nearby Garden of the Hundred Thousand shivered, shedding some of their perfect dangling blossoms. And I closed my eyes, inhaling so that I would not whoop for joy.

"Sieh?" Shahar's voice, alarmed and puzzled. Her ancestors had known this sensation, but no Arameri in a hundred years had felt it. I opened my eyes and smiled at her, so fondly that she blinked and almost smiled back.

"My father returns," I whispered.

Beyond us, Yeine turned; she was smiling, too. Itempas—he had turned away from us, gazing off toward the palace as if it was suddenly the most interesting of sights. But I saw the stiffness in his shoulders, the effort that it took him to stay relaxed.

Nahadoth faded into view near Yeine, a storm weaving itself from nothingness into a semblance of mortal flesh. The shape that he took was an homage to his time of suffering: male, pale, the tendrils of his substance bleeding away like drifting, living smoke. (There had been a mortal body within that smoke once: Ahad. Did he shiver now, somewhere in the city below, feeling the nearby presence of his old prisoner?) Nahadoth's shape was the only thing that had not changed since the days of his enslavement, for I felt his power now, gloriously whole and terrible, a weight upon the very air. Chaos and darkness, pure and unleashed.

There were murmurs and cries of alarm within the group of Arameri as Nahadoth manifested, though Remath quelled them with a glare. Making an example of herself, she stepped forward. I did not think less of her for pausing to steel herself.

I did think better of Shahar, though, who took a deep breath and moved away from us, hurrying to her mother's side. Remath glanced back at her, forgetting to hide her surprise. Shahar inclined her head in taut reply. She had, after all, met Nahadoth before. Together, both women proceeded to join the two gods.

Deka did not attempt to join them. He had folded his arms and begun to shift from foot to foot, throwing frowns at Itempas and then at me, generally radiating unhappiness. It was not difficult to guess at the source of his distress: the Three walked among us, even if they were not quite complete, and Deka was not stupid enough to believe they had all come merely to build the Arameri's vacation home. No doubt he guessed now why I had been so upset the night before.

I came for you, Itempas had said.

I folded my arms across my chest as well, but this was not defensive. It just took effort to steel myself against hope.

Then the conversation was done, and Yeine looked up at all of us, nodding once in absent reply to something Remath said. Her eyes met mine across the forecourt just as, beyond her, the horizon flared gold with the sun's first delicate rays. For just an instant—as fleeting as the dawn itself—her form changed, becoming something indescribable. My mind tried to define it anyway, using images and sensations that its mortal perceptions could encompass. A phantasm of herself drawn in silver-pastel mist. A vast and impossible landscape, dominated by a whole forest of trees as great as the one that cradled us now. The scent and taste of ripe fruit, tooth-tender and succulently sweet. For a moment I ached with most unfilial yearnings: lust for her, jealousy for Naha, and pity for Tempa because he had gotten to taste her only once.

Then the moment passed, and Yeine was herself again, and her smile was for me alone, her first and favorite son. I would not give up that specialness for all the world.

"Time to go," she said.

And suddenly we were no longer in Sky.

"We" being all of us, gods and Arameri, right down to the servants and baggage. One moment we were in Sky's forecourt, and the next, the forty or so of us were somewhere else in the world, transported by a flick of Yeine's will. It was later here; the dawn had advanced into full morning, but I paid little attention to this. I was too busy laughing at the Arameri, most of whom were stumbling or gasping or otherwise trying not to panic, because *we stood atop an ocean*. Waves surrounded us, an endless plain of gently heaving emptiness. When I looked down, I saw that our feet dented the water, as though someone had laid a thin and flexible coating between the liquid and our shoes. When the waves bobbed beneath us, we bobbed with them but did not sink. Some of the Arameri fell over, unable to adjust. I chuckled and braced my feet apart, balancing easily. The trick was to lean forward and rely on one's core, not the legs. I had skated oceans of liquefied gas, long ago. This was not so different.

"Bright Father help us!" cried someone.

"You need no help," Itempas snapped, and the man fell over, staring at him. Tempa, of course, was rock-steady upon the waves.

"Will this do?" Yeine asked Remath. Remath, I was amused to see, had solved the problem of maintaining balance and dignity by dropping to one knee again.

"Yes, Lady," Remath replied. A swell passed beneath us, making everyone rise and then drop several feet. Yeine, I noted, did not move as this occurred; the dent beneath her feet simply deepened as the water rose and flowed around her. And the swell died the instant it drew near Nahadoth, the wave's force dissipating into scattered, pointless motion.

"Where are we?" Shahar asked. She had knelt as well, following Remath's lead, but even this seemed difficult for her. She did not look up as she spoke, concentrating on remaining at least somewhat upright.

It was Nahadoth who answered. He had turned to face the sun, narrowing his eyes with a faint look of distaste. It did not harm him, however, because it was just one small star, and it was always night somewhere in the universe.

"The Ovikwu Sea," he said. "Or so it was last called, long ago."

I began to chuckle. Everyone nearby looked at me in confusion. "The Ovikwu," I said, letting my voice carry so they could all share the joke, "was a landbound sea in the middle of the Maroland—the continent that once existed where we now stand." The continent that had been destroyed by the Arameri when they'd been foolish enough to try and use Nahadoth as their weapon. He'd done what they wanted, and then some.

Deka inhaled. "The *first* Sky. The one that was destroyed."

Nahadoth turned—and paused, gazing at him for far too long a breath. I tensed, my belly clenching. Did he notice the familiarity of Deka's features, so clearly etched with Ahad's stamp? If he realized what Deka was, what Remath and Shahar were... Would he listen if I pleaded for their lives?

"The first Sky is directly below," he said. And then he looked at me. *He knew.* I swallowed against sudden fear.

"Not for long," said Yeine.

She raised a hand in a graceful beckoning gesture toward the sea beneath us. The Three can bring new worlds into existence at will; they can set galaxies spinning with a careless breath. It took Yeine no effort to do what she did then. She didn't need to gesture at all. That was just her sense of theater.

But I think she'd overestimated the mortal attention span. No one noticed *her* once the first stones burst from the sea.

It was Deka who murmured for a bubble of air to form around all of us, warding off the now-churning waves and spray. Thus we were safe, able to watch in undisturbed awe as jagged, seaweed-draped and coral-encrusted chunks of daystone—the smallest the size of the Arms of Night—rose beneath and around us. Rubble undisturbed for centuries: it rose now, tumbling upward, stone piling atop stone and fusing, walls forming and shedding debris, courtyards rising beneath our feet to take the place of the heaving waves, structure shaping itself from nothingness.

Then it was done, and the spray cleared, and we looked around to find ourselves standing atop glory.

Take a nautilus shell; cut it cross section. Gently elevate its swirling, chambered tiers as they approach the tight-bound center, culminating at last in a pinnacle on which we all stood. Note its asymmetrical order, its chaotic repetition, the grace of its linkages. Contemplate the ephemerality of its existence. Such is the beauty that is mortal life.

This was not Sky, old or new. It was smaller than both its predecessor palaces and deceptively simpler. Where those earlier structures had been built compact and high, this palace hugged the ocean's surface. Instead of sharp spires piercing the sky, here there were low, smoothly sloping buildings, joined by dozens of lacy bridges. The foundation—for the palace had been built atop a kind of convex platform—was many-lobed and odd, with spars and indentations jutting out in every direction. Its surface gleamed in the dawn light, white and nacreous as pearl, the only similarity between it and Sky.

I could feel the power woven into every sweeping balustrade, keeping the massive edifice afloat—but there was more to it than magic. Something about the structure itself worked to maintain its buoyancy. If I had still been a god, I might have understood it, for there are rules even where we are concerned, and it was Yeine's nature to seek balance. Perhaps the magic harnessed the ocean's waves in some new way or absorbed the power of the sun. Perhaps the foundation was hollow. Regardless, it was clear this new palace would float, and with some assistive magic would travel readily across the ocean. It would defend the precious cargo within its walls, if only because no mortal army could assail it.

While the mortals turned about, most of them speechless with awe, the rest making sounds of shock and delight and incomprehension, I strode across the drying daystone of the central platform. Yeine and Nahadoth turned to face me.

"Not bad," I said. "Bit *white*, though, isn't it?"

Yeine shrugged, amused. "You were thinking gray walls? Do you *want* them all to kill themselves?"

I looked around, considering the vast but monotonous surrounding oceanscape. Faintly I could hear surf and wind; aside from that there was silence. I grimaced. "Point. But that doesn't mean they should have to endure the same boring, austere sameness of the previous two palaces, does it? They're yours now. Find some way to remind them of that."

She thought a moment. Nahadoth, however, smiled. Suddenly the daystone beneath our feet softened, turning to thick black loam. Everywhere I looked—on railings, edging the bridges—the daystone had remolded itself into troughs of soil.

Yeine laughed and went to him, a teasing look in her eye. "A hint?" She extended her hand, and he took it. I could not help noticing the easy camaraderie between them and the sudden softness of Nahadoth's cabochon eyes when he gazed at her. His ever-changing face grew still, too, becoming a different kind of familiar: brown-skinned and angular and Darren. I fought the urge to glance at Deka, to see if he had noticed.

"We have always built better together than alone," Naha said. Yeine leaned against him, and the soft dark tendrils of his aura swept forward to surround her. They did not touch her, but they did not have to.

A movement at the corner of my vision drew my attention. Itempas had turned away from his siblings' intimacy, watching me instead. I gazed back at him in his solitude, surprised to feel sympathy instead of the usual anger. We two outcasts.

Then I spied Shahar, standing near Dekarta. He was alight as I had never seen him, turning and turning to try and take in the whole of the palace. It looked as though he would never stop grinning. I thought of the adventure novels he'd loved so as a child and wished I was still god enough to enjoy this pleasure with him.

Shahar, more subdued, was smiling, too, glancing now and again at the spirals, but mostly she was just watching him. Her brother, whom she'd lost for so long, come back to her at last.

And purely by chance as I watched them, they noticed

me. Deka's grin grew wider; Shahar's small smile lingered. They did not join hands as they walked over to me, stepping carefully over the soft soil, but the bond between them was obvious to anyone who knew how love looked. That this bond included me was equally obvious. I turned to them, and for a long and wondrous moment, I was not alone.

Then Yeine said, "Come, Sieh," and the moment ended.

Shahar and Deka stopped, their smiles fading. I saw understanding come. They had made me mortal so I could be their friend. What would happen to us once I was a god again?

A hand touched my shoulder, and I looked up. Itempas stood there. Ah, yes; he had loved mortals, too, over the years. He knew how it felt to leave them behind.

"Come," he said gently.

Without another word, I turned my back on Dekarta and Shahar and went with him.

Yeine and Nahadoth met us, and their power folded around us, and we vanished just as the first green shoots began to push up from the soil.

18

In the name of Itempas
We pray for light.
We beg the sun for warmth.
We diffuse the shadows.
In the name of Itempas
We speak to give meaning to sound.
We think before we act.
We kill, but only for peace.

THE CHAMBER IN WHICH WE APPEARED was not far from
the others. Still in the new palace, in fact—one of the
smaller, delicate nautilus chambers that had formed on
the palace's outermost edges, covered over by prism glass.
As soon as we appeared in it, I knew what it really was: a
pocket of space made different from the world around it,
ideal for scrivening or channeling magic without spreading the magic's effects to the surrounding structure. Deka
would love these when he found them.

Nahadoth and Yeine faced Itempas, who gazed back at
them. No expression on any face, though this meant little,
I knew, for they had never needed words to speak. Too

much of what they needed to exchange was emotion in any case. Perhaps that was why, when Nahadoth spoke, he kept his words brief and his manner cool.

"Until sunset," he said. "You will have that much parole."

Itempas nodded slowly. "I will attend to Sieh at once, of course."

"When sunset comes and you return to mortal flesh, you will be weak," Yeine added. "Be sure you prepare."

Itempas only sighed, nodding again.

It was an intentional cruelty. They had granted him parole for my sake, but we needed his power for only a moment. For them to allow a whole day of freedom beyond that, when they would only snatch it back at the day's end, was just their way of turning the knife again. He deserved it, I reminded myself, deserved it in spades.

But I will not pretend it didn't trouble me.

Then there was a shimmer, all that my mortal mind could perceive, and the whole world sang clean when they stripped the mortal covering from him and cast it away. Itempas did not cry out, though he should have. I would have. Instead he only shuddered, closing his eyes as his hair turned to an incandescent nimbus and his clothes glowed as if woven from stars and—I would have laughed, if this had not been sacred—his boots turned white. Even with my dull mortal senses, I felt the effort he exerted to control the sudden blaze of his true self, the wash of heat that it sent across the surface of reality, tsunamis in the wake of a meteor strike. He stilled it all, leaving only profound silence.

Would I do as well, when I was a god again? Probably not. Most likely I would shout and jump up and down, and maybe start dancing across any planets nearby.

Soon, now.

When the blaze of Itempas's restoration had passed, he paused for a moment longer, perhaps composing himself. I braced myself when he focused on me, as he had promised. But then, almost imperceptibly—I would not have noticed if I hadn't known him so well—he frowned.

"What is it?" asked Yeine.

"There is nothing wrong with him," Itempas replied.

"Nothing wrong with me?" I gestured at myself, with my man's hand. I'd had to shave again that morning and had nicked my jaw in the process. It still *hurt*, damn it. "What is there about me that *isn't* wrong?"

Itempas shook his head slowly. "It is my nature to perceive pathways," he said. An approximation of what he meant, since we were speaking in Senmite out of respect for my delicate mortal flesh. "To establish them where none exist and to follow those already laid. I can restore you to what you are meant to be. I can halt that which has gone wrong. But nothing about you, Sieh, is wrong. What you have become..." He looked at Yeine and Nahadoth. He would never have done anything so undignified as throw up his hands, but his frustration was a palpable thing. "He is as he should be."

"That cannot be," said Nahadoth, troubled. He stepped toward me. "This is not his nature. His growth damages him. How can this be *meant*?"

"And who," asked Yeine, speaking slowly because she was not as practiced as the other two at rendering our concepts into mortal speech, "has meant it?"

They looked at each other, and belatedly I realized the gist of their words. I would not be regaining my godhood today. Sighing, I turned away from them and went over to the curving nacre wall. I sat down against it and propped my arms on my knees.

And, quite predictably, things went very bad, very fast.

"This cannot be," Nahadoth said again, and I knew his anger by the way the little chamber suddenly dimmed despite the bright morning sunlight filtering through its glass ceiling. Only the chamber dimmed, however, rather than the whole sky. Clever Yeine, planning for her brothers' tempers. If only I had not been trapped in the chamber with them.

Nahadoth stepped toward Itempas, his aura weaving itself darker and thinner, becoming a glow that no mortal eyes should have been able to see by any law of nature—but of course he defied such laws, so the blackness was plain to all.

"You have always been a coward, Tempa," he said. The words skittered around the chamber's walls, darting, striking in echoes. "You pressed for the demons' slaughter. You fled this realm after the War and kept our children away, leaving us to deal with the mess. Shall I believe you now when you say you cannot help my son?"

I waited for the explosion of Itempas's fury and all the usual to follow. They would fight, and Yeine would do as Enefa had always done and keep their battle contained, and only when they were both exhausted would she try to reason with them.

I was so tired of this. So tired of all of it.

But the surprise was mine. Itempas shook his head slowly. "I would do no less than my best by our child, Naha." Only the faintest of emphasis on *our*, I noticed, where once he would have made a show of possession. He did not look at me, but he didn't have to. Every word that Itempas spoke had meaning, often in multiple layers. He knew, as I did, that his claim on me was precarious at best.

I frowned at him, wondering at this newfound humility; it did not at all seem like the Tempa I knew. Nor did his calm in the face of Nahadoth's accusation. Nahadoth frowned at this, too, more in suspicion than surprise.

And then something else unexpected happened: Yeine stepped forward, looking at Nahadoth with annoyance. "This serves no purpose," she snapped. "We did not come here to rehash old grievances." And then, before Nahadoth could flare at her, she touched his arm. "Look to our son, Naha."

Startled out of anger, Nahadoth turned to me. All three of them looked at me, in fact, radiating a combination of pity and chagrin. I smiled back at them, bleak in my despair.

"Nicely done," I said. "You only forgot I was here for half a minute."

Nahadoth's jaw tightened. I took an obscure pride in this.

Yeine sighed, stepping between her taller brothers with a glare at each, and came to my side. She crouched beside me, balancing on her toes; as usual she wore no shoes. When I did not move, she shifted to sit against me, her head resting on my shoulder. I closed my eyes and pressed my cheek against her hair.

"There is another option," Nahadoth said at last, breaking the silence. He spoke slowly, reluctantly. Change should not have been difficult for him, but I could see that this was. "When we are of one accord, all things become possible."

Again, I expected a reaction that Itempas did not provide. "Sieh's restoration is something we all desire." He spoke stiffly because change *was* difficult for him. Yet he made the effort anyway, even though it was an extreme suggestion: to bring together the Three as they had not done since the dawning of the universe. To remake reality, if that was what it took to remake *me*.

To this, I had no snide remark. I stared at them, Naha and Tempa, standing side by side and trying, for my sake, to get along.

Yeine lifted her head, which forced me to do the same. "I am willing, of course," she said to them, though she sounded concerned. "But I have never done this before. Is there danger to Sieh?"

"Some," said Itempas.

"Perhaps," said Nahadoth.

At Yeine's frown, I touched her hand, explaining as I had done for Shahar and Deka. "If the Three's accord is not total"—I nodded toward Itempas and Nahadoth, not needing to be subtle in my meaning—"if there is any hint of discord between you, things could go very wrong."

"How wrong?"

I shrugged. I had not seen it happen myself, but I understood the principle. It was simple: their will became reality. Any conflicts in their respective desires manifested as natural law—inertia and gravity, time and perception, love and sorrow. Nothing that the Three did was subtle.

Yeine considered this for a long moment. Then she reached up to caress my hair. As a boy, I had loved for her to do this. As a man, I found it awkward. Patronizing. But I tolerated it.

"Then there is danger," she said, troubled. "I want what *you* want. And it seems to me that what you want is not entirely clear."

I smiled sadly. Itempas's eyes narrowed. He and Nahadoth exchanged a knowing look. That was nice, actually. Like old times. Then they remembered that they hated each other and focused on me again.

It was ironic, really, and beautiful in its way. The problem was not them but me. The Three walked the world again and had come together in the hope of saving me. And I could not be saved, because I was in love with two mortals.

Yeine sighed. "You need time to think." She got to her feet, brushing unnecessarily at her pants, and faced Nahadoth and Itempas. "And we have business of our own to discuss, Sieh. Where shall we send you?"

I shook my head, rubbing my head wearily. "I don't know. Somewhere else." I gestured vaguely at the palace. "I'll make my own way." I always did.

Yeine glanced back at me as if she'd heard that last thought, but like a good mother, she let it pass unremarked. "Very well."

Then the world blurred, and I found myself sitting in a large open chamber of the new palace. Templelike, its ceiling arched high overhead, thirty or forty feet away. Vines dangled from its cornices and wended down the curving pillars. In the handful of minutes since we'd left, Yeine's power had thoroughly permeated the palace and covered it in green. The daystone was no longer precisely white, either: one wall of the chamber faced the sun, translucent, and against the bright backdrop I saw white stone marbled with something darker, gray shading to black. The black was studded with tiny white points, like stars. Perhaps they would glow, too, come night.

Deka sat there on his knees, alone. What had he been doing, praying? Holding vigil while my mortality passed away? How quaint. And how unsubtle of Yeine, to send me to him. I would never have figured her for a matchmaker.

"Deka," I said.

He started, turned, and frowned at me in surprise. "Sieh? I thought—"

I shook my head, not bothering to get up. "I have unfinished business, it seems."

"What—" No. Deka was too smart to ask that question. I saw understanding, elation, guilt, and hope flow across his face in a span of seconds before he caught himself and put his Arameri mask in place instead. He got to his feet and came over, offering a hand to help me up, which I took. When I was up, however, there was a moment of awkwardness. We were both men now, and most men would have stepped apart after such a gesture, putting distance between themselves so as to maintain the necessary boundaries of independence and camaraderie. I did not move away, and neither did Deka. Awkwardness passed into something entirely different.

"We were thinking about what to name this palace," he said softly. "Shahar and I."

I shrugged. "Seashell? Water?" I had never been much for creative naming. Deka, who had taste, grimaced at my suggestions.

"Shahar likes 'Echo.' She'll have to run it past Mother, of course." So fascinating, this conversation. Our mouths moved, speaking about things neither of us cared about, a verbal mask for entirely different words that did not need to be said. "She thinks this will make a good audience chamber." Another grimace, this one more delicate.

I smiled. "You disagree?"

"It doesn't feel like an audience chamber. It feels..." He shook his head, turning to face a spot beneath the translucent swirl-wall. I took his meaning. There was a votive atmosphere to this chamber, something difficult to define. There should have been an altar in that spot.

"So tell her," I said.

He shrugged. "You know how it is. Shahar is still...
Shahar." He smiled, but it faded.

I nodded. I didn't really want to talk about Shahar.

Deka's hand brushed mine, tentative. This was something he could have played off as an accident, if I let him.
"Perhaps you should bless this place. It's a trick, of a sort,
or it will be. The real home of the Arameri, leaving Sky as
a decoy..."

"I can't bless anything anymore, except in the poetic
sense." I took his hand, growing tired of the game. No
semblance of just-friends anymore. "Shall I become a god
again, Deka? Is that what you want?"

He flinched, thrown by my directness, his mask cracking. Through it I saw need so raw that it made me ache in
sympathy. But he abandoned the game, too, because that
was what the moment deserved. "No."

I smiled. If I had still been a god, my teeth would have
been sharp. "Why not? I could still love you, as a god." I
stepped closer, nuzzling his chin. He did not take this bait
or the verbal bait I offered next. "Your family would love
you better, if I were a god. *Your* god."

Deka's hands gripped my arms, tight. I expected him
to thrust me away, but he didn't. "I don't care what they
want," he said, his voice suddenly low, rough. "*I want* an
equal. I want to be *your* equal. When you were a god, I
couldn't be that, so... So help me, yes, some part of me
wished you were mortal. It wasn't deliberate, I didn't
know what would happen, but I don't regret it. So Shahar's not the only one who betrayed you." I flinched, and
his hands tightened, to the threshold of pain. He
leaned closer, intent. "As a child, I was nothing to you. A
game to pass the time." When I blinked in surprise, he

laughed bitterly. "I told you, Sieh. I know everything about you."

"Deka—" I began, but he cut me off.

"I know why you've never taken a mortal lover as more than a passing whim. Even before mortals were created, you'd lived so long, seen so much, that no mortal could be anything but an eyeblink in the eternity of your life. That's if you were willing to try, and you weren't. *But I will not be nothing to you*, Sieh. And if I must change the universe to have you, then so be it." He smiled again, tight, vicious, beautiful. Terrifying.

Arameri.

"I should kill you," I whispered.

"Do you think you could?" Unbelievable, his arrogance. Magnificent. He reminded me of Itempas.

"You sleep, Deka. You eat. Not all my tricks need magic."

His smile grew an edge of sadness. "Do you really *want* to kill me?" When I didn't answer—because I didn't know—he sobered. "What *do* you want, Sieh?"

And because I was afraid, and because Yeine had asked the same question, and because Deka really did know me too well, I answered with the truth.

"N-not to be alone anymore." I licked my lips and looked away—at the altar-less floor, at a nearby pillar, at the sun diluted by swirls of white and black and gray. Anywhere but at him. I was so very, very tired. I had been tired for an age of the world. "To have... I want... something that is *mine*."

Deka let out a long, shaky sigh, pressing his forehead against mine as if he'd just won some victory. "Is that all?"

"Yes. I want—"

And then there was no repeating what I wanted,

because his mouth was on mine and his soul was in me and it was frightening to be invaded—and exhilarating and agonizing. Like racing comets and chasing thought-whales and skating along freezing liquid air. It was better than the first time. He still kissed like a god.

Then his mouth was on my throat, his hands tugging open my shirt, his legs pushing us back back back until I stopped against one of the vine-covered pillars. I barely noticed despite the breath being knocked out of me. I was gasping now because he'd bitten me just over my lower rib cage, and that was the most erotic sensation I'd ever felt. I reached out to touch him and found hot mortal skin and humming tattooed magic, free of the encumbering cloth as he stripped himself. There are so many ways to make magic. I tapped a cadence over his shoulders, and hot, raw power seared up my arms in response. I drank it in and moaned. He had made himself strong and wise, a god in mortal flesh, for me, me, me. Was he right? I had always avoided mortals. It made no sense for a being older than the sun to want a creature that would always be less than a child, in relative terms. But I did want him; oh gods, how I wanted him. Was that the solution? It was not my nature to do what was wise; I did what felt good. Why should that not apply to love as well as play?

Had I truly been fighting myself all this time?

Movement on the edge of my vision pulled me out of the haze of Deka's teeth and hands. I focused on reality and saw Shahar, in the entryway of the marbled chamber. She had stopped there, framed by the corridor beyond, illuminated by the swirling sun. Her eyes were wide, her face paler than ever, her lips a flat white line. I remembered those lips soft and open, welcoming, and in spite of everything, I craved her again. I stroked Deka's straight

hair and thought of hers coiling round my fingers and—
Gods, no, I would go mad if I kept this up.

Something that was mine. I looked down at Deka,
who'd crouched at my feet, licking the bite on my ribs as I
shuddered. His hands cupped my waist, as gentle as if I
were made of eggshell. (I was. It was called mortal flesh.)
Beautiful, perfect boy. Mine.

"Prove it," I whispered. "Show me how much you love
me, Deka."

He looked up at me. I realized he knew Shahar was
there. Of course; the bond between us. Perhaps that was
why she'd come here, too, at this precise moment, out of
the whole vast empty palace. I was lonely. I needed. That
need drew them to me now, just as my need had drawn
them on a long-ago day in Sky's underpalace. We had
shared something powerful when we took our oath, but
the connection had been there even beforehand. That
could not be broken by something so paltry as betrayal.

All this was in Deka's eyes as he gazed up at me. I do
not know what he saw in mine. Whatever it was, though,
he nodded once. Then he rose, never taking his hands off
me, and turned me gently to face the pillar. When he
spoke into my ear, the words were gods' language. That
made me believe them, and trust him, because they could
be nothing but true.

"I'll never hurt you," he said, and proved it.

Shahar left sometime during what followed. Not
immediately. She stayed for a long while, in fact, listening
to my groans and watching while I stopped caring about
her, or even being aware of her presence. Perhaps she even
lingered after I pulled her little brother to the floor and
made a proper altar of it, wringing sweat and tears and
songs of praise from him, and blessing him with pleasure

in return. I didn't know. I didn't care. Deka was my only world, my only god. Yes, I used him, but he wanted me to. I would worship him forever.

I was exhausted afterward. Deka wasn't tired at all, the bastard. He sat up awhile, using the floor to idly trace the outlines of sigils that he intended to draw into the new palace's substance as part of its first layer of arcane protection. Apparently teams of soldiers and scriveners had already begun exploring the palace and mapping its wonders. He told me about this while I lay in a stupor. It was as though he'd gorged himself on my vitality, leaving me little better than a husk. Then it occurred to me that during our lovemaking, it had been he who'd drawn us out of the world and back; his kisses, not mine, had woven our souls together. He was still one-eighth of a god. I was all mortal.

If this was how mortals usually felt when a god was done with them, I felt fresh guilt for all my past dalliances.

Eventually I recovered, however, and told Deka that I needed to leave. All the highbloods were selecting apartments in the uppermost central spirals of the palace—the old pattern from Sky. It would be easy for me to find him later. There was an uncomfortable moment when Deka gave me a long and silent perusal before replying, but whatever he saw in my face satisfied him. He nodded and rose to get dressed himself.

"Be careful," was all he said. "My sister may be dangerous now."

I thought that was probably true.

I found Itempas less than a half hour before sunset. As I'd suspected, he'd taken up residence on the wide central platform where we'd first arrived, which had become a meadow of bobbing sea grass in the meantime. This palace had not been configured to exalt him; nevertheless, the highest center point of anything was a natural place for him to settle.

He stood facing the sun, his legs braced apart and arms folded, unmoving, though he must have sensed my approach. The grass whispered against my pant legs as I walked, and I saw that the grass nearest Itempas had turned white. Typical.

I did not see Nahadoth or Yeine or feel their presence nearby. They had abandoned him again.

"Want to be alone?" I asked, stopping behind him. The sun had almost touched the sea in the distance. He could count the remaining moments of his godhood on one hand. Maybe two.

"No," he said, so I sat down in the grass, watching him.

"I've decided that I want to remain mortal," I said. "At least until...you know. Close to. Ah. The end. Then the three of you can try to change me back." Unspoken was the fact that I might change my mind again then and choose to die with Deka. It was a choice that not every god got to make. I was very fortunate.

He nodded. "We felt your decision."

I grimaced. "How unromantic. And here I was thinking that was an orgasm."

He ignored my irreverence out of long habit. "Your love for those two has been clear to all of us since your transformation into mortal, Sieh. Only you have resisted this knowledge."

I hated it when he got sanctimonious, so I changed the subject. "Thanks for trying, by the way. To help me."

He sighed gently. "I wonder, sometimes, why you think so little of me. Then I remember."

"Yes. Well." I shrugged, uncomfortable. "Is Glee coming to fetch you?" Unspoken: *when you are mortal again?*

"Yes."

"She really loves you, you know."

He turned, just enough so that I could see his face. "Yes."

I was babbling, and he had noticed. Annoyed, I stopped talking. The silence collected around us, comfortable. In the old days, I had only ever liked being quiet around him. With anyone else, the urge to fill the silence with chatter or movement was overwhelming. He had never needed to command me to be still. Around him, I just wanted to.

We watched the sun inch toward the horizon. "Thank you," he said suddenly, surprising me.

"Hmm?"

"For coming here."

At this, I sighed and shifted and rubbed a hand over my hair. Finally I got up, coming to stand beside him. I could feel the radiant warmth of his presence, skin tightening even from a foot away. He could blaze with the fire and light of every sun in existence, but most times he kept the furnace banked so that others could be near him. His version of a friendly invitation—because naturally he would never, ever just *say* he was lonely, the fool.

And somehow, I had never, ever noticed that he did this. What did that make me? His twice-fool son, I supposed.

So I stayed there beside him while we watched the last curve of the sun flatten into an oblong, then puddle against the edge of the world, and finally melt away. The instant this happened, Itempas gasped, and I felt a sudden swift wave of heat, as of something rushing away. What remained in its wake was human, ordinary, just a middle-aged man in plain clothes and worn boots (brown again, ha ha!) with too much hair for practicality. And when he toppled backward like an old broken tree, unconscious in the aftermath of godhood, it was I who caught him, and eased him to the floor, and cradled his head in my lap.

"Stupid old man," I whispered. But I stroked his hair while he slumbered.

Would that things could have ended there.

A moment after I'd settled down with Itempas, I felt a presence behind me and did not turn. Let Glee think what she would of me with her father. I was tired of hating him. "Make him decorate his hair," I said, more to make conversation than anything else. "If he's going to wear his hair in a Teman style, he ought to do it right."

"So," said Kahl, and I went rigid with shock. His voice was soft, regretful. "You have forgiven him."

What—

Before the thought could form, he was in front of me, on Itempas's other side, with one hand poised in a way that made no sense to me—until he plunged it down, and too late I remembered that Glee had been protecting him from this very thing.

By that point, Kahl's hand was up to the wrist in Itempas's chest.

Itempas jerked awake, rigid, his face a rictus of agony. I did not waste time screaming denial. Denial was for mortals. Instead I grabbed Kahl's arm with all my strength, trying to keep him from doing what I *knew* he was about to do. But I was just a mortal, and he was a godling, and not only did he rip Itempas's heart out in a blur of splattering red, but he also threw me across the platform in the process. I rolled to a halt amid the salt-sweet stench of bruised sea grass, barely three feet from the edge. There were steps wending around the platform, but if I'd missed those, it was a long way—several hundred feet—to the base of the palace.

Dazed, I struggled upright and discovered that my arm was dislocated. As I finished screaming from this, I looked up and found Kahl standing between me and Itempas's corpse. The heart was in his hand, dripping; his expression was implacable.

"Thank you," he said. "I've been hunting him for years now. His demon daughter is good at hiding. I knew that if I watched *you*, however, I would eventually get my chance."

"What—" Hard to think around pain. If mortals could do it, I could, damn it. I ground my teeth and spoke through them. "What in the infinite hells is *wrong* with you? You know that won't kill him. And now Naha and Yeine will be after you." I was not a god anymore. I could not call them with my thoughts. What could I do, as a mortal, facing the god of vengeance in the moment of his triumph? Nothing. Nothing.

"Let them come." So familiar, that arrogance. Where had I seen it before? "They haven't found me yet. I can complete the mask now and take it back from Usein." He lifted Itempas's heart, peering intently at it, and for the first time I saw him smile in unreserved pleasure. His lips drew back, showing a hint of canine—

—sharp teeth, so much like—

"Only a spark left. Just enough, though."

I understood then, or thought I did. What Kahl had sought was not Itempas's mere blood or flesh, but the pure bright power of the god of light. As a mortal, Itempas had none, and in his true form he was too powerful. Only now, in the space between mortality and immortality, was

Itempas both vulnerable and valuable—and I, powerless, was no sufficient guardian. Glee had been right not to trust me with him, though not for the reasons she feared.

"You're going to take the mask from Usein?" I struggled to sit up, holding my arm. "But I thought..."

No. Oh, no. I had been so wrong.

A mask that conferred the power of gods. But Kahl had never meant for a mortal to wear it.

"You can't." I could not even imagine it. Once upon a time, there were three gods who had created all the realms. Less than three and it would all end. *More* than three and— "You can't! If the power doesn't rip you apart—"

"Are you concerned?" Kahl lowered the heart, his smile fading. There was anger in him now; all his earlier reticence and sadness had vanished. He had accepted his nature at last, waxing powerful in the moment of his triumph. Even if I had been my old self, I would have felt fear. One did not challenge the elontid at such times. "Do you care about me, Sieh?"

"I care about *living*, you demonshitting fool! What you're planning..." It was a nightmare that no godling would admit dreaming. The Maelstrom had given birth to three gods down the course of eternity. Who knew if—or when—it might suddenly belch forth another? What we thought of as the universe, the collection of realities and embodiments that had been born from the Three's warring and loving and infinitely careful craft, was too delicate to survive the onslaught of a Fourth. The Three themselves would endure, and adapt, and build a new universe that would incorporate the new one's power. But everything of the old existence—including godlings and the entire mortal realm—would be gone.

There was a blur and suddenly Kahl was before me. To be more precise, his foot was on my chest, and I was on the ground being crushed beneath it. With my good hand I scrabbled for his booted foot but could gain no purchase on the fine, god-conjured leather. The only reason I could still breathe at all was the soil beneath my back: my torso had sunk into it rather than simply collapsing.

Kahl leaned over me, adding pressure to my lungs. Through watering eyes I saw his: narrow, deep-set slashes in the plane of his face, like Teman eyes. Like mine, though far colder. And they were green, too, like mine.

—like Enefa's—

"Are you afraid?" He cocked his head as if genuinely curious, then leaned closer. I could almost hear my ribs groan, on the brink. But when I forced my face back up, muscles straining, throat bulging, I forgot all about my ribs. Because now Kahl was close enough that I could see his eyes clearly, and when his pupils flickered into narrow, deadly slits—

—eyes like Enefa's no no EYES LIKE MINE—

I tried to scream.

"It's far too late for you to care about me, Father," he said.

The word fell into my mind like poison, and the veil on my memory shredded into tatters.

Kahl vanished then, and I do not remember what happened after that. There was a lot of pain.

But when I finally awoke, I was thirty years older.

BOOK FOUR

No Legs at Midnight

HERE IS WHAT HAPPENED.

In the beginning there were three gods. Nahadoth and Itempas came first, enemies and then lovers, and they were happy for all the endless aeons of their existence.

Enefa's coming shattered the universe they had built. They recovered, and welcomed her, and built it again—newer, better. They grew strong together. But for most of that time, Nahadoth and Itempas remained closer to each other than to their younger sister. And she, in the way of gods, grew lonely.

So she tried to love me. But because she was a god and I merely a godling, our first lovemaking nearly destroyed me. I tried again—I have always been hardheaded, as the Maro say—and would have kept trying if Enefa, in her wisdom, had not finally realized the truth: a godling cannot be a god. I was not enough for her. If she was ever to have something of her own, she would have to win one of her brothers away from the other.

She succeeded, many centuries later, with Nahadoth. This was one of the events that led to the Gods' War.

But in the meantime, she did not wholly spurn me. She

was not a sentimental lover, but a practical one, and I was the best of the god-children she had yet produced. I would have been honored, when she decided to make a child from my seed—

—if the existence of that child had not almost killed me.

So she took steps to save both of us. First she tended to me, as I lay disintegrating within the conflagration of my own unwanted maturity. A touch, a reweaving of memory, a whisper: forget. As the knowledge that I was a father vanished, so, too, did the danger, and I was cured.

Then she took the child away. I do not know where; some other realm. She sealed the child into this place so that it—he—Kahl—could grow up in safety and health. But he could not escape, and he was alone there, because keeping the secret from me meant keeping Kahl unknown to the other gods.

Perhaps Enefa visited him to prevent the madness that comes of isolation. Or perhaps she ignored and observed him while he cried for her, one of her endless experiments. Or perhaps she took him as a new lover. No way to know, now that she is dead. I am just father enough to wonder.

Still, because the fact of Kahl's existence did not change, this has led to our current problem. Her delicate chains in my mind, the heavy bars on Kahl's prison: both were loosened when Enefa died in Tempa's trembling hands. Those protections held, however, until Yeine claimed the remnant of Enefa's body and soul for her own. This "killed" Enefa at last. The chains were broken, the bars snapped. Then Kahl, son of death and mischief, Lord of Retribution, was loosed upon the realms to do as he would. And it was only a matter of time before my memory returned.

Just as well, I suppose, that I am already dying.

19

I DID NOT FEEL at all well when I woke.

I lay in a bed, somewhere in the new palace. It was nighttime, and the walls glowed, though far more strangely than they had in Sky. Here the dark swirls in the stone reduced the light, though the flecks of white within each indeed gleamed like tiny stars. Beautiful, but dim. Someone had hung lanterns from looping protrusions on the walls, which seemed to have been created for that purpose. I almost laughed at this, because it meant that after two thousand years, the Arameri would now have to use candles to see by, like everyone else.

I didn't laugh because something had been shoved down my throat. With some effort I groped about my face and found some sort of tube in my mouth, held in place with bandages. I tried to tug it loose and gagged quite unpleasantly.

"Stop that." Deka's hand came into my view, pushing mine away. "Be still, and I'll remove it."

I will not describe what the removal felt like. Suffice it to say that if I had still been a god, I would have cursed Deka to three hells for putting that thing in me. Though only the nicer hells, since he'd meant well.

Afterward, as I sat panting and trying to forget the fear that I might die choking on my own vomit, Deka moved to the edge of the bed beside me. He rubbed my back gently and slowly. A warning. "Feel better?"

"Yes." My voice was rough, and my throat dry and sore, but that would fade. I was more troubled by the awful weakness in every limb and joint. I looked at one of my hands and was stunned: the skin was dry and loose, more wrinkled than smooth. "What..."

"You needed nourishment." He sounded very tired. "Your body had begun to devour itself. One of my scriveners came up with this. I think it saved your life."

"Saved—"

And then I remembered. Kahl. My—

forget

My mind shied away from both the thought and my mother's warning, though it was too late for either. The knowledge was free, the damage done.

"Mirror." I whispered it, hoarse.

One appeared nearby: full-length, on a wheeled wooden pivot stand. I had no idea how it had been conjured. But when Deka got up and tilted it toward me, I forgot the mystery of the mirror. I stared at myself for a long, long time.

"It could have been much worse," Deka said, while I sat there. "We—the scriveners—didn't know what was wrong with you. Our warning-scripts led us to you. Then Lord Itempas revived and told us what needed to be done. I was able to design a negation-script to work in tandem with a loop-interrupt..." He trailed off. I wasn't listening, anyway. It had worked; that was all that mattered. "We stopped the age acceleration. Then we repaired what we could. Three of your ribs were broken, your sternum was cracked, one lung punctured. There was some bruising to your heart, a dislocated shoulder..."

He stopped again when I reached out to touch the mirror.

My face was still handsome, at least, though no longer boyishly pretty. This was not my doing. My body was growing how it wanted now, and I could have ended up pudgy and bald. I'd gone gray mostly at the temples, though there was plenty threaded through the rest of my hair, which was long again, tangling into knots on the sheets behind me. The shape of my face was not so different, just softer. Temans tended to age well in that respect. The texture of my skin, however, was thicker, dryer, weathered, even though it had seen little of the outdoors. There were deep-set lines around my mouth, finer ones at the corners of my eyes, and I was looking decidedly grizzled, though thankfully someone had shaved me. If I kept my mouth shut and dressed right, I might be able to do "distinguished."

When I lowered my hand, it took more effort to move. Slower reflexes, softer muscles. I was skinny again, though not nearly as bad as after the last mortaling. The food tube had kept me in healthy flesh, but it was definitely weaker, less resilient flesh.

"I'm too old for you now," I said, very softly.

Deka pushed aside the mirror, saying nothing. That silence hurt, because I took it to mean he agreed with me. Not that I blamed him. But then Deka lay down beside me and pulled me to lie with him, draping an arm across my chest. "You need to rest."

I closed my eyes and tried to turn away from him, but he wouldn't let me, and I was too tired to struggle. All I could do was turn my face away.

"Aren't you too old to sulk, too?"

I ignored him and sulked anyway. It wasn't fair. I had wanted so much to make him mine.

Deka sighed, nuzzling the back of my neck. "I'm too tired to talk sense into you, Sieh. Stop being stupid and go to sleep. There's a lot going on right now, and I could use your help."

He was the strong one, young and brilliant, with a bright future. I was nothing. Just a fallen god and a terrible father. (Even to think this hurt, grinding agony throughout my body like a headache with serrated teeth. I bit my lip and focused on loneliness and self-pity instead, which was better.)

But I was still tired. Deka's arm, draped over my chest, made me feel safe. And though it was an illusion, doomed like all things mortal, I resolved to enjoy it while I could, and slept again.

When I woke next, it was morning. Sunlight shone through the walls; the bedroom was illuminated in shades of white and green. Deka was gone from beside me. Glee was in the room instead, sitting beside the bed in a big chair.

"I knew it was a mistake to trust you," she said.

I was feeling stronger, and my temper, at least, had not mellowed with age. I sat up, creaky, stiff, and glared at her. "Good morning to you, too."

She looked as tired as Deka, her clothing more disheveled than I had ever seen it, though still neat by the standards of average mortals. But when the daughter of Itempas wears unmatched clothing with her blouse half undone at the top, she might as well be a beggar from the Ancestors' Village. She had, as perhaps a final concession to exhaustion, bottled her thunderstorm of hair rather than style it with her usual careless confidence: a tie pulled it into a fluffy bun at the nape of her neck. It did not suit her.

"All you had to do," she said tightly, "was shout Yeine's name. It was twilight; she would have heard you. She and Naha would have come and dealt with Kahl, and that would have been that."

I flinched, because she was right. It was the sort of thing a mortal would have thought to do. "Well, where the hells were you?" This was a weak riposte. Her failure did not negate mine.

"*I* am not a god. I didn't know he'd been attacked." She sighed, lifting a hand to rub her eyes. Her frustration was so palpable that the very air tasted bitter. "Father didn't use his sphere to summon me until Kahl was long gone. His first thought, upon returning to life, was of *you*."

If I had still been a child, I would have felt a small and petty pleasure at this hint of her jealousy. But my body was older now; I could no longer be childish. I just felt sad.

"I'm sorry," I said. She only nodded, bleak.

Because I felt stronger, I took in more of my surroundings this time. We were in the bedchamber of an apartment. I could see another room beyond the doorway, brighter lit; there must have been windows. The walls and floors were bare of personal touches, though I glimpsed clothes hanging neatly in a large closet across the room. Some of them were the ones Morad had given me before we'd left Sky. Apparently Deka had told the servants I was living with him.

Pushing aside the covers, I got to my feet, slowly and carefully, as my knees hurt. I was naked, too, which was unfortunate as I seemed to have sprouted hair from an astonishing variety of body parts. Glee would just have to endure, I decided, and made my way to the closet to dress.

"Did Dekarta explain what has happened?" Glee had composed herself; she sounded brisk and professional again.

"Aside from me taking a great flying leap toward death? No." All my clothes had been made for a younger man. They would look ridiculous on me now. I sighed and pulled on the most boring of what I found and wished for shoes that might somehow ease the ache in my knees.

Something flickered at the edge of my vision. I turned, startled, and saw a pair of boots sitting on the floor. Each had good, stiff leather about the ankles, and when I picked one up, I saw it had thick padding in the sole.

I turned to Glee and held up the boot in wordless query.

"Echo," she said. "The palace's walls listen."

"I...see." I did not.

She looked fleetingly amused. "Ask for something—or even think of it with enough longing—and it appears. The palace seems to clean itself as well, and it even rearranges furniture and decor. No one knows why. Some remnant of the Lady's power, perhaps, or some property that has been permanently built in." She paused. "If it is permanent, there will be little need for servants here, going forward."

And little need for the age-old divisions between high-bloods and low, among Arameri family members. I smiled down at the boot. How like Yeine.

"Where is Deka?" I asked.

"He left this morning. Shahar has kept him busy since Kahl's attack. He and the scriveners have been setting up all manner of defensive magics, internal gates, and even scripts that can move the palace, though not with any great speed. When he hasn't been here, tending you, he's been working."

I paused in the middle of pulling on pants. "How long have I been, er, incapacitated?"

"Almost two weeks."

More of my life slept away. I sighed and resumed dressing.

"Morad has been busy organizing the palace's operations and preparing sufficient living quarters for the high-bloods," Glee continued. "Ramina has even put the courtiers to work. Remath has begun transferring power to Shahar, which requires endless paperwork and meetings with the military, the nobles, the Order..." She shook her head and sighed. "And since none of those are permitted to come here, the palace's gates and message spheres have seen heavy use. Only Remath's orders keep Shahar here, and no doubt if Deka were not First Scrivener and essential to making the palace ready, she would have him visiting fifty thousand kingdoms as her proxy."

I frowned, going to the mirror to see if anything could be done about my hair. It was far too long, nearly to my knees. Someone had cut it already, I suspected, because given my usual pattern it should have been long enough to fill the room by this point. I willed scissors to appear on a nearby dresser, and they did. Almost like being a god again.

"Why the urgency?" I asked. "Has something happened?" I hacked clumsily at my hair, which of course offended Glee. She made a sound of irritation, coming over to me and taking the scissors from my hand.

"The urgency is all Remath's." She worked quickly, at least. I saw hanks of hair fall to the floor around my feet. She was leaving it too long, brushing my collar, but at least I wouldn't trip on it now. "She seems convinced that the transition must be completed sooner rather than later. Perhaps she has told Shahar the reason for her haste; if so, Shahar has not shared this knowledge with the rest of us." Glee shrugged.

I turned to her, hearing the unspoken. "How has Shahar been, then, as queen of her own little kingdom?"

"Sufficiently Arameri."

Which was both reassuring and troubling.

Finishing, Glee brushed off my back and set the scissors down. I looked at myself in the mirror and nodded thanks, then immediately ran fingers through my hair to make it look messier. This annoyed Glee further; she turned away, her lips pursed in disapproval. "Shahar wanted to be informed when you were up and about, so I let a servant know when you began to stir. Expect a summons shortly."

"Fine. I'll be ready."

I followed Glee out of the bedchamber and into a wide, nicely apportioned room of couches and sidebars that smelled of Deka, though it did not at all *feel* like him. No books. One whole wall of this room was a window, overlooking the bridge-linked tiers of the palace and the placid ocean beyond. The sky was blue and cloudless, noonday bright.

"So what now?" I asked, going to stand at the window. "For you and Itempas? I assume Naha and Yeine are searching for Kahl."

"As are Ahad and his fellow godlings. But the fact that they have not yet found him—and did not, prior to his attack—suggests he has always had some means of hiding from us. Perhaps he simply retreats to wherever Enefa kept him hidden before now. That worked well enough for millennia."

"Darr," I said. "The mask was there."

"Not anymore. Immediately after leaving here, Kahl went to Darr and took the mask. To be precise, he forced a young Darren man to pick up the mask, and took *him*. The Darre are furious; when Yeine arrived, searching for Kahl, they told her everything." Glee folded her arms, the expression on her face very familiar. "Apparently Kahl approached Usein Darr's grandmother, more than fifty years ago. He showed them how to combine the art of mask making with scrivening techniques and godsblood, and they took it further still. In exchange, he claimed the best of their mask makers and had them work on a special project for him. He *killed* them, Sieh, when they'd done whatever work he needed. The Darre say the mask grew more powerful—and Kahl grew less able to approach it himself—with every life he gave it."

I knew what Kahl was doing now. That sickening churn of wild, raw power I'd felt near the mask, like a storm—the Three had been born from something like that. A new god could be made from something similar.

But he'd killed mortals to give it power? That I didn't understand. Mortals were children of the Maelstrom, it was true; we all were, however distant. But the power of the Three was as a volcano to mortals' candleflames. Mortal strength was so much lesser than ours as to be, well, nothing. If Kahl wanted to create himself anew as a god, he would need far more power than that.

I sighed, rubbing my eyes. Didn't I have enough to worry about? Why did I have to deal with all these mortal issues, too?

Because I am mortal.

Ah, yes. I kept forgetting.

Glee said nothing more, so I experimented with wishing for food, and the precise meal I wanted—a bowl of soup and cookies shaped like cute prey animals—appeared on a nearby table. No need for servants indeed, I mused as I ate. That would serve the family's security interests well, as they would have no need to hire non-Arameri. There would always be a need for certain tasks to be done, though, like running errands, and the Arameri were the Arameri. Those with power would always find some way to exert it over those who didn't. Yeine was naïve to hope that such a simple change might free the family of its historic obsession with status.

Still... I was glad for her naïveté. That was always the nicest thing about having a newborn god around. They were willing to try things the rest of us were too jaded even to consider.

The knock at the door came just as I finished eating. "Come."

A servant stepped inside, bowing to both of us. "Lord Sieh. Lady Shahar requests your presence, if you are feeling better."

I looked at Glee, who inclined her head to me. This could have meant anything from *hurry up* to *hope she doesn't kill you*. With a sigh, I rose and followed the servant out.

Shahar had not chosen the Temple as her seat of power. (Already it had acquired capital-letter status in my heart, because what I had done with Deka there was holy.) The servant led us instead to a chamber deep within the palace's heart, directly below the central high platform that had already come to be called the Whorl. Deka and his crew had been busy, I saw as we walked. Transport-sigils had been painted at intervals throughout the palace's corridors and painted over with resin in order to protect them from scuffing or wear. They did not work quite like the lifts in Sky—standing on one sent a person anywhere they willed themselves to go within the palace, not merely up and down. This was awkward if one had never been to a particular location. When I asked the servant about this, he smiled and said, "The first time we go anywhere, we go on foot. Steward Morad's orders." Just the kind of eminently sensible thing I expected of her, especially given that with servants so sparse, she could not afford to lose even one to oblivion.

Since the servant had been to the audience chamber before, I allowed him to control the magic, and we appeared in a space of cool, flickering light. Echo was more translucent than Sky, reflecting more of whatever colors surrounded it. By this I guessed immediately that we were somewhere beneath the waterline of the palace—which was confirmed as we passed a row of windows. I saw a great expanse of glimmering, shadow-flickering blueness and a passing curious fish. I grinned in delight at Shahar's cleverness. Not only would her audience chamber be safer underwater than the rest of the palace, but also any visitors—the few who would be permitted to see her in person—would instantly be awed by the alien beauty of the fishes'-eye view. There was a certain symbolism to the choice as well, as the Arameri now served the Lady of Balance. Shahar's safety would depend on the strength of the walls and windows and the equilibrium they could maintain against the weight of the water. It was perfect.

And even though I am a god, it was I who stopped when we entered the audience chamber, staring about in awe.

The chamber was small, as befit a space that would never be used by many people. Echo would have little need of the tricks that Sky had employed to intimidate and impress visitors, like vaulted ceilings and proportions meant to make supplicants feel unimportant before the great stone throne. This room was shaped like Echo itself: a descending spiral, though with small alcoves surrounding the depressed central space. In the alcoves, I glimpsed some of the soldiers who had come with us, at guard. Then I noticed more shadowy figures interspersing them, these crouched and oddly still. The ever-elusive Arameri assassins.

A poor choice, I decided. They made it too obvious that Shahar felt the need to guard herself from her own family.

When I finally stopped boggling, I noticed that Deka had preceded me. He knelt before the chamber's depression, not looking up, though he'd probably heard me. I stopped beside him, emphatically *not* kneeling. The seat we faced was almost humble: just a wide, curving stool lined with a cushion, low-backed. Yet the room was structured so that every eye was drawn to it, and all of the flickering oceanlight coming through the chamber's windows met in overlapping waves there. Had Shahar been sitting on the stool, she would have seemed unworldly, especially if she sat still. Like a goddess herself.

Instead, she stood near one of the room's windows, her hands behind her back. In the cool light she was almost unnoticeable, the folds of her pale gown lost amid flickering blueness. Her stillness troubled me—but then, what about this little scene didn't? I had spent centuries in chambers like this, facing Arameri leaders. I knew danger when I sensed it.

When the servant knelt to murmur to Shahar, she nodded and then raised her voice. "Guards. Leave."

They exited with no hesitation. The assassins did so by slipping out through small doors in each alcove, which the servant also used to leave at Shahar's quiet command. Presently, she and I and Dekarta were alone. Deka rose to his feet then, glancing once at me; his face was unreadable. I nodded to him, then slipped my hands into my pockets and waited. We had not seen Shahar since that moment in the Temple, when she had witnessed our claiming of each other.

"Mother has accelerated the schedule again," Shahar said, not turning to us. "I asked her to reconsider, or at least send more help. She has agreed to do the latter; you will receive ten scriveners from the Sky complement by tomorrow afternoon."

"That will do more harm than good," Deka said, scowling. "New people need to be trained, shown around, supervised. Until they're ready, that will slow down my teams, not speed up the work."

Shahar sighed. I could hear the weariness in her voice, though I also heard her struggle to contain it. "It was the only concession I could gain, Deka. She's like a heretic these days, filled with a fervor no rational person can comprehend."

In this I also heard a hint of sourness that I was certain she only revealed because we would have detected it anyway. Was she upset about Remath's decision to turn from the Itempan faith? A pointless concern, given all our other troubles.

"Why?"

"Who can say? If I had the time to conspire against her, I might accuse her of madness and seek backers within the family for a coup. Though perhaps that's why she's sent me here, where I'm less of a danger." She laughed once, then turned—and paused, staring at me. I sighed while she took in my new, middle-aged shape.

It surprised me that she smiled. There was nothing malicious in it, just compassion and a hint of pity. "You *should* look like my father," she said, "but with that look of disgust on your face, it's clear you're still the same bratty little boy we met all those years ago."

I smiled in spite of myself. "I don't mind so much," I said. "At least I'm done with adolescence. Never could stand it; if I don't want to kill someone, I want to have sex with them."

Her smile faded, and I remembered: I had lain with her while we were both adolescents. Perhaps she had fond memories of what I now joked about. A mistake on my part.

She sighed, turning to pace. "I will have to rely on you, both of you, more than ever. What is happening now is unprecedented. I've checked the family archives. I truly don't know what Mother is thinking." She stopped at last, pressing fingers against her forehead as if she had a terrible headache. "She's making me the family head."

There was a moment of silence as we both processed her words. Deka reacted before I did, stricken. "How can you be head if she still lives?"

"Precisely. It's never been done." She turned to us suddenly, and we both flinched at the raw misery in her face. "Deka...I think she's preparing to die."

Deka went to her at once, ever the loving brother, taking her elbow. She leaned on him with such utter trust that I felt unexpected guilt. Had she come seeking us for comfort that night, only to find us comforting one another, uninterested in her? What had she felt, watching us make love while she stood alone, friendless, hopeless?

For just an instant, I saw her again at the window, stock-still, her hands behind her back. I saw Itempas gazing at the horizon, stock-still, too proud to let his loneliness show.

I went to them and reached for her, hesitating only at the last moment. But I had not stopped loving her, either. So I laid a hand on her shoulder. She started and lifted her head to look at me, her eyes bright with unshed tears. They searched mine, seeking—what? Forgiveness? I wasn't certain I had that in me to give. But regret—yes, that I had.

Naturally, I could not let such a powerful moment pass without a joke. "And here I thought *I* had problem parents." It wasn't a very good joke.

She chuckled, blinking quickly against the tears and trying to compose herself. "Sometimes I wish I still wanted to kill her." It was a better joke, or would have been if there had been a grain of truth in it. I smiled anyway, though uncomfortably. Deka did not smile at either joke—but then Remath had no interest in him, and he probably *did* want to kill her.

It seemed Deka was thinking along the same lines. "If she steps down in favor of you," he said, all seriousness, "you will have to exile her."

Shahar flinched, staring at him. *"What?"*

He sighed. "No beast can function with two heads. To have two Arameri palaces, two Arameri rulers..." He shook his head. "If you cannot see the potential danger in that, Shahar, you aren't the sister I remember."

She was, and she could. I saw her expression harden as she understood. She turned away from us, going back to the window and folding her arms across her breasts. "I'm surprised you've suggested only exile. I would have expected a more permanent solution from you, Brother."

He shrugged. "Mother doubtless expects something along those lines herself. She's not a fool, and she's trained you well." He paused. "If you didn't love her, I would suggest it. But under the circumstances..."

She laughed once, harshly. "Yes. Love. So inconvenient."

She turned then, looking at both of us, and suddenly I

tensed again, because I *knew* that look. I had worn it too many times, in too many shapes, not to recognize it on another being. She was up to no good.

Yet when she focused on me, the look softened. "Sieh," she said. "Are we friends again?"

Lie. The thought came to me so strongly that for an instant I thought it was not my own. Deka, perhaps, sending his words into my mind as gods could. But I knew the flavor of my own thoughts, and this had the particular bitter suspicion that came of years spent with this mad family and aeons of life amid my own madder one. She wanted the truth, and the truth would hurt her. And she was too powerful now, too dangerous, for me to hurt with impunity.

For the sake of what we'd once had, however, she deserved the truth, painful or not.

"No," I said. I spoke softly, as if that would ease the blow. She stiffened, and I sighed. "I can't trust you, Shahar. I need to trust the people I call friend." I paused. "But I understand why you betrayed me. Perhaps I would even have made the same choice, in your position; I don't know. I'm not angry about it anymore. I can't be, given the result."

And then I did something stupid. I looked at Deka and let my love for him show. He blinked, surprised, and I added insult to injury by smiling. It would hurt so much, leaving him, but he did not need an old man for a lover. Such things mattered for mortals. I would do the mature thing, preserve my dignity, and step aside before our relationship grew too awkward.

I have always been a selfish fool. I thought only of myself in that moment, when I should have thought of protecting him.

Shahar's face went utterly blank. It was as though someone had thrust a knife into her and cut out her soul, leaving only a cold and implacable statue in her place. But it was not empty, this statue. Anger had filled its hollows.

"I see," she said. "Very well. If you cannot trust me, then I can hardly allow myself to trust you, can I?" Her eyes flicked over to Deka, still cold. "That puts me in a difficult position, Brother."

Deka frowned, puzzled by the change in Shahar's manner. I, however, was not. It was all too easy to see what she meant to do to her brother, in her rage at me.

"Don't," I whispered.

"Dekarta," she said, ignoring me, "it pains me to say this, but I must ask that you accept a true sigil."

When Deka stiffened, she smiled. I hated her for that.

"I, of course, would never presume to dictate your choice of lover," she said, "but in light of Sieh's history, the many Arameri he has slain through his tricks and deceptions—"

"I don't believe this." Deka was trembling, fury clawing through the shock on his face. But beneath that fury was something much worse, and again I knew it by experience. Betrayal. He had trusted her, too, and she had broken his heart as she'd broken mine.

"Shahar." I clenched my fists. "Don't do this. Whatever you feel toward me, Deka is your brother—"

"And I am being generous even to let him live," she snapped. She walked away from us, going to sit on the stool. There, she was poised and implacable, her slim form washed in ice-water light. "He just implied that I should kill the head of this family. Clearly he needs the restrictions of a true sigil, lest he plot further treachery."

"And this would have nothing to do with me fucking your little brother instead of you—" My fists clenched. I

stepped forward, intending...gods, I didn't know. To grab her arm and make her see reason. To shout into her face. She tensed as I came near, though, and the sigil on her brow turned to white light. I knew what that meant, had felt the whip's sting too often in the past, but that had been a mortal lifetime ago. I was not prepared when a slash of raw magic threw me across the room.

It didn't kill me. Didn't even hurt much, compared to the agony that Kahl's revelation had caused. The blast threw me upside down against the window; a passing squid seemed fascinated by my shoelaces on the glass. What amused me, even as I lay there dazed and struggling to right myself, was that Shahar's sigil had only treated me as a threat *now*, in my useless mortal form. She had never truly feared me when I was a god.

Deka pulled me up. "Tell me you're all right."

"Fine," I said muzzily. My knees hurt more, and my back was killing me, but I refused to admit that. I blinked and managed to focus on Shahar. She hovered, half standing, above her seat. Her eyes were wide and stricken. That made me feel better, at least. She hadn't meant it.

Deka meant it, however, as he let me go and got to his feet. I felt the black pulse of his magic, heavy as a god's, and thought for a moment that I heard the echoing sibilance of the air as he turned to face his sister.

"Deka," she began.

He spoke a word that cracked the air, and thunder roiled in its wake. She cried out, arching backward and clapping both hands over her forehead, half falling over her seat. When she struggled upright a moment later, there was blood on her fingers and streaking her face. She lowered her trembling hand, and I saw the raw, scorched wound where her semisigil had been.

"Mother is a fool," Deka said, his voice echoing and cold. "I love you, and she thinks that keeps you safe from me. But I would rather kill you myself than watch you become the kind of monster this family is infamous for producing." His right arm levered away from his side, stick-straight, though his hand hung loose, the backs of his fingers caressing the air like a lover. I remembered the meaning of the markings on that arm and realized he really was going to kill her.

"Deka..." Shahar shook her head, trying to clear blood from her eyes. She looked like the victim of some disaster, though the disaster had not yet struck. "I didn't... Sieh, is he all...I can't see."

I touched Deka's other arm and found the muscles as tight as woven rope. Power tingled against my fingers, through his shirt. "Deka. Don't."

"You would do the same, if you still could," he snapped.

I considered this. He knew me so well. "True. But it would be wrong for you."

That caused his head to whip toward me. *"What?"*

I sighed and stepped in front of him, though the power that coiled around him pressed warningly against my skin. Scriveners were not gods. But Deka was not just a scrivener, and it was as a brother-god that I touched his arm and gently, firmly, guided it back to his side. Gestures were a form of communication. Mine said, *Listen to me,* and his power withdrew to consider my suggestion. I saw his eyes widen as he realized what I had done.

"She is your sister," I said. "You're strong, Deka, so strong, and they are fools to forget that you're Arameri, too. Murder is in your blood. But I know you, and if you kill her, it will destroy you. I can't let you do that."

He stared at me, trembling with warring urges. I have

never before seen such deadly rage mingled with loving sorrow, but I think it must have been what Itempas felt when he killed Enefa. A kind of madness that only time and reflection can cure—though by then, usually, it is too late.

But he listened to me and let the magic go.

I turned to Shahar, who had finally gotten the blood out of her eyes. By the look on her face, she had only just begun to realize how close she'd come to death.

"We're leaving," I said. "I am, anyway, and I'm going to ask Deka to come with me. If you've decided that we're your enemies, we can't stay here. If you're wise, you'll leave us be." I sighed. "You haven't been very wise today, but I suspect that's a onetime aberration. I know you'll come to your senses eventually. I just don't feel like waiting around for it to happen."

Then I took Deka's hand, looking up at him. His expression had gone bleak; he knew I was right. But I would not press him. He'd spent ten years trying to get back to his sister, and she'd undone that in ten minutes. Such things were not easy for any mortal to bear. Or any god, for that matter.

Deka's hand squeezed mine, and he nodded. We turned to leave the audience chamber. Shahar stood behind us. "Wait," she said, but we ignored her.

When I opened the door, however, everything changed.

We stopped in surprise at the noise of many voices, raised and angry. Beyond the main corridor, I glimpsed soldiers running and heard shouts. Immediately before us was Morad, her face red with fury. She was shouting at the guards, who'd crossed pikes in front of the chamber's entrance. When the door opened, the guards started, and Morad grabbed at one of the pikes, half yanking it away before the guard cursed and tightened his grip.

"Where is Shahar?" she demanded. "I *will* see her."

Shahar came up behind us. It was a measure of Morad's agitation that she did not blink at the sight of the heir's bloody face. "What has happened, Morad?" I heard the thinness of the calm veneer on Shahar's voice. She had composed herself, just.

"Maskers have attacked Shadow," Morad said.

We stood there, stunned into silence. Behind her, a troop of soldiers came tearing around the corner, running toward us. Wrath was behind them, walking with the ominous deliberation of a general preparing for war. All around us I could feel a hollow thrum as whatever protective magics Deka's scriveners had put into place came alive. Seals for the gates, invisible walls to keep out foreign magics, who knew what else.

"How many maskers?" asked Shahar. She spoke more briskly now, all business.

After the worst had passed, I would remember this moment. I would see the false calm on Morad's face, and hear the real anguish in her voice, and pity her all the more. A servant and a queen were as doomed as a mortal and a god. Some things could not be helped.

"*All of them,*" Morad said.

20

Ashes, ashes, we all fall DOWN!

IT WAS THE STILLNESS that made them so frightening.

It was not easy to view city streets and crowds via a seeing sphere. The spheres were made to display nearby faces, not vast scenes. And what Wrath's lieutenant in Shadow had to show us, by slowly panning his sphere in a circle, was vast.

There were dozens of maskers.

Hundreds.

They filled the streets. In the Promenade, where normally pilgrims jostled with street performers and artists for space, there were only maskers. Along the Avenue of Nobles, right up to the steps of the Salon: maskers. Just visible amid the trees and flowers of Gateway Park: maskers. Approaching from South Root, their shoes stained by street muck: maskers.

We could see many fleeting forms that were not maskers, most of them hurrying in the opposite direction, some of them carrying whatever they could on horses or wheelbarrows or their own hunched backs. The people of

Shadow were no strangers to magic, having lived among godlings for decades and in the shadow of Sky for centuries. They knew trouble when they smelled it, and they knew the appropriate response: run.

The maskers did not molest the unmasked. They moved in silence and unison, when they moved. Most of them stopped moving when they reached the center of Shadow, then just stood there, utterly still. Men and women, a few children—not many, thank me—a few elders. No two masks were alike: they came in white and black; some were marbled like Echo's substance; some were red and cobalt blue and stony gray. Some were painted porcelain, some clay and straw. Many were in the High Northern style, but quite a few displayed the aesthetics and archetypes of other lands. The variation was astonishing.

And they were all looking up at Sky.

We—Shahar and Dekarta and I, and a good number of the highbloods and servants—stood in what would doubtless come to be called the Marble Hall, given the usual Amn naming conventions. For some reason known only to Yeine, the walls of the chamber were streaked with a deep rust color, interspersing white and gray, which made the whole room look washed in blood. There was some wry symbolism in this, I suspected; some element of Yeine's morbid sense of humor. I was apparently too mortal to get the joke.

Wrath was gone, though his soldiers were present, guarding the doors and the balcony. It had been his suggestion to gather all the highbloods together; easier to guard. While we waited for him to say when we could leave—no time soon, I gathered—some servant had brought the large seeing sphere from the scriveners' storage, setting it up on the room's single long table. Through this, we were able to behold the ominous stillness in the streets of Shadow.

"Are they waiting for something?" asked a woman who bore a halfblood mark. She stood near Ramina. He put a comforting hand on her back while she stared at the hovering image.

"Some signal, perhaps," he replied. For once, he was not smiling. But long minutes passed, and there was no movement on the part of the maskers. The person panning the sphere stood atop the Salon's steps. On either end of the arc swing we could glimpse Arameri soldiers, clad in the white armor of the Hundred Thousand Legions, hastily setting up barricades and preparing for a defensive battle. Even in such brief glimpses, however, we saw enough to despair. The bulk of the Arameri army was outside the city, in a vast complex of permanent barracks and bases stationed a half day's ride away. Everyone had assumed that the attack, when it came, would be from beyond the city. The army was no doubt marching and riding and gating into the city as fast as it could now, but those of us who had seen the maskers in action knew that it would take more than soldiers to stop them.

I turned to Shahar, who stood on one of the elevated tiers around the chamber's edge. She had wrapped her arms around herself as if cold; her expression was too blank to be intentional. In the whole room, where her relatives clustered in twos and threes and comforted each other, she stood alone.

I considered for a moment, then stepped away from Deka and went to her. Her head turned sharply toward me as I approached. She was not at all in shock. A subtle shift transformed her posture from the lost girl of a moment before to the cold queen who had tried to enslave her brother. But I saw the wariness in her. She had lost that battle.

Deka watched me go to her but did not join us.

"Shouldn't you contact Remath?" I asked. I kept my tone neutral.

She relaxed fractionally, acknowledging my unspoken offer of truce. "I've tried. Mother hasn't answered." She looked away, through the translucent walls, at the lowering sun. West, toward Sky. "There's no point, in any case. The army is there and under Mother's command as it should be, along with the bulk of the scrivener and assassin corps and the nobles' private forces. Echo is barely functional and understaffed as it is. We have no help to offer."

"Not all support must be material, Shahar." It still felt strange to remember that Remath and Shahar loved each other. I would never get used to Arameri behaving like normal people.

She glanced at me again, not so sharply this time. Considering. Then Ramina said, "Something's happening," and we all grew tense.

There was a blur in the air, a few feet above and to one side of the image we'd been watching. The soldiers reached for their weapons. The highbloods gasped and one cried out. Deka and the other scriveners tensed, some pulling out premade, partially drawn sigils.

Then the image resolved, and we saw Remath. The image was angled oddly—over her shoulder and slightly behind her. The sphere must have been set into her stone seat.

Facing her, in Sky's audience chamber, was Usein Darr.

Shahar caught her breath and moved down the steps, as if she meant to step through the image and aid her mother.

The soldiers in Sky's audience chamber had drawn their weapons, swords and pikes and crossbows. They did not attack, however. Remath must have warned them off, though two of her guards, Darre women, had moved to stand between Remath and Usein, crouching with hands on their knives. Usein stood proud and fearless at the center of the room, ignoring the guards. She had come unarmed, though she did wear traditional Darre battle dress: a leather-wrapped waist, a heavy fur mantle that marked her as a battlefield commander, and armor made of thin plates of flakespar—a light, strong material the Darre had invented a few decades back. She looked taller when she wasn't pregnant.

"I take it we have you to thank for the spectacle below," said Remath. She drawled the words, sounding amused.

Usein inclined her head. I thought she would speak in Darre, given her nationalism, but she used clear, ringing Senmite instead. "It is not our preferred way of doing battle, we in the north. To use magic, even our own, feels cowardly." She shrugged. "But you Arameri do not fight fair."

"True," said Remath. "Well, then. I expect you have demands?"

"Simple ones, Arameri." Family name only was the way Darre addressed formidable opponents, a mark of respect by her terms. To Amn, of course, it was blatant disrespect. "I—and my allies, who would be here if it had not taken all our dimmers and magicians to get even one person through your barriers—demand that your family give up its power and all trappings thereof. Your treasury: fifty percent of it is to be given to the Nobles' Consortium, to be distributed equally among the nations of the world. Thirty percent will go to the Order of Itempas and all established faiths that offer public services. You may retain twenty percent. You may no longer address the Nobles' Consortium. It is for them to say whether Sky-in-Shadow can retain its representative. Disband your army and distribute its generals among the kingdoms; relinquish your scriveners and spies and assassins and all your other little toys." Her eyes flicked toward the Darre guards, full of contempt. I did not see whether the women reacted to this or not. "Send your son back to the Litaria; you don't want him anyway." (Nearby, Deka's jaw flexed.) "Send your daughter to foster in some other kingdom for ten years so that she can learn the ways of some people other than you murderous, high-handed Amn. I will leave the choice of kingdom to you." She smiled thinly. "But Darr would welcome her and treat her with such respect as she is capable of earning."

"*Like hells* will I live among those tree-swinging barbarians," snapped Shahar, and the other highbloods murmured in angry agreement.

Usein went on. "In short, we demand that the Arameri become just another family and leave the world to rule itself." She paused, looking around. "Oh. And leave this palace. Sky's presence profanes the Lady's Tree—and frankly, the rest of us are tired of looking up at you. You will henceforth dwell on the ground, where mortals belong."

Remath waited a moment after Usein fell silent. "Is that all?"

"For now."

"May I ask a question?"

Usein lifted an eyebrow. "You may."

"Are you responsible for the murders of my family members?" Remath spoke lightly, but only a fool would not have heard the threat underneath. "*You* in the plural, obviously."

For the first time, Usein looked unhappy. "That was not our doing. Wars of assassination are not our way." Left unspoken was that wars of assassination were very much the Amn way.

"Whose, then?"

"Kahl." Usein smiled, but it was bleak. "Kahl Avenger, we call him—a godling. He has been of great help to us, me and my forbears and our allies, but it has since become clear that this served his own agenda. He merely used us. We have broken ways with him, but I'm afraid the damage is done." She paused, her jaw tightening briefly. "He has killed my husband and numerous members of our Warriors' Council. Perhaps that will seem a consolation to you."

Remath shook her head. "Murder is never a thing to be celebrated."

"Indeed." Usein regarded Remath for a long moment, then bowed to her. It was not a deep bow, but the respect in the gesture was plain. An apology, unspoken. "Kahl has been declared an enemy by the peoples of the north. But that does not negate our quarrel with you."

"Naturally." Remath paused, then inclined her head, a show of great respect in Amn terms, since the ruler of the Amn had no need to bow to anyone. By Darre standards, it was probably an insult.

"Thank you for your honesty," Remath added. "Now, as to the rest, your demands regarding my family: no."

Usein raised her eyebrows. "That's all? 'No'?"

"Were you expecting anything else?" I could not see Remath's face well, but I guessed that she smiled.

Usein did, too. "Not really, no. But I must warn you, Arameri: I speak for the people of this world. Not all of them would agree with me, I will admit, as they have spent too many centuries under your family's control. You have all but crushed the spirit of mortalkind. It is for their sake that I and my allies will now fight to revive it—and we will not be merciful."

"Are you certain that's what you want?" Remath sat back, crossing her legs. "The spirit of mortalkind is contentious, Usein-ennu. Violent, selfish. Without a strong hand to guide it, this world will not know peace again for many, many centuries. Perhaps ever."

Usein nodded, slowly. "Peace is meaningless without freedom."

"I doubt the children who starved to death, before the Bright, would agree."

Usein smiled again. "And I doubt the races and heretics your family have destroyed would consider the Bright *peace*." She made a small gesture of negation with her hand. "Enough. I have your answer, and you will soon have mine." She lifted a small stone that bore a familiar mark. A gate sigil. She closed her eyes, and a flicker later she was gone.

The lower image—of Shadow and the silent maskers—jolted abruptly, drawing our eyes. There was a brief blur of motion, which grew still as the soldier who held the sphere set it down. We saw him then, a young man in heavy armor marked with seven sigils: one on each limb, one on his helmet, one on his torso, and one on his back. Simple magic of protection. He held a pike at the ready, as did the other men—all in the same armor—that we could see. Their armor was white. I suppose Remath hadn't gotten around to reequipping her army to symbolize the family's new divine allegiance.

And beyond them, the maskers had begun to move. Slowly, silently, they walked toward the soldiers that we could see. I could only assume that beyond the image, the scene was being repeated throughout Shadow. All of the masks that we could see, in every color, were tilted upward, paying no attention to the soldiers before them. Fixed on Sky.

"How does she command them?" Deka murmured, frowning as he peered at the image. "We were never able to determine…"

His musings were drowned out by noise from both images. Out of view, someone shouted to the soldiers, and the battle began as volleys of crossbow bolts shot toward the masked ranks. Already we could see that the bolts did almost nothing. The maskers continued forward with arrows jutting from chests, legs, abdomens. A handful went down as their masks were split or cracked, but not enough. Not nearly enough.

In the higher image, Remath barked orders to the soldiers in her audience chamber. We saw hurried movement, chaos. Amid this, however, Remath rose from her throne and turned to face it. She leaned forward and touched something we could not see. "Shahar."

Shahar started, coming forward. "Mother? You must come here, of course. We are ready to accommodate—"

"No." Her quiet negative struck Shahar silent, but Remath smiled. She was calmer than I had ever seen her. "I have had dreams," she said, speaking softly. "I've always had them, for whatever reason, and they have always, always, come true. I have dreamt this day."

I frowned in confusion. Dreams that came true? Was that even possible for mortals? Remath *was* a godling's granddaughter…

In the image below her face, the maskers charged forward, running now. The sphere's range was too small to capture more than a segment of chaos. For brief stretches there was nothing to see, interspersed with blurring glimpses of shouting men and still, inhuman faces. We barely noticed. Shahar stared at her mother, her face written with anguish as if there were no one else in the room, nothing else that she cared about. I put a hand on her shoulder because for a moment it looked as though she might climb onto the table to reach Remath. Her shoulder, beneath my hand, was taut and trembling with suppressed tension.

"You must *come here*, Mother," she said tightly. "No matter what you've seen in some dream—"

"I have seen Sky fall," said Remath, and Shahar jerked beneath my hand. "And I have seen myself die with it."

In the other image, the one in the large sphere, there were screams. A sudden loud concussion that I thought might have been an explosion. And suddenly the sphere was jostled from its place, falling toward the Salon steps. We heard the crunch as it broke, and then the image vanished. The other image—Remath's image—shuddered a moment later, and she looked around as people exclaimed in alarm behind her. They had felt the explosion, too.

"Why did you have the Lady build Echo, if not to come here?" Shahar was shaking her head as she spoke, wordless negation despite her effort to speak reasonably. *"Why would you do this, Mother?"*

"I have dreamt of more than Sky." Remath suddenly looked away from Shahar, her gaze settling on me and Deka. "I have seen *all existence* fall, Lord Sieh. Sky is merely the harbinger. Only you can stop it. You and Shahar and you, my son. All three of you are the key. I built Echo to keep you safe."

"Mother," said Deka in a strained voice. "This—"

She shook her head. "There's no time." She paused suddenly, looking away as a soldier came close and murmured to her. At her nod, he hurried away, and she looked at us again, smiling. "They are climbing the Tree."

Someone in the Marble Hall cried out. Ramina, his face taut, stepped forward. "Remath, gods damn it, there's no reason for you to stay if—"

Remath sighed, with a hint of her usual temper. "I told you, I have seen how this must go. If I die with Sky, there is hope. My death becomes a catalyst for transformation. There is a future beyond it. If I flee, it all ends! The Arameri fall. The *world* falls. The decision is quite simple, Ramina." Her voice softened again. "But... will you tell her... ?"

I wondered at this as Ramina's jaw flexed. Then I remembered: Morad. She wasn't present, no doubt trying to assist Wrath in preparing for the possibility of an attack. I hadn't realized Ramina knew about them, but then, I supposed, he was the only one Remath could have trusted with the secret. No doubt Morad knew about Ramina fathering Remath's children, too. The three of them were bound together by love and secrets.

"I'll tell her," Ramina said at last, and Remath relaxed.

"I will, too," I said, and she started. Then, slowly, she smiled at me.

"Lord Sieh, are you beginning to like me?"

"No," I said, folding my arms. It was Morad whom I liked. "But I'm not a *complete* ass."

She nodded. "You love my son."

It was my turn to flinch. Very carefully I avoided looking at Deka. What the hells was she doing? If any of us got through this, the whole family would find some way to use my relationship with Deka against him. Perhaps she simply thought he could handle it.

"Yes," I said.

"Good." She glanced at Deka, then away, as if she could not bear to look at him. From the corner of my eye, I saw his fists clench. "I could protect only one of them, Lord Sieh. I had to make a choice. Do you understand? But I... I did what I could. Perhaps someday, you..." She faltered silent, throwing another of those darting glances at her son. I looked away so that I wouldn't see what passed between them, and saw others doing the same around the room. This was too intimate. The Arameri had changed indeed since the old days; they no longer liked to see pain.

Then Remath sighed and faced me again, saying nothing. But she knew, I felt certain. I nodded, minutely. *Yes, I love Shahar, too.* For whatever good that did.

It seemed to satisfy Remath. She nodded back. As she did this, there was another shudder in Sky, and the image began to flicker. Deka muttered something in gods' language and the image stilled, but I could see the instability of the message. Color and clarity wisped away from the image's edges like smoke.

"Enough." Remath rubbed her eyes, and I felt sudden sympathy for her. When she lifted her head again, her expression held its usual briskness. "The family and the world are yours now, Shahar. I have no doubt that you will do well by both."

The image vanished, and silence fell.

"No," Shahar whispered. Her knuckles, where her hands gripped the chair, were a sickly white. *"No."*

Deka relented at last and came over. "Shahar—"

She rounded on him, her eyes wild. My first thought was, *She's gone mad.*

My second thought, when she grabbed Deka's hand, then mine, and I realized her intent in the same instant

that magic washed through me like the arc of light that
heralds a star's birth—

—was *demonshit, not again.*

We became We.

As one, We reached forth with Our hand, unseen and
yet vast, and picked up the bobbing, lonely mote that was
Echo. And it was as one that We sent that mote west, hur-
tling across the world so rapidly that it should have killed
everything inside. But part of Us (Deka) was smart
enough to know that such speed was fatal for mortals, and
We shaped the forces of motion around the mote accord-
ingly. And another part of Us (me) was wise in the ways
of magic, and that part murmured soothingly to the forces
so they would be appeased, or else they would have backlashed violently against such abuse. But it was the will—
Shahar, Shahar, O my magnificent Shahar—who drove us
forward, her soul fixed on a singular intent.

Mother.

We all thought this—even I, who hated Remath, and
even Deka, whose feelings toward her were such a morass
that no mortal language could encompass it. (The First
Tongue could: *maelstrom.*) And for all of Us, *mother*
meant different things. For me it was a soft breast, cold
fingers, the voice of a god with two faces—Naha, Yeine—
whispering words of love. For Shahar it was fear and hope
and cold eyes warming, fleetingly, with approval, and a
single hug that would reverberate within her soul for the
rest of her life. For Deka—ah, my Deka. For Deka,
mother meant Shahar, a fierce little girl standing between
him and the world. It meant a child-godling with old, tired
eyes, who had nevertheless taken the trouble to smile
kindly at him, and stroke his hair, and help him be strong.

For this, We kept control.

The palace slowed as We approached Sky-in-Shadow. We saw everything, everywhere within the scope of Our interest. On the ground just outside the city: a small force of warriors, northerners from many nations. Usein Darr was among these, sitting on the back of a small, swift horse, watching the city through a long contraption of lenses that made the distant seem closer. Like a nautilus spiral, We cycled inward, seeing all the sane folk of the city evacuating, bottlenecks of traffic on every major street. Further in: a dead masker. Beside his body crouched a woman, alone, weeping. *(Mother.)* In. Godlings in the streets, helping their chosen, helping any who asked, doing what they could, not doing enough. We have always been far better at destroying than protecting. Further in. Maskers now, the ones whose bodies had been old or infirm; they straggled behind their more able comrades, hobbling toward the Tree. In, in. Dead soldiers here, in the sigil-marked white of the Hundred Thousand Legions. They littered the Salon steps, lay disemboweled on the Promenade stones, hung from the windows of nearby buildings—one with a crossbow still in his hand, though his head was gone. In.

The World Tree.

Its trunk was infested with tiny, crawling mites that had once been thinking mortals. The maskers climbed with a strength that mortal flesh should not have possessed—and indeed, a few of them did not. We saw them fall, the magic burning out their bodies. But more of them clung securely to the thick, rough bark, and more still made the climb, steadily. It was only a half-mile to Sky, straight up. Some of the maskers were more than halfway there.

Shahar saw this and screamed DIE and We screamed
with her. We swept Our infinite hand over the Tree,
knocking the insects away: dozens, hundreds. Because
they were already dead, some got up and began climbing
again. We crushed them. Then We turned outward again,
rushing, raging, toward Usein and her warriors. We were
greedy for the taste of their fear.

They were afraid, We saw when We reached them, but
not of Us.

We whirled and saw what they saw: Kahl. He stood in
the air over the city, gazing down at what his machinations had wrought. He looked displeased.

We were much stronger. Exulting, We raised Our hand
to destroy—

—*my son*—

—and stopped, frozen. Indecisive, for the first time,
because of me.

We had no flesh, so Kahl did not see Us. His lips tightened at the scene below. In one hand, We saw, was the
strange mask. It was complete now—and yet not. Kahl
could hold it with no apparent discomfort, but the thing had
no power. Certainly nothing that could forge a new god.

He raised a hand, and it is my fault, not Ours, *mine*, for
I am a god and I should have *known* what he was about to
do. But I did not think it, and the lives lost will haunt my
eternal soul.

He sent forth power as a hundred whipcord serpents.
Each wove through buildings and stone and sought its
lair: a tiny, barely visible notch in all of the masks, so
small as to be subliminal. (We knew across time. We saw
Kahl doing a god's work, whispering into the dreams of
the sleeping *dimyi* artists, inspiring them, influencing
them. We saw Nsana the Guide turn, sensing the intrusion

upon his realm, but Kahl was subtle, subtle. He was not discovered.)

We saw all of the masks glow blue-white—

—and then *explode*.

Too many. Too close to the base of the Tree, where We had swept the bodies. We screamed as We understood and rushed back, but even gods are not omnipotent.

Roiling fire blossomed at the World Tree's roots. The shock wave came later, like thunder, echoing. (Echo, Echo.) The great, shuddering groan of the Tree rose slowly, so gradually that We could deny it. We could pretend that it was not too late right up until the World Tree's trunk split, sending splinters like missiles in every direction. Buildings collapsed, streets erupted. The screams of dying mortals mingled with the Tree's mournful cry, then were drowned out as the Tree listed slowly, gracefully, monstrously. It fell away from Shadow, which We thought was a blessing—until the Tree's crown, massive as mountains, struck the earth.

The concussion rippled outward in a wave that destroyed the land in every direction as far as mortal eyes could see.

We saw Sky shatter into a hundred thousand pieces.

And high above Us, his face a mask of savage triumph to contrast the mask in his hands: Kahl. He raised the mask over his head, closing his eyes. It shone now, glimmering and shivering and changing—replete, at last, with the million or more mortal lives he had just fed it. Its ornamentation and shape flared to form a new archetype—one suggesting implacability and fathomless knowledge and magnificence and quintessential power. Like Nahadoth and Itempas and Yeine, if one could somehow strip away their personalities and superficialities to leave only the distilled meaning of them. That meaning was *God*: the mask's ultimate form and name.

We felt the mask call out, and We felt something answer, before Kahl vanished.

We dissolved then. Shahar's grief, Deka's anguish, my horror—all the same emotion, but the respective reverberations were too powerful individually to meld into the whole of Us. With what remained of Us, We (I) remembered belatedly that We were in a flying palace that had been built as a floating palace, and either way it would not do well as a falling palace. So We (I) looked around and spied the Eyeglass Lake, a boring little body of water in the middle of even more boring farmland. It would do. Into this, carefully, We deposited the delicate shell that was Echo. Usein would be pleased, at least: the Eyeglass was small and unassuming, nothing compared to the ocean's vast grandeur. Only a mile of distance would now separate the palace from the shore; people could swim to it if they wanted. Remath's plan to isolate the Arameri had backfired. The Arameri, such as remained, would be henceforth more accessible than ever, and far, far closer to the earth.

Then We were gone, leaving only Deka and Shahar and I, who stared at one another as the power drained away. We fell as one and sought solace in the void together.

21

THINGS CHANGED.

Deka and Shahar woke a day later. I, for reasons I can only guess at, slept for a week. I was reinstalled in Deka's quarters and reintroduced to my old friend the feeding tube. I had aged again. Not much this time; just ten years or so. This put me in my early to mid-sixties, by my guess. Not that a few years really mattered, at that age.

In the week that I slept through, the war ended. Usein sent a message to Echo the day after Skyfall. She did not surrender, but in light of the tragedy, she and her allies were willing to offer a truce. It was not difficult to read between the lines of this. Her faction had intended the deaths of the Arameri and their soldiers, and perhaps some abstract deaths in the future as mortalkind devolved to its endless warring. No one, not even a hardened Darre warrior, had been prepared for the fallen Tree, the shattered city, or the wasteland that was now central Senm. I am told that the northerners joined in the rescue operations, and they were welcome—even though they'd inadvertently caused the disaster. Everyone who could help was welcome, in those first few days.

The city's godlings did what they could. They had

saved many by transporting them out of the area when the first explosions began. They saved more by mitigating the damage. The Tree's roots had nearly torn free of the earth when it fell. If the stump had uprooted, there would have been no rubble from which to rescue survivors, only a city-sized freshly turned grave. The godlings worked tirelessly thereafter, entering the most damaged parts of the city and sniffing out the fading scents of life, holding up sagging buildings, teaching the scriveners and bonebenders magic that would save many lives in the days to follow. Godlings from other lands came to help, and even a few from the gods' realm.

Despite this, of all the mortals who had once populated Sky-in-Shadow, only a few thousand survived.

Shahar, in her first act as the family head, did something at once stupid and brilliant: she ordered that Echo be opened to the survivors. Wrath protested this vehemently and finally prevailed in getting Shahar and the rest of the highbloods to relocate to the center of the palace—the Whorl and its surrounding buildings, which could be guarded by Wrath's men and the handful of remaining soldiers who had come with the survivors. The rest of Echo was ceded to wounded, heart-lost mortals, many of them still covered in dust and blood, who gratefully slept in beds that made themselves and ate food that appeared whenever they wished for it. These were small comforts, and no consolation, given what they had suffered.

In the days that followed, Shahar convened an emergency session of the Nobles' Consortium and blatantly asked for help. The people of Shadow could rebuild, she said, with time to heal and sufficient assistance. But more than goods and food, they would need something the Arameri could not provide: *peace*. So she asked the assembled nobles to put aside their differences with each other and the Arameri and to remember the best principles of the Bright. It was, I am told, an amazing, stirring speech. The proof of this lies in the fact that they listened to her. Caravans of supplies and troops of volunteers began arriving within the week. There was no more talk of rebellion—only for the time being, but even that was a significant concession.

They may have been motivated by more than Shahar's words, however. There was a new object in the sky, and it was drawing closer.

A week after I woke, when I was feeling strong enough, I left Echo. Some godling—don't know which—had stretched a tongue of daystone from the palace's entrance to the lakeshore, wide enough for carriages and pack animals. Nowhere near as elegant as Sky's Vertical Gate, but it worked. Deka, who needed a break from the frenetic work of the past few weeks, decided to come with me. I considered trying to persuade him otherwise, but when I turned to him and opened my mouth, he gave me such a challenging look that I closed it again.

It took us an hour to walk over the bridge, and we spoke little on the way. In the distance we could see the humped, distorted shape of the fallen Tree through the morning haze. Neither of us looked in that direction often. Closer by, a fledgling city had already begun to develop around Echo and its lake. Not all the survivors wanted to live in Echo, so they had built tents and makeshift huts on the shore in order to stay close to family or new-made friends in the palace. A kind of market had developed amid this camp as a result, not far from the bridge's terminus. Deka and I rented two horses from a caravanner who'd set up a stall—two fine mounts for the young man and his grandfather, the proprietor said, trying to be friendly—and began our journey, which would supposedly take only a day. We had no escorts or guards. We were not that important. Just as well; I wanted privacy to think.

The road we'd chosen to take, once the main thoroughfare between the city and its surrounding provinces, was badly damaged. We rode across humped pavement and patches of rubble that forced us to dismount frequently and check the horses' hooves for stones. In one place the road simply split, falling away into a chasm that was unpleasantly deep. I was fine with going around it; there was nothing but ruined farmland in the vicinity, so it wasn't as though the detour would take long. Deka, however, in a rare show of temper, spoke to the rocks and got them to form a narrow, solid bridge across the gap. We crossed before I muttered something to Deka along the lines that he should really be less quick to use magic to solve problems. He only looked at me, and I hunched. It had just seemed like the sort of thing an older man should say to a younger one.

We moved on. By afternoon, we reached the outskirts of the city. It was harder going here, and the damage slowed us down. Every street that had once been cobbled was rubble; the sidewalks were death traps, where we could even find streets. I caught a glimpse of the utter ruin that was South Root and despaired. There was a chance, a slim one, that Hymn and her family had gotten out before Skyfall. I would pray for Yeine to watch over them, alive or dead.

We did not want the city itself in any case, so it was easier to skirt around the worst parts, using the outlying districts to make our way. These had been the homes and estates of the middling wealthy—too poor to build onto the World Tree's trunk but rich enough to buy the better sunlight that could be had farther from the roots. This made things easier, because they had wide lawns and dirt paths that the horses could manage. There was plenty of sunlight now.

Eventually we reached the trunk itself, a long, low mountain laid along the earth, as far as the eye could see. We surprised our first survivors here, since the rest of the area had been thoroughly abandoned: scavengers, picking through the ruins of the mansions that had once been attached to the Tree. They glared at us and pointedly fingered hatchet handles and machetes. We courteously gave them a wide berth. Everyone was happy.

Then we reached Sky. Where, to my surprise, we were not alone.

We smelled Ahad's reeking cheroot before we saw him, though the scent was different this time. My nose was not what it had been, so it was only when I got close that I understood he'd put cloves in the thing to make the smell less offensive. I realized why when I noticed that the smoke was mingled with Glee Shoth's hiras-flower perfume.

They likely heard the horses before we came into sight but did not bother to alter their position, so we found Ahad draped atop one of the nearer, smaller piles of rubble as though it was a throne. Behind him was Glee. He leaned back against her, his head pillowed on her breasts. She had propped one elbow on a smooth piece of daystone, her free hand idly combing his loose hair. His expression was as cold as usual, but I didn't buy it this time. There was too much vulnerability in his posture, too much trust in the way he'd let Glee hold his weight. I saw too much wariness in his eyes. He could not hide some things from me, which was probably why he hadn't bothered to try. But he would kill me, I suspect, if I dared to comment on it. So I didn't.

"If you've come to dance on this grave, you're too late," he said as we dismounted and came to look up at them. "I already did it."

"Good," I said, nodding to Glee, who nodded silently back. (She, unlike Ahad, did not bother to hide the pride she felt in him. And there was a decided smug possessiveness in the way she stroked his hair that reminded me fleetingly of Itempas, back when he'd held Nahadoth's affections.) I stretched and grimaced as my knees twinged after the long ride. "I'm not really up to dancing anymore."

"Yes, you do look like shit, don't you?" He exhaled a long, curling stream of smoke, and I saw him consider whether to hurt me further. There were so many ways he could have done it with a casual comment. *So it turns out you're an even worse father than I thought*, or perhaps *Glad to know I wasn't your first mistake*. I braced myself as best I could, though there was really nothing I could do. According to Deka, I was still aging faster than I should have been, perhaps ten days for every one. Merely knowing that I was a father was a relentless poison that would kill me in a year, two at the most. Not that any of us had so long to wait.

Ahad said nothing, to my relief. Either he was feeling magnanimous, or Glee had begun to mellow him. Or perhaps he simply saw no point under the circumstances.

"Hello," said Deka. He was staring at Ahad, and belatedly I remembered that I'd never gotten around to telling him about his origins. My long-lost son's attempt to destroy the universe had been a bit distracting.

Ahad sat up, eyeing the boy. After a moment, a slow

smile spread across his face. "Well, well, well. You would be Dekarta Arameri."

"I am." Deka said this stiffly, trying and failing to conceal his fascination. They did not look wholly alike, but the resemblance was close enough to defy coincidence. "And you are?"

Ahad spread his arms. "Call me 'Grandpa.' "

Deka stiffened. Glee threw an exasperated look at the back of Ahad's head. I sighed and rubbed my eyes. "Deka... I'll explain later."

"Yes," he said. "You will." But he folded his arms and looked away from Ahad, and Ahad uttered a sigh of disappointment. I wasn't sure whether he really minded Deka's disinterest or was just using another opportunity to needle the boy.

We fell silent then, as was proper at graveside.

I gazed at the great piles of tumbled daystone and slipped my hands into my pockets, wondering at the feelings within me. I had loathed Sky for all the years of my incarceration. Within its white walls I had been starved, raped, flayed, and worse. I had been a god reduced to a possession, and the humiliation of those days had not left me despite a hundred years of freedom.

And yet... I remembered my orrery, and En pulsed in gentle sympathy against my chest. I remembered running through Sky's wild, curving dead spaces, making them my own. I had found Yeine here; without thinking, I began to hum the lullaby I had once sung her. It had not been all suffering and horror. Life is never only one thing.

Ahad sighed above me. Sky had been his home once. Deka touched my hand; same for him. None of us mourned alone, for however long that mourning might last.

Above us, halfway between the sun and the faint, early

risen moon, we could all see the peculiar smudge that had grown steadily larger since the day of Kahl's victory. It was not a thing that could be described easily, in either Senmite or the gods' language. A streaking transparency. A space of wavering nothingness, leaving nothingness in its wake. We could feel it, too, like an itch on the skin. Hear it, like words sung just out of hearing—but it would not be long now before we all heard it, more clearly than any sane being would want. Its roar would eclipse the world.

The Maelstrom. Kahl had summoned It, and It was coming.

After a time, during which the sun set and the early stars began to show, Ahad sighed and got to his feet, turning to help Glee to hers. They flickered to the ground, which made Deka start, then inhale as his suspicions were confirmed. Ahad winked at him, then sobered as he turned to me.

"The others think they can ride out whatever happens in the gods' realm," he said softly. "I have my doubts, but I can't blame them for trying." He hesitated, then glanced at Glee. "I'm staying here."

It was an admission I would never have expected from him. Glee was mortal; she could not survive in our realm. When I glanced at Glee, to see if she understood how profound a change she had worked on him, she nodded minutely, lifting her chin in a blatantly protective challenge. Ahad was not the only one of us who could cause pain with a comment.

I had no interest in hurting Ahad, however. I'd done enough to him.

"Perhaps a more productive line of conversation is *saving* this realm, rather than fleeing it," said Deka, and by the edge in his voice, I knew I would get an earful when we were alone. But Ahad shook his head, growing uncharacteristically serious.

"There's no saving it," he said. "Not even the Three can command the Maelstrom. At best, they can stand aside while It punches through the realms, and rebuild from whatever's left. Not that that does us much good." He shrugged and sighed, looking up at the sky. The smudge was just as visible at night, a waver against the carpet of stars. Beyond It, however, the stars were gone. There was nothing but black void.

"My father believes it is worthwhile to try and save this realm," said Glee. Deka stared at her, probably guessing more secrets. I really should have told him everything beforehand. More stupidity on my part.

"Yeine and Nahadoth, too, if I know them at all." I sighed. "But if they could have stopped it, they would have done so by now."

I did not add that I had prayed to both, more than once, in the preceding nights. They had responded with silence. I tried not to worry about what that meant.

"Well, we'd better get going. Just came to wish the old hell good-bye." Ahad's cheroot had finally burned down. He dropped the butt to the ground and stubbed it out with his toe, throwing one final glance at Sky's tumbled bulk behind us. The daystone still glowed at night, ghostly soft radiance to contrast the torn emptiness in the sky above. A fitting marker for mortalkind's grave, I decided. Hopefully Yeine and Naha would find some way to preserve it when the world was gone.

And Itempas, my mind added to Yeine's and Naha's names, though of course that was less certain. Perhaps they would let him die with the rest of us. If they were going to, this would be the time.

"We will see you again," Glee said. I nodded, noticing at last that they were holding hands.

Then they vanished, leaving me alone with Deka. "Explain," he snapped.

I sighed and looked around. It was well and truly night. I hadn't figured on the journey taking as long as it had. We had no supplies with which to make camp. It would be horse blankets on the ground instead. My old bones were going to love that.

"Let's get comfortable first," I said. His jaw flexed as though he would have preferred to argue, but instead he turned to the horses, bringing them closer to the daystone pile so that they could have some shelter from the wind.

We set up on what had been the foundation of a house, blown clean away by the force of the Tree's fall. A few small pieces of daystone had landed here, so we gathered them into a pile for light, and Deka murmured a command that made them generate heat as well. I laid out our blankets separately, whereupon Deka promptly moved his over next to mine and pulled me into his arms.

"Deka," I began. We had shared his bed since my last mortaling, but both of us had been too tired for anything but sleep. Convenient for putting off necessary conversations, but they could not be put off forever. So I took a deep breath and prayed briefly to one of my brothers for strength. "You don't have to pretend. I know how it is for young men, and—"

"I think," he said, "you've been stupid enough lately, Sieh. Don't make things worse."

At this I tried to sit up. I couldn't because he wouldn't let me and because my back complained fiercely when I tried. Too much time on horseback. "What?"

"You are still the child," he said quietly, and I stopped

struggling. "And the cat, and the man, and the monster who smothers children in the dark. So you're an old man, too; fine. I told you, Sieh, I'm not going anywhere. Now lie down. I want to try something."

More out of shock than any real obedience, I did as he bade me.

He slid a hand under my shirt, which made me blush and splutter. "Deka, gods—"

"Be still." His hand stopped, resting on my chest. It was not a caress, though my stupid old body decided that it was and further decided that perhaps it was not so old after all. I was grateful; at my age there were no guarantees that certain bodily processes still worked.

Deka's expression was still, intent. I had seen the same concentration from him when he spoke magic or drew sigils. This time, however, he began to whisper, and his hand moved in time with his words. Puzzled, I listened to what he was saying, but they were not words. It was not our language, or any language. I had no idea what he was doing.

I felt it, though, when words began tickling their way along my skin. When I jumped and tried to sit up, Deka pressed me down, closing his eyes so that my twitching would not distract him. And I *did* twitch, because it was the most peculiar sensation. Like ants crawling over my flesh, if those ants had been flat and made of sibilance. That was when I noticed the soft black glow of Deka's marks—which were more than tattoos, I realized at last. They always had been.

But something was not right. The marks he whispered into my flesh did not linger. I felt them wend around my limbs and down my belly, but as soon as they settled into place, they began to fade. I saw Deka's brow furrow, and after a few moments of this he stopped, his hand on my chest tightening into a fist.

"I take it that didn't go as expected," I said quietly.

"No."

"What *did* you expect?"

He shook his head slowly. "The markings should have tapped your innate magic. You're still a god; if you weren't, your antithesis wouldn't affect you. I should be able to remind your flesh that its natural state is young, malleable, embodied only by your will...." His jaw tightened, and he looked away. "I *don't* understand why it failed."

I sighed. There had been no real hope in me, probably because he hadn't told me what he was doing ahead of time. I was glad for that. "I thought you wanted me mortal."

He shook his head again, his lips thinning. "Not if it means you dying, Sieh. I never wanted that."

"Ah." I put my hand over his fist. "Thank you for trying, then. But there's no point, Deka, even if you could fix me. Godlings are fragile compared to the Three. When the Maelstrom breaks this universe, most likely we—"

"Shut up," he whispered, and I did, blinking. "Just shut up, Sieh." He was trembling and there were tears in his eyes. For the first time since his childhood, he looked lost and lonely and more than a little afraid.

I was still a god, as he had said. It was my nature to comfort lost children. So I pulled him to me, intending to hold him while he wept.

He pushed my hands aside and kissed me. Then, as though the kiss had not been sufficient reminder that he was no child, he sat up and began tugging my clothes off.

I could have laughed, or said no, or pretended disinterest. But it was the end of the world, and he was mine. I did what felt good.

We would all die in three days, but there was so much that could be done in that time. I was not a true mortal; I knew better than to take Enefa's gift for granted. I would savor every moment of my life that remained, suck its marrow, crunch its bones. And when the end came... well, I would not be alone. That was a precious and holy thing.

In the morning, we returned to Echo. Deka went to look in on his scriveners and ask again whether they had found some miracle that could save us all. I went in search of Shahar.

I found her in the Temple, which had finally been dedicated as such. Someone had put an altar in it, right on the spot where Deka and I had first made love. I tried not to think lewd thoughts about human sacrifice as I stopped before it, because I refused to be a *dirty* old man.

Shahar stood beyond the altar, beneath the colored swirl that now cast faintly blue light on us, like that of the cloudless sky outside. Her back was to me, though I was certain she'd heard me approach. I'd had to speak to four guards just to get into the room. She did not move until I spoke, however, and then she started, coming out of whatever reverie she'd lapsed into.

"Friends lie," I said. I spoke softly, but my voice echoed in the high-ceilinged chamber. It was deeper now, with a hoarse edge that would only get worse as I grew older. "Lovers, too. But trust can be rebuilt. You *are* my friend, Shahar. I shouldn't have forgotten that." She said nothing. I sighed and shrugged. "I'm a bastard, what do you expect?"

More silence. I saw the tightness of her shoulders. She folded her arms across her chest. I had seen enough women cry that I recognized the warning signs and decided to leave. But just as I reached the doorway, I heard, "Friends."

I stopped and looked back. She held up her right hand—the one that had held mine, years ago when we'd taken our oath. I rubbed a thumb across my own tingling palm and smiled.

"Friends," I said, raising my own. Then I left, because there was something in my eyes. Dust, probably. I would have to be more careful in the future. Old men had to take good care of their eyes.

22

...and they all lived happily ever after.
The end.

THE WORLD REMAINED SURPRISINGLY calm as the Maelstrom grew to dwarf the sun in the sky. This was not at all what I had expected. Mortal humans are only a few languages and eccentricities removed from mortal beasts, and it is the nature of beasts to panic at the approach of danger.

There were some beastly acts. No looting—the Order-Keepers had always been quick to execute thieves—but many cases of arson and vandalism as mortals destroyed property to vent their despair. And there was violence, of course. In one of the patriarchal lands, so many men slaughtered their wives and children before killing themselves that one of my siblings got involved. She appeared in the capital wreathed in falling leaves and let it be known that she would personally carry the souls of such murderers to the worst of the infinite hells. Even then the killings did not stop entirely, but they did decrease.

All this was nothing to what could have been. I had

expected...I don't know. Mass suicide, cannibalism, the total collapse of the Bright.

Instead, Shahar married Datennay Canru of Tema. It was a small and private ceremony, as there had not been time to prepare for anything better. At my prompting, she asked Deka to administer the rites as First Scrivener, and at my prompting, Deka agreed. There were no apologies exchanged. They were both Arameri. But I saw that she was contrite, and I saw that Deka forgave her. Then Shahar had the Order of Itempas spread word of the event by crier and runner and news scroll. She hoped to send a message by her actions: *I believe there will be a future.*

Canru agreed readily to the marriage, I think, because he was more than a bit in love with her. She...well, she had never stopped loving me, but she genuinely liked him. We all sought our own forms of comfort in those days.

I spent my nights in Deka's arms and was humbly grateful for my fortune.

So the world went on.

Until its end.

We gathered at dawn on the final day: Arameri, notables from Tema and other lands, commonfolk from Shadow, Ahad and Glee, Nemmer and a few of the other godlings who had not fled the realm. The Whorl was not as high as Sky had been, but it was as good a vantage point as any. From there, the heavens were a terrible, awe-inspiring sight. More than half of the sky had been devoured by the swirling, wavering transparency. As the sun rose and passed into the space of change, its shape turned sickly and distorted, its light flickering on our skins like a campfire. This was not an illusion. What we saw was literal, despite the impossibility of the angles and distance. Even

Tempa's rules for physics and time had been distorted by the Maelstrom's presence. Thus we beheld the slow and tortured end of our sun as it was torn apart and drawn into the great maw. There would be light for a while longer, and then darkness such as no mortal had ever seen. If we lasted that long.

I held Deka's hand as we stood gazing at it, unafraid.

Alarmed gasps from the center of the Whorl meadow drew my attention: Nahadoth and Yeine had appeared there amid the bobbing sea grass. The gathered folk stumbled back from them, though some quickly knelt or began weeping or calling out to them. No one shushed them, for hope had never been a sin.

I dragged Deka with me as I pushed through the crowd. Between Nahadoth and Yeine was Itempas; they had brought him. All three of them looked grim, but they would not have come without reason. Nahadoth might act without purpose, but Yeine tended not to, and Itempas had never done so.

They turned to me as I reached them, and I was suddenly sure of it. "You have a plan," I said, squeezing Deka's hand hard.

They looked at each other. Beyond the Three, Shahar stepped out of the crowd as well, Canru in her wake. He stopped, gazing at them in awe. Shahar came forward alone, her fists tight at her sides.

Itempas inclined his head to me. "We do."

"What?"

"Death."

If I had not spent countless eternities enduring his manner, I would have screamed at this. "Can you be more specific?"

There was the faintest twitch of Itempas's lips. "Kahl has called the Maelstrom to join with him," he said. "He

will have to appear in order to take It into himself and—
he hopes—use Its power to become a god. We will kill
him and offer It a new seat of power instead." He spread
his hands, indicating himself.

I caught my breath, horrified as I understood. "No.
Tempa, you were born from the Maelstrom. To return to
It—"

"I have chosen this, Sieh." His voice cut across mine,
soothing, definitive. "It is the fate my nature demands. I
have felt the possibility since Kahl's summoning. Yeine
and Nahadoth have confirmed it." Behind him, Yeine's
face was unreadable, serene. Nahadoth...he was almost
the same. It was not his nature to contain himself, however. He could not hide his unease entirely, not from me.

I scowled at Itempas. "What is this, some misguided
attempt at atonement? I told you a century ago, you stubborn fool, nothing can make up for your crimes! And
what good does it do for you to sacrifice yourself, if your
death will cause everything to end anyway?"

"The Maelstrom may cease Its approach if It fulfills
Kahl's purpose," Itempas replied. "In this case, creating a
new god. We believe the form that this new god takes will
depend on the nature and will of the vessel." He shrugged.
"I will see that what is created is a fitting replacement for
myself."

I stumbled back, and Deka put a hand on my shoulder
in concern. It was the same conjunction of power and will
that had forged Yeine into a new Enefa, and where that
had been wild, a series of not-quite-accidental coin-
cidences, now Itempas hoped to control a similar event.
But whatever god was created in his place, however
stick-in-the-mud that new one might turn out to be, *Itempas* would die.

"No," I said. I was trembling. "You can't."

"It's the only solution, Sieh," said Yeine.

I stared at the two of them, so set in their resolve, and did not know what I felt in that moment. Not so long before, I would have rejoiced at the idea of a new Itempas. Even now it was a temptation, because I might have forgiven him and I might still love him, but I would never forget what he had done to our family. Nothing would ever be the same for any of us. Would it not be easier, somehow—*cleaner*—to start over with someone new? Knowing Itempas, the idea had some appeal for him, too. He did like things neat.

I turned to Nahadoth, hoping for—something. I didn't know what. But Nahadoth, damn him, wasn't paying attention to any of us. He had turned away to gaze at the swirling sky. Around him, the dark wreathing tendrils of his presence wheeled in a slow, matching dance. Inching higher, in random increments, as I watched. Toward the Maelstrom.

Wait—

Itempas spoke his name sharply, before my thoughts could crystallize into fear. Yeine, surprised by this, frowned at both her brothers. For a moment, I saw incomprehension in her face, and then her eyes widened. But Naha only smiled, as if it amused him to frighten us. And he kept looking up at the Maelstrom, as if It was the most beautiful sight in the mortal realm.

"Perhaps we should do nothing," Nahadoth said. "Worlds die. Gods die. Perhaps we should let *all* of it go, and start anew."

Start anew. My eyes met Yeine's across the drift of Naha's blackness. Deka's hand tightened on my shoulder; he understood, too. The unsteady tremor of sorrow that edged Nahadoth's voice. The way his shape kept blurring in time with the Maelstrom's perturbations, resonating with its terrible, churning song.

But there was no fear in Itempas's face as he took a step toward Nahadoth. He was smiling, in fact—and I marveled, because even though he was trapped in mortal flesh, his smile somehow had all the old power. Nahadoth, too, reacted to this. He lowered his gaze to focus on Itempas, his own smile fading.

"Perhaps we should," Itempas said. "That *would* be easier than repairing what's broken."

The drifting curls of Nahadoth's substance grew still. They shifted aside as Itempas approached Nahadoth, allowing him near—but also curving inward, and sharpening into jagged, irregular scythes. Fanged jaws ready to close on Itempas's so-powerless flesh. Itempas ignored this blatant threat, continuing forward and, finally, stopping before him.

Behind him, Glee stood stiff and wide-eyed. I held my breath.

"Will you die with me, Nahadoth?" he asked. His voice was low, but it carried; we all heard it, even over the twisting, growing shriek of the Maelstrom. "Is that what you want?"

Beyond them, perhaps only I saw Yeine's expression tighten, though she said nothing. Anyone could see the delicacy of the spell Tempa had woven, more fragile still because it was nothing but words. He had no magic. No weapons at all for this battle, save the history between them, good and ill.

Nahadoth did not answer, but then he didn't need to. There were faces he wore only when he meant to kill. They are beautiful faces—destruction is not his nature, just an art he indulges—but in my mortal shape I could not look upon them without wanting to die, so I fixed my eyes on Itempas's back. Somehow, despite *his* mortal shape, Tempa could still bear Naha's worst.

"The new one," Tempa said, very softly. "I'll make certain he's worthy of both of you."

Then he lifted his hands—I clamped down on my tongue to keep from blurting a warning—and cupped Nahadoth's face. I expected his fingers to fall off, for the black depths around Naha had grown lethal, freezing flecks of snow from the air and etching cracks into the ground beneath their feet. It probably did hurt Itempas; they always hurt each other. This did not stop him from leaning close and touching his lips to Nahadoth's.

Nahadoth did not return the kiss. Itempas might as well have pressed his mouth to stone. Yet the fact that it had occurred at all—that Nahadoth permitted it, that it was Itempas's farewell—made it something holy.

(I clenched my fists and fought back tears. I was too old for sentimentality, damn it.)

Itempas pulled away, his sorrow plain. But as he stood there, his hands hiding Nahadoth's face from any view but his own, Naha showed him something. I couldn't see what, but I could guess, because there were faces Naha wore for love, too. I had never seen the one he'd shaped for Itempas, because Itempas guarded that face jealously, as he had always done with Naha's love. But Itempas inhaled at the sight of whatever Naha showed him now, closing his eyes as if Naha had stricken him one last, terrible blow.

Then he stepped back, and as his hands fell away, Nahadoth's face resumed its ordinary, shifting nature. With this, Naha turned his back on all of us, his cloak retracting sharply to form a tight, dark sheath around him. Itempas might as well not have been there anymore.

But he did not look up at the sky again.

When Itempas mastered himself, he glanced at Yeine and nodded. She regarded him for a long, weighted moment, then finally nodded in return. I let out a breath, and Deka did, too. I thought perhaps even the Maelstrom grew quieter for a moment, but that was probably my imagination.

But before I could digest my own relief and sorrow, Nahadoth's head jerked sharply upward—but not toward the Maelstrom, this time. The blackness of his aura blazed darker.

"*Kahl,*" he breathed.

High above—the same place from which he'd struck down the World Tree—a tiny figure appeared, wreathed in magic that trembled and wavered like the Maelstrom.

Before I could think, however, I was nearly floored by the furnace blast of Yeine's rage. She wasted no time in deciding to act; the air simply rippled with *negation of life*. I flinched, in spite of myself, as death struck Kahl, my son—

—my unknown, unwanted, unlamented son, whom I would have mentored and protected if I had been able, whose love I would have welcomed if I'd been given the choice—

—did *not* die. Nothing happened.

Nahadoth hissed, his face twitching reptilian. "The mask protects him. He stands outside this reality."

"Death is reality everywhere," Yeine said. I had never heard such murderousness in her voice.

There was a shudder beneath us, around us. The towns-folk cried out in alarm, fearing another cataclysm. I thought I knew what was happening, though I could no longer sense it: the earth beneath us had shifted in response to Yeine's hate, the whole planet turning like some massive, furious bodyguard to face her enemy. She spread her hands, crouching, the loose curls of her hair whipping in a gale that no one else felt, and her eyes were as cold as long-dead things as they fixed on Kahl.

On my son. But—

Nahadoth, his face alight, laughed as her power rose, even as the inimical nature of it forced him to step back. Even Itempas stared at her, pride warring with longing in his gaze.

This was as it should be. It was what I had wanted all along, really, for the Three to reconcile. But—

—to kill my son!

No. That I hadn't wanted.

Deka glanced at me and caught my hand suddenly, alarmed. "Sieh!" I frowned, and he lifted a hank of my hair for me to see. It had been brown streaked thickly with white; now the white predominated. The few remaining brown strands faded to colorlessness as I watched. It was longer, too.

I looked up at Deka and saw the fear in his eyes. "I'm sorry," I said. And I truly was, but... "I never wanted to be a poor father, Deka. I—"

"Stop it." He gripped my arm. "Stop speaking, stop thinking about him. You're killing yourself, Sieh."

So I was. But it would have happened anyway. Damn Enefa; I would think what I liked, mourn as I wished for the son I had never known. I remembered his fingers on the back of my neck. He would have forgiven me if he could have, I think, if forgiveness had not been counter to his nature. If my weakness had not left him to suffer so much. Everything he'd become was my fault.

There was a crack of displaced air as Yeine vanished. I could not see what followed—my eyes were not what they had been, and I seemed to be developing cataracts. But there was another crack from high above, a thunder of echoes, and then Nahadoth tensed, his smile fading. Itempas stepped up beside him quickly, his fists clenched. "No," he breathed.

"No," Nahadoth echoed, and then he, too, was gone, a flicker of shadow.

"What's happening?" I asked.

Deka squinted above us, shaking his head. "Kahl. It isn't possible. Dear gods, how is he—" He caught his breath. "Yeine has fallen. Now Nahadoth—"

"What?"

But there was no time to consider this, because suddenly the space where Nahadoth and Yeine had been was filled again, and we all fell to our knees.

Kahl wore the God Mask, and the power that it radiated was the worst thing I had ever felt in my life. Worse, even, than the day Itempas forced me into mortal flesh, and that had been like having all my limbs broken so that I could be stuffed into a pipe. Worse than seeing my mother's body, or Yeine's when she died her mortal death. My skin crawled; my bones ached. All around me I heard others falling, crying out. The mask was *wrong*—the emulation of a god, extraneous and offensive to existence itself. In its incomplete form, only godlings had been able to feel the wrongness, but now the God Mask radiated its hideousness to all children of the Maelstrom, mortal and immortal alike.

Deka moaned beside me, trying to speak magic, but he kept stuttering. I struggled to stay on my knees. It would have been easier to just lie down and die. But I forced my head up, trembling with the effort, as Kahl took a step toward Itempas.

"You're not the one I would have chosen," he said, his voice shivering. "Enefa was the original target of my vengeance. I would thank you for killing her, in fact, but here and now, you are the easiest of the Three to kill." He stepped closer, raising a hand toward Itempas's face. "I'm sorry."

Itempas did not back up or drop to the ground, though I saw how the ripple of power around Kahl pressed at him. It likely took everything he had to stay upright, but that was my bright father. If pride alone had been his nature, no force in the universe could ever have stopped him.

"Stop," I whispered, but no one heard me.

"*Stop*," said another voice, loud and sharp and furious. Glee.

Even with my failing eyesight, I could see her. She was on her feet as well, and it was not a trick of the light: a pale, faint nimbus surrounded her. It was easier to see this because the sky had grown overcast, stormclouds boiling up from the south as a brisk wind began to blow. We could no longer see the Maelstrom, except in snatches when the clouds parted, but we could hear It: a hollow, faint roar that would only grow louder. We could feel It, too, a vibration deeper than the earth that Yeine had shaken. A few hours, a few minutes; no telling when It would arrive. We would know when It killed us.

Itempas, who had not stepped away from Kahl, stumbled now as he turned to stare at his daughter. There were many things in Glee's eyes in that moment, but I did not notice them for staring at her eyes themselves, which had gone the deep, baleful ember of a lowering sun.

Kahl paused, the God Mask turning slightly as he peered at her. "What is it that you want, mortal?"

"*To kill you*," she replied. Then she burst into white-hot flame.

All the mortals nearby screamed, some of them fleeing for the stairs. Itempas threw up an arm as he was flung farther back. Ahad, beside her, cried out and vanished, reappearing near me. Even Kahl staggered, the blur around him bending away from the sheer blazing force of her. I could feel the heat of her fire tightening my skin from where I was, ten feet away. Anyone closer was probably risking burns. And Glee herself...

When the flames died, I marveled, for she stood clad all in white. Her skirt, her jacket—dear gods, even her *hair*. The light that surrounded her was almost too bright to look at. I had to squint through watering eyes and the shield of my hand. For an instant I thought I saw rings, words marching in the air, and in her hands...no. It could not be.

In her hands was the white-bladed sword that Itempas had used to cleave apart Nahadoth's chaos and bring design and structure to the earliest iteration of the universe. It had a name, but only he knew it. No one could wield it but him; hells, no one else had ever been able to get *near* the damned thing, not in all the aeons since he'd created time. But Itempas's daughter held it before her in a two-handed grip, and there was no doubt in my mind that she knew how to use it.

Kahl saw this, too, his eyes widening within the mask's slits. But of course he feared it; he had disrupted the order of all things, bringing the Maelstrom where it did not belong and claiming power he had no right to possess. In a contest of strength, he could endure, even against Nahadoth and Yeine—but there is more to being a god than strength.

"Control," said Itempas. He had drawn as close as he could, anxious to advise his daughter. "Remember, Glee, or the power will destroy you."

"I will remember," she said.

And then she was gone, and Kahl was, too, both of them leaving a melted, glowing trough across the Whorl's grassy plain.

Then two more streaks shot across the horizon in that direction, moving to join the battle: Nahadoth and Yeine.

Without Kahl's power to crush me, I struggled to my feet. Damned knees hurt like someone had lined the joints with broken glass. I ignored the pain and grabbed for Deka, then dragged him over to Ahad. "Come on," I said to both of them.

Ahad tore his eyes from the dwindling, shining mote that his lover had become. In the distance, plates of spinning darkness swirled out of nowhere, converging on a point. A massive, jagged finger of stone shot up from the earth, hundreds of feet into the sky in seconds. The second Gods' War had begun, and it was an awesome sight—even if, this time, it would leave far more than just the mortal realm in ruins.

"What?" Ahad looked dazed when I gripped his arm.

"Help me get Itempas," I said. When he simply stared at me, I jabbed him in the ribs with my gnarled fist. He glared; I stepped closer to shout into his face. "Pay attention! We have to go. With that kind of power in play, Glee won't last long. Nahadoth and Yeine might be able to stop him, I hope, we can pray, but if not, he's going to come back here." I pointed at Itempas, who was also staring after Glee, his fists clenched.

Finally understanding, Ahad caught my arm. I was holding Deka. There was a flicker as we moved through space, and then Ahad had Itempas by the arm as well. Itempas looked startled, but cottoned on faster than Ahad had; he did not fight. But then Ahad frowned. "Where can we go that he won't find us?"

I almost wailed the words. "Anywhere, anywhere, you fool!" The planet was going to die. All reality was beginning to falter, bleeding out through the mortal wound that the Maelstrom had punched into its substance. All we could do was start running, anywhere we could, and hope that Kahl did not catch up. Though if he did... "Dear gods, I hope you've found your nature by now."

Ahad's face went too impassive. "No."

"Demonshitting *brak'skafra*—" There was a hollow whoosh behind me, louder even than the Maelstrom's growing roar, and Deka turned quickly, barking a command to counter whatever I'd stupidly unleashed. The sound went silent; Deka glared at me. "Sorry," I muttered.

"Anywhere," Ahad said, but he was looking away from us. Something bloomed against the horizon like a round, white sun. I wanted to cheer for magnificent demon girls, but the light died too quickly for me to feel comfortable, and then Ahad took us away from the palace.

With his attention so thoroughly divided, I should have realized where we would end up. When the world resolved around us, we stood on tumbled white stones littered with the debris of everyday life: torn bedsheets, broken perfume bottles, an overturned toilet. Looming high overhead: broken, wilting limbs as thick as buildings.

"Sky?" I rounded on Ahad, wishing for once that I had a cane. I had to shout to be heard over the rising cacophony, but that was fine, because I was furious. "You brought us to *Sky*, you stupid son of a demon? What were you *thinking*?"

"I—"

But whatever Ahad might have retorted died in his mouth as his eyes widened. He whirled, looking north, and we all saw it. A great amorphous blotch of blackness was fading from view, but against its contrast we could see a tiny, blazing white star.

Falling, and winking out of sight as it fell.

Ahad took a great, shuddering breath, and the air around him turned the color of a bruise. The sound that he made was less a word than an animal, maddened shriek. For an instant he became *something else*, shapeless and impossible, and then we were all flung sprawling as daystone and Tree wood and the air itself whipped into an instant tornado around him. He was a god, and his will forged reality. All the matter nearby hastened to do his bidding.

Then he was gone, and all the debris that had been blasted away in his wake pelted onto whatever body parts we'd been foolish enough to turn upright.

I pushed myself up slowly, trying to get a broken Tree branch off my back and daystone dust out of my mouth. My hands hurt. Why did my hands hurt? I'd never had arthritis on any of the previous occasions I'd become old. Then again, that had been old age as I'd imagined it; perhaps the reality was simply more unpleasant than I'd thought.

Hands grabbed me, helping me up: Deka. He pushed the branch away, then pushed my hair out of my face; it was waist-long now, though thin and stringy white. No matter how old I got, the stuff kept growing. Why couldn't I go bald, damn it?

"Should've seen that coming," I muttered as he helped me to my feet.

"Seen what?"

Then Itempas was there, also helping me. Between the two of them, I was able to scramble over the jagged, unstable stones of the fallen Sky. "That one." Itempas nodded in the direction Ahad had gone. In another life I would have laughed at his refusal to use Ahad's borrowed name. "Apparently, his nature has something to do with love."

No wonder it had taken Ahad so long to find himself. He had lived the past century in the antithetical prison of his own apathy—and his centuries of suffering in Sky had probably not predisposed him to attempt love, even when the opportunity came along. But Glee…I bit my lip. In spite of everything, I prayed that she would be all right. I did not want to lose my newest sister, and I did not want this other, surrogate son of mine to discover himself through grief.

It is not an easy thing to climb a pile of rubble the size of a small city. It is harder when one is a half-blind old man of eighty or so. I kept having to stop and catch my breath, and my coordination was so poor that after a few close calls and nearly broken ankles, Itempas stepped in front of me and told me to climb onto his back. I would have refused, out of pride, but then Deka, damn him, picked me up bodily and forced me to do it. So I locked my arms and legs round Itempas, humiliated, and they ignored my complaints and resumed climbing.

We did not speak as the Maelstrom's roar grew louder. This was not merely because of the noise but also because we were waiting, and hoping, but as we kept climbing and the moments passed, that hope faded. If Yeine and the others had been able to defeat Kahl, they would have done it by now. The universe still existed; that meant the two gods were alive at least. Beyond that, no news was not good news.

"Where can we go?" Deka had to shout to be heard.

All around us was a charging, churning monstrosity of sound. I made out bird whistles and men shouting as if in agony, ocean surf and rock grating against metal. It did not hurt our ears—not yet—but it was not pleasant either.

"I can take us away once, maybe twice," he said, and then looked ashamed. "I don't have a god's strength, or even..." He looked toward where Glee had fallen. I hoped Ahad had managed to catch her. "But anywhere in the mortal realm, Kahl will find us. Even if he doesn't—"

We all paused to look up. High above, the clouds had begun to boil and twist in a way that had nothing to do with weather patterns. Would the great storm stop there in the sky, once It reached the place from which It had been summoned? Or would It simply plow through and leave a void where the earth had been?

Back to Echo, then. Deka and I could join with Shahar again, attempt to control what we had done only by instinct before... but even as I thought this, I dismissed it. Too much discord between Shahar and Deka now; we might just make things worse. I leaned my head on Itempas's broad shoulder, sighing. I was tired. It would be easier, so much easier, if I could just lie down now and rest.

But as I thought this, suddenly I knew what could be done.

I lifted my head. "Tempa." He had already stopped, probably to catch his breath, though he would never admit such a thing. He turned his ear toward me to indicate that he was listening. "How long does it take you to return to life when you die?"

"The time varies between ten and fifty minutes." He did not ask why I wanted to know. "Longer if the circumstances that caused me to die remain present—I revive, then die again immediately."

"Where do you go?" He frowned. It was hard to make

my voice work at this volume. "While you're dead. Where do you go?"

He shook his head. "Oblivion."

"Not the heavens? Not the hells?"

"No. I am not dead. But I am not alive, either. I hover between."

I wriggled to get down, and he set me on my feet. I nearly fell at once; the circulation in my legs had been cut off by his arms, and I hadn't even felt it. Deka helped me to sit on a rough piece of what—I think—had once been a part of the Garden of the Hundred Thousand. Groaning, I massaged one of my legs, nodding irritably for Deka to take the other, which he did.

"I need you to die," I said to Tempa, who lifted an eyebrow. "Just for a while." And then, using as few words as I could to save my voice, I told them my plan.

Deka's hands tightened on my calf. He made no protest, however, for which I was painfully grateful. He trusted me. And if he helped me, I would be able to pull my biggest trick ever.

My last trick.

"Please," I said to Tempa.

He said nothing for a long moment. Then he sighed, inclining his head, and took off his coat, handing it to me.

Then, as coolly as though he did such things every day, he looked around, spying a thin, fine extrusion jutting up from the pile. A piece of the Wind Harp: it was a wickedly sharp spear perhaps four feet long, angled straight up in the air. Tempa examined it, flicked away a scrap of faded cloth that had wrapped around its tip, and yanked it to the side, jostling loose a good bit of rubble while he positioned it to his liking. When he'd gotten it to about a forty-five degree angle, he nodded in satisfaction—and fell forward onto it, sliding down its shaft until friction or bone or gods knew what stopped him short. Deka cried out, leaping to his feet, though it was too late and he'd known it was going to happen anyhow. He protested because that was just the kind of man he was.

I reached up to take Deka's hand, and he turned to me, his face still writ in lines of horror. How had an Arameri been born with a soul as perfect as his? I was so glad I'd lived to see it, and to know him.

He proved his worth again when grim determination replaced horror in his eyes. He helped me to my feet, handing me Tempa's coat, which I put on. The wind had risen to a gale, and I was a skinny, frail old man.

We both looked up then, startled, as a sound like wailing horns filled the sky and the clouds tore apart. Above us, filling the sky, a new and terrible god appeared: the Maelstrom. What we saw was not Its true self, of course, which was vaster than all existence, let alone a single world. Like everything that entered the mortal realm, It had shaped an approximation of Itself: churning clouds, the sun stretched into glowing candy, a string of floating pieces of worlds and shattered moons trailing in Its wake. In Its boiling surface, we could see ourselves and the world around us, a reflection distorted and magnified. Our faces screamed; our bodies broke and bled. The imminent future.

Deka turned his back to me and crouched. Speech was no longer possible now. Soon our ears would rupture, which would be a blessing, because otherwise the roar would destroy our sanity. I climbed onto Deka's back, pressing my face into his neck so that I could breathe his scent one last time. Ignoring my sentimentality, he closed his eyes and murmured something. I felt the markings on his back grow hot and then cold against my chest.

Gods do not fly. Flying requires wings and is ineffi-
cient in any case. We leap, and then stick to the air. Anyone can do it; most mortals just haven't learned how.
There's a trick to it, see.

Deka's first leap took us nearly into the Maelstrom. I
groaned and clung to him as the thunder of the storm
above us grew so great that I lost the feeling in my hands,
nearly lost my grip entirely. But then, somehow, Deka corrected his error, arcing down now toward the gods' battle.

Which was not over. There was a flash of darkness, and
we passed through a space of coldness: Nahadoth. Then
warm air, redolent of spores and rotting leaves: Yeine.
Both still alive, and still fighting—and winning, I was glad
to see. They had dissipated their forms, corralling Kahl in
a thickening sphere of combined power so savage that I
urged Deka to stop well away, which he did. At the center
of this sphere was Kahl, raging, blurring, but contained.
The God Mask had made him one of them, temporarily,
but no false god could challenge two of the Three for long.
To win, Kahl would have to make his transformation permanent. To do that, he would need strength he didn't have.

Which was why I, his father, offered that to him now. I
closed my eyes and, with everything that I was, sent my
presence through the ethers of this world and every other.

The swirling, searing forms of Yeine and Nahadoth
stopped, startled. Kahl spun within the shell that held him,
and I thought that his eyes marked me from within the mask.

Come, I said, though I had no idea whether he could
hear my voice. I prayed it, shaping my thoughts around
fury, to make sure. My poor Hymn, whom I'd never been
able to bless. All the dead of Sky-in-Shadow. Glee and
Ahad. And he wanted Itempas, my father? No. It was not
difficult to summon a craving for vengeance in my own

heart. Then, carefully, I masked this with sorrow. That wasn't hard to dredge up either.

Come, I said again. *You need power, don't you? I told you to accept your nature. Enefa threw you in a hole somewhere, left you forgotten and forsaken, for me. You cannot forgive me for that. Come, then, and kill me. That should give you the strength you need.*

Within his glimmering prison, Kahl stared at me—but I knew I'd baited the trap well. He was Vengeance, and I was the source of his oldest and deepest pain. He could no more resist me than I could a ball of string.

He hissed and flexed what remained of his power, a miniature Maelstrom straining to break free. Then I felt the unstable surge of his elontid nature, amplifying the God Mask and waxing powerful enough that the shell Naha and Yeine had woven around him cracked into smoking fragments. Then he came for me.

This was my gift to him, father to son. The least I could offer, and far less than I should have done.

My Deka; he never wavered, not even when the outermost edges of Kahl's blurring rage struck and began to shred his skin. We both screamed as our bones snapped, but Deka did not drop me. Not even when Kahl wrapped his arms around both of us, tearing us apart by sheer proximity, in an embrace that he'd probably intended as a parody of love. Perhaps there was even a bit of real love in it. Vengeance was nothing if not predictable.

Which was why, with the last of my strength, I reached into Itempas's coat, pulled out the dagger coated with Glee Shoth's blood, and shoved it into Kahl's heart.

He froze, his green, sharpfold eyes going wide within the God Mask. The power around him went still, as the calm within a storm.

My hands were bleeding, mangled claws, but thankfully they were still the hands of a trickster. I snatched the God Mask from Kahl's face. This was easy, as he was already dead. As it came away, his face, so like mine, stared at me with empty eyes. Then all three of us began to fall, separating. Kahl slid off the knife as we twisted in the air. I hung on to it by sheer force of will.

But there came a jolt, and I found Yeine leaning into the diminishing plane of my vision.

"Sieh!" Such was her voice that I could hear her even over the great storm. I felt her power gather to heal me.

I shook my head, having no strength to talk. I had enough left, just, to raise the God Mask to my face. I saw her eyes widen when I did this, and she tried to grab my arms. Silly former mortal. If she had used magic, she could have stopped me.

Then the mask was on me.

It was on me.

IT WAS ON ME AND I—

I—

—smiled. Yeine had released me, crying out. I'd hurt her. I hadn't meant to. We gods just have opposing natures.

She fell, and Deka fell. Yeine would be all right. Deka would not, but that was fine, too. It had been his choice. He had died like a god.

Nahadoth coalesced before me, just beyond the range of my painful, vibrating aura. His face was a study in betrayal. "Sieh," he said. I had hurt him, too. He looked at me the way he looked at Itempas these days. That was worse than what I'd done to Yeine. I felt sudden pity for my bright father and prayed—to no one in particular—that Nahadoth would forgive him soon.

"What have you done?" he demanded.

Nothing, yet, my dark father.

I won't say I wasn't tempted. I had what I'd yearned for. It would be easy, so easy, to go and kill Tempa with the knife, as he had killed Enefa long ago. Easy, too, to absorb the Maelstrom, make the transformation permanent, take Itempas's place. I could be Naha's lover in earnest then, and share him with Yeine, and make all of us a new Three. I heard a song promising this in the Maelstrom's ratcheting scream.

But I was Sieh, the whim and the wind, the Eldest Child and Trickster, source and culmination of all mischief. I would not tolerate being some cheap imitation of another god.

So I turned, the power coming easily as my flesh remembered itself. A beautiful feeling, greater than anything I had ever known, and this wasn't even real godhood. Closing my eyes, I spread my arms and turned to face the Maelstrom.

"Come," I whispered with the voice of the universe.

And It came, Its wild substance passing into me through the filter of the God Mask. Remaking me. Fitting me into existence like a puzzle piece—which worked only because Itempas's temporary absence had left a void. Without that, my presence, a *Fourth*, would have torn it all apart. In fact, when Itempas next awoke, the sundering would begin.

Thus I raised the knife coated with my son's blood. There was plenty of Glee's left, too, I hoped—though really, there was only one way to find that out.

I drove the knife into my breast, and ended myself.

23

IN THE SKY ABOVE, just when it seemed the Maelstrom would crush everything, It suddenly winked out of existence, leaving a painful silence.

As I pushed myself up from where I'd been curled on the ground, my hands clamped over my ears, Lord Nahadoth appeared, carrying my brother. Then came Lord Ahad, bringing a newly revived Lord Itempas and a badly wounded Glee Shoth. A moment later, Lady Yeine arrived, bearing Sieh.

I am Shahar Arameri, and I am alone.

I issued an edict to the Consortium, summoning them to Echo, and to this I added a personal invitation for Usein Darr, and any allies that she chose to bring. To make my position clear, I phrased the note thus: *To discuss the terms of the Arameri surrender.*

Mother always said that if one must do something unpleasant, one should do it wholeheartedly and not waste effort on regret.

I invited representatives from the Litaria as well, and the Merchants' Guild, and the Farmers' Collective, and the Order of Itempas. I even summoned a few beggars from Ancestors' Village, and artists from Shadow's Promenade. As Lord Ahad was indisposed—he would not leave the bedside of Glee Shoth, who had been healed but slept in deep exhaustion—I included an invitation to several of the gods of Shadow, where they could be located. Most of them, not entirely to my surprise, had remained in the mortal realm as the disaster loomed. It was not the Gods' War again; they cared about us this time. To wit, Ladies Nemmer and Kitr responded in the affirmative, saying that they would attend.

The Litaria's involvement meant that all parties could gather quickly, as they sent scriveners forth to assist those mortals who could not hire their own. Within less than a day, Echo played host to several hundred of the world's officials and influencers, decision makers and exploiters. Not everyone who mattered, of course, and not enough of those who didn't. But it would do. I had them gather in the Temple, the only space large enough to hold them all. To address them, I stood where my brother and my best friend had shown me how to love. (I could not think of that and function, so I thought of other things instead.)

And then I spoke.

I told everyone there that we, the Arameri, would give up our power. Not to be distributed among the nobles, however, which would only invite chaos and war. Instead, we would give the bulk of our treasury, and management of our armies, to a single new governing body that was to consist of everyone in the room or their designated representatives. The priests, the scriveners, the godlings, the merchants, the nobles, the common folk. All of them. This body—by vote, edict, or whatever method they chose—would rule the Hundred Thousand Kingdoms in our place.

To say that this caused consternation would be understating the case.

I left as soon as the shouting began. Unconscionable for an Arameri ruler, but I no longer ruled. And like most mortals who had been near the Maelstrom that day, my ears were sensitive, still ringing despite my scriveners' healing scripts. The noise was bad for my health.

So I sought out one of the piers of Echo. A few hadn't been damaged by the palace's precipitous flight from ocean to lake. The view from here was of the lakeshore, with its ugly, sprawling survivors' encampment—not the ocean I craved or the drifting clouds I would never stop missing. But perhaps those were things I should never have gotten used to in the first place.

A step behind me. "You actually did it."

I turned to find Usein Darr standing there. A thick bandage covered her left eye and that side of her face; one of her hands had been splinted. There were probably other injuries hidden by her clothing and armor. For once I saw none of Wrath's constantly hovering guards about, but Usein did not have a knife in her good hand, which I took as a positive sign.

"Yes," I said, "I did it."

"Why?"

I blinked in surprise. "Why are you asking?"

She shook her head. "Curiosity. A desire to know my enemy. Boredom."

By my training, I should never have smiled. I did it anyway, because I no longer cared about my training. And because, I was certain, it was what Deka would have done. Sieh, I suspected, would have gone a step further, because he always went a step further. Perhaps he would have offered to babysit her children. Perhaps she would even have let him.

"I'm tired," I said. "The whole world isn't something one woman should bear on her shoulders—not even if she wants to. Not even if she has help." And I no longer did.

"That's it?"

"That's it."

She fell silent, and I turned back to the railing as a light breeze, redolent of algae and rotting crops and human sorrow, wafted over the lake from the land beyond. The sky was heavily overcast as if threatening a thunderstorm, but it had been so for days without rain. The lords of the sky were in mourning for their lost child; we would not see the sun or the stars for some time.

Let Usein knife me in the back, if she wished. I truly did not care.

"I am sorry," she said at length. "About your brother, and your mother, and..." She trailed off. We could both see the Tree's corpse in the distance; it blocked the mountains that had once marked the horizon. From here, Sky was nothing more than tumbled white jewels around its broken crown.

" 'I was born to change this world,' " I whispered.

"Pardon?"

"Something the Matriarch—the first Shahar—reportedly said." I smiled to myself. "It isn't a well-known quote outside the family, because it was blasphemous. Bright Itempas abhors change, you see."

"Hmm." I suspected she thought I was mad. That was fine, too.

After a time, Usein left, probably returning to the Temple to battle for Darr's fair share of the future. I should have gone, too. The Arameri were, if nothing else, the royal family of the numerous and fractious tribes of the Amn race. If I did not fight for my people, we might be short-changed in the time to come.

So be it, I decided, and hitched up my gown to sit against the wall.

It was Lady Yeine who found me next.

She appeared quietly, seated on the railing I had just leaned against. Though she looked the same as always—relentlessly Darren—her clothing had changed. Instead of pale gray, the tunic and calf-pants she usually wore were darker in color. Still gray, but a color that matched the lowering stormclouds above. She did not smile, her eyes olive with sorrow.

"What are you doing here?" she asked.

If one more person, mortal or god, asked me that question, I was going to scream.

"What are *you* doing here?" I asked in return. An impertinent question, I knew, for the god to whom my family now owed its allegiance. I would never have dared it with Lord Itempas. Yeine was less intimidating, however, so she would have to deal with the consequences of that.

"An experiment," she said. (I was privately relieved that my rudeness did not seem to bother her.) "I am leaving Nahadoth and Itempas alone together for a while. If the universe comes apart again, I'll know I made a mistake."

If my brother had not been dead, I would have laughed. If her son had not been dead, I think she would have, too.

"Will you release him?" I asked. "Itempas?"

"It has already been done." She sighed, drawing up one knee and resting her chin on it. "The Three are whole again, if not wholly united, and not exactly rejoicing at our reconciliation. Perhaps because there *is* no reconciliation; that will take an age of the world, I imagine. But

who knows? It has already gone faster than I expected."
She shrugged. "Perhaps I'm wrong about the rest, too."

I considered the histories I had read. "He was to be
punished for as long as the Enefadeh. Two thousand years
and some."

"Or until he learned to love truly." She said nothing
more. I had seen Itempas weep beside the body of his son,
silent tear tracks cleansing the blood and dirt from his
face. This had been nothing meant for a mortal's eyes, but
he had permitted me to see it, and I was keenly conscious
of the honor. At the time, I'd had no tears of my own.

And I had seen Lord Itempas put a hand on the shoulder of Lord Nahadoth, who knelt beside Sieh's corpse
without moving. Nahadoth had not shaken that hand off.
By such small gestures are wars ended.

"We will withdraw," Lady Yeine said, after a time of
silence. "Naha and Tempa and I, completely this time. There
is much work to be done, repairing the damage that the
Maelstrom did. It takes all our strength to hold the realms
together, even now. The scar of Its passage will never fade
completely." She sighed. "And it has finally become clear to
me that our presence in the mortal realm does too much
harm, even when we try not to interfere. So we will leave
this world to our children—the godlings, if they wish to
stay, and you mortals, too. And the demons, if there are any
left or any more born." She shrugged. "If the godlings get
out of hand, ask the demons to keep them in line. Or do it
yourselves. None of you are powerless anymore."

I nodded slowly. She must have guessed my thoughts,
or read them in my face. I was slipping.

"He loved you," she said softly. "I could tell. You drove
him half mad."

At that, I did smile. "The feeling was mutual."

We sat then, gazing at the clouds and the lake and the broken land, both of us thinking unimaginable thoughts. I was glad for her presence. Datennay tried, and I was growing to care for him, but it was hard to keep the pain at bay some days. The Mistress of Life and Death, I feel certain, understood that.

When she got to her feet, I did, too, and we faced each other. Her tiny size always surprised me. I thought she should have been like her brothers, tall and terrible, showing some hint of her magnificence in her shape. But that was what I got for thinking like an Amn.

"Why did it begin?" I asked. And because I was used to how gods thought and that question could have triggered a conversation about anything from the universe to the Gods' War and everything in between, I added, "Sieh. How did we make him mortal? Why did we have such power over him, with him? Was it because…" It was difficult for me to admit, but I'd had the scriveners test me, and they had confirmed my suspicions. I was a demon, though the god-killing potency of my blood was negligible, and I had no magic, no specialness. Mother would have been so disappointed.

"It had nothing to do with you," Yeine said softly. I blinked. She looked away, sliding her hands into her pockets—a gesture that tore at my heart, because Sieh had done it so often. He'd even looked like her, a little. By design? Knowing him, yes.

"But what—"

"I lied," she said, "about us staying wholly out of the mortal realm. There will be times in the future when we'll have no choice but to return. It will be our task to assist the godlings, you see, when the time of metamorphosis comes upon them. When they become gods in their own right."

I jerked in surprise. "Become... what? Like Kahl?"

"No. Kahl sought to force nature. He wasn't ready for it. Sieh was." She let out a long sigh. "I didn't begin to understand until Tempa said that whatever Sieh had become, he was *meant* to become. His bond with you, losing his magic—perhaps these are the signs we'll know to watch for next time. Or perhaps those were unique to Sieh. He was the oldest of our children, after all, and the first to reach this stage." She looked at me and shrugged. "I would have liked to see the god he became. Though I still would have lost him then, even if he'd lived."

I digested this in wonder and felt a little fear at the implications. Godlings could grow into gods? Did that mean gods, then, could grow into things like the Maelstrom? If they could somehow live long enough, would mortals become godlings?

Too many things to think about. "What do you mean, you would have lost him if he'd lived?"

"This realm can abide only three gods. If Sieh had survived and become whatever he was meant to be, his fathers and I would have had to send him away."

Death or exile. Which would I have preferred? *Neither. I want him back, and Deka, too.* "But where could he have gone?"

"Elsewhere." She smiled at my look, with a hint of Sieh's mischief. "Did you think this universe was all there was? There's room out there for so much more." Her smile faded then, just a little. "He would have enjoyed the chance to explore it, too, as long as he didn't have to do it alone."

The Goddess of Earth looked at me then, and suddenly I understood. Sieh, Deka, and I; Nahadoth, Yeine, and Itempas. Nature is cycles, patterns, repetition. Whether by chance or some unknowable design, Deka and I had begun Sieh's transition to adulthood—and perhaps, when the chrysalis of his mortal life had finally split to reveal the new being, he would not have transformed alone.

Would I have wanted to go with him and Deka, to rule some other cosmos?

Just dreams now, like broken stone.

Yeine dusted off her pants, stretched her arms above her head, and sighed. "Time to go."

I nodded. "We will continue to serve you, Lady, whether you're here or not. What prayers shall we say for you at the dawn and twilight hour?"

She threw me an odd look, as if checking to see if I was joking. I wasn't. This seemed to surprise and unnerve her; she laughed, though it sounded a bit forced.

"Say whatever you want," she said finally. "Someone might be listening, but it won't be me. I have better things to do."

She vanished.

Eventually I wandered back into the palace, and to the Temple, where the assembly was breaking up at last. Merchants and nobles and scriveners drifted down the hall in knots, still arguing with each other. They ignored me completely as I came to the Temple entrance.

"Thanks for leaving," said Lady Nemmer as she emerged looking thoroughly disgruntled. "We got exactly one thing done, aside from setting a date for a future useless meeting."

I smiled at her annoyance; she scowled back, the room growing oddly shadowed. But she wasn't really angry, so I asked, "And the thing you got done was?"

"We chose a name." She waved a hand, irritable. "A pretentious and needlessly poetic one, but the mortals outnumbered Kitr and I, so we couldn't vote it down. *Aeternat.* It's one of our words. It means—"

I cut her off. "I don't need to know, Lady Nemmer. Please convey to whoever's speaking for this Aeternat that they should inform me when they're ready for the transfer of military command and funds."

She looked at me in real surprise, then finally nodded. We turned at the sound of someone calling my name from down the corridor: Datennay. He'd sat in on the Aeternat's session. I would have to quickly dissuade him from doing that, now that he was my husband. Beyond him was Ramina, who watched me with a solemn sorrow in his expression that I understood completely. He caught my eye over the heads of a gaggle of shouting priests and smiled, however, inclining his head in approval. It warmed me. I would need to have his true sigil removed sometime soon.

And I would need to send a note to Morad, I reminded myself. She'd quit her position and gone home to southern Senm, to no one's surprise. I still hoped to entice her back eventually; competent stewards were hard to find. I would not press Morad, however. She deserved the time and space to mourn in her own way.

While Datennay approached, I inclined my head to Nemmer in farewell. "Welcome to ruling the world, Lady Nemmer. I wish you enjoyment of it."

She spoke a godword so foul that one of the nearby lanterns turned to melted metal-and-oil sludge and crashed to the floor. As I walked away, I heard her cursing again—in some mortal tongue this time, more softly, as she bent to clean up the mess.

Datennay met me halfway down the hall. He hesitated before offering me his hand. Once, I had discouraged him from displaying affection in public. Now, however, I took his hand firmly, and he blinked in surprise, flashing a smile.

"These people are all mad," I said. "Take me away from here."

As we walked away, something pulsed hot between my breasts, and I remembered I had forgotten to tell Lady Yeine about the necklace we'd found on Sieh's body. The cord had been broken, half the smaller beads lost to whatever had snapped it, but the central bead—the peculiar yellow one—was fine. It was surprisingly heavy, and sometimes, if I was not imagining things, it became oddly warm to the touch. I had put the thing on a chain around my own neck, because I felt better wearing it. Less alone.

Lady Yeine would not mind if I kept it, I decided. Then I stroked the little sphere as if to comfort it, and walked on.

CODA

Shahar Arameri died in bed at the age of seventy, leaving two daughters and a son—half-Teman fullbloods unmarked by any sigil—to carry on the family. The Arameri still owned many businesses and properties, and they remained one of the most powerful clans on the Senm continent. They just had less. Shahar's children immediately began scheming to get more upon her death, but that is a matter for other tales.

The godling Ahad, called Beloved by his fellow godlings, watched over Glee Shoth for the entire year that she slept after her legendary battle with Kahl. When she finally awoke, he took her away from Echo and the new city developing around its lake. They settled in a small northwestern Senm town, where they spent some years looking after an elderly, blind Maro woman until her death. There they remained for another hundred years or so, never marrying, raising no children, but always together. She lived a long time for a mortal, and gave him a proper name of his own before she died. He tells no one that name, it is said, guarding it like something precious and rare.

Those mortals who worshipped the Goddess of Earth

claimed ownership of the corpse of the World Tree. By the time of Shahar's death, they had excavated and preserved enough of its trunk to house a small city, which began to call itself World. They lived in the Tree and on it, said their prayers at the skeleton of its roots, dedicated their sons and daughters to its broken branches. Fires, and fire-godlings, were not allowed in this city. They lit their chambers at night with pieces of Sky.

The Aeternat...well. It was not eternal. But that, too, is a matter for other tales.

So many tales, really. They are sure to be exciting. A shame that I will get to hear none of them.

I? Oh, yes.

When Shahar exhaled her last breath I awakened, midwifed into existence by her mortality. My first act was to turn in space and time and kiss Deka awake, beside me. Then I called to my En, and it shot across realities and blazed into joyous, welcoming life somewhere far, far beyond the realms of the Three. It would be the seed-star of a new realm. *Our* realm. It sent out great arcing plumes of fire, silly little ball of gas, and I petted it silent and promised it worlds to warm just as soon as I'd taken care of other business.

Then we found Shahar, and gathered her up, and took her with us. She was, to say the least, surprised. But not displeased. We are together now, the three of us, for the rest of forever. I will never be alone again.

My name is not Sieh, and I am no longer a trickster. I will think of a new name and calling, eventually—or some one of you, my children, will name me. Make of me, of us, whatever you wish. We are yours until time ends, and perhaps a little beyond.

And we will all create such wonderful new things, you and we, out here beyond the many skies.

A Glossary of Terms

~~Ahad:~~ A niwwah godling living in ~~Shadow~~; proprietor of the Arms of Night brothel.

Amn: Most populous and powerful of the Senmite races.

Antema: Capital of the largest province of the Teman Protectorate.

~~Arameri:~~ *ASSHOLES* Ruling family of the Amn; advisors to the Nobles' Consortium; ~~servants of Itempas~~. *ASSHOLES ASSHOLES ASSHOLES ASSHOLES ASSHOLES ASSHOLES ASSHOLES ASSHOLES ASSHOLES Asshole*

shooky shooky smell like **Arms of Night:** A brothel in the South Root neighborhood of Shadow, known to cater to an exclusive clientele.

Blood sigil: The mark of a recognized Arameri family member.

Bright, the: The time of Itempas's solitary rule, after the Gods' War. General term for goodness, order, law, righteousness. *HA, HA, HA*

Darkwalkers: Worshippers of the Nightlord.

Datennay Canru: Pymexe (heir) to Lady Hynno of the Teman Triadice; a friend of Shahar and Dekarta Arameri.

Dekarta Arameri: Twin brother of heir Shahar Arameri. Named for a former head of the family. *DO YOU LOVE ME?*

Demon: Children of ~~unions~~ unions between gods/*I WILL SHOW YOU* godlings and mortals. Mortal, though they ~~may~~ possess innate magic equivalent to that of godlings in strength, or greater. *COME AND*

Dimmer: An artist skilled in dimyi.

Dimyi: The art of mask making; a specialty of High North.

Easha: East Shadow.

Echo: A palace.

Elontid: The second ranking of godling. *BLAH BLAH BLAH BLAH* The imbalancers, born of the inequality between gods and godlings, or the instability of Nahadoth and Itempas. Sometimes as powerful as gods, sometimes weaker than godlings. *VNRS SUCK*

EN! The best friend a godling ever had.

Enefa: One of the Three. ~~Former~~ Goddess of Earth, creator of godlings and mortals, Mistress of Twilight and Dawn (deceased).

Eyem-sutah: A niwwah godling living in Shadow. Lord of the Lanes (of commerce).

Gateway Park: A park built around Sky and the World Tree's base. *CRAZY*

Glee Shoth: A Maroneh woman; ~~girlfriend~~ of Ahad. *WHO HAS NO TASTE*

God: Immortal children of the Maelstrom. The Three.

Godling: Immortal children of the Three. Sometimes also referred to as *gods*. *?*

Godsblood: A popular and expensive narcotic. Confers heightened awareness and temporary magical abilities on consumers. *EAT OF MY FLESH AND THY SOUL SHALL BE FORFEIT*

Gods' realm: All places beyond the universe. *you are here*

Gods' War: An apocalyptic conflict in which Bright Itempas claimed rulership of the heavens after defeating his two siblings.

Gray, the: The "middle city" of Sky-in-Shadow, situated atop the World Tree's roots. Includes servants, suppliers, and crafters, and the mansions they serve (which encircle the Tree's trunk) by means of a network of steam-driven escalators.

Heavens, Hells: Abodes for souls beyond the mortal realm.

High North: Northernmost continent. A backwater.

Hundred Thousand Kingdoms, the: Collective term for the world since its unification under Arameri rule.

Hymnesamina: A girl living in the South Root neighborhood of Shadow. *with a truly stupid hat.*

Interdiction, the: The period after the Gods' War when no godlings appeared in the mortal realm, per order of Bright Itempas.

Islands, the: Vast archipelago east of High North and Senm.

Itempan: General term for a worshipper of Itempas. Also used to refer to members of the Order of Itempas.

Itempas: One of the Three. The Bright Lord; master of heavens and earth; the Skyfather. *I HATE YOU FOREVER* godling.

Kitr: A manasat godling who lives in Shadow. The Blade.

Lil: An elontid godling who lives in Shadow. The Hunger.

Maelstrom: The creator of the Three. Unknowable.

Magic: The innate ability of gods and godlings to alter the material and immaterial world. Mortals may approximate this ability through the use of the gods' language.

Maroland, the: Smallest continent, which once existed to the east of the islands; site of the first Arameri palace. Destroyed by Nahadoth.

Mnasat: The third ranking of godlings; godlings born of godlings. Generally weaker than godlings born of the Three.

Mortal realm: The universe, created by the Three.

Nahadoth: One of the Three. The Nightlord.

Nemmer: A niwwah godling who lives in Shadow. The Lady of Secrets.

Nimaro Reservation: A protectorate of the Arameri, established after the Maroland's destruction.

Niwwah: The first ranking of godlings, born of the Three; the Balancers. More stable but sometimes less powerful than the elontid.

Nobles' Consortium: Ruling political body of the Hundred Thousand Kingdoms.

Nsana: A niwwah godling; the Dreammaster.

Order of Itempas: The priesthood dedicated to Bright Itempas. In addition to spiritual guidance, also responsible for law and order, education, public health, and welfare. Also known as the Itempan Order.

Order-Keepers: Acolytes (priests-in-training) of the Order of Itempas, responsible for maintenance of public order.

Pilgrim: Worshippers of the Gray Lady who journey to Shadow to pray at the World Tree.

Previt: One of the higher rankings for priests in the Order of Itempas.

Promenade, the: Northernmost edge of Gateway Park in East Shadow.

Pymexe: (masculine; feminine is *pymoxe*) Heir to one of the three ruling positions in the Teman Triadice.

Not hereditary; Triadic heirs are chosen at an early age, after a rigorous selection process involving official examinations and interviews.

Ramina Arameri: A fullblood; half brother of Remath Arameri.

Remath Arameri: Current head of the Arameri family; mother of Shahar and Dekarta.

Salon: Headquarters for the Nobles' Consortium.

Script: A series of sigils, used by scriveners to produce complex or sequential magical effects.

Scrivener: A scholar of the gods' written language.

Semisigil: A modern version of the Arameri blood sigil, modified to remove anachronistic scripts.

Senm: Southernmost and largest continent of the world.

Senmite: The Amn language, used as a common tongue for all the Hundred Thousand Kingdoms.

Shadow: The city beneath Sky.

Shahar Arameri: Current heir of the Arameri Family. Also high priestess of Itempas at the time of the Gods' War. Matriarch of the Arameri family.

Sieh: A godling, also called the Trickster. Eldest of all the godlings.

Sigil: An ideograph of the gods' language, used by scriveners to imitate the magic of the gods.

Sky: The palace of the Arameri family.

Sky-in-Shadow: Official name for the palace of the Arameri and the city beneath it.

Teman Protectorate, the: A Senmite kingdom.

Time of the Three: Before the Gods' War.

True sigil: An Arameri blood sigil in the traditional style.

T'vril Arameri: A former head of the Arameri family.

Usein Darr: A Darren warrior; heir to the Baron Darr.

Wesha: West Shadow.

White Hall: The Order of Itempas's houses of worship, education, and justice.

World Tree, the: An evergreen tree estimated to be 125,000 feet in height, created by the Gray Lady. Sacred to worshippers of the Lady.

Wrath Arameri: Captain of the White Guard in Sky.

Yeine: One of the Three. The current Goddess of Earth, Mistress of Twilight and Dawn.

Acknowledgments

Going to keep it short this time. This is the longest novel I've ever written, after all, and I'm plum tuckered out.

I need to thank you.

Seriously. That's not just pretentious "I'd like to thank all the little people" bullshit. A writer is a writer whether she's read or not, but no writer can have a career in this business unless she satisfies her readers. And really, even that's not enough, not in these days of the long tail and a quarter-million new titles published per year in the United States alone. A writer needs readers who will find other readers, and grab them by the arm, and say to them, *Read this book right now.* She needs readers who will post reviews on retailer sites and argue with other readers over their ratings; readers who will select her work for their monthly book club meetings and discuss it over tea and cake; readers who will Tweet about the book's surprises; readers who'll put the book on a literature syllabus. She even needs people who'll rant that they hate the book—because those kinds of strong reactions make people curious.

The opposite of liking is not disliking, after all. The opposite of liking is apathy.

All new writers have Something to Prove—me more than most, maybe. But because so many of you have been anything but apathetic, I know I've done a good job. So thank you. Thank you. Thank you.

extras

orbit

meet the author

N. K. Jemisin

N. K. JEMISIN is a career counselor, political blogger, and would-be gourmand living in New York City. She's been writing since the age of ten, although her early works will never see the light of day. Find out more about the author at www.nkjemisin.com.

short story

Not the End

By N. K. Jemisin

THE FIRE HAD GONE out again, I noticed as I came upstairs from my basement art studio. The whole first floor was already cold. It was the damned chimney damper, I was sure. The thing had been dodgy since that time Cingo had tried to repair it himself. Must've jammed entirely; we were lucky the whole house wasn't full of smoke.

I stopped at the top of the stairs, catching my breath and feeling annoyed. Not at the snuffed fire. My daughter, and the man who passed for my son-in-law, did not get cold; their room was on the first floor, but I doubted they would even notice. I wasn't even annoyed at Cingo, because he was fifty years dead and it was a testament even to his inept repairs that they'd lasted this long. Nor was I annoyed at myself, given that sentimentality had kept me from getting Cingo's folly fixed in all this time. My irritation had no focus, other than perhaps the cold, which made my hands ache more than usual, or the climb up the basement stairs, which had left me breathless. Back when I'd lived in Shadow, I could've climbed a dozen flights of steps in a day and barely felt them. But that had been a long, long, long time ago. Lifetimes.

Maybe that was the problem: I was just too damned old.

I didn't feel like going to bed. Silence from the room down the hall. I was the only one awake in the house. Impossible not to feel lonely at such an hour, with even the air gone quiet and still. It was right and proper to sleep; my restlessness profaned the cycles that Lady Yeine had woven throughout the mortal realm. But I didn't much care if I profaned anything of *hers*, all things considered.

Finally I wandered toward the back porch and stepped outside, though it was even colder on the porch and I wore nothing but a tatty old nightgown and housecoat. A few minutes wouldn't kill me, and Glee wasn't around to glower disapprovingly. I folded my arms and tucked in my hands, and tilted my face up to the moonlight that I could feel as the most delicate of pressures against my skin. Even after all these years, I still wasn't used to seeing nothing when I looked up.

And even after all these years, I still always glanced toward the muckbins, eventually. Habit. But this time I froze as I felt something contrast the ambient predawn stillness. Something *more* still, and heavy, and solid as a boulder that had suddenly appeared out of nowhere in the middle of my backyard. No, not a boulder; a mountain. Bigger. Incomprehensibly immense—yet contained, perfectly so, within the comparatively tiny space between my porch and the muckbin gate.

Terrifying. Impossible. Familiar. I drew in a long, careful breath, and was proud that it did not shake.

"May I assume," I said softly, out of respect for the stillness, "that your presence means there's been some relaxing of the rules?"

For a moment there was only silence in response. I wondered, of course, if I'd been wrong. One does get funny notions after a certain age. At least if I was hallucinating, though, there was no one around to catch me at it.

Then he spoke. Same voice, even and soft, tenor. "Not so much a relaxation as..." I imagined, rather than heard, the infinite sift of his thoughts, choosing among a million languages and a thousand suitable phrases, of which a dozen were all equally appropriate for the moment. "...a reordering of priorities."

I nodded. Put my hands on the porch railing, lightly, so he wouldn't realize I needed it to stand. Just resting my hands. "All that business with the Maelstrom, then? They tell me you acquitted yourself well."

"Sufficiently." I could not help smiling at his perfectionism. He was closer now. Not on the porch yet, still on the ground below, probably on the cobble path that led to my garden terraces. I had not heard his feet move. Which meant...

"I am free now," he said, in the same moment that I guessed it. "Permanently."

I nodded. "After only a century and change. Congratulations."

"It was not my doing. But I am grateful, nevertheless." He moved closer again, right in front of where I stood at the railing. I could feel him looking up at me. Studying me, perhaps remembering the beauty I had once been. "I feared I would not see you again."

At this I could not help a single laugh, which sounded more harsh than it should have in the still air. "And here I feared you *would*. You couldn't just appear at my deathbed, could you? That would've been nice and romantic—fulfilling a last wish, saying good-bye to an old flame. No, now I've got to live on for however damned long, creaky and half toothless..." I shook my head. "Demons."

"Ephemerality is meaningless, Oree." Gods, gods, his voice. I had forgotten how nice it sounded, my name, when he spoke it. "You remain the same in all essential ways."

"But I'm *not* the same. *You're* not the same. My name is Desola now, remember? Oree Shoth is long dead." My hands had tightened on the railing. I forced them to relax. "Ephemerality is meaningless except to us mortals. Being mortal for a hundred years should've taught you that."

He smiled. I had forgotten that, too. The way I'd always been able to feel him. "It did. But I do not change."

I sighed and lifted my hands to blow on them. At least I had an excuse for shaking the way I was, in all this damned cold.

He moved again. I heard him this time, his footsteps heavy and sure on the cobbles. Then on the porch steps. Then on the porch itself, hollow, measured thuds along the old wood. Then he was beside me, right there, and my whole left side tingled at the warmth of his presence. I felt warmer all over, in fact, as though I stood beside a chimney. A tall, breathing chimney that gazed at me like I was the only person in the world who mattered.

I let out a deep sigh, and it was shaky this time. "I got married, you know. A local man. We were together almost forty years." Unnecessarily, I added, "That's a long time, for mortals."

In fact, Cingo had been with me long enough to notice that I was not aging—not at the rate I should have, anyhow. By the end he'd been making jokes about trophy wives, and I'd finally remembered that my father had been the same, young-looking even when he was old. And I had begun to mourn early, because by then I'd known I would have to move to a new town, give up everything and start over yet again, as soon as Cingo died. Couldn't have people asking questions or making gossip. I still had nightmares about T'vril Arameri coming to get me—though that was foolish because he was decades dead, too, and his descendants had done a thorough job of stomping all over his grave. My secrets had probably died with him. Probably.

Cingo had come with me to this town, helped me pick out a new house. Fixed the damn chimney, however badly. And then he'd died, commanding me to find someone else so I wouldn't be lonely. I hadn't obeyed.

My companion nodded. "You were happy with him. Good."

"As happy as anyone can be after forty years of marriage." But I had been very happy. Cingo had been just what I'd needed, steady and reliable. I'd just wished he'd lived longer. I sighed again, inadvertently relaxing in the warmth, which made me feel boneless and sleepy. Perhaps that was why I said what I meant, instead of what was tactful. "I knew better than to wait for you."

I'd meant it to hurt, but he gave no sign that it did. "That was a wise decision." A pause. Everything he did had meaning. "You've had no husband since, Glee mentioned."

As bad as her father, that girl, both of them forever meddling in people's lives and expecting them not to mind. Then I scowled, hearing the implication underneath his words. Everything he said had *more than one* meaning. "No. And that had nothing to do with *you*. I just didn't want to outlive another man, pretend to be something other than what I was...Darkness and daylight, you're still a bastard, aren't you?"

He didn't answer, because his silence was answer enough. As was his presence, even though I was sure it couldn't mean what I feared it meant. (Hoped it meant? No no no.) But I knew him, I *knew* him, and it was not his nature to act without purpose. He had done so occasionally back then, but that was only because he'd been broken. Symptoms of a greater malaise. Now he was whole, and he was here, and I needed to figure out why.

I could've just asked him. He would've told me. But I was not the bold girl I had been. With age comes caution, and perhaps cowardice. I changed the subject. "Did Glee know you were planning this?"

"We never discussed it."

I nodded. No answer was its own answer. "She's recovered well, if you're wondering. Her magic is still weak, but physically, she's almost as good as she was before the coma." I stretched my shoulders, unable to keep myself from basking in the warmth. "That man of hers is a piece of work, but he'll walk through all the hells for her."

I heard the faint movement of his shrug. "He is a child of Nahadoth. That will make him...difficult." I did not imagine the sour note that entered his tone. It made me smile that he liked our daughter's choice no better than I did.

"You would know." Which made the next question hard to avoid. "Speaking of Nahadoth...and Yeine, I suppose..."

His voice grew as matte-soft as the predawn air for a moment. "We mourn our son. We repair the damage done by the Maelstrom. We contemplate the full complexity of existence, now that its shape has been revealed to us." He paused. "Nahadoth does not forgive me, and Yeine does not trust me. It is possible this cycle will not repeat in the expected permutation."

"Sorry to hear that," I said, and meant it. However incomprehensible his words, I had heard the pain in them. He was a family man at heart. "But if the Nightlord and Gray Lady still aren't keen on you, then why—" Ah, but he had said. Priorities. The Maelstrom running amok. Loss and horror. For some things, terrible things, even an estranged lover was better than none. But being tolerated, even needed, was not the same thing as being welcomed home. "Well. Sorry."

He shrugged. I wondered what he was wearing. It sounded creaky, like leather, though it smelled only of his usual (I had never forgotten *that*) dry-spice-hot-metal scent.

"They will do you no harm," he added. "Regardless of how long I stay."

And there it was.

Bastard. Idiot asinine infuriating son of a demon.

"Don't. Be. *Ridiculous*," I snapped. "This isn't some soppy tale for noble ladies. I raised your child, made a new life for myself, outgrew even that—all *without you*. I don't need you now."

"Glee has made us both proud. And you have never *needed* me."

"Damn straight." His agreement made me even more irritable. I turned to face him, orienting on all that radiant warmth. Had he always been so big? Maybe I'd shrunken. I hated that he was immortal, that I was not, that my entire life had been nothing but a moment to him—to be resumed, as if without interruption, as soon as the moment passed. "I don't *want* you, either. My life has been magnificently god-free for decades, and I like it this way. I've even begun to hope that I will die a quiet, boring death."

"God-free?" I heard him shift a little. Turning, I guessed, to glance at the house's western window. Glee's room.

"He's in Glee's life, not mine. I'm just the old woman who sneaks him cheroots and pretends she doesn't hear when he has sex with her daughter. He doesn't matter, Shi—"

I faltered to silence, appalled at what I had almost called him, even though...I was talking to him as if... but if he was here, then he could not be...

Damn. Five minutes in his presence and I couldn't even *think* simply anymore.

His smile was like the moon's reflected sunlight on my skin. "Most gods have many names. I, however, have only ever accepted one. Before you."

For a moment I was touched. Then I sighed and rubbed my eyes with one hand. The memory of pain, and weariness, were making me foolish.

"I'm too old for this," I murmured. "I don't need this kind of madness in my life anymore."

He said nothing, turning away slightly to face the yard and the trees beyond it. I waited, growing angry as the silence wore on, because he wasn't bothering to argue with me and I wanted him to. When it finally became clear that he wouldn't, I opened my mouth to tell him to leave and never return.

Before I could speak the words, however, they died in my mouth. Because, faint against the darkness, I could suddenly see something. Him, a pale shadow, pulsing in a gradual rhythm that in no way resembled a heartbeat; too slow. Too even and precise. Building, though— brightening—with each passing moment.

Dawn. I had forgotten, but...oh, gods. I had not allowed myself to think about this for so long. I didn't even watch Glee when it happened to her, because she was too much his daughter as it was and at dawn it was impossible to forget. How I'd missed the sight of morning magic.

He turned to me, now that I could see him, letting me absorb the changes. His hair was long; that was the strangest thing. It had been cabled like a Teman's, the great mass of it falling out of sight behind his shoulders in a heavy mantle, the forelocks tied neatly back from his face. He wore a long leather coat, and boots, both of which matched his hair in color. His face—I stared at this the longest, trying to understand why it was not quite what I remembered. And then I knew. There was a little less firmness to the jaw, a crow's-foot or two around the eyes, and his hairline was just a bit farther back than it had been. He hadn't overdone it. There were just enough details to suggest the passage of time, the earning of wisdom. Distinguished strength.

Of course. It wouldn't do for an old woman to take up with a man who looked half her age; that would be scandalous. The Bright Lord of Order would naturally be concerned about propriety.

I groaned. "I thought you didn't change?"

"Ephemerality is—"

"Yes, yes, I *know.* Did you give yourself rheumatism and a bad back, too? Since ephemerality is so meaningless."

He looked amused at my reaction, but his gaze was serious. "I will bring no madness into your life, Oree," he said, very gently. "Quiet, serenity, the comfort of routine... these things are my nature, after all." He paused, his expression hardening in warning. "As is stubbornness."

I closed my eyes and turned away from him, though he had not yet reached sufficient brightness that I had to. "Barging into my life and insisting that I accept you—"

"Are the most expedient means to achieve what we

both desire," he finished, with so-familiar curtness. "You said a quiet, boring death. You did not include *lonely*."

At this I stiffened, wishing that I had my stick. It would've done no good whatsoever, and I didn't need it; I knew the porch like my own hand. But it would've given me something to clench, as I tried my damnedest to set him on fire by will alone. I was out of practice with magic. It didn't work.

"I can't stop you," I snapped. "You've made your wishes clear. But I will not tolerate your lying to me. Do as you like around the house—Glee will be pleased to see you, at least—but leave me alone." I walked to the door and tried to open it. Predictably, it would not budge.

"I do not lie," he said. There was, to my surprise, no anger in his tone. He almost sounded hurt, but that was likely my imagination.

I turned back, sighing. "What we both desire? Do you think I'm a fool? You're free, Sh—" I shook my head and laughed. "*Itempas*. The Three are whole once more. So you're in the doghouse for the next aeon or two; you know that won't last forever. And you." I gestured at him as he stood there, shining, so bright I could barely look at him, so beautiful that he made my heart ache. I wanted to cry. Hadn't done that in years. Damn him. "You come here, to the back end of beyond in the mortal realm, and say you want to keep some old woman company in her last days? You expect me to believe that's anything but pity?"

He stared at me for a moment, then sighed with an almost human exasperation. "Oree Shoth, you were a devout Itempan, once. Tell me, when has *pity* ever been my nature?"

I paused then, because this was true.

"Nor is it my nature," he added, sounding positively

testy now, "to waste time. If I had no desire to be with you, or if I meant only to attend your death, I would simply kill you to get it over with and return to the gods' realm."

There was that. He was nothing if not practical.

"Moreover," he added, clasping his hands behind his back with the air of a man delivering a report, "you have become a thoroughly unpleasant, disrespectful, and irrational creature—as I correctly predicted you would when we first met. Why would it, therefore, trouble me in any way to spend some trifle of time with you? As you suggest, I could readily go elsewhere."

I pursed my lips, furious now. "Open this gods-damned door."

The door lock unlatched itself with a loud clack. I put my hand on it and paused, as his hand landed on mine. It was visible, but no longer radiant, though it should have been. I could feel the dew lifting. The sun had begun to warm the air with the crest of dawn. In the old days, by this point, he would have been shining too brightly to see. Now he had control of himself. He grew only bright enough for my comfort.

"Perhaps you should even be grateful," he murmured, his irritation gone now. "If not for my siblings, I would have been here with you all this time. I imagine we would have found one another insufferable by this point." His thumb stroked the back of my hand suddenly, and I jumped, my heart doing a shameful little flutter. I was too old, far too old, for thoughts like this. He was going to kill me.

Then I registered his words and could not help laughing. He was right. A hundred years with him would have driven me insane.

"Shall I offer more rebuttals to your protests, Oree?"

He had stepped close to take my hand; his breath stirred my hair. "Must we continue this needless discussion?"

A faint breeze crossed the deck then, stirring my housecoat and reminding me of how cold the morning was. I'd forgotten, with him so close and warm.

I turned to him, and though I could see him, I lifted my hand to his face. My fingers explored the lines of his flesh, still familiar after decades and other faces and my own forgetfulness. His eyes shut, the lashes brushing my fingertips. I remembered how once, so very long ago, before the diapers and the wedding and the garden terraces and the town council and all the mundanities I'd surrounded myself with, a god had leaned his cheek into the palm of my hand. That moment was as vivid in my mind as if it had been yesterday.

It *was* yesterday, to him. And was that so terrible a thing, really? In his eyes, I wasn't even old.

"I get to call you Shiny again," I said softly. "Or anything else I want. And you can't get angry about it. Make it a law of the universe, in fact. You can do that now, can't you?"

Something washed across my vision, subtle but powerful, an outward wave of transformation. He sounded smug. "A small price to pay."

He hadn't heard the nicknames I was already thinking up. A hundred years might be nothing to him, but I was mortal after all—fickle, changeable, easily bored. Hopefully he was strong enough to deal with that now.

I sighed and turned the door handle, heading into the kitchen. He followed me in, closing the door behind us. I paused for a moment to listen, biting my bottom lip.

He took off his long coat and hung it on the hook behind the door. He wiped his feet.

Something that I had not known was tensed inside me went soft and still. I let out a slow, heavy breath, and he lifted an eyebrow, perhaps sensing the significance of the moment. Perhaps he even understood it. I didn't really care if he did or not.

"Sit down," I said, nodding toward the table. "You look like you could use a good meal." He was a better cook than I was, I remembered. But that was all right. I would treat him like a guest for one day. He could start doing the cooking again tomorrow.

He sat while I headed for the pantry. We began again.

introducing

If you enjoyed
THE KINGDOM OF GODS,
look out for

THE KILLING MOON

Book One of the Dreamblood series

by N. K. Jemisin

IN THE CITY-STATE OF GUJAAREH, *peace is the only law.
Along its ancient stone streets, where time is marked by
the river's floods, there is no crime or violence. Within
the city's colored shadows, priests of the dream-goddess
harvest the wild power of the sleeping mind as magic,
using it to heal, soothe... and kill.*

*But when corruption blooms at the heart of Gujaareh's
great temple, Ehiru—most famous of the city's
Gatherers—cannot defeat it alone. With the aid of his
cold-eyed apprentice and a beautiful foreign spy, he must
thwart a conspiracy whose roots lie in his own past. And
to prevent the unleashing of deadly forbidden magic, he*

must somehow defeat a Gatherer's most terrifying neme-
sis: the Reaper.

In the dark of dreams, a soul can die. The fears we con-
front in shadows are as reflections in glass. It is natural
to strike a reflection which offends, but the glass cuts; the
soul bleeds. The Gatherer's task is to save the soul, at any
cost.

(Wisdom)
* * *

In the dark of waking, a soul has died. Its flesh, however,
is still hungrily, savagely alive.

The Reaper's task is *not* to save.
* * *

The barbarians of the north taught their children to fear
the Dreaming Moon, claiming that it brought madness.
This was a forgivable blasphemy. On some nights, the
moon's strange light bathed all Gujaareh in oily swirls of
amethyst and aquamarine. It could make low-caste hovels
seem sturdy and fine; pathways of plain clay brick
gleamed as if silvered. Within the moonlight's strange
shadows, a man might crouch on the shadowed ledge
of a building and be only a faint etching against the marbled gray.

In this land, such a man would be a priest, intent upon
the most sacred of his duties.

More than shadows aided this priest's stealth. Long
training softened his footfalls against the stone; his feet
were bare in any case. He wore little altogether, trusting
the darkness of his skin for camouflage as he crept along,
guided by the sounds of the city. An infant's cry from a
tenement across the street; he took a step. Laughter from
several floors below his ledge; he straightened as he

reached the window that was his goal. A muffled cry and the sounds of a scuffle from an alley a block away; he paused, listening and frowning. But the disturbance ended as sandals pattered on the cobblestones, fading into the distance, and he relaxed. When the love-cries of the young couple next door floated past on a breeze, he slipped through the curtains into the room beyond.

The bedchamber: a study in worn elegance. The priest's eyes made out graceful chairs upholstered in fraying fabrics and wood furnishings gone dull for lack of polish. Reaching the bed, he took care to avoid shadowing the face of the person who slept there—but the old man's eyes opened anyhow, blinking rheumily in the thin light.

"As I thought," said the old man, whose name was Yeyezu. His hoarse voice grated against the silence. "Which one are you?"

"Ehiru," said the priest. His voice was as soft and deep as the bedchamber's shadows. "Named Nsha, in dreams."

The old man's eyes widened in surprise and pleasure. "So that is the rose's soul-name. To whom do I owe this honor?"

Ehiru let out a slow breath. The old man had awakened too harshly. It was always more difficult to bestow peace once a tithebearer had been frightened; that was why the law commanded Gatherers to enter dwellings in stealth. But Yeyezu was not afraid, Ehiru saw at once—so he chose to answer the old man's question, though he preferred to do his work without conversation.

"Your eldest son submitted the commission on your behalf," he said. From the hipstrap of his loinskirt he plucked free the jungissa: a thumb-long, polished stone like dark glass, which had been carved into the likeness of a cicada. Yeyezu's eyes tracked the jungissa as Ehiru raised it; the stones were legend for their rarity as well as their power, and few of Hananja's faithful ever saw one. "It was considered and accepted by the Council of Paths, then given to me to carry out."

"Finally," Yeyezu said, and closed his eyes.

So Ehiru bent and kissed the old man's forehead. Fevered skin, delicate as papyrus, smoothed under his lips. When he pulled away and set the jungissa in place of his kiss, the stone quivered at a flick of his fingernail and then settled into a barely visible vibration. Yeyezu sagged into sleep, and Ehiru laid his fingertips on the old man's eyelids to begin.

In the relative quiet of the city's evening, the room sounded only of breath: first Ehiru's and Yeyezu's, then Ehiru's alone. Amid the new silence—for the jungissa had stopped vibrating with the dream's end—Ehiru stood for a few moments, letting the languor of the newly collected dreamblood spread within him. When he judged the moment right, he drew another ornament from his hip—this one a small hemisphere of obsidian whose flat face had been embossed with an oasis rose, the crevices tamped full of a powdered ink. He pressed the carving carefully into the skin of Yeyezu's bony, still chest, setting his signature upon the artwork of flesh. The smile that lingered on the elder's cooling lips was even more beautiful.

"Dreams of joy always, my friend," he whispered, before pulling away the bedsheet and arranging Yeyezu's limbs into a peaceful, dignified position. Finally, as quietly as he'd entered, he left.

Now flight: along the rooftops of the city, swift and silent. A few blocks from Yeyezu's house Ehiru stopped, dropping to the ground in the lee of an old broken wall. There he knelt amid the weeds and trembled. Once, as a younger man, he would have returned to the Hetawa after such a night's work, overwhelmed with joy at the passing of a rich and full life. He was no longer a young man. He was stronger now; he had learned discipline. Most nights he could perform a second Gathering, and occasionally a third if circumstances required—though doing that would leave him giddy and half a-dream, barely able to function in the waking realm. Even a single soul's dreamblood could still muddle his wits, for how could he not exult at the passing of such a rich life? Yet for the sake of other suffering souls, it was necessary to try. Twice he attempted to count fours and failed at only 256. Pathetic. At last, however, his thoughts settled and the tremors ceased.

With some irritation he saw that Dreaming Moon had reached zenith, her bright expanse glaring from the sky's center like a great striped eye; the night was half over. Faster to cross this part of the city on the ground than by rooftop. After a moment's pause to turn his loindrapes and don several ear-cuffs—for not even the poorest man in Gujaareh went without some ornamentation—Ehiru left the old wall and walked the streets as a man of no particular caste, nondescript in manner, taking care to slouch in order to lessen his stature. At such a late hour he saw only caravanners making the final preparations for a journey on the morrow, and a yawning guardsman, doubtless headed for a night shift at one of the city gates. None of them noticed him.

The houses became less dense once he reached the high-caste district. He turned down a side street lit poorly with half burned-out lanterns, and emerged amid a gaggle of young shunha men who reeked of a timbalin house and a woman's stale perfume. They were laughing and staggering together, their wits slowed by the drug. He trailed in their wake for a block before they even marked his presence and then slipped aside, down another side street. This one led to the storage barn of the guesthouse he sought. The barn doors stood open, barrels of wine and twine-wrapped parcels in plain view along the walls— unmolested; Gujaareh's few thieves knew better. Slipping into the shadows here, Ehiru removed his show-jewelry and turned his drapes once more, rolling them so they would not flap. On one side, the drapes bore an unassuming pattern, but on the other—the side he wore now—they were black.

The day before, Ehiru had investigated the guesthouse. As shrewd as any merchant-casteman, the house's proprietor kept his tower open year-round to cater to wealthy foreigners, many of whom disliked relocating during the spring floods. This tithebearer—a northern trader—had a private room in the tower, which was fortunately separated from the rest of the building by a flight of steep stairs. Hananja made way when She wanted a thing done.

Within the house, the kitchen was dim, as was the serving chamber beyond. Ehiru moved past the communal table and through the house's atrium garden, slowing as he turned aside fronds of palms and dangling ferns. Beyond the garden lay the sleeping chambers. Here he crept most stealthily of all, for even at such a late hour there could be guests awake, but all of the rooms' lanterns remained shuttered and he heard only slow, steady breathing from each curtained entrance. Good.

As he climbed the tower steps, Ehiru heard the trader's unpeaceful snores even through the room's heavy wooden door. Getting the door open without causing its hinges to creak took some doing, but he managed it while privately damning the outland custom of putting doors on inner chambers. Inside the room, the trader's snores were so loud that the gauze curtains around his bed shivered in vibration. No wonder the proprietor had put him in this room. Still, Ehiru was cautious; he waited until a particularly harsh snort to part the curtains and gaze down at his next commission.

This close, the scent of the man mingled rancid sweat, stale grease, and other odors into a pungent mix that left Ehiru momentarily queasy. He had forgotten the infrequent bathing habits of people from the north. Though the night was cool, the northerner—a trader from the Bromarte people, the commission had specified, though in truth Ehiru had never been able to tell one northern tribe from another—sweated profusely, his pale skin flushed and rash-prickled as if he slept in high noon's swelter instead of the post-midnight cool. Ehiru studied that face for a moment, wondering what peace might be coaxed from the dreams of such a man.

There would be something, he decided at last, for Hananja would not have chosen him otherwise. The man was lucky; She did not often bestow Her blessings upon foreigners.

The Bromarte's eyes already flickered beneath their lids; no jungissa was necessary to send him into the proper state of sleep. Laying fingers on the man's eyelids, Ehiru willed his soul to part from flesh, leaving its seat of connection—the umblikeh—in place so that he could follow it back when the time came. The bedchamber had become a shadow-place, colorless and insubstantial, when Ehiru opened his soul's eyes; a part of the space between dreaming and waking, unimportant. Only one thing had meaning in this halfway place: the delicate, shimmering red tether that emerged from somewhere near the Bromarte's collarbone, and trailed away into nothingness. Showing the path his soul had taken on its journey to Ina-Karekh, the land of dreams. It was a simple matter for Ehiru to follow the same path *out* and then *in* again.

When he opened his soul's eyes this time, the dream of the Bromarte revealed itself. Charleron of Wenkinsclan, came the name to Ehiru's consciousness, and he absorbed the name's foreignness and as much as he could of the person who bore it. Not a soul-name, but that was to be expected. Bromarte parents named their children for the hopes and needs of the waking world, not protection in sleep. By the reckoning of this Charleron's people, his was a name of ambition. A name of *hunger*. And hunger was what filled the Bromarte's soul: hunger for wealth, hunger for respect, hunger for things even he himself could not name. Reflected in the dreamscapes of Ina-Karekh, these hungers had coalesced into a great yawning pit in the earth, its walls lined with countless disembodied, groping hands. Assuming his usual dream-form, Ehiru floated down through the hands and ignored their silent, scrabbling, blind need as he searched.

And there, at the bottom of the well of hands, weeping with fear and helplessness, knelt the manifestation of the unfortunately named Bromarte man. He cringed between sobs, trying and failing to twist away from his own creations as the hands plucked at him again and again. They did him no harm and were only moderately frightening— but this was nevertheless the bile of dreams, Ehiru judged: black and bitter, necessary for health but unpleasant to the senses. He absorbed as much of it as he could for the Sharers, for there was much use in dreambile even if Charleron might not agree. But he reserved space within himself for the most important humor, which after all was why he had come.

And as they always did, as the Goddess had decreed they must, the bearer of Hananja's tithe looked up and saw Ehiru in his true, unadulterated shape.

"Who are you?" the Bromarte demanded, distracted momentarily from his terror. A hand grabbed his shoulder and he gasped and flinched away.

"Ehiru," he said. He considered giving the man his soul-name and then decided against it. Soul-names meant nothing to heathens. But to his surprise, the Bromarte's eyes widened as if in recognition.

"*Gualoh*," the Bromarte said, and through the filter of their shared dream, a whiff of meaning came to Ehiru. Some kind of frightening creature from their nightfire tales? He dismissed it; barbarian superstition.

"A servant of the Goddess of Dreams," Ehiru corrected, crouching before the man. Hands plucked nervously at his skin and loincloth and the twin braids that dangled from his nape, responding to the Bromarte's fear of him. "You have been chosen for Her. Come, and I will shepherd you to a better place than this, where you may live out eternity in peace." He extended his hand.

The Bromarte leapt at him.

The movement caught Ehiru by such surprise that he almost failed to react in time—but no common man could best a Gatherer in dreaming. With a flick of his will, Ehiru banished the well of hands and replaced it with an innocuous desert of wind-waved dunes. This afforded him plenty of room to sidestep the Bromarte's headlong rush. The Bromarte ran at him again, roaring obscenities; Ehiru opened and then closed the ground beneath the Bromarte's feet, dropping him to the waist in sand.

Even thus pinned, the Bromarte cursed and flailed and wept, grabbing handsful of the sand to fling at him—which Ehiru simply willed away. Then, frowning in puzzlement, he crouched to peer into the Bromarte's face.

"It's pointless to fight," he said, and the Bromarte flinched into stillness at the sound of his voice, though Ehiru had kept his tone gentle. "Relax, and the journey will go soft." Surely the Bromarte knew this? His people had been trading goods and seed with Gujaareh for centuries. In case that was the source of the Bromarte's panic, Ehiru added, "There will be no pain."

"Get away from me, gualoh! I'm not one of you mudgrubbers; I don't need you feeding on my dreams!"

"It is true that you aren't Gujaareen," Ehiru replied. Without taking his attention from the man, he began adjusting the dreamscape to elicit calm. The clouds overhead became wispy and gentle, and he made the sand around the Bromarte's dreamform finer, pleasant against the skin. "But foreigners have been Gathered before. The warning is given to all who choose to live and do business within our capital's walls: Hananja's city obeys Hananja's Law."

Something of Ehiru's words finally seemed to penetrate the Bromarte's panic. His bottom lip quivered. "I, I don't want to die." He was actually weeping, his shoulders heaving, so much that Ehiru could not help pitying him. It was terrible that the northerners had no narcomancy. They were helpless in dreaming, at the mercy of their nightmares, and none of them had any training in the sublimation of fear. How many had been lost to the shadowlands because of it? They had no Gatherers, either, to ease the way.

"Few people desire death," Ehiru agreed. He reached out to stroke the man's forehead, brushing thin hair aside, to reassure him. "Even my countrymen, who claim to love Hananja, sometimes fight their fate. But it's the nature of the world that some must die so that others may live. You will die—early and unpleasantly if the whore's disease you brought to Gujaareh runs its course. And in that time you might not only suffer but spread your suffering to others. Why not die in peace and spread life instead?"

"Liar." Suddenly the Bromarte's face was piggish, his small eyes glittering with hate. The change came so abruptly that Ehiru faltered to silence, startled. "You call it a blessing of your Goddess, but I know what it really is." He leaned forward; his breath had gone foul. *"It gives you pleasure."*

Ehiru drew back from that breath and the fouler words. Above their heads, the wispy clouds stopped drifting. "No Gatherer kills for pleasure."

"No Gatherer kills for pleasure." The Bromarte drawled the words, mocking. "And what of those who *do*, Gatherer?" The Bromarte grinned, his teeth gleaming momentarily sharp. "Are they Gatherers no longer? There's another name for those, yes? Is that how you tell your lie?"

Coldness passed through Ehiru; close on its heels came angry heat. "This is obscenity," he snapped, "and I will hear no more of it."

"Gatherers comfort the dying, yes?"

"Gatherers comfort those who believe in peace, and welcome Hananja's blessing," Ehiru snapped. "Gatherers can do little for unbelievers who mock Her comfort." He got to his feet and scowled to himself in annoyance. The man's nonsense had distracted him; the sand rippled and bubbled around them, heaving like the breath of a living thing. But before he could resume control of the dream and force the Bromarte's mind to settle, a hand grasped his ankle. Startled, he looked down.

"They're using you," said the Bromarte.

Alarm stilled Ehiru's mind. "What?"

The Bromarte nodded. His eyes were gentler now, his expression almost kind. As pitying as Ehiru himself had been a moment before. "You will know. Soon. They'll use you to nothing, and there will be no one to comfort *you* in the end, Gatherer." He laughed and the landscape heaved around them, laughing with him. "Such a shame, Nsha Ehiru. Such a shame!"

Gooseflesh tightened Ehiru's skin, though the skin was not real. The mind did what it had to do to protect the soul at such times, and Ehiru suddenly felt great need of protection—for the Bromarte *knew his soul-name*, though he had not given it.

He jerked away from the man's grip and pulled out of his dream in the same reflexive rush. But to Ehiru's horror, the clumsy exit tore free the tether that bound the Bromarte to his flesh. Too soon! He had not moved the Bromarte to a safer place within the realm of dreams. And now the soul fluttered along in his wake like flotsam, twisting and fragmenting no matter how he tried to push it back toward Ina-Karekh. He collected the spilled dreamblood out of desperation but shuddered as it came into him sluggishly, clotted with fear and malice. In the dark between worlds, the Bromarte's last laugh faded into silence.

Ehiru returned to himself with a gasp, and looked down. His gorge rose so powerfully that he stumbled away from the bed, leaning against the windowsill and sucking quick, shallow breaths to keep from vomiting.

"*Holiest mistress of comfort and peace...*" He whispered the prayer in Sua out of habit, closing his eyes and still seeing the Bromarte's dead face: eyes wide and bulging, mouth open, teeth bared in a hideous rictus. What had he done? *Oh Hananja, forgive me for profaning Your rite.*

He would leave no rose-signature behind this time. The final dream was never supposed to go so wrong— certainly not under the supervision of a Gatherer of his experience. He shuddered as he recalled the reek of the Bromarte's breath, like that of something already rotted. Yet how much fouler had it been for the Bromarte, who had now been hurled, through Ehiru's carelessness, into the nightmare hollows of Ina-Karekh for all eternity? And that only if enough of his soul had been left intact to return.

Yet even as disgust gave way to grief, and even as Ehiru bowed beneath the weight of both, intuition sounded a faint warning in his mind.

He looked up. Beyond the window rose the rooftops of the city, and beyond those the glowing curve of the Dreamer sank steadily toward the horizon. Waking Moon peeked around its larger curve. The city had grown still in the last moments of moonlight; even the thieves and lovers slept. All except himself—

—and a silhouette, hunched against the cistern on a nearby rooftop.

Ehiru frowned and pushed himself upright.

The figure straightened as he did, mirroring his movement. Ehiru could make out no details aside from shape: male, naked or nearly so, tall and yet oddly stooped in posture. Indeterminate features and caste, indeterminate intent.

No. That much, at least, was discernible. Ehiru could glean little else from the figure's stillness, but *malevolence* whispered clearly in the wind between them.

The tableau lasted only a moment. Then the figure turned, climbed the cistern's rope to its roof, and leapt onto an adjoining building and out of sight. The night became still once more. But not peaceful.

Gualoh, echoed the Bromarte's voice in Ehiru's memory. Not an insult, he realized, staring at where the figure had been. A warning.

Demon.